MOURN NOT YOUR DEAD

Superintendent Duncan Kincaid of Scotland Yard did not relish investigating the murder at Holmbury St Mary, for the man who had been beaten to death in his own home was Commander Alastair Gilbert of the Metropolitan Police. Neither his wife Claire, nor her teenage daughter Lucy can think of anyone who would want to murder Gilbert, but it soon becomes clear that few in the village had any affection for the stern policeman. Did Gilbert merely interrupt a thief at work? Or is there someone with more sinister motives within the sleepy suburban village...

MOURN NOT YOUR DEAD

MOURN NOT YOUR DEAD

by
Deborah Crombie

Magna Large Print Books
Long Preston, North Yorkshire,
England.

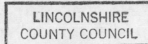
British Library Cataloguing in Publication Data.

Crombie, Deborah
  Mourn not your dead.

  A catalogue record for this book is
  available from the British Library

  ISBN 0-7505-1175-3

First published in Great Britain by Macmillan, an imprint
of Macmillan General Books, 1996

Copyright © 1996 by Deborah Crombie

Cover illustration © Last Resort Picture Library

The right of Deborah Crombie to be identified as the author
of this work has been asserted by her in accordance with
the Copyright, Designs and Patents Act, 1988

Published in Large Print 1997 by arrangement with Macmillan
Publishers Ltd.

Magna Large Print is an imprint of
Library Magna Books Ltd.
Printed and bound in Great Britain by
T.J. International Ltd., Cornwall, PL28 8RW.

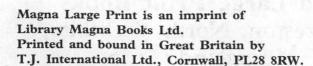

For DIANE, DALE, JIM, VIQUI, JOHN, and RICKEY, who have once again read the book in progress with much patience and insight. Thanks, you guys.

Acknowledgements

Special thanks are due to my friend Paul Styles (former chief inspector, Cambridgeshire Constabulary), who tried to keep me on the straight and narrow, and is not responsible for any deviations I may have made from proper police procedure for the sake of *story*. Diane Sullivan, RN, BSN, certified flight registered nurse, provided details on injuries and related first aid; Carol Chase vetted the manuscript; and David and Gill Hill, owners of Bulmer Farm in Holmbury St Mary, Surrey, provided me with maps, information, and warm hospitality while I was researching this book.

Although the village of Holmbury St Mary and its church do indeed exist, all the characters portrayed in this novel are entirely a product of the author's imagination.

Chapter One

His office seemed to shrink as he paced. The walls drew in, their angles distorted by the elongated shadows cast from the swivel lamp on his desk. The Yard always felt a bit eerie at night, as if the very emptiness of the rooms had a presence. He stopped at the bookcases and ran his finger along the spines of the well-thumbed books on the top shelf. Archaeology, art...canals...crime reference... Many of them were gifts from his mother, sent in her continual quest to remedy what she considered his lack of a proper education. Although he'd tried to group them alphabetically by subject, there were a few inevitable strays. Kincaid shook his head—would that he could order his life even half as well as he did his books.

He glanced at his watch for the tenth time in as many minutes, then crossed to his desk and sat down very deliberately. The call that had brought him in had been urgent—a high-ranking police officer found murdered—and if Gemma didn't arrive soon he'd have to go on to the crime scene without her. She'd not been in to work since she had left his flat on

Friday evening. And although she had called in and requested leave from the chief superintendent, she had not answered Kincaid's increasingly frantic calls over the past five days. Tonight Kincaid had asked the duty sergeant to contact her, and she'd responded.

Unable to contain his restlessness, he rose again and had reached to pull his jacket from the coat stand when he heard the soft click of the latch. He turned and saw her standing with her back to the door, watching him, and a foolish grin spread across his face. 'Gemma!'

'Hello, guv.'

'I've tried and tried to ring you. I thought something must have happened—'

She was already shaking her head. 'I went to my sister's for a few days. I needed some time—'

'We have to talk.' He moved a step nearer and stopped, examining her. She looked exhausted, her pale face almost transparent against the copper of her hair, and the skin beneath her eyes held faint purple shadows. 'Gemma—'

'There's nothing to say.' She slumped, resting her shoulders against the door as if she needed its support. 'It was all a dreadful mistake. You can see that, can't you?'

He stared at her, astonishment freezing

12

his tongue. 'A mistake?' he managed finally, then wiped a hand across his suddenly dry lips. 'Gemma, I don't understand.'

'It never happened.' She took a step towards him, entreating, then stopped as if afraid of his physical proximity.

'It did happen. You can't change that, and I don't want to.' He went to her then and put his hands on her shoulders, trying to draw her to him. 'Gemma, please, listen to me.' For an instant he thought she might tilt her head into the hollow of his shoulder, relax against him. Then he felt her shoulders tense under his fingers and she pulled away.

'Look at us. Look at where we bloody are,' she said, thumping a fist against the door at her back. 'We can't do this. I've compromised myself enough already.' She took a ragged breath and added, spacing the words out as if to emphasize their weight, 'I can't afford it. I've my career to think of...and Toby.'

The phone rang, its short double *brr* echoing loudly in the small room. He stepped back towards his desk and fumbled for the receiver, bringing it to his ear. 'Kincaid,' he said shortly, then listened for a moment. 'Right, thanks.' Replacing the handset in the cradle, he looked at Gemma. 'Car's waiting.' Sentences formed and dissolved in his mind, each sounding more futile than the last. This was not the time or the place to discuss it, and he would only embarrass them both by going on about it now.

Finally, he turned away and slipped into his jacket, using the moment to swallow his disappointment and compose his features in as neutral an expression as he could manage. Facing her again, he said, 'Ready, Sergeant?'

Big Ben struck ten o'clock as the car sped south across Westminster Bridge, and in the back seat beside Gemma, Kincaid watched the lights shimmer on the Thames. They sat in silence as the car zigzagged on through South London, inching its way towards Surrey. Even their driver, a usually chatty young PC called Williams, seemed to have caught their mood, remaining hunched in taciturn concentration over the wheel.

Clapham had vanished behind them when Gemma spoke. 'You'd better fill me in on this one, Guv.'

Kincaid saw the flash of Williams's eyes as he cast a surprised glance at them in the rearview mirror. Gemma should have been briefed, of course, and he roused himself to answer as ordinarily as possible. Gossip in the ranks would do neither of them any good. 'Little village near Guildford. What's it called, Williams?'

'Holmbury St Mary, sir.'

'Right. Alastair Gilbert, the division commander at Notting Dale, found in his kitchen with his head bashed in.'

He heard Gemma draw a sharp breath, then she said with the first spark of interest he'd heard all evening, 'Commander Gilbert? Jesus. Any leads?'

'Not that I've been told, but it's early days yet,' Kincaid said, turning to study her.

She shook her head. 'There will be an unholy stink over this one, then. And aren't we the lucky coppers, having it land in our laps?' When Kincaid snorted in wry agreement, she glanced at him and added, 'You must have known him.'

Shrugging, he said, 'Didn't everyone?' He was unwilling to elaborate in front of Williams.

Gemma settled back into her seat. After a moment she said, 'The local lads will have been there before us. Hope they haven't messed about with the body.'

Kincaid smiled in the dark. Gemma's possessiveness over bodies always amused him. From the beginning of a case, she considered the corpse her personal property and she didn't take unnecessary interference kindly. Tonight, however, her

15

prickliness brought him a sense of relief. It meant she had engaged herself in the case, and it allowed him to hope that their working relationship, at least, was not beyond salvage. 'They've promised to leave it until we've had a chance to see things *in situ.*'

Gemma nodded in satisfaction. 'Good. Do we know who found him?'

'Wife and daughter.'

'Ugh.' She wrinkled her nose. 'Not at all nice.'

'At least they'll have a WPC to do the hand-holding,' Kincaid said, making a half-hearted attempt to tease her. 'Lets you off the hook.' Gemma often complained that female officers were good for more than breaking bad news to victims' families and offering comforting shoulders, but when the task fell to her she did it exceptionally well.

'I should hope so,' she answered and looked away towards her window, but not before he thought he saw her lips curve in a smile.

A half-hour later they left the A road at Abinger Hammer, and after a few miles of twisting and turning down a narrow lane, they entered the sleepy village of Holmbury St Mary. Williams pulled on to the verge and consulted a scribbled sheet of directions under the map light. 'When the road curves left we stay straight on, just to the right of the pub,' he muttered as he put the car into gear again.

'There,' said Kincaid, wiping condensation from his window with the sleeve of his coat. 'This must be it.'

Turning to look out of her window, Gemma said, 'Look. I've never seen that particular sign before.' He heard the pleasure in her voice.

Kincaid leaned across her just in time to catch a glimpse of a swinging pub sign showing two lovers silhouetted against a smiling moon. Then he felt Gemma's breath against his cheek and caught the faint scent of peaches that always seemed to hover about her. He sat back quickly and turned his attention ahead.

The lane narrowed past the pub, and the blue flashing of the panda cars' lights lit the scene with an eerie radiance. Williams brought their car to a halt several yards back from the last car and almost against the hedge on the right, making allowance, Kincaid guessed, for the passing of the coroner's van. They slid from the car, stretching their cramped legs and huddling closer into their coats as the November chill struck them. A low mist hung in the still air, and plumes of condensation formed in front of their faces as they breathed.

A constable materialized before them in the lane, Cheshire Cat-like, the white checks on his hatband creating a dog-toothed smile. Kincaid identified them, then peered through the gate from which the constable had come, trying to make out features in the dark bulk of the house.

'Chief Inspector Deveney is waiting for you in the kitchen, sir,' said the constable. The gate moved silently as he opened it and led them through. 'There's a path just here that goes round the back. The scene-of-crime lads will have some lamps rigged up shortly.'

'No sign of forced entry?'

'No, sir, nor any tracks that we've been able to see. We've been careful to keep to the stones.'

Kincaid nodded in approval. When his eyes adjusted to the dimness within the precincts of the garden wall, he could see that the house was large and stolidly Tudor. Red brick, he thought, squinting, and above that black-and-white half timbering. Not the real thing, surely—more likely Victorian, a representation of the first migration of the well-off into suburbia. A faint light shone through the leaded panes in the front door, echoed by faint glints from the upstairs windows.

Carefully he knelt and touched the grass. The lawn that separated them from the house felt as smooth and dense as black velvet. It seemed that Alastair Gilbert had lived very well.

The flagged path indicated by the constable took them along the right side of the house, then curved around to meet light spilling out from an open door. Beyond it Kincaid thought he could see the outline of a conservatory.

A silhouette appeared against the light, and a man came down the steps towards them. 'Superintendent?' He extended his hand and grasped Kincaid's firmly. 'I'm Nick Deveney.' An inch or so shy of Kincaid's height and near his age, Deveney flashed them a friendly smile. 'You're just in time to have a word with the pathologist.' He stepped aside, allowing Kincaid, Gemma and the still-silent Williams to enter the house before him.

Kincaid passed through a cloakroom, registering a few pairs of neatly aligned wellies on the floor and mackintoshes hanging from hooks. Then he stepped through into the kitchen proper and halted, the others piling up at his back.

The kitchen had been white. White ceramic floors, white ceramic walls, set off by cabinets of a pale wood. A detached part of his mind recognized the cabinets as something he had seen when planning the refitting of his own kitchen—they were free-standing, made by a small English firm, and quite expensive. The other part of his mind focused on the body of Alastair Gilbert, sprawled face down near a door on the far side of the room.

In life, Gilbert had been a small, neat man known for the perfection of his tailoring, the precision of his haircuts, the gloss upon his shoes. There was nothing neat about him now. The metallic smell of blood seemed to lodge at the back of Kincaid's nose. Blood matted Gilbert's dark hair. Blood had splattered, and smeared, and run in scarlet rivulets across the pristine white floor.

A small sound, almost a whimper, came from behind Kincaid. Turning, he was just in time to see a pasty-faced Williams push his way out through the door, followed by the faint sound of retching. Kincaid raised an eyebrow at Gemma, who nodded and slipped out after Williams.

A woman in surgical overalls knelt beside the body, her profile obscured by a shoulder-length fall of straight, black hair. She hadn't looked up or paused in her work when they had entered the room, but now she sat back on her heels and regarded Kincaid. He came nearer and squatted, just out of the blood's path.

'Kate Ling,' she said, holding up her

gloved hands. 'You won't mind if I don't shake?'

Kincaid thought he detected a trace of humour in her oval face. 'Not at all.'

Gemma returned and dropped down beside him. 'He'll be all right,' she said softly. 'I've sent him along to the duty constable for a cuppa.'

'Can't tell you much,' Dr Ling said as she began stripping off her gloves. 'Blood's not congealing, as you can see.' She gestured at the body with the deflated latex fingers of an empty glove. 'Possibly taking some sort of anticoagulant. From the body temperature I'd say he's been dead four or five hours, give or take an hour or two.' Her eyelid drooped in a ghost of a wink. 'But look at this,' she added, pointing with a slender index finger. 'I think the weapon has left several crescent-shaped depressions, but I'll know more when I get him cleaned up.'

Looking closely, Kincaid thought he detected fragments of skull in the blood-matted hair, but no crescent shapes. 'I'll take your word for it, Doctor. Any defence wounds?'

'Not that I've found so far. All right with you if I have him moved now? The sooner I get him on the table, the more we'll know.'

'It's your call, Doc.' Kincaid stood up.

21

'The photographer and the scene-of-crime lads would like to move the live bodies out as well,' said Deveney, 'so they can get on with things.'

'Right.' Kincaid turned to him. 'Can you fill me in on what you've got so far? Then I'd like to see the family.'

'Claire Gilbert and her daughter came home around half-past seven. They'd been away several hours, doing some shopping in Guildford. Mrs Gilbert parked the car in the garage as usual, but as they came across the back garden towards the house they saw that the back door stood open. When they entered the kitchen they found the commander.' Deveney nodded towards the body. 'Once she'd ascertained there wasn't a pulse, Mrs Gilbert called us.'

'In a nutshell,' said Kincaid, and Deveney smiled. 'So what's the theory? Did the wife do it?'

'There's nothing to suggest they had a fight—nothing broken, no marks on her. And the daughter says they were shopping. Besides—' Deveney paused. 'Well, wait till you meet her. I've had her check the house, and she says she can't find a few items of jewellery. There have been a few thefts reported in the area recently. Petty things.'

'No suspects in the thefts?'

Deveney shook his head.

'All right, then. Where are the Gilberts?'

'I've a constable with them in the sitting room. I'll take you through.'

Pausing in the doorway for a final glimpse of the body, Kincaid thought of Alastair Gilbert as he had seen him last—lecturing from a podium, extolling the virtues of order, discipline, and logical thinking in police work—and he felt an unexpected stirring of pity.

Chapter Two

As they entered the sitting room, Kincaid gathered a quick impression of deep red walls and understated elegance. A fire burned in the grate, and across the room a plainclothes constable sat in a straight-backed chair with a teacup balanced on his knee, looking not at all uncomfortable. From the corner of his eye, Kincaid saw Gemma's eyes widen as she took in the male hand holder, then his attention was drawn to the two women seated side by side on the sofa.

Mother and daughter—the mother fair, small-boned, and delicate of feature; the daughter a darker copy, her long, thick hair framing a heart-shaped face. Above her pointed chin her mouth looked disproportionately large, as if she hadn't quite grown into it. Why had he thought of the Gilberts' daughter as a child? Although his wife appeared considerably younger, Gilbert had been in his mid-fifties, and certainly they might have had a grown, or nearly grown, daughter.

The women looked up enquiringly, their faces composed. But the perfection of the little tableau was marred by Claire Gilbert's clothes. The front of her white turtle-necked sweater was decorated with a Rorschach stain of dried blood, and the knees of her navy trousers bore darker splotches as well.

The constable had set down his cup and crossed the room to have a murmured word with his boss. Deveney nodded at him as he left the room, then turned back to the women and cleared his throat. 'Mrs Gilbert, this is Superintendent Kincaid and Sergeant James from Scotland Yard. They'll be helping us in our inquiries. They'd like to ask you a few questions.'

'Of course.' Her voice was low and almost hoarse, huskier than Kincaid had expected for a woman of her size, and controlled. But when she leaned forward to set her cup on the low table, her hand trembled.

Kincaid and Gemma took the two

armchairs opposite the sofa, and Deveney shifted the constable's chair so that he sat beside Gemma.

'I knew your husband, Mrs Gilbert,' Kincaid said. 'I'm very sorry.'

'Did you?' she asked in a tone of bright interest. Then she added, 'Would you like some tea?' The low table before her held a tray with a pot and some extra cups and saucers. When Kincaid and Gemma both murmured affirmatives, she leaned forward and poured a little into her own cup, then sat back, looking around vaguely. 'What time is it?' she asked, but the question didn't seem to be directed to anyone in particular.

'Let me do that for you,' said Gemma after a moment, when it became clear that tea was not forthcoming. She filled two cups with milk and strong tea, then glanced at Deveney, who shook his head.

Accepting a cup from Gemma, Kincaid said, 'It's very late, Mrs Gilbert, but I want to go over one or two things while they're clear in your mind.'

The carriage clock on the mantelpiece began to chime midnight. Claire stared at it, frowning. 'It is late, isn't it? I hadn't realized.'

The daughter had been sitting so quietly that Kincaid had almost forgotten her presence, but now she shifted restlessly, drawing his attention. Her clothes made a rustling sound against the sofa's cream-and-red striped chintz as she repositioned herself, turning towards Claire and touching her knee. 'Mummy, please, you must get some rest,' she said, and from the entreaty in her voice Kincaid guessed that it was not the first time she'd made the request. 'You can't keep on like this.' She looked at Kincaid and added, 'Tell her, Superintendent, please. She'll listen to you.'

Kincaid examined her more closely. She wore a bulky jumper over a tight black miniskirt, but in spite of the sophistication of her clothes, there was an unfinished quality about her that made Kincaid revise his estimate of her age down to late teens, perhaps even younger. Her face looked pinched with stress, and as he watched she rubbed the back of her hand against her lips as if to stop them quivering. 'You're absolutely right—' He paused, realizing he didn't know her name.

Obligingly, she filled it in for him. 'I'm Lucy. Lucy Penmaric. Can't you—' A muffled yelping came from somewhere nearby and she paused, listening. Kincaid heard the frustration in the sound, as if the dog had given up hoping for a response. 'That's Lewis,' she said. 'We had to shut him in Alastair's study to keep him from...you know, getting into things.'

'A very good idea,' Kincaid said absently as he added what he'd just heard to his assessment of the situation. Her name wasn't Gilbert, and she referred to the commander as 'Alastair'. A stepdaughter rather than a daughter. He thought of the man he had known and realized what had struck him as odd. Try as he might, he couldn't quite manage to imagine Gilbert relaxed before a fire, a large (from the sound of it) dog sprawled comfortably at his feet. Nor did this room, with its rich velvets and chintzes and the deep pile of a Persian carpet under their feet, seem a likely habitat for a dog. 'I wouldn't have thought of Commander Gilbert as a dog man,' he ventured. 'I'm surprised he allowed a dog in the house.'

'Alastair made us—'

'Alastair preferred that we confine Lewis to his kennel,' interrupted Claire, and Lucy looked away, her face losing the brief spark of animation he'd seen when she spoke of the dog. 'But under the circumstances...' Claire smiled at them, as if excusing a lapse in manners, then looked around vaguely. 'Would you like some tea?'

'We're quite all right, Mrs Gilbert,' he said. Lucy was right: her mother needed rest. Claire's eyes had the glazed look of impending collapse, and her coherence seemed to fade in and out like a weak radio signal. But even though he knew he couldn't press her much further, he wanted to ask a few more questions before letting her go. 'Mrs Gilbert, I realize how difficult this must be for you, but if you could just tell us exactly what happened this evening, we can get on with our inquiries.'

'Lucy and I ran into Guildford for some shopping. She's studying for her A levels, you see, and needed a book from Waterstone's in the shopping centre. We poked about a bit in the shops, then walked up the High Street to Sainsbury's.' Claire stopped as Lucy stirred beside her, then she looked at Deveney and frowned. 'Where's Darling?'

Gemma and Kincaid glanced at each other, Kincaid raising a questioning eyebrow. Deveney leaned over and whispered, 'The constable who was with them. His name is Darling.' Turning to Claire, he said, 'He's still here, Mrs Gilbert. He's just gone to give the other lads a hand for a bit.'

Tears filled Claire's eyes and began to run down the sides of her nose, but she made no move to wipe them away.

'After you'd finished your shopping, Mrs Gilbert,' Kincaid prompted after a moment, 'what did you do then?'

28

She seemed to focus on him with an effort. 'After? We drove home.'

Kincaid thought of the quiet lane where they had left their car. 'Did anyone see you? A neighbour, perhaps?'

Claire shook her head. 'I don't know.'

While they talked, Gemma had unobtrusively pulled her notebook and pen from her bag. Now she said softly, 'What time was this, Mrs Gilbert?'

'Half-past seven. Maybe later. I'm not quite sure.' She looked from Gemma to Kincaid, as if for reassurance, then spoke a little more forcefully. 'We weren't expecting Alastair. He had a meeting. Lucy and I had bought some pasta and ready-made sauce at Sainsbury's. A bit of a treat, just for the two of us.'

'That's why we were surprised to find his car in the garage,' added Lucy, when her mother didn't continue.

'What did you do then?' Kincaid asked.

After a quick glance at Claire, Lucy went on. 'We put Mum's car in the garage. When we came around the corner of the garage into the garden we could see the door standing—'

'Where was the dog?' asked Kincaid. 'What's his name—Lewis?'

Lucy stared at him as if she didn't quite understand the question, then said, 'He was in his run, in the back garden.'

29

'What kind of dog is Lewis?'

'A Lab. He's brilliant, really lovely.' Lucy smiled for the first time, and again he heard that flash of proprietary pride in her voice.

'Did he seem upset in any way? Disturbed?'

Mother and daughter glanced at each other, then Lucy answered. 'Not then. It was only later, when the police came. He got so frantic we had to bring him into the house.'

Kincaid set his empty cup on the table, and Claire's body jerked slightly as the china clinked. 'Let's go back to when you saw the open door.'

The silence stretched. Lucy moved a bit nearer her mother.

The fire settled and a shower of sparks rose, then flickered out. Kincaid waited another heartbeat, then spoke. 'Please, Mrs Gilbert, try to tell us exactly what happened next. I know that you've already been through this with Chief Inspector Deveney, but you might remember some tiny detail that could help us.'

After a moment Claire took Lucy's hand and cradled it between her own, but Kincaid couldn't tell if she was extending support or receiving comfort. 'You saw. There was blood...everywhere. I could smell it.' She drew a deep, shuddering breath, then continued. 'I tried to lift him. Then I realized...I had some first-aid training, years ago. When I couldn't find a pulse, I dialled nine-nine-nine.'

'Did you notice anything unusual as you came into the house?' asked Gemma. 'Anything at all in the kitchen that wasn't quite where it should be?'

Claire shook her head, and the lines of exhaustion seemed to deepen around her mouth.

'But I understand you've reported some things missing from the house,' said Kincaid, and Deveney gave him a quick nod of confirmation.

'My pearls. And the earrings Alastair gave me on my birthday...he had them specially made.' Claire sank back against the sofa cushion and closed her eyes.

'It sounds as if they must have been quite valuable,' said Gemma.

When Claire didn't stir, Lucy glanced at her, then answered, 'I suppose they were. I don't know, really.' She pulled her hand free of her mother's and held it out in a pleading gesture. 'Please, Superintendent,' she said, and at the distress in her voice the dog began to bark, scrabbling against the door with his claws.

'Do shut him up, Lucy,' said Claire, but her voice was listless, and she didn't move or open her eyes.

31

Lucy sprang up, but even as she did so the dog's barking faded to a whimper, then subsided altogether. She sank back to the edge of the sofa, looking in mute appeal from her mother to Kincaid.

'Only one more thing, Lucy, I promise,' he said softly, then he turned to Claire. 'Mrs Gilbert, do you have any idea why your husband came home early?'

Claire pressed her fingers to her throat and said slowly, 'No. I'm sorry.'

'Do you know who he was meet—'

'Please.' Lucy stood up, shivering. She crossed her arms tightly beneath her breasts and said through chattering teeth, 'She's said already. She doesn't know.'

'It's all right, darling,' said Claire, rousing herself. With an apparent effort, she pushed herself to the edge of her seat. 'Lucy's right, Superintendent. It's not—it wasn't Alastair's habit to share details about his work. He didn't tell me whom he intended seeing.' She stood up, then swayed. Lucy reached out to support her, and as she was the taller of the two, her arm fitted easily around her mother's shoulders.

'Please, Mummy, do stop,' she said, then she looked at Kincaid. 'Let me take her upstairs now.' Her voice held more question than command, and she seemed to Kincaid very much a child playing an adult's part.

'There must be someone you can call,' said Gemma, standing and touching Lucy's arm. 'A neighbour? A relative?'

'We don't need anyone else. We can manage,' Lucy said a little abruptly. Then her brief bravado seemed to dissolve as she added, 'What should I do about the house...and things? What if...?'

Deveney answered her gently, but without patronizing her. 'Please don't worry, Miss Penmaric. I'm sure that whoever did this won't come back. And we'll have someone here all night, either outside or in the kitchen.' He paused for a moment, and they heard a faint whimpering. 'Why don't you take the dog upstairs with you, if it makes you feel more comfortable?' he suggested, smiling.

Lucy gave it grave consideration. 'He'd like that.'

'If there's nothing else...' Claire's speech had begun to slur, yet in spite of her exhaustion she still maintained a semblance of graciousness.

'That's all for tonight, Mrs Gilbert. And Lucy. Thank you for your patience,' said Kincaid as he stood beside Deveney and Gemma, and they all watched silently as mother and daughter left the room.

When the door had swung shut, Nick Deveney shook his head and ran his fingers through the early grey streaking his hair at

33

the temple. 'I'm not sure I'd have held up as well, under the circumstances. Lucky for them, isn't it, that they have each other?'

The scene-of-crime team was still busily at work in the kitchen, but Alastair Gilbert's body had been removed. The drying blood had smeared in streaks and swirls, like a child's exercise in fingerpaints. Excusing himself to speak to one of the SOCOs, Deveney left Kincaid and Gemma standing in the doorway.

Kincaid felt the adrenalin that had sustained him for the last few hours ebbing. Glancing at Gemma, he found her studying him. Her freckles, usually an almost imperceptible dusting against her fair skin, stood out in sharp contrast to her pallor. He suddenly felt her exhaustion as if it were his own, and the familiar, intimate awareness of her ran through him like a shock. As he lifted a hand to touch her shoulder, she started to speak, and they both froze. They had lost the ease of it, all their carefully established camaraderie had gone, and it seemed to him as if she might misconstrue even his small gesture of comfort. Awkwardly, he dropped his hand and shoved it in his pocket, as if removing it from temptation. As Deveney came back to them, Gemma abruptly excused herself and left the kitchen by the cloakroom door without meeting his eyes again.

'Dr Ling said she'd schedule the post-mortem first thing tomorrow at Guildford Mortuary.' As he spoke, Deveney slumped against the doorframe and watched with an abstracted expression as one of the civilian techs scraped up a blood sample from the floor. 'Can't be soon enough, as far as the brass are concerned. I'll have the plods out door-to-door at first light—' He paused, and for the first time his expression was wary as he glanced at Kincaid. 'That is, if it meets with your approval.'

The chain of command when the Yard was called in to work with a regional force could be a bit tricky. Although technically Kincaid outranked Deveney, he had no wish to antagonize the local man at the outset. Nick Deveney seemed an intelligent and capable copper, Kincaid thought as he nodded assent, and he'd be more than happy to let him run his end of things without interference. 'You'll be following up on this intruder business?'

'Maybe at daylight we'll find he's left half-inch-deep footprints all over the garden,' Deveney said, grinning.

Kincaid snorted. 'Along with a set of perfect prints on the door-knob and a criminal record a mile long. We should be so lucky. How early is first thing, by the way?' he asked, yawning and rubbing his hand across the stubble on his chin.

'Sevenish, I would imagine. Kate Ling doesn't seem to need sleep. Exists on a combination of coffee and formaldehyde fumes,' said Deveney. 'But she's good, and we were lucky to get her on the scene tonight.' As Gemma rejoined them, Deveney included her with a quick smile. 'Listen, why don't you send your driver back to London with your car? I've made arrangements to put you up at the local—you did come prepared to stay?' When they nodded, he continued. 'Good. We'll send someone to take you to the mortuary in the morning. And then—' He broke off as a plainclothes officer beckoned him from the cloakroom door. With a sigh he pushed off from the wall. 'Back in a tick.'

'I'll see to Williams,' said Gemma a little too quickly, and left Kincaid standing alone. For a few moments he watched the technicians and the photographer, then he edged around their work area until he reached the refrigerator. Opening it, he bent over and examined the contents. Milk, juice, eggs, butter, and, tucked haphazardly on to the bottom shelf, a package of fresh pasta and a plastic container of Alfredo sauce, bearing the Sainsbury deli's seal. Neither container had been opened.

'I found some bread and cheese. Made

the ladies some sandwiches,' said a voice above his head.

Kincaid stood and turned, and found himself looking up at the rosy-cheeked visage of Police Constable Darling. 'Ah, the minder,' he murmured, then at the constable's blank look he added more loudly, 'Very thoughtful of you...' He couldn't quite bring himself to add the surname.

'Add hunger to shock and exhaustion and they'd have been in a right state,' Darling said seriously, 'and there didn't seem to be anyone else to look after them.'

'No, you're quite right. Usually, helpful and nosy neighbours materialize out of the woodwork in this sort of situation. Relatives, too, as often as not.'

'Mrs Gilbert said both her parents were dead,' volunteered Darling.

'Did she now?' Kincaid studied the constable for a moment, then gestured towards the hall door. 'Here, let's have a word where it's a bit quieter.' When they reached the relative calm of the passageway, he continued. 'You sat with Mrs Gilbert and her daughter for quite some time, didn't you?'

'Several hours, I'd say, in between the chief inspector's comings and goings.'

A lamp on the telephone table lit

Darling's face from below, revealing a few lines on his brow and crinkles at the corners of his blue eyes. Perhaps he was not as young as Kincaid had first thought. 'You seem to have taken this in your stride,' Kincaid said, his curiosity piqued by the man's self-possession.

'I grew up on a farm, sir. I've seen death often enough.' He regarded Kincaid for a moment, then blinked and sighed. 'But there is something about this one. It's not just Commander Gilbert being a senior officer and all. Or the mess, exactly.' Kincaid raised an eyebrow and Darling went on, hesitantly. 'It's just that it all seems so...inappropriate.' He shook his head. 'Sounds stupid, I know.'

'No, I know what you mean,' Kincaid answered. Not that *appropriate* was a word he'd be likely to apply to any murder, but something about this one struck a distinctly jarring note. Violence had no place in such an ordered and well-kept life. 'Did Mrs Gilbert and Lucy talk to each other while you were with them?' he asked.

Darling settled his broad shoulders against the wall and focused on a point beyond Kincaid's head for a moment before replying. 'Now that you mention it, I can't say that they did. Or only a word or two. But they both talked to me. I offered to ring someone for them, but Mrs Gilbert said no, they'd be all right on their own. She did say something about having to tell the commander's mother, but it seems she's in a nursing home and Mrs Gilbert thought it best to wait until tomorrow. Today, that is,' he added, glancing at his watch, and Kincaid heard the beginnings of fatigue in his voice.

'I won't keep you, Constable.' Kincaid smiled. 'And I can't speak for your guv'nor, but I'm about ready to salvage what little sleep I can from this night.'

Late as the hour was, a few lights still burned in the pub. Deveney rapped sharply on the glass pane of the door, and in a moment a shadowy form slid back the bolts.

'Come in, come in,' the man said as he opened the door. 'Take the chill off. I'm Brian Genovase, by the way,' he added, holding out a hand to Kincaid and Gemma in turn as they crowded in behind Deveney.

The pub was surprisingly small. They had entered directly into the right-hand alcove, where a handful of tables surrounded a stone hearth. To their left the length of the bar occupied the pub's centre, and beyond that a few more tables were grouped to make up the dining area.

'It's kind of you to wait up, Brian,'

Deveney said as he went to the hearth and stood rubbing his hands above the still-glowing embers.

'Couldn't sleep. Not with wondering what was going on up there.' Genovase tilted his head towards the Gilberts'. 'The whole village is buzzing, but no one quite had the nerve to brave the cordon and bring back a report. I gave it a try, but the constable on the gate persuaded me otherwise.' As he spoke he slipped behind the bar, and Kincaid saw him more clearly. A large man with dark hair going grey and the beginnings of a belly, he had a pleasant face and quick smile. 'You'll need something to warm you up from the inside,' he said, pulling a bottle of Glenfiddich from the shelf, 'and while you're at it you can tell me all that's fit to print. So to speak.' He flashed a grin at them and favoured Gemma with a wink.

They'd followed him to the bar, unresisting as lemmings drawn towards the cliff. As Genovase tilted the bottle over the fourth glass, Gemma suddenly put out a restraining hand. 'No, thank you, but I don't think I can manage it. I'm just about out on my feet. If you'll just tell me where to put my things—'

'I'll show you,' Genovase said, putting down the bottle and wiping his hands on a towel.

'No, please, I'm sure I can manage,' Gemma said firmly, shaking her head. 'You've put yourself out enough as it is.'

Shrugging good-naturedly, Genovase gave the appearance of recognizing a stubborn set of mind when he saw it. 'Round the bar, up the stairs, down the corridor, last door on the right.'

'Thanks. Good night, then.' Focusing on the empty space between Kincaid and Deveney, she added, 'I'll see you in the morning.'

A dozen excuses to call her back, to go up with her, froze on the tip of Kincaid's tongue. Anything he did would make them both look foolish and might arouse the very speculation they couldn't afford, so he sat on in miserable, silent frustration until she disappeared through the door at the far end of the bar. Deveney, too, had watched her, and seemed to have trouble drawing his gaze from the empty doorway.

Genovase raised his glass. 'Cheers. This is on the house, Nick, so you'll not get me for breaking the licensing laws, but I expect to be paid in kind.'

'Fair enough,' Deveney agreed. Then he said, 'Ah, that'll do nicely,' as the first sip of whisky went down. 'You heard that someone did for Commander Gilbert, I take it?'

Genovase nodded. 'But Claire and Lucy—they're all right, aren't they?'

'Shocked, but fine other than that. They found the body.'

Relief and distress battling in his face, Genovase said, 'Oh, lord,' and rubbed at an invisible spot on the bar with his towel. 'Was it bad? What—?' The small negative movement of Deveney's head stopped him. 'Out of bounds? Sorry.'

'We won't be releasing full details for a bit,' said Deveney with practised diplomacy.

It would be difficult to keep anything under wraps for long in a village this size, Kincaid knew, but they'd try until the house-to-house enquiries were finished, just in case someone let slip they knew something they shouldn't.

'You were friendly with the Gilberts?' Deveney asked Genovase, sliding forward on his stool so that he could rest his elbows on the bar.

'It's a small village, Nick. You know how it is. Claire and Lucy are well liked.'

Kincaid took another sip of his drink and said casually, 'And the commander wasn't?'

Brian Genovase looked wary for the first time. 'I didn't say that.'

'No, you didn't.' Kincaid smiled at him. 'But is it true?'

After a moment's consideration, Genovase said, 'Let me put it this way—Alastair Gilbert didn't go out of his way to make himself popular around here. Not one of the beard-and-wellie brigade, not by a long chalk.'

'Any particular reason?' Kincaid asked. Gilbert hadn't gone out of his way to make himself popular with his officers, either, not if Kincaid's experience with him was any indication. He had seemed, in fact, to enjoy making the most of his superiority.

'Not really. An accumulation of small misunderstandings, amplified by the gossip mill. You know how it is,' he said again, 'place like this, things get blown out of proportion sometimes.' Obviously unwilling to say more, Genovase finished his drink in one swallow and set his glass down.

Deveney followed suit and sighed. 'I'm not looking forward to this, I can tell you that. Better you than me in the hot seat, mate,' he added, glancing at Kincaid. 'You're welcome to it.'

'Thanks,' Kincaid said with considerable irony. He finished his own drink more slowly, finding comfort in the burn as it went down, then stood and retrieved his coat and bag. 'That's it for me, I'm afraid.' He looked at his watch and swore. 'Hardly worth going to bed.'

'You're last on the left, Mr Kincaid,' said Genovase. 'And I'll have a bit of breakfast for you in the morning.'

Kincaid had said his thanks to both and turned to go when Deveney touched him on the arm and said quietly, 'Your sergeant—Gemma. She's not married, I take it?'

It was a moment before Kincaid found his tongue, managed to say reasonably enough, 'No. No, she's not.'

'Is she...um, unattached, then?'

'That,' said Kincaid through clenched teeth, 'is something you'll have to ask her yourself.'

Chapter Three

The hurt had been evident on his face. Gemma hadn't expected it, and it had almost caused her to lose her resolve. During the days she'd spent hiding at her sister's, watching Toby play in the park with his cousins and thinking furiously of what she should do, she'd managed to convince herself that he would be glad to ignore what had happened, relieved, even grateful. So she had prepared her little speech, giving him a graceful out that he

44

would accept with a slightly embarrassed grin, and rehearsed it so often in her mind she could almost hear him saying, 'Of course, you're absolutely right, Gemma. We'll just go on as before, shall we?'

Experience should have taught her that Duncan Kincaid never behaved quite as expected. Shivering a little in the cold room, she turned back the bed and laid out her nightdress. She fumbled in her carryall until she found the zip bag containing her toothbrush and cleanser and turned resolutely towards the door.

Then suddenly, limply, she sat down on the edge of the bed. How could she have been foolish enough, in the days that had passed like aeons since the night at his flat, to think she could grant herself an instant immunity to his physical presence? Memory had flooded back with a jolt like a boxer's punch the moment she saw him, leaving her breathless and shaken. It had been all she could do to hold on to her wavering defences, and now she couldn't bear the thought of bumping into him in the corridor outside her room. She had no armour left—a kind word, a gentle touch, and she would be undone.

But she must get to bed, or she would feel even less capable of dealing with things in the morning. So she listened, alert for the creak of a tread on the stairs or the sound of a door opening. Reassured by the silence, she slipped from her room and tiptoed down the hall to the bathroom.

When she emerged a few minutes later, the door to the room opposite the bathroom was closing. She stopped, heart thumping, chiding herself for being absurd, until the glimpse before the door swung shut assured her that the person inside was not Kincaid. Frowning, she tried to fit together pieces of the brief image—curling fair hair falling over a surprisingly masculine pair of shoulders. She shrugged and returned to her room, letting herself in with a grateful sigh.

And if, once she had put on her warm nightdress and tucked herself under the puffy duvet, there was a kernel of disappointment hidden in the relief, she buried it deeper still.

The sight of the Royal Surrey County Hospital did nothing to brighten the atmosphere in the small car. Gemma studied the sprawl of muddy-brown brick, wondering why it had not occurred to the architects that ill people might need a bit of cheering up.

'I know,' said Will Darling, as if he'd read her thoughts. 'It's bloody institutionally awful. It's a good hospital, though. They combined several smaller facilities when they built this one, and it offers just about every sort of care you could imagine.'

Darling had arrived at the pub just as Gemma and Kincaid had finished their breakfasts. They had eaten in uncomfortable silence, served by an equally subdued Brian Genovase. 'Not much of a morning person,' he'd said with a shadow of last night's smile. 'Goes with the territory.' The breakfast had been good, though—the man could still cook even when his social skills were not at their best—and Gemma had forced herself to eat, knowing she'd need the sustenance to get through the day.

'The Chief Inspector should have been here before us,' said Darling, scanning the parked cars as he pulled the car around to the back of the hospital and stopped it in a space near the mortuary doors. 'I'm sure he'll be along in a minute.'

'Thanks, Will.' Kincaid stretched as he emerged from the cramped back seat. 'At least we get to enjoy the view while we wait, unlike the clientele.' He nodded towards the unremarkable glass doors.

Gemma slid from the car and moved a few steps away, considering the prospect. Perhaps if you were inside the building looking out, it wasn't such a bad place after all. The hospital was high on the hill rising to the west of Guildford, and below, the red-brick town hugged the curve of the River Wey. Pockets of mist still hovered over the valley, muting trees ablaze with autumn. To the north, higher still, the tower of the cathedral rose against a flat grey sky.

'It's a new cathedral, did you know that?' asked Darling, coming to stand beside her. 'Begun during the war and consecrated in nineteen sixty-one. You don't often have a chance to see a cathedral built in our lifetime.' Glancing at Gemma, he amended with a smile, 'Well, perhaps not yours. But it's lovely, all the same, and well worth a visit.'

'You sound very proud of it,' said Gemma. 'Have you always lived here?' Then she added, with the frankness he seemed to inspire, 'And you can't be old enough to have seen it built, either.'

Chuckling, he said, 'Got me to rights, there. I was born on consecration day, as a matter of fact. May seventeenth, nineteen sixty-one. So the cathedral always had a special significance for us—' He broke off as a car pulled up beside theirs. 'Here's the chief, now.'

Suddenly aware that Kincaid had been standing quietly against the car, listening to their conversation, Gemma flushed with embarrassment and turned away.

The few hours' sleep seemed to have

48

rejuvenated Nick Deveney. He hopped out of the battered Vauxhall and came over to them with a quick apology. 'Sorry about that. I live south of here, in Godalming, and there was a bit of a holdup on the Guildford road.' His breath formed a cloud of condensation as he rubbed his hands together and blew on them. 'Heater's out in the bloody car.' He gestured towards the doors. 'Shall we see what Dr Ling has in store for us this morning?' Smiling at Gemma, he added, 'Not to mention getting warm.'

They trailed Deveney through the maze of identical white-tiled corridors, passing no one, until they reached another set of double doors. A very official-looking sign above them read AUTHORIZED PERSONNEL ONLY—RING BELL FOR ADMITTANCE, but the doors stood slightly ajar and Deveney pushed on through them. A faint smell of formalin tickled Gemma's nose, and then she heard the murmur of a voice. Following the sound to the autopsy room, they found Kate Ling sitting on a stool with a clipboard on her lap, drinking coffee from a large thermal mug. 'Sorry, my assistant's off with flu, and I couldn't be bothered manning the portals. And it's not as if anyone's dying to get in here,' she added, looking at Deveney as if waiting for his groan.

Deveney shook his head in mock amazement, then turned to the others, who had squeezed into the small room behind him, none of them venturing too close to the white-sheeted form on the table. 'Did you know that all pathologists have to undergo a special initiation into the Order of Bad Puns? Won't let 'em practise without it. The doc here is a Grand Master and loves to show off.' He and Kate Ling grinned at each other, completing what was obviously a practised and much-enjoyed routine.

'Just finishing up my notes on the external,' Ling said, scribbling a few more words, then setting her pad aside.

'Anything interesting?' Deveney asked. He studied the pad as if he might decipher it upside down, although Gemma thought it unlikely that the doctor's scrawl was legible even right side up.

'Lividity corresponds perfectly with the position of the body, so I'd say he wasn't moved. Of course, we expected that from the blood spatter, but they pay me to be thorough.' She gave them a wry smile over the rim of her mug as she drank, then continued, 'So if we calculate the drop in body temperature using the temperature of the Gilberts' kitchen, I'd say he was killed between six and seven o'clock.' Swivelling around towards the counter top behind her, Ling exchanged her coffee for a new pair of latex gloves. As she pulled them on, she added thoughtfully, 'One odd thing, though. There were some tiny rips in the shoulders of his shirt. Not large enough that I could hazard a guess as to what made them or why.' Sliding from the stool, she checked the voice-activated mike hanging over the autopsy table, then lifted the lid from the stainless-steel instrument box on a nearby rolling trolley. 'All set, then? You'll need to gown and glove.' She regarded them quizzically. 'You lot are jammed in here like sardines in a can. I'll need some elbow room.'

Will Darling touched Gemma on the shoulder. 'I can take a hint when I hear it. Come on, Gemma, we'll wait in the corridor. Let them have all the fun.'

Having appropriated two folding chairs from a nearby room, Will set them up just outside the post-mortem room door and left Gemma for a moment. 'I'll find us a cuppa,' he said over his shoulder as he disappeared down the corridor.

Gemma sat, her eyes closed and her head leaning against the wall. She felt a little resentful of having been so easily excluded, yet she was glad not to have to summon the resources watching an autopsy always required. With half her mind she

51

listened to the murmur of voices and the clink of instruments, imagining the methodical exploration of Alastair Gilbert's body, while with the other half she thought about Will Darling.

He had an easy assurance not consistent with his rank, yet there was no aggressiveness to it, and no sense of the desire to impress one's superiors that she so often saw and knew she'd been guilty of herself. And there was something comfortable about him, maybe even comforting—something more than the sense of ease provided by his friendly, slightly snub-nosed face, but she couldn't quite put her finger on it.

She opened her eyes as he reappeared beside her, holding two steaming polystyrene cups. Expecting institutional sludge, she tasted the tea, then looked at him in surprise. 'Where'd you get this? It's actually decent.'

'My secret,' Will answered as he settled himself beside her.

Kate Ling's voice came clearly through the open door. 'Of course, we were fairly certain from the blood velocity and external examination of the head wounds that we were looking at blunt force trauma, but let's see what things look like when we get under the scalp.'

In the silence that followed, Gemma

cradled the hot cup in her hands, taking an occasional sip of tea. She knew that Dr Ling would be peeling Gilbert's scalp from his skull, folding it forward over his face like a grotesque mask in reverse, but it seemed distant, not logically connected to the feel of the chair's cold metal against her back and thighs or the faint shapes she fancied she saw in the distempered wall opposite.

Her eyelids drooped and she blinked, fighting the fuzzy blanket stealing over her. But her lethargy had the overwhelming quality born of exhaustion and emotional stress, and Dr Ling's words floated disjointedly in and out of a haze.

'...blow just behind the right ear...several overlapping blows nearer the crown...all slightly to the right...never be sure—some lefties perform gross motor skills with their right hand.'

Gemma's eyes flew open as she felt Will's fingers against her hand. 'Sorry,' he said softly. 'You were about to tip your cup.'

'Oh. Thank you.' She grasped it more firmly in both hands, making a huge effort to stay alert and concentrate, but the voice began again, its precise intonation as soporific as a warm bath. When Will took the cup from her slack hands a few minutes later, she couldn't manage a protest. The words came to her now with a clarity and an almost physical presence, as if their existence outweighed all surrounding stimuli.

'...most likely conclusion is that the blow behind the ear was the first, struck from behind, and the others followed as he fell. Ah, now take a look at this...see the half-moon shape of the indentation in the bone? Just here? And here? Let's take a measurement just to be sure, but I'd be willing to bet that's the imprint of a common or garden-variety hammer...quite characteristic. Nasty things, hammers, though you wouldn't think it. Never forget a case I had in London—a little old lady living alone, never done anyone a moment's harm in her life, opens her door one day and some bloke bashes her in the side of the head so hard with a hammer it lifts her right out of her slippers.'

'Did they catch him?' Some part of Gemma's mind recognized the voice as Deveney's.

'Within a week. Silly bugger wasn't too bright, talked about it all round the pubs. Hang on a bit while I take some tissue samples.'

Gemma heard a saw, and a moment later smelled the sickening odour of burning bone, but still she couldn't reach the surface of consciousness.

'...commander's medical records, by the way, he was taking an anticoagulant. Had heart surgery two years ago. Let's see how well things had held up.'

In the silence that followed Gemma drifted deeper still. Muttered phrases such as 'constricted arteries' and 'type-A personality' no longer had any meaning, then awareness of the post-mortem faded away all together.

When Will nudged her with a whispered 'They're finishing up now, Gemma,' she jerked awake with a gasp. She had dreamed that Kincaid stood before her with his most mischievous grin, and in his hand he held a hammer, wet with blood.

For the first time Gemma saw Holmbury St Mary in full light. The pub faced an immaculate triangle of green, with the Gilberts' lane to the right and the church on its left. Across the green, a few rooftops and red-brick gables peeked from among the trees.

Deveney had gone back to Guildford Police Station to oversee incoming reports, delegating Will Darling to drive Gemma and Kincaid back to the Gilberts'. 'Meet you there in an hour and we'll compare notes,' he'd said as he got into his car and gave a mock shiver. 'Looks like I won't be getting the bloody thing in the shop any time soon.'

Will parked in the car park behind the pub, and they walked across the lane slowly, studying the house and its surroundings as they went. The thick hedge almost met over the curved iron gate, and above it only the upper floor of the house showed, black beams against white-trimmed red brick, creeper softened. 'A suburban fortress,' Kincaid said softly as Will nodded to the uniformed constable on duty at the gate. 'And it didn't protect him.'

'Any too curious onlookers?' Will asked the constable.

'I've passed through a couple of neighbours wanting to help, but that's been it.'

'No press?'

'A few sniffers is all.'

'Won't be long, then,' said Will, and the constable agreed resignedly.

'I hope Claire Gilbert and her daughter are ready for a siege,' said Kincaid as they took the path towards the back of the house. 'The media won't let this go easily.'

When they reached the cloakroom door, Kincaid hesitated, then said, 'Gemma, why don't you and Will find Mrs Gilbert and take a detailed statement of her movements yesterday afternoon, so that we can run a check. I'll be along in a bit.' Gemma started to protest, but he had already turned away, and for a moment she stood watching him walk across the garden towards the dog's run. Then, sensing that Will was watching her, she turned and opened the cloakroom door a little more forcefully than necessary.

The white-tiled kitchen floor winked at Gemma as she entered, its glossy surface pristine, unmarred. Someone had cleaned away the blood.

Gemma looked suspiciously at Will, remembering he'd made some excuse to stay behind when they'd left for the pub last night, but he merely gave her an innocent smile. The fingerprint technician was still busily dusting the cabinet surfaces, but aside from that Gemma could almost imagine it an ordinary room on an ordinary day, waiting for the smell of toast and coffee and sleepy breakfast chatter. A colourful placemat and napkin lay on the table in front of the garden window, along with a copy of *The Times*. The paper bore yesterday's date, Gemma discovered when she examined it, yet she didn't remember seeing it last night—she barely remembered noticing the breakfast alcove. That wouldn't do at all, she told herself, and interrupted Will's quiet conference with the technician more sharply than she'd meant.

'Mrs Gilbert made herself a cup of tea, said she'd be in the conservatory if anyone wanted her,' the fingerprint man said in answer to Gemma's question, then went back to his tuneless whistling.

Remembering the glassed extension she'd seen from the garden, Gemma led the way through the kitchen and turned to the right. She tapped lightly on the door at the end of the hall, and when she heard no answer after a moment, opened the door and looked in.

Although a profusion of green plants gave the room the proper conservatory ambience, it was obviously very much lived in. Two squashy sofas faced each other, separated by a low table covered with books and newspapers. A woolly rug drooped from one sofa back, and a pair of reading glasses sat jauntily on a side table. A pair of Doc Martens peeked from under the other sofa, the first sign Gemma had seen that Lucy Penmaric lived in this house.

Claire Gilbert sat in the corner of the near sofa with her back to the door, stockinged feet curled up beneath her, a yellow legal pad in her lap. Her gaze rested not on the pad, however, but on the garden, and even when Will and Gemma stepped into the room she didn't stir.

'Mrs Gilbert?' Gemma said softly, and

then Claire turned her head with a start.

'I'm sorry. I was miles away.' She gestured at the pad in her lap. 'There are so many things to be done. I thought I'd make a list, but I can't seem to keep at it.'

'We need to ask you a few questions, if you don't mind,' said Gemma, directing a silent and unflattering epithet towards Kincaid for leaving her with this task. She never grew inured to the grief of bereaved relatives, had in fact given up hope of becoming so.

'Sit down, please.' Claire slipped her feet into her shoes and smoothed her skirt over her knees.

'You're looking a bit better this morning,' said Will as he sat down on the sofa opposite her. 'Did you sleep, then?'

'I didn't think I possibly could, but I did. Strange, isn't it, how the body makes its own decisions.' She did look better, less drawn and fragile, her skin porcelain-fine even in the mercilessly clear morning light.

'And Lucy?' he asked as Gemma sat beside him and took out her notebook.

Claire smiled. 'I found the dog stretched out on the bed with her this morning, but she didn't stir even when I took him out. I insisted she take a sedative last night. She's stubborn as a mule, though you wouldn't think it to look at her, and she doesn't like to admit when she's reached her limit.'

'Takes after her mum, does she?' said Will with a familiarity that Gemma, daunted by Claire Gilbert's rather formal good manners, would have found impossible to attempt. She remembered Claire's distress when she realized Will had left the room last night, and marvelled that he had managed to establish such rapport in only a few hours.

Claire smiled. 'Perhaps you're right. Though I was never as single-minded about things as Lucy. I fluffed my way through school, although I dare say I could have done better if I'd had some idea what I wanted to do. Dolls and house...' she added softly, looking out into the garden again and pleating the fabric of her skirt with her fingers.

'I'm sorry?' said Gemma, not sure she'd heard correctly.

Focusing on her, Claire smiled apologetically. 'I was one of those little girls who played house and nursed her dolls. It never occurred to me that marriage and family might not be the centre of my life, and my parents encouraged that, my mother especially. But Lucy... Lucy's wanted to be a writer since she was six years old. She's always worked hard at school, and now she's studying to sit her mocks in preparation for her A levels in the spring.'

Will leaned forward, and Gemma noticed absently that the elbow of his tweed jacket was wearing thin. 'She goes to the local comprehensive, then?' he asked.

'Oh, no,' Claire answered quickly, then she seemed to hesitate for a moment before continuing. 'She's a day student at the Duke of York School. I suppose I'll have to ring the headmaster sometime today and explain what's happened.' Exhaustion seemed to wash over her at the thought. Her mouth quivered, and for a moment she covered it with her fingers. 'I think I'm managing well enough until I have to tell someone, and then...'

'Isn't there someone who can make these calls for you?' Gemma asked, as she had before, but hoping that with rest Claire would have reconsidered.

'No.' Claire straightened her shoulders. 'I won't have Lucy do any of it. This is difficult enough for her as it is. And there's no one else. Alastair and I were both only children. My parents are dead, and Alastair's father. I've been to his mother already this morning, first thing. She's in a nursing home near Dorking.'

Gemma felt a rush of sympathy for Claire Gilbert. Telling an old woman that her only son was dead could not

61

have been easy, yet Claire had done what was necessary, alone and as quickly as possible. 'I'm sorry. That must have been very difficult for you.'

Claire gazed out of the window again, touching her fingers to the silk scarf at her throat. In the reflected light her pupils shrank to pinpoints, and her irises were as gold as a cat's. 'She's eighty-five and physically a bit frail, but her mind's still sharp. Alastair was very good to her.'

In the silence that followed they heard Lewis give a sharp, playful bark, then came a good-natured shout from Kincaid. Claire gave a tiny, startled jerk and dropped her hand to her lap. 'I'm sorry,' she said, looking at them again. 'Where were we?'

'If you could just tell us a little more about your movements yesterday afternoon and evening?' Gemma uncapped her pen and waited, but Claire seemed puzzled.

'I'm sorry,' she said again. 'I'm afraid I don't understand.'

'You said you and Lucy did some shopping,' prompted Gemma. 'Where exactly did you go?'

'But what difference could it possibly—' Claire's protest died as she looked at Will.

He shook his head gently. 'How can we know at this point what's important and what isn't? Some detail, something someone said, something you saw, could prove the glue that holds all the pieces together, so please be patient.'

After a moment, Claire said, 'Oh, all right,' with some grace and settled back into the sofa. 'I'll give it a try.

'About half-past four we left the house and drove into Guildford. Lucy drove— she's only had her licence a few months and likes to practise whenever she can. We left the car in the Bedford Road car park and crossed over the pedestrian bridge to the Friary.'

'A shopping precinct,' Will explained to Gemma. 'A conversion of the old Friary Meaux brewery site, very upmarket.'

Claire smiled a little at Will's description. 'I suppose it is, but I have to confess that I like it. Staying warm and dry while one goes round the shops has its advantages.' Her smile faded as she returned to her story. 'Lucy needed a book from Waterstone's...she's reading Hardy for one of her exams, I think. After that...' She rubbed her forehead, then gazed out of the window for a moment. Gemma and Will waited patiently until she sighed and began again. 'We bought some coffee at the speciality shop, then a bottle of Badedas at Boots. After that we window-shopped for a bit, then had some tea at the restaurant in the court,

I can't think of its name. It's absurd. I seem to have these gaps in my mind where things I know perfectly well should be, but instead there's a perfect blank. I remember when—' Claire paused on the shudder of an indrawn breath, then gave a sharp shake of her head. 'Never mind. It doesn't matter now. Lucy and I left the centre from the far side and walked up the High Street to Sainsbury's, where we picked up a few things for our dinner. By the time we finished and drove home it was almost half-past seven.'

Gemma's pen flew over the page until she caught up, but before she could frame a question, Claire spoke again. 'Must I...the next bit...must I go over it again?' Her hand hovered near her throat again, and Gemma saw her fingers tremble slightly. She had small, slender hands, with fine, unmarked skin, and although her nails were very short, they were buffed to a healthy pink.

'No, Mrs Gilbert, not just now,' said Gemma a bit absently as she thumbed back through her notes. When she reached the beginning of the interview she paused, then looked up at Claire Gilbert. 'But tell us about the earlier part of the afternoon. You didn't say what you were doing before going to Guildford.'

'I'd been at work, of course,' Claire said with a touch of impatience. 'I'd just got home minutes before Lucy arrived back from school—oh, my God...' Her hand flew to her mouth. 'I didn't ring Malcolm. How could I have forgotten to ring Malcolm?'

'Malcolm?' Will raised an eyebrow.

'Malcolm Reid.' Claire rose and went to the window, where she stood looking out into the garden, her back to them. 'It's his shop—his business—and I work in the shop, but I also do some consulting.'

Forced to turn around awkwardly, Gemma squinted at Claire's outline, haloed by the light. 'Consulting?' She hadn't thought of Claire Gilbert working, had automatically categorized her as a pampered housewife with no duties more demanding than attending meetings at the Women's Institute, and now she chided herself for her carelessness. Assumptions in an investigation were dangerous—and an indication that she didn't have her mind on her job. 'What sort of business is it?' she added, resolving to give Claire Gilbert her undivided attention.

'Interior design. The shop's in Shere— it's called Kitchen Concepts, but kitchens aren't all we do.' Claire glanced at her watch and frowned. 'It's just getting on for nine o'clock—Malcolm won't have missed me yet.' The smooth fall of her fair hair caught the light as she shook her head, and when she spoke her voice wavered for the first time. 'Telling Gwen was all I could think of from the time I woke this morning, then once I'd done that...I feel such a ninny—' She broke off suddenly and laughed. 'When have you heard that expression? My mother used to say that.' Her laughter stopped as suddenly as it had begun and she sniffed.

Will had taken advantage of Claire's retreat to the window to rise and explore the room. He'd wandered over to a dresser that stood against the back wall and now idly rearranged a collection of seashells. 'You mustn't be too hard on yourself,' he said, turning to Claire. 'You've had a dreadful shock and you can't expect to go on as if nothing has happened.'

'Those are Lucy's.' Coming to stand beside him, Claire picked up a small green-and-red-speckled shell and turned it in her hands. 'She had a book about the seaside she loved as a child, and she's collected shells ever since. This one's called Christmas. Apt, isn't it?' She replaced the shell, aligning it carefully, then gave an odd little shake of her head, as if to clear it. 'I keep thinking that Alastair would expect me to cope, and then I remember...' Her words trailed off and she stood for a moment, staring at the shells, her hands hanging limply at her sides. Then, seeming to gather herself with an effort, she turned to them and smiled. 'I'd better ring Malcolm as soon as possible. The shop opens at half-past and I'd not want him to hear it from someone else.'

Gemma gave in gracefully. 'Thank you, Mrs Gilbert,' she said as she tucked her notebook into her bag and stood. 'You've been very helpful. We'll leave you to get on with things.' The rote phrases came easily, while underneath she wondered furiously where in hell Kincaid had got to and what he could have been doing poking about in the garden all this time. Claire came with them to the door, and as Gemma stepped into the hall Will stopped and murmured something to her that Gemma didn't quite catch.

The fingerprint technician had packed up his equipment and gone, leaving only his dust to mar the impression that normal life in the Gilbert household would resume at any time. The light came more strongly through the bay window, highlighting the motes dancing in the air. Gemma went to the window and looked out into the garden—there was no sign of Kincaid.

'What's next?' asked Will as he came

in from the hall. 'Where's our super got himself off to?'

Gemma thanked whatever guardian angel made her bite her lip rather than venting her bad temper, because just at that moment Kincaid came in through the cloakroom door and smiled broadly at them both. 'Waiting for me? Sorry. I got a bit carried away in the garden shed.' He wiped a smudge of dirt from his forehead and brushed ineffectually at the cobwebs on his jacket. 'How did you—'

'Was the dog giving you a hand?' interrupted Gemma. As soon as the words left her mouth she heard their shrewishness and would have called them back if she could. Flushing with shame, she drew a breath to explain, apologize, and then she saw that in his left hand he held a hammer.

The hall door flew open and Claire Gilbert came in as if propelled, her cheeks pink stained. 'Malcolm says they've been round to the shop already,' she said breathlessly, looking from one of them to the other in appeal. 'People saying things and reporters. They're coming here. The reporters are coming here—' Her gaze fixed on Kincaid, the quick colour drained from her face and she crumpled upon the white tiles.

Chapter Four

For a large man, Will Darling moved with surprising swiftness. He managed to reach Claire before her head made contact with the floor, and now knelt beside her, supporting her head and shoulders against his knees. As Gemma and Kincaid hovered over them anxiously, Claire's eyelids fluttered open and she moved her head restlessly. 'I'm sorry,' she said as she focused on their faces. 'I'm sorry. I can't think what happened.'

She struggled to sit up, but Will restrained her gently. 'Keep your head down a bit longer. Just relax now. Still feel woozy?' When she shook her head, he raised her a few inches. 'We'll do it a little at a time,' he continued as he eased her into a sitting position and then into one of the breakfast area chairs.

'I'm so sorry,' Claire said once more. 'How dreadfully silly of me.' She rubbed at her face with trembling hands, and although some colour had returned to her cheeks, she remained unnaturally pale.

Kincaid pulled a chair away from the table and sat facing her. 'I didn't frighten

69

you with that, did I?' he asked, gesturing towards the hammer which he'd placed carefully on the nearby counter top. He'd rubbed absently at the cobwebs in his hair, and now a chestnut lock fell in a comma on his forehead. With one eyebrow raised in concern, he looked deceptively, dangerously innocent, and Gemma found herself feeling sorry for Claire Gilbert. 'It's only the old hammer from your garden shed. A bit the worse from neglect, I'm afraid,' he added with a rueful smile, brushing at the sleeves of his jacket again.

'You don't think...that's what Alastair...' Claire shivered and hugged herself.

'From the layer of dust I'd say it had been months since anyone touched that hammer, but we'll need to run some tests just to be sure.'

Claire closed her eyes and took a breath, exhaling slowly. Tears began to slip beneath her closed lids as she spoke. 'It did frighten me. I don't know why. Last night they asked me over and over if I knew what might have been used, if there was anything missing, but I couldn't think. The garden shed never even occurred to me...'

Having seen her maintain her control when almost incoherent with shock and exhaustion, Gemma felt surprised at Claire's distress, yet thought she understood. Even though she had dealt with the bloody aftermath, Claire hadn't wanted to imagine what had happened to her husband. Her mind had avoided it until she confronted a physical reminder. Funny how the mind played tricks on you. 'Mrs Gilbert,' Gemma began, wanting to offer some comfort, 'don't—'

'Please don't keep on calling me that,' said Claire with sudden vehemence. 'My name is Claire, for God's sake.' Then she covered her face with her hands, muffling small hiccuping sobs.

With a warning shake of his head, Will mouthed, 'Let her cry.' He went to the refrigerator, and after a moment's rummaging, retrieved a loaf of bread, butter, and marmalade. Popping two slices in the toaster, he assembled plate and cutlery, putting things together so efficiently that by the time Claire's tears had subsided, her belated breakfast was ready.

'You've been living on tea,' he said accusingly. 'That's all you've had this morning, isn't it?' Without waiting for her answer, he went on. 'And you barely touched your food last night. You can't go on this way and expect to cope, now can you?' As he spoke he spread the butter and marmalade, then handed Claire a slice of toast.

Obediently she took a small bite.

Will sat beside her, watching with such concentration that Gemma could almost hear him urging Claire to chew and swallow, chew and swallow.

After a moment Kincaid caught Gemma's eye and motioned towards the garden. She followed a pace behind him through the narrow cloakroom, careful not to bump against him, determined not to notice the faint smell of his soap, his aftershave, his skin. But she couldn't help seeing that his hair needed cutting—he'd forgotten, as he often did, and it was beginning to creep over the edge of his collar at the back.

A wave of irrational anger swept through her, as if those wayward hairs had deliberately meant to offend her. When they reached the garden, she pounced on the first unrelated grievance that came to mind. 'Did you have to upset Claire Gilbert like that? She's been through enough as it is, and the least we can do is—'

'The least we can do is try to find out who killed her husband,' he interrupted sharply. 'And that means covering every possibility, however unlikely. And how was I supposed to know that the sight of the garden shed hammer would send her into a dead faint?' he added, sounding aggrieved. 'Either that or my face needs an overhaul.' He tried on a smile, but when she merely scowled back at him he said crossly, 'What the hell is the matter with you, Gemma?'

For a moment they stared at each other. She wondered how he could ask such a stupid question, then realized she didn't know the answer. All she could sort from the jumble of her feelings was that she wanted her confusion to go away, her world to right itself again. She wanted things to be as they were, safe and familiar, but she didn't know how to make it so.

She turned away and walked across the grass to the dog's run. Lewis wagged his tail in happy greeting, and she touched his nose through the wire mesh.

Kincaid's voice came from behind her, neutral now. 'And have you forgotten that the spouse is always the most likely suspect?'

'There's no evidence,' Gemma said, hooking her fingers through the fence. 'And besides, she has an alibi.'

'Too true, I'm afraid. Who's this Malcolm fellow Claire mentioned, by the way?' When she'd told him, he considered for a moment, then said, 'We'd best divide up the labour for the rest of the day. You and Will go over her tracks in Guildford. I'll wait here for Deveney, then perhaps we'll have a word with Malcolm Reid before we tackle the village.' He waited, and when she didn't answer, didn't turn, he said, 'We'll keep a PC on the gate until

73

the furore dies down, so Claire won't have to deal with the press unless she goes out. I hope that puts your mind at rest,' he added as he walked away, and he didn't quite manage to suppress the sarcasm.

Buckled into the passenger seat of Will's car, Gemma fumed silently. Who the hell did Duncan Kincaid think he was, ordering her about like some raw recruit? He hadn't discussed it with her, hadn't asked her opinion, and when a small voice in her head suggested that perhaps she hadn't given him the opportunity, she said aloud, 'Shut up.'

'Sorry?' said Will, taking his eyes off the curve of the road to give her a startled glance.

'Not you, Will. I'm sorry, I was thinking out loud.'

'Not a very pleasant conversation you were having,' he said, sounding amused. 'Want to add a third party?'

'It seems to me you take on enough without adding my troubles,' Gemma answered in an attempt to change the subject. 'How do you do it, Will? How can you stay objective when you seem to feel such empathy for the people involved?' She hadn't meant to speak so plainly, but something about him eased the normal safeguards off her tongue. Hoping he hadn't taken offence, she glanced at him, but he met her eyes and smiled.

'I have no trouble remaining objective when I'm presented with evidence of wrongdoing. But until then I see no reason why I shouldn't treat people with as much decency and consideration as possible, especially when they've been through an experience as difficult as Claire Gilbert's and her daughter's.' He looked at her again and added, 'You've brought out my upbringing. Sorry. I didn't mean to preach. My mum and dad were staunch supporters of the Golden Rule, though people don't set much stock by it nowadays.'

He kept his attention on the road after that, for they had reached the A25 and the morning traffic was heavy.

Gemma watched him curiously. She didn't often hear men talk willingly of their parents. Rob had been ashamed of his—hardworking tradespeople with unpolished accents—and she'd been furious with him when she'd heard him tell someone once that they were dead. 'Will...earlier you said the cathedral always *had* special significance, and just then you said your parents *were*...are your parents dead, then?'

Will coaxed the car around a grumbling farm lorry before answering. 'Two years ago, Christmas-time.'

'An accident?'

'They were ill,' he said. Then with a grin he added, 'Tell me about your family, Gemma. I couldn't help noticing the set of plastic keys in your handbag.'

'Very professional of me, isn't it? But if I don't keep them handy Toby loses the real thing,' and before she knew it she had launched into a detailed account of Toby's latest escapades.

The snapshot showed Claire and Lucy together, arms round one another, laughing into the camera, against a background that looked like the pier at Brighton. Gemma had borrowed it from a frame on the dresser in the conservatory. The spotty-faced assistant at Waterstone's studied it, then tossed his hair back and looked at Gemma and Will with bright, intelligent eyes. 'Nice bird. Bought a copy of *Jude the Obscure*. Wasn't inclined to stay for a chat, though.'

'You do mean the daughter?' said Gemma a bit impatiently.

'The younger one, yeah. Though the other's not bad, either,' he added with another considering glance at the photo.

'And you're sure you didn't see them both?' Gemma fought the urge to snatch the photo back, sure that he was smudging it with his fingerprints.

He tilted his head and eyed them speculatively. 'Can't swear to it, can I? It was a fairly busy afternoon, and I might not have even remembered her, if she hadn't come to the register.' With an exaggerated little sigh of regret he returned the photo to Gemma.

Will, leafing idly through the volume on the sales table beside the register, looked up. 'What time was it?'

For a moment the boy dropped his pose as he thought. 'After four, because that's when I take my break, and I remember I'd had it already. Nearer than that I can't say.'

'Thanks,' said Gemma, making an effort to sound as if she meant it, and Will gave him a card with the usual instructions to call them if he remembered anything else.

'Prat,' said Gemma under her breath as they left the shop.

'You're not feeling very charitable this morning, are you?' Will asked as they dodged shoppers laden with bags and parcels. 'Your boy will be just like that in a few years.'

Recognizing the tease, Gemma said, 'God forbid,' and smiled. 'He'd better not be. I hate men who *leer*. And boys.'

As they continued down their list of shops, the spotty-faced boy grew more appealing in retrospect. No one else had any recollection of mother or daughter, together or alone. 'At least we're warm and dry, which is more than some can say,' offered Will, dragging Gemma's attention from the window of a boutique. They'd parked the car in the Bedford Road car park, just as Claire had done, and crossed over Onslow Street into the Friary by the covered pedestrian walkway. Gusts of wind had shaken the bridge as the first drops of rain slicked the street below.

'Mmmm,' she answered, eyes on the dress in the window again. It was short, clingy, and black, the kind of dress she never bought, never had occasion to wear.

'Nice dress. You'd look great in it.' Will studied her, and she felt conscious of her unremarkable trousers and jacket. 'How long has it been since you've bought something you didn't need for work?'

Gemma frowned. 'I can't remember. And I've never had a dress like that.'

'Go on,' Will urged, grinning. 'Treat yourself. Have a quick look while I ring the station and check in.'

'You're a bad influence, Will. I shouldn't, I really shouldn't...' She was still grumbling as Will waved at her and ambled off in the direction of the phone box, but there didn't seem much point without an audience. Will was uncannily on the mark. She

78

bought good-quality, serviceable clothes, neutral enough to wear over and over, conservative enough not to hinder her career prospects—and she suddenly hated them. 'The condemned went quietly,' she said under her breath and entered the shop.

She emerged feeling a decade older—the teenage sales assistant had been dreadfully condescending—and considerably lighter in her bank balance. Thrusting the plastic carrier bag at Will, she said accusingly, 'I can't go around making inquiries carrying my shopping. Now what will I do?'

'Roll it up and put it in your handbag.' Will demonstrated patiently. 'You could hide an army in this thing. I've never understood why women don't get permanently lopsided from carrying around the equivalent of a suitcase all day.' He looked at his watch. 'We've still Sainsbury's to try, but I'm starving. Let's get a bite of lunch first, and maybe the rain will stop.'

After some debate they settled on the fish and chip shop in the food court and carried their trays to one of the moulded plastic tables in the common area. Will tucked into his food with relish, but with the first bite of fish, grease coated Gemma's mouth and ran down her throat, threatening to gag her with its rancid slickness. She pushed the tray away, and when Will looked up and frowned she snapped, 'Don't lecture me, Will. I'm not hungry. And I hate mushy peas.' She pushed at the distasteful mess with the prongs of her plastic fork.

When he returned to his lunch without comment, Gemma felt a rush of shame. 'I'm sorry, Will. I'm not usually like this. Really. It must be something about this case. Makes me feel all jumpy. And it'll be worse once the press get hold of it.'

'Sensitive, are you?' Will said as he loaded his fork with fish and peas, adding a chip for good measure. 'It's your guv and mine who'll have to tread carefully. Heads could roll if things aren't sorted out fast enough to please the powers that be. I'd just as soon not be in their shoes. Give me door-to-door in the rain any day.' He smiled and she felt restored to his good graces.

When he'd mopped up the last of his lunch, she said, 'Sainsbury's then?'

'And afterwards we'll stop in at the station and you can get acquainted with the lads in the incident room.'

Neither the deli assistant nor the checkout girl at Sainsbury's proved the least bit helpful. Gemma and Will came out into the High Street again discouraged, but at least Will had got his wish and the rain had receded to a soft drizzle. The pavements were thronged with shoppers, and a columned passageway held banks of flower-stalls. At the bottom of the steep street, Gemma could see the soft colours of the trees lining the river-banks.

'You'll have to see it in better circumstances,' said Will.

'It's lovely when the sun shines, and there's a first-class museum in the castle.'

'You're mind reading again, Will.' Gemma ducked away from a woman wielding an umbrella. 'It is a pretty town, even in the rain. Good place to grow up,' she said, thinking of Toby learning to fend for himself in the London streets.

'But I didn't—not in Guildford itself, anyway. We lived in a village near Godalming. I'm a farm boy—can't you tell?' He held up a broad hand for her inspection. 'See all those scars? A little tangle with the hay baler.' Touching the pale streak that sliced through his eyebrow, he added, 'Barbed wire, that one. My parents must have despaired of raising me to adulthood in one piece.'

'You're an only child,' Gemma said, guessing.

'A late blessing, they always said, in spite of the trips to the doctor's surgery.'

It was on the tip of Gemma's tongue to ask him what had become of the farm, but something in his expression stopped her. They walked the rest of the way back to the car park in silence.

Having asked Will to run her back to Holmbury St Mary in case she was needed, she felt a fool when the constable on the Gilberts' gate said that Kincaid and Deveney hadn't returned, nor had Kincaid left her a message.

'I've some phone calls to make,' she assured Will. 'I'll wait at the pub.' She waved him off with a smile, then slowly crossed the road. The rain had stopped, but the tarmac felt greasy beneath her feet and moisture hung heavily in the air.

The odour of stale cigarette smoke lingered inside the pub, but there was no sign of human presence. Gemma waited for a few minutes, warming her hands at the embers of the lunchtime fire. Her stomach rumbled emptily, and once she'd become aware of it, the pang quickly became ravenous hunger. Another trip to Surrey flashed in her memory, a day when she and Kincaid had shared sandwiches in a tea-shop garden, then walked along the river-bank.

Unshed tears smarted behind her eyelids. 'Don't be a stupid bloody cow,' she said aloud. Lack of sleep and low blood sugar, that's all that was wrong with her—nothing that a snack and nap wouldn't fix, and she might as well take advantage of the time on her own. Scrubbing at her eyes, she marched over to the bar, but the reconnaissance didn't turn up so much as a packet of stale crisps. She had some biscuits in her overnight bag—they would have to do.

She'd trudged halfway up the stairs, feeling as though her calves carried lead weights, when a body flew around the landing and cannoned into her. As the blow against her right shoulder spun her round, she lost her footing and sat down with a thump.

'Oh, God! I'm sorry. I didn't see you coming—are you all right?' The flying body resolved itself into an anxious-faced young man, broad-shouldered and sporting shoulder-length tumbling blond curls. He peered up at her, holding out a hand as if he weren't sure whether to help her or protect himself from her ire.

'I saw you last night,' she said, still too dazed to come up with anything more appropriate, 'when I came out of the bathroom.'

'I'm Geoff.' He dropped his hand and ventured a smile. 'Look, are you sure you're all right? I didn't hurt you? I didn't know anyone else was around—' Rolling his eyes, he added under his breath, 'Brian'll have my head on a platter.'

Gemma looked down, past his tatty sweater and jeans. He wore thick socks but no shoes. No wonder she hadn't heard him. 'I'm fine, really. I wasn't paying attention, either.' She studied him, liking his oval face and clear grey eyes. Although the moustache adorning his upper lip was a mere downy wisp, Gemma thought he must be in his mid-twenties, at the least. Tiny lines had begun to radiate from the corners of the eyes, and the creases between nose and mouth spoke of accumulated living.

Her stomach rumbled again, loudly enough for him to hear, and she groaned. 'If you can tell me how to rustle up something to eat around here, I'll call us even.'

'Come down to the kitchen and I'll make you a sandwich,' he said, looking pleased to be let off the hook so easily.

'You will? But...are you sure it's okay?' As she wondered why a guest would be so free with the pub's kitchen, a wave of light-headedness swept over her.

They stared at one another in consternation for a moment, then his face cleared and he said, 'I live here. I should have said. It's Geoff Genovase—Brian's my dad.'

The information took a moment to click into place, then she said, 'Oh, of course.

84

Silly of me not to have twigged.' Now that she knew, she could see it in the set of his shoulders, the shape of his head, the quick flash of his smile. 'That's all right, then.'

A little unsteadily, she followed him down to the kitchen. He seated her at a small table wedged into a space near the gas cooker, then opened the refrigerator and studied the contents. 'Cheese and pickle okay? That's what I was thinking of having.'

'Lovely.' As he rummaged in the fridge, she looked around the room. The kitchen was small but professionally equipped, from the stainless-steel cooker to the scarred work table.

Geoff sliced the crumbly cheddar and assembled the ingredients with the deftness of one who had grown up helping out in the kitchen, and in a few moments carried two plates of thick wholemeal sandwiches to the table. 'Go ahead,' he urged her. 'Don't be polite. I've put the kettle on, and I'll have us some tea in a minute.' As Gemma bit into her sandwich, he ran hot water into a brown earthenware pot to warm it. She made herself chew slowly, closing her eyes and tasting the buttery richness of the cheddar against the dark, sweet sharpness of the pickle. After the first few bites she felt her muscles begin to relax.

Geoff emptied the warm water from the pot and spooned in tea. With his back to her, he said, 'You're the lady copper, aren't you? Brian told me you came last night.' He added boiling water from the kettle on the cooker, then brought the pot and two mugs to the table. 'Milk?' Mouth too full to speak, Gemma nodded, and he returned to the fridge for a pint bottle. 'Sugar's on the table,' he said as he slid into the chair across from her.

'Did you know him?' Gemma asked, having managed to swallow. 'Commander Gilbert, I mean.'

''Course I did. Place like this, you can't *not* know people.' Even around a mouthful of bread and cheese, his tone held disgust.

'It must be hard for you,' said Gemma, her curiosity aroused, 'living in such a small village, I wouldn't think there'd be a lot going in the way of social life.'

Lots of young people stayed on with their parents when they couldn't find work—it was an economic fact of life. There'd been times after Rob left that she'd been afraid she and Toby might have to go back to her parents' small flat above the bakery, and the idea had horrified her. Geoff merely shrugged and said, 'It's all right.'

'The sandwich is super,' she said, washing down a bite with a mouthful of the tea he'd poured her. When he gave her a gratified smile, she ventured, 'What do you do? For a job, I mean?'

He waited until he'd finished chewing before answering. 'Oh, this and that. Mostly I help Brian out around the pub.' Pushing away from the table, he stood up and reached into the cupboard above the cooker. 'Look.' He selected a packet of biscuits and held it out for her inspection. 'I know just what we need to finish up.'

'Chocolate digestives?' Gemma said with a sigh of contentment. 'The plain ones, too. My favourite.' She ate in silence for a few minutes, and when she'd finished her sandwich, she separated a biscuit from the stack and nibbled on its edge. Geoff had undoubtedly shied away from the personal—she'd try the general again. 'You must have been pretty shocked when you heard about the commander. Were you here last night?'

'I was in my room, but Brian saw the pandas go by, lights and sirens. He called me down to take over the bar—it was John's night off—then he went straight across the road, but they wouldn't let him through. "There's been an accident" was all they'd tell him, and he came back in a right state. We didn't know until Nick Deveney sent a constable over to make arrangements for you that it was the commander, not Lucy or Claire.'

'And that made a difference, did it?' asked Gemma, thinking how much people revealed unwittingly, just by the construction of their sentences, their emphasis on certain words.

'Of course it did.' Geoff sat back in his chair and crossed his arms. 'Like I said, it's a small place, and everybody knows everybody, especially neighbours. Lucy's a nice kid, and Claire...everyone likes Claire.'

Odd, thought Gemma, if Claire Gilbert was so well thought of, that she had leaned on Will Darling rather than accepting comfort from a sympathetic neighbour. 'But not Alastair Gilbert?' she asked. 'You didn't mind so much about him?'

'I didn't say that.' Geoff frowned at her, their pleasant camaraderie definitely damaged. 'It's just that he's not *here*—I mean he wasn't here—what with his job and being in London most of the time.'

'I knew him,' said Gemma, putting her elbows on the table and propping her chin in one hand. She wondered why she hadn't mentioned it to Kincaid, then shrugged. She hadn't felt inclined to volunteer anything remotely personal.

'He was my super at Notting Hill when I first joined the Force,' she continued.

Geoff relaxed, looking interested and settling more comfortably into his chair, as if Gemma's admission had put them back on equal footing. Sipping her tea, she said, 'But I didn't really *know* him, of course—there were more than four hundred officers at Notting Hill, and I was too lowly to come to his attention. He might have spoken ten words to me in all that time.' The man she remembered seemed to have little connection to the body sprawled so messily on the Gilberts' kitchen floor. He'd been small and neat, soft-spoken and particular in his dress and his diction, and had occasionally given little pep talks to the ranks about the importance of rules. '"A tight ship," my sergeant used to say. "Gilbert runs a tight ship." But I don't think he meant it kindly.'

'He did like things his way.' Geoff broke another biscuit in two and popped one half into his mouth. Indistinctly, he said, 'He was always at odds with the village council over something, wanting them to enforce the parking restrictions round the green, things like that.' The second biscuit half followed the first, then he refilled both their cups. 'And he had a row with the doctor a couple of weeks ago. If you can call it rowing when no one raises his voice.'

'Really?' Gemma sat up a bit. 'What about?'

'I don't know. I didn't actually hear it. It was a Saturday, see, and I do some odd jobs for the doctor. When I went up to the kitchen door to ask her about the compost, he was just leaving. But something had happened—you know how you can tell sometimes, like bad feeling stays in the air. And Doc Wilson had that tight-lipped look.'

'Her? I mean she?' said Gemma, trying to sort out her cases.

'This is a very feminist village—lady doctor and lady vicar. And I don't think the Commander got on with either of them.'

Gemma remembered that Gilbert's manner to the women under his command had bordered on condescending, and he'd been notorious for overlooking female officers for promotions.

'I can't wait to meet them,' she said, toying with the idea of stealing a march on Kincaid by interviewing the doctor.

'This afternoon?' Geoff studied her with concern. 'You look all in, if you don't mind my saying so.'

'Thanks.'

Her evident sarcasm made Geoff blush. 'I'm sorry. It's just that—you know what I mean. You look tired, is all.'

She relented. 'It's okay. Maybe I will go up to my room for a bit. And thanks for looking after me. I'd have caved in, I think, if you hadn't rescued me.'

'Any time, fair damsel.' He stood and gave a little bow. Gemma laughed, thinking doublet and hose would have suited him and imagining his fair curls under a plumed hat.

She followed him up the stairs, and when they reached the door of his room, he stopped. 'Tell me if you need anything else. I'm at your—'

His words faded out of Gemma's perception. A computer sat on a desk across his room, and she stood staring, fascinated by the image on the screen. 'What is it?' she asked, without taking her eyes from the picture. Mist seemed to swirl in the eerie, three-dimensional scene, but she could make out a turreted castle, and through one of its doorways a vista of green grass and a path leading towards a mountain.

'It's a role-playing game, an adventure. A girl finds herself transported to a strange land, and she must survive by her wits, her skills, and her small knowledge of magic. Only by following a certain path and collecting talismans can she discover the secrets of the land, and then she will have the power to stay or to go back to our world.

'You can play. I'll show you.' He touched her arm but Gemma shook her head, resisting the enchantment.

'I can't. Not now.' Pulling her gaze away, she focused on his face. 'What does she choose, in the end?'

He regarded her, the expression in his grey eyes unexpectedly serious. 'I don't know. That all depends on the player.'

Chapter Five

Kincaid stood alone in the Gilberts' kitchen, listening to the sound of the ticking clock. It hung above the refrigerator, and the large black hands and numerals against its white face were impossible to miss, reminding him that time was indeed fleeting. He should be concentrating on Alastair Gilbert's murder, rather than wanting to punch his fist against the wall in frustration every time he thought about Gemma. After her outburst in the garden, she had left for Guildford without speaking an unnecessary word to him. What in hell had he done now? At least, he thought with a flare of satisfaction, he hadn't sent her traipsing off around the county with Nick Deveney, after the way he'd leered at her last night.

Sighing, Kincaid ran a hand through his hair. There was nothing for it but to get on with things as best he could. Glancing automatically at his watch, he shrugged in irritation. He bloody well knew what time it was, and as long as he had to wait for Nick Deveney and had the ground floor of the house to himself, he might as well have a look round.

Entering the hall, he stood quietly for a moment, orienting himself. For the first time he noticed the higgledy-piggledy nature of the house—a step here, a step down there—every room seemed to exist on a different level. The exposed beams in the walls were canted at slightly tipsy angles. For a moment he fancied he heard an echo of the kitchen clock, then traced the insistent ticking to a grandfather clock half hidden in an alcove beneath the stairs. To his untrained eye, it looked old and probably quite valuable. A family heirloom, perhaps?

Nearest the kitchen lay the sitting room they had used last night, and a quick glance showed it quiet and empty, the fire burned down to cold ash. Continuing down the hall towards the front of the house, he opened the next door and peered in.

He'd found the commander's study, without a doubt. Entering and looking about, he felt that the room was almost a parody of a masculine retreat—the walls not covered with bookshelves were dark panelled, a green-shaded lamp cast a pool of light on a massive desk, the sofa set before the heavily curtained windows was covered in a deep red tartan. Moving closer, he studied the light oblongs on the dark walls—hunting prints, of course. The sound of the heavy clock on the desk mimicked his heartbeat, and for a moment he imagined the entire house ticking to its own internal rhythm. 'Bloody hell!' Swearing aloud broke the spell, and he banished thoughts of the Edgar Allan Poe story from his mind.

Crossing to the desk, Kincaid found the surface as tidy as expected, but a photo in a silver frame made him pause and lift it for a better look. This was an Alastair Gilbert he'd never seen, in shirt-sleeves, smiling, with his arm around a small white-haired woman. Mother and son? He replaced the photo, filing in his mind the thought that interviewing the elder Mrs Gilbert might prove useful.

The top drawer held the usual office paraphernalia, neatly arranged, and the side drawers, tidy ranks of files that would have to wait for someone else to give them a detailed going-over. Unsatisfied with such meagre results, Kincaid went through the drawers again, and the more careful search revealed a leather-bound book tucked behind the files in the right-hand drawer. Removing it carefully, he opened it on the blotter. It was a desk diary, with the usual engagement notations and a few unidentified phone numbers written in a neat, pencilled hand. How like Gilbert not to have risked making a mistake in ink!

Kincaid turned a few more pages. The day before Gilbert's death held an ambiguous '6:00', accompanied by a question mark and another pencilled phone number. Had Gilbert met someone, and if so, why? He'd have to leave it to Deveney's team to run checks on all the notations while he concentrated on the interviews. Closing the book, he'd placed it on the desktop when a voice startled him.

'What are you doing?'

Lucy Penmaric stood in the doorway, arms crossed, heart-shaped face creased in a frown. In jeans and sweatshirt she looked younger than she had the night before, less sophisticated, and her pale face bore tiny creases, as though she'd just got up. 'I heard a noise—I was looking for my mother,' she said before he could answer.

Not wanting to talk to Lucy from behind

Gilbert's desk, Kincaid closed the drawer and came around it before he said, 'I think she's upstairs having a rest. Can I help?'

'I didn't think to look there,' she said, rubbing her face as she went to curl up in the corner of the tartan sofa. 'I can't seem to wake up properly—my brain's gone all fuzzy.'

'I imagine it's the sleeping pill. If you're not used to them they can make you feel a bit hung over.'

Lucy frowned again. 'I didn't want to take it. I only agreed so Mum would rest. Is she...is she all right this morning?'

Kincaid felt no compunction in editing out Claire's fainting spell in the kitchen. 'Coping reasonably well, under the circumstances. She went to visit your grandmother first thing.'

'Gwen? Oh, poor Mum,' said Lucy, shaking her head. 'Gwen's not my real grandmother, you know,' she added in an instructive voice. 'Mummy's parents are dead, and I don't get to see my dad's very often.'

'Why not? Doesn't your mother get on with them?' Kincaid settled himself against the edge of the desk, willing to see where the conversation might lead.

'Alastair always had some reason why I shouldn't go, but I like them. They live near Sidmouth, in Devon, and you can walk to the beach from their house.' Lucy twirled a strand of hair around her finger as she sat quietly for a moment, then she said, 'I remember when my dad died. We lived in London then, in a flat in Elgin Crescent. The building had a bright yellow door—I remember when we came back from walks I could see it from a long way away, like a beacon. We had the top-floor flat, and a cherry tree blossomed just outside my window every spring.'

If he'd thought about Claire Gilbert's first husband at all, he would have assumed they'd divorced, but then what were the odds that a woman in her forties would find herself twice widowed? 'It sounds lovely,' he said softly after Lucy fell silent for so long he feared she'd retreated where he couldn't follow.

'Oh, it was,' said Lucy, coming back to him with a little shiver. 'But cherry blossoms always make me think of death now. I dreamed of them last night. I was covered in them, suffocating, and I couldn't wake myself up.'

'Is that when your father died? In the spring?'

Lucy nodded, then pushed her hair away from her face and tucked it behind one ear. She had small ears, Kincaid thought, delicate as seashells. 'When I was five I was really ill with a high fever one night.

Dad went out to the all-night chemist in the Portobello Road to get something for me, and a car hit him at the zebra crossing. Now it's all mixed up in my head—the police coming to the door, Mum crying, the scent of the cherry blossom from my open window.'

So Claire Gilbert had not only been widowed but had faced a husband's sudden death once before. Remembering the days when giving an occasional death notification had been part of his duties, he imagined the scene from the officers' viewpoint—light spilling out from the flat on a soft April evening, the pretty young blonde wife at the door, apprehension growing in her face as she took in the uniforms. Then out with it, baldly, 'Ma'am, we're sorry to tell you that your husband is dead,' and she would stagger as if she'd been slapped. They'd been taught to do it that way in the Police College, kinder to get it over with, supposedly, but that never made it any easier.

Lucy sat with her hair twined around her finger again, staring at one of the hunting prints behind Gilbert's desk. When Kincaid said, 'I'm sorry,' she didn't respond, but after a moment began to speak without looking at him, as if continuing a conversation.

'It feels odd, sitting here. Alastair didn't

like us to come in this room, particularly me. His sanctum, he called it. I think women somehow spoiled the atmosphere.

'My dad was a writer, a journalist. His name was Stephen Penmaric, and he wrote mostly about conservation for magazines and newspapers.' She looked at Kincaid now, her face animated. 'He had his office in the box room of our flat, and there must not have been enough room because I remember there were always stacks of books on the floor. Sometimes if I promised to be really quiet, he'd let me play in there while he worked, and I built things with the books—castles, cities. I liked the way they smelled, the feel of the covers.'

'My parents had a book-shop,' said Kincaid. 'Still do, in fact. I played in the stock-room, and I used books for building blocks too.'

'Really?' Lucy looked up at him, smiling for the first time since she'd described her dog the night before.

'Honestly.' He smiled back, wishing he could keep that expression on her face.

'How lovely for you,' she said a bit wistfully. Tucking her feet up on the sofa, she wrapped her arms around her calves and rested her chin on her knees. 'It's funny. I hadn't thought about my dad so much in years.'

'I don't think it's funny at all. It's perfectly natural under the circumstances.' He paused, then said carefully, 'How do you feel about what's happened, about your stepfather's death?'

She looked away, her finger back in her hair again. After a bit she said slowly, 'I don't know. Numb, I suppose. I don't really believe it, even though I saw him. They say seeing is believing, but it's not really true, is it?' With a quick glance at the door, she added, 'I keep expecting him to walk in any minute.' She shifted restlessly, and Kincaid heard voices from the back of the house.

'I think that's probably Chief Inspector Deveney, looking for me. Will you be all right on your own for a bit?'

With a return of some of the spirit she'd shown last night, she said, 'Of course I'll be all right. And I'll look after Mummy when she gets up.' She jumped up from the sofa with the fluidity of the very young and had reached the door before he framed a reply.

As she turned back to him, he said, 'Lewis will be glad to see you,' and was rewarded by one more brilliant smile.

'Have you noticed,' Kincaid said to Nick Deveney as they wound their way through the series of lanes that lay between villages, 'that no one seems to be grieving for Alastair Gilbert? Even his wife seems to be shocked but not distraught.'

'True enough.' Deveney flashed his lights at an oncoming car and backed into the nearest passing place. 'But that doesn't give us a motive for murder. If that were the case, my ex-mother-in-law would be dead twenty times over.' He pulled out into the road again. 'Hope you don't mind the short-cut. Actually, I'm not sure it *is* a short-cut, but I like driving through the hills. Beautiful, isn't it?' Storm clouds had gathered in the west, but as he spoke a shaft of sun broke through, illuminating the air deep in the woods. Deveney glanced in his rear-view mirror. 'I'll bet they're getting a soaking in Guildford,' he said, then pointed at the elaborate gates of an estate as they passed. 'Look. It's people like that who keep this part of Surrey from being overrun by tourists. They come here from London, bringing their money with them, so that we don't really need to boost our economy by encouraging trippers.' Shrugging, he added, 'But it's a double-edged sword. Although they buy property and use services, many of them are never really accepted by the locals, and that generates some conflicts.'

'And that was true of Gilbert, too? He certainly fitted the classic commuter profile,' Kincaid said as they came around a curve and gaps in the trees revealed a sweeping view across the North Downs.

'Oh, definitely, I'd say, and he was treated with a mixture of disdain and flattery. I mean, after all, you don't really want to kill the goose that lays the golden eggs, do you? You just don't want it to think it can sit at your table.'

Kincaid gave a snort of laughter. 'I suppose not. Do you think Gilbert was aware that he wasn't accepted, probably would never be accepted? Did it matter to him?'

Shrugging, Deveney said, 'I didn't really know him personally, just spoke with him a few times at police functions.' Changing gear, he added, 'I only know Brian Genovase because we played in the same over-the-hill rugby league.' The road had descended quickly from the hills, and now became a narrow street with picture-postcard cottages either side. 'Holmbury St Mary is quite unspoilt, while this village is competing for the "prettiest village in England" title. That's the Tillingbourne River,' he added as they crossed a clear stream, 'star of many a postcard.'

'It's not too bad, surely,' Kincaid said as Deveney deftly parked against the kerb. He'd seen a rather flowery tea-shop but nothing else that seemed out of the ordinary.

'No, but I'm afraid the tarting up is inevitable.'

'Cynic.' Kincaid followed Deveney out of the car, flexing toes that had suffered from the failure of the Vauxhall's heating system.

Laughing, Deveney agreed, then added, 'I'm too young to sound like such an old codger. Must be divorce has a tendency to sour a man's outlook. Now this shop is certainly not a bad thing'—he gestured at a sign reading KITCHEN CONCEPTS—'and it wouldn't be possible without commuters like Alastair Gilbert. It would never occur to the local farmers to have their kitchens refitted in Euro-chic.'

The window showed them colourful expanses of tile interspersed with gleaming copper fittings. Kincaid, who had refitted the kitchen in his Hampstead flat using mostly do-it-yourself materials, opened the door with some anticipation. A wellie-clad woman holding carrier bags stood chatting with a man near a display of cabinet fronts, but their conversation came to an awkward halt as Kincaid and Deveney entered.

After a moment the woman said, 'Well, I'll be off then. Cheerio, Malcolm.' She gave them a bright, interested glance as she squeezed out of the door, holding her shopping to her chest like a bulging shield. What was the use of being out of uniform,

Kincaid often wondered, when you might as well be wearing a sign on your chest that said POLICE?

Deveney had his warrant card out, and introduced himself and Kincaid as Malcolm Reid came forward to greet them. Kincaid was happy to play second fiddle for a bit, as it gave him a chance to observe Claire Gilbert's employer. Tall, with short silvery-blond hair and evenly tanned skin that spoke of a recent holiday in a warmer clime, Reid spoke in a soft, unaccented voice. 'You've come about Alastair Gilbert? It's absolutely dreadful. Who would do such a thing?'

'That's what we're attempting to find out, Mr Reid,' said Deveney, 'and we'd appreciate any help you can give us. Did you know Commander Gilbert personally?'

Reid put his hands in his pockets before answering. He wore good-quality trousers, Kincaid noticed, and along with the grey pullover and discreet navy tie they created just the impression needed for Reid's position—not too casual for the owner of a successful business, not too formal for a small village. 'Well, of course I'd met him. Claire had Val—that's my wife, Valerie—and me to dinner once or twice, but I can't say that I knew him well. We didn't have much in common.' He gestured at the showroom, his expression slightly amused.

'But surely Gilbert was interested in his wife's career?' said Kincaid.

'Look, let's have a seat, shall we?' Reid led them to a desk at the rear of the showroom and waved them into two comfortable-looking visitors' chairs before seating himself. 'That's not an easy question.' He picked up a pencil and watched it meditatively while he rolled it between his fingers, then looked up at them. 'If you want an honest answer, I'd say he only tolerated Claire's job as long as it didn't interfere with his social schedule or his comforts. Do you know how Claire came to work for me?' He put the pencil down and leaned back in his chair. 'She came to me as a client, when Alastair finally gave her permission to decorate their kitchen. The house is Victorian, you know, and what little had been done to it had been done badly, as is so often the case. Claire had been nagging him for years, and I think he only gave in when their entertaining reached such a scale that it embarrassed him for guests to see the kitchen.'

For a man who professed not to know Gilbert well, Reid had certainly managed to build up an active dislike of him, Kincaid thought as he nodded encouragingly.

'Claire hadn't any design training,' continued Reid, 'but she had natural talent, which is even better in my book. When we started her kitchen she was brimming with imaginative *and* workable ideas—they don't always go together, you see—and when she came to the shop she'd help other customers, too.'

'And you didn't mind?' Deveney asked a bit sceptically.

Reid shook his head. 'Her enthusiasm was contagious. And the customers liked her ideas, which increased my sales. She's very good, though you'd never know it by looking at their house.'

'What's wrong with their house?' Deveney scratched his head in bewilderment—whether real or feigned Kincaid couldn't guess.

'Too stuffily traditional for my taste, but Alastair kept a tight rein on things and that's what he liked. It was his idea of middle-class respectability.'

Reid's judgement certainly seemed to fit Gilbert as Kincaid had known him. As an instructor he had been unimaginative, insisting on rules where flexibility might have been more productive, attached to traditions simply because they were traditions. His curiosity aroused, he asked Reid, 'Do you know anything about Gilbert's background?'

106

'I believe his father managed a dairy farm near Dorking, and Gilbert attended the local grammar school.'

'So the native came back,' mused Kincaid. 'I find that rather surprising. But then, his mother's in a home nearby, isn't she?' he asked, leaning forward to remove a business card from a holder on Reid's desk. The shop's name stood out artfully, dark green print against a cream background, with phone number and address in a smaller typeface. Kincaid slipped it into his jacket pocket.

'The Leaves, just on the outskirts of Dorking. Claire visits her several times a week.'

'Tell us about Mrs Gilbert's schedule yesterday, if you don't mind, Mr Reid.' Deveney's tone made it plain that this was a command and only framed as a request for politeness's sake.

Sitting forward again, Reid touched the pencil he'd put down on the blotter. Mimicking Deveney, he asked, 'Why should I, if you don't mind me asking? Surely you can't think Claire had anything to do with Gilbert's death?' He sounded genuinely shocked.

'It's a normal part of our inquiries,' soothed Deveney. 'You should know that from watching the telly, Mr Reid. We have to ask about everyone who was closely connected with Commander Gilbert.'

Reid crossed his arms and regarded them steadily for a moment, as if he might refuse, then he sighed and said, 'Well, I still don't like it, but I can't see any harm in it because there was nothing out of the ordinary. Claire came in around ten and spent the day in the shop, helping customers, dealing with some outstanding orders for materials. I was out for an appointment early in the afternoon, and Claire left before I'd got back, a bit after four. She and Lucy had planned some shopping, I believe.' He paused for a moment, then added, 'We don't run a military ship around here, as you may have gathered.'

'And when did you find out that Gilbert was dead?' asked Kincaid, remembering Claire Gilbert's words before she'd fainted.

'Some of the locals were waiting when I unlocked the shop door this morning. They'd heard it from the postman, who'd heard it from the newsagent. "Somebody did for Alastair Gilbert last night—bashed his head in and left him in a pool of his own blood," were the exact words, I believe,' he added with a grimace.

Deveney thanked him, and they took their leave, Kincaid with a backward glance at the stainless-steel arch of the German mixer-tap he hadn't been able to afford for his own kitchen sink.

'Terrific,' Deveney said with weary resignation as they got into the car. 'So much for keeping the cause of death under our hats until we've interviewed the villagers. That's life in the country for you.'

The last customer, a garrulous old woman named Simpson, stood chatting long after she'd paid for her meagre purchases. Madeleine Wade, who included proprietorship of the village shop among her many ventures, listened absently to the latest tabloid scandal while she closed out the till. All the while she thought longingly of curling up in her snug upstairs flat with a glass of wine and the *Financial Times*. The 'pink paper', as she always thought of it, was her secret vice and the last relic from her former life. She read it every day, tracking her investments, then tucked it away out of sight of her clients—no point in disillusioning the dears.

Mrs Simpson, having received no more encouragement than the occasional nod, finally sputtered to a halt, and Madeleine saw her out with relief. Over the years she'd learned to be more comfortable with people, forced herself to develop an armour impervious to all but the most open revulsion, but it was only when alone that she felt truly at peace. It became her solace, her reward at the end of the day, and she anticipated it with the same eagerness an alcoholic awaits his first drink.

She saw him as she finished locking the door. Geoff Genovase stood half in the shadow of The White Hart next door, hands in his pockets, waiting. When he moved, the light from the street-lamp glittered on his fair hair.

His fear reached her then. Palpable and intense, it enveloped him like a dense cloud.

She'd sensed it before, a dim undercurrent —sensed also the careful control that kept it in check. What had caused this explosion of terror? Madeleine hesitated, her desire to help warring with her fatigue and her need for solitude, then felt a pang of shame. She'd come to this village after a lifetime of running away, intending to offer whatever aid her talents might provide, and such selfishness must be crushed by discipline.

Whatever had triggered Geoff's distress, he'd come to her for comfort, and she could not refuse. She stepped forward, lifting a hand to call out to him, but he had melted into the shadows.

When a knock at Gemma's door brought

no response, Kincaid went back to his room and scribbled a note telling her he'd be in the bar and that Deveney would be meeting them for drinks and dinner. He slipped the scrap of paper under her door and waited for a moment, still hoping for a quiet word with her, but when there was no stir of movement he turned away and went slowly downstairs.

He and Nick Deveney had spent an unproductive afternoon at Guildford Police Station, reading reports and sparring with the media, and it had left the lingering taste of frustration. 'A pint of Bass, please, Brian,' he said as he slid on to the only unoccupied bar stool. 'A good crowd for a Thursday evening,' he added as Brian placed the pint glass on a mat.

'It's that nasty out,' Brian answered as he drew a pint for another customer. 'Always good for business.'

The rain had come on steadily with the dark, but Kincaid suspected that the pub's popularity this evening had as much to do with exchanging gossip as sheltering from the weather. Although he had to admit that as refuges went, the atmosphere was pleasant enough. A pub never felt right empty. It needed the movement of bodies and the rise and fall of voices in order to come into its own. This was his first opportunity to judge the Moon

111

under the proper circumstances. Swivelling around on his stool, he liked what he saw: comfortable without too much tarting up. There were velvet covers on the stools and benches, a dark-beamed ceiling, a few brasses, a few copper pieces in the dining area, flowered red-trimmed curtains shutting out the night, and the wood fire radiating warmth within.

A man in an oiled jacket squeezed in between Kincaid and the next stool, handing his glass to Brian to be refilled. He spoke without preamble, as if continuing a discussion. 'Well, he may have been a right bastard, Bri, but I never thought it would have come to that.' He shook his head. 'Can't even feel safe in our own bloody beds these days.'

Brian gave a quick, involuntary glance in Kincaid's direction, then said noncommittally as he pulled the pint, 'He wasn't in his bed, Reggie, so I doubt we need worry about ours.' He wiped away the foam that had overflowed the glass and slid it across the bar before nodding at Kincaid and adding, 'This is Superintendent Kincaid, down from London to look into things.'

The man gave Kincaid a brusque acknowledgement, muttering something that sounded like, 'Our own lads do well enough,' before making his way back to his table.

Brian leaned across the bar and said earnestly to Kincaid, 'Don't mind Reggie. He'd find fault with sunshine in May.' But the buzz of conversation around Kincaid had died, and he felt himself the target of glances both interested and wary.

It was a relief when Deveney came in a few minutes later, shaking the water droplets from his rain hat before stuffing it into his overcoat pocket. Just as Kincaid stood up to greet him, the table nearest the fire emptied and they took it over with alacrity.

When Deveney had returned from the bar with his pint, Kincaid lifted his in salute. 'Cheers. You've just had a vote of confidence from the locals.'

'Wish I felt I deserved it.' Sighing, Deveney rotated his shoulders and neck. 'What a hell of a day. As much as I hated paperwork at school, why I ever—' His eyes widened as he looked towards the far end of the room, then he smiled. 'The day just improved considerably.' Following his gaze, Kincaid saw Gemma edging her way through the crowd. 'Why can't my sergeant look like that?' Deveney complained with an air of much-practised martyrdom. 'I'll complain to the chief constable, take it all the way to the top.' But Kincaid barely heard him. The dress was black and long-sleeved, but there any pretence of demureness ended, for the fabric clung to Gemma's body until it stopped midway down her thighs. She seldom wore her hair loose, but tonight she had left it so, and her fair skin looked pale as cream within its copper frame.

'Close your mouth,' Deveney said with a grin as he got up to fetch Gemma a chair.

'Gemma,' Kincaid began, not knowing what he meant to say, and the lights went out.

For an eerie moment a hush fell over the pub, then the voices rose in a wave—questioning, exclaiming.

'Just hold on,' Brian called out. 'I'll get the lanterns.' The wavering flame of his cigarette lighter disappeared through the door at the far end of the bar. Within moments he had three emergency lanterns lit and placed throughout the room.

The lamplight cast a soft yellow glow, and Deveney smiled at Gemma with unabashed pleasure. 'I'd say that was perfect timing. You look even lovelier by lamplight, if that's possible.'

At least she had the grace to blush, Kincaid thought as she murmured something unintelligible. 'No, let me get it,' Deveney said as Kincaid rose to get Gemma a drink. 'It's easier for me to get out.'

Kincaid sank back on to his bench and regarded her, unsure what he might say without antagonizing her. Finally he offered, 'Nick's right, you do look wonderful.'

'Thanks,' she said, but instead of meeting his eyes she fidgeted with the empty ashtray and looked towards the bar. 'I wonder where Geoff is? That's Brian's son,' she explained, turning back to Kincaid. 'I met him this afternoon, and from what he told me I thought he'd be helping out behind the bar.'

Appearing once more from the kitchen, Brian announced, 'I've been on to the Electricity Board. There's a transformer down between Dorking and Guildford, so it may be quite some time before we have power again. Not to worry,' he interrupted the buzz that was beginning, 'the cooker's gas, so most of the menu is still on.'

'That's a relief,' Deveney said as he returned with Gemma's vodka and orange, and the dinner menu. 'I'm starved. Let's see what Brian can do at a pinch.' When they'd made their decisions and settled back with their drinks, he said to Kincaid, 'I had a message from the chief constable waiting when I got back to the station. The gist of it was he expects to see something concrete, and there were a few phrases thrown in like "residents' peace of mind"

115

and "image of the force".'

Both Kincaid and Gemma pulled faces. It was familiar 'authority-speak' and had little to do with the mechanics of an investigation. 'You're still keen on your intruder theory, Nick?' asked Kincaid.

'It's as good as anything else we've got.' Deveney shrugged.

'Then I'd suggest we start by interviewing everyone in the village who's reported things missing. We'll have to eliminate the possibility of a connection before we can move on. Do we have a list from today's house-to-house?'

Just then Brian brought their salads. Once he'd set them on the table, he wiped his perspiring brow. 'Can't imagine what's kept John,' he said. Then he added, 'He helps out behind the bar, and I'm that strapped without him tonight.'

'But what about Geoff?' asked Gemma.

'Geoff? What has Geoff got to do with it?' Brian said impatiently, then hurried away as another customer called to him.

'But—' Gemma said to his retreating back, then subsided, a flush creeping up her cheekbones. 'I know he said he worked for his dad, and it seemed a logical assumption that he tended bar.'

'So what do you make of Geoff, then?' asked Deveney, drawing attention from her embarrassment, and she launched into an account of their meeting that afternoon.

Kincaid listened, watching her animated face and hands as she talked to Deveney, and felt more excluded by the minute. He toyed with the ubiquitous cress and iceberg lettuce of his salad, wondering if he had really known her at all. Had he lain next to her, felt her skin against his, her breath on his lips? He shook his head in disbelief. How could he have been so wrong about what had happened between them?

The word 'quarrel' pulled him back to the conversation and he said, 'What? I'm sorry.'

'Geoff told me that he overheard Gilbert and the village doctor quarrelling a couple of weeks ago,' Gemma answered a bit too patiently, as if Kincaid were a not-too-bright child. 'But he didn't know what it was about, only that they both seemed angry and upset.'

'It's odd,' she added a moment later as she speared a tomato wedge with her fork. 'I don't remember ever seeing Gilbert angry. There was just this sort of unspoken knowledge that if he spoke even more quietly than usual, you were in big trouble.'

'What?' Kincaid said again, glass halfway to his mouth. 'You knew him? You worked under Alastair Gilbert?' He felt a complete fool as Deveney looked at them with a puzzled expression.

'He was my super when I was a rookie at Notting Hill,' Gemma said dismissively. 'I didn't know it was important.' In the awkward silence that followed, she added, 'I think we should definitely interview this doctor first thing tomorrow, along with the burglary victims.'

'Wait, Gemma,' said Kincaid. 'Someone needs to get on to Gilbert's office, check out that end of things. And you'll be needing to look after Toby. Why don't you go up to London tomorrow, and Nick and I will do the interviews here?'

She didn't speak as she pushed her plate away and carefully laid down her knife and fork, but the look she gave him could have frozen lava.

Chapter Six

Morning commuters packed the Dorking to London train. 'There is no direct service from Guildford,' Will Darling had explained to Gemma when he'd picked her up from the pub. 'So there's usually a bit of a crush.' Gemma bumped against more than one briefcase before she reached the only available seat. The immense woman

118

opposite left no room for Gemma's knees and she had to wedge herself in sideways. But as the train came to life with a jerk, she settled herself against the window contentedly enough, grateful for the journey's quiet minutes.

A good night's sleep had restored some of her perspective, and as Will dropped her at the station she'd apologized again for yesterday's behaviour.

'Don't give it another thought,' he'd assured her, his friendly face unperturbed. 'It's a difficult case for us all. It'll do you good to get home for a bit.'

She'd had every intention of apologizing to Kincaid, too, but he and Deveney had left for a meeting at Guildford Police Station before she came down for breakfast. Over solitary toast and boiled egg she tried to convince herself that she really hadn't any reason to feel guilty. Kincaid had excused himself after dinner with a too polite reserve, and she'd been left to fend off the good-natured Deveney.

She hadn't deliberately set out to make Kincaid jealous—she'd always despised women who used such tactics—but Deveney's interest and Kincaid's growing discomfort had fuelled her like water on a grease fire. In the more sober light of day, she realized she'd have to be a bit more careful with Nick Deveney. He was an attractive single man, but to have him making overtures was the last thing she needed just now. And Kincaid—the reasons she had enjoyed making him squirm didn't bear too close an examination.

Deliberately, she turned her attention to more comfortable subjects.

Now, as the Surrey countryside gradually disappeared into the suburban sprawl of London, she thought about Alastair Gilbert, who had taken this same train every morning. She pictured him sitting where she sat, watching the world with careful eyes, briefcase close to his lap. What had he thought about as the miles clicked away? Or had he buried himself in his *Times* and not thought at all? Had any of the other passengers noticed his absence, wondered what had happened to the small, dapper man? Her eyes drifted closed until the squeal of brakes announced their arrival at Victoria.

Gemma walked up Victoria Street towards Buckingham Gate, taking her time, enjoying the thin sunshine that had followed last night's downpour. As she turned into Broadway, she found the sight of the Yard surprisingly welcome. For once, its stark aspect proved comforting, and it felt good to be on firm ground again.

Having made a brief report to Chief Superintendent Childs, she appropriated

Kincaid's office, but found none of her usual satisfaction in it. It allowed her the peace she needed to organize her day, however, and soon she had made an appointment with Commander Gilbert's staff officer, Chief Inspector David Ogilvie, and was on her way to the Divisional Headquarters in Notting Dale.

She remembered Ogilvie from her Notting Hill days, before he, like Gilbert, had transferred to divisional headquarters. He'd been an inspector then, and she'd felt a bit frightened of him. His dark, hawkish looks had made his reputation as a ladies' man plausible, but he seldom smiled, and his tongue was known to be as sharp as the jut of his nose.

Steeling herself for an unpleasant interview, she introduced herself to the duty officer and sat down in the reception area to wait until Ogilvie sent for her. Much to her surprise, Ogilvie appeared himself a few moments later, hand outstretched in welcome. He hadn't changed much, she thought, studying him as she shook his hand. Flecks of grey had appeared in his thick, dark hair, and the angles of his face were a bit more prominent, his body a little leaner.

He led her to his office, seated her cordially, then surprised her again by taking the initiative before she could get out her notebook and pen. 'This business about Alastair Gilbert is shocking. I don't think any of us have quite taken it in yet. We keep waiting for someone to tell us it was all a mistake.' He paused while he aligned some loose papers on his desk, then gazed at her directly.

His eyes were a very dark, pure grey, set off to perfection by the charcoal herringbone of his jacket. Gemma looked away. 'I'm sure it must be hard for you, having worked with—'

'You were part of the team called to the scene,' he interrupted, ignoring her condolence. 'I want you to tell me what happened.'

'But you'll have seen a report—'

Shaking his head, he leaned towards her, his dark eyes dilated. 'That's not good enough. I want to know what it looked like, what was said, down to the last detail.'

Gemma felt a prickle of sweat break out under her arms. What in hell was he playing at? Was this some sort of test of her abilities? And was she obliged to answer him? The silence stretched, and she shifted uncomfortably in her chair. What harm could it do, after all? He had access to the incident files anyway, and she needed to establish some sort of rapport with him. She took a deep breath and began.

Ogilvie sat very still while she talked, and when she'd finished he relaxed back into his chair and smiled at her. 'I see we trained you very well at Notting Hill, Sergeant.' Gemma started to speak, but he held up his hand. 'Oh, yes, I remember you,' he said, and his grin grew wolfishly wide. 'You were quite determined to get on, and it seems that you have. Now what can I do for you, since you've been so obliging? Will you be wanting to go through the things in the commander's office?'

'I'd like to ask you some questions first.' Having succeeded in retrieving her pen and notebook, Gemma flipped to a new page and headed it with determination. 'Had you noticed anything different about the commander's behaviour recently?'

Ogilvie swivelled his chair towards the window a little and appeared to give the matter serious thought. After a moment he shook his head. 'No, I can't say that I did, but then I knew Alastair for many years and I could never have guessed what he was feeling at any given time. He was a very private person.'

'Any difficulties at work? Could someone have threatened him?'

'You mean some villain threatening to do

for the copper as nicked 'im? I do believe you've been watching the telly, Sergeant.' Ogilvie gave a bark of amusement and Gemma flushed, but before she could retort, he said, 'As you are aware, Gilbert had little to do with day-to-day operational policing. And as he was always better at administration than tactics, I dare say it suited him.' He stood up with a swift grace that increased Gemma's impression of his fitness. 'I'll take you—'

'Chief Inspector.' Gemma didn't budge from her chair. 'Tell me about the commander's last day, please. Did he do anything out of the ordinary?'

Rather than sit down again, Ogilvie went to the window and fiddled absently with the lever on the blinds. 'As far as I can remember he was in and out of departmental meetings all day. The usual drill.'

'It was only two days ago, Chief Inspector,' Gemma said softly.

He turned back to her, hands in his trouser pockets, and smiled. 'Perhaps I'm getting old, Sergeant. And I had no reason to pay particular attention to the commander's movements that day. Have a word with the departmental secretary, why don't you? And I know Alastair kept a desk diary. He liked to know where he stood.' As he came around the desk and opened the door, he said, 'I'll just get you started.'

Gemma smiled and thanked him, all the while aware of a distinct feeling that she'd been led a merry dance.

Alastair Gilbert's office furnishings befitted a commander. Good-quality carpeting covered the floor, and the furniture was the impressive sort only senior officers could requisition. A heavy bookcase against one wall held volumes of philosophy and military history as well as police manuals, but other than that Gemma found the room devoid of personality. Of course, she hadn't really expected Gilbert to accumulate the flotsam that cluttered most people's work spaces, but the order of this room was not even marred by family photographs. With a sigh she settled down to work.

Not until her stomach growled did she realize she'd missed lunch by several hours. She replaced the papers in the last file and levered herself up from the floor, her joints stiff and aching. Her fingertips felt dry and grimy from handling so many pieces of paper, but her search had yielded absolutely nothing of interest. Gilbert's meticulous appointment book merely outlined a day that sounded as dull as she felt at that moment.

He had started his last morning with a senior officers' briefing, then taken care of his correspondence. Before lunch he'd met with a representative from the local council and after lunch with officials from local pressure groups and the Crown Prosecution Service. There was no reference to an after-work meeting, nor had there been any notation for the evening before.

Stretching and smothering a yawn, Gemma conceded for the first time that Kincaid might have a point in not wanting further promotion. She retrieved her handbag from beneath the desk and went to find the loo.

Feeling better once she'd washed her hands and splashed water on her face, she emerged from the building to find the sun miraculously still shining. She stood still and tilted her face up, soaking in the faint warmth obliviously until the door flew open and someone bumped her from behind. 'Sorry,' she said automatically, taking in an impression of a stocky female body in a blue uniform, then the face clicked into focus and she gasped. 'Jackie? I can't believe it! Is it really you?' After a moment's laughing and hugging, she held her friend at arm's length and studied her. 'It is you. I'd swear you haven't changed a bit.'

She and Jackie Temple had been in the

same class at the Police College, and when they were both posted to Notting Hill a pleasant acquaintanceship had merged into real friendship. They stayed close, even when Gemma transferred from Uniform to CID, but since Gemma had been posted to the Yard they'd seen each other very rarely. Now she realized with a shock that she hadn't spoken to Jackie since she'd been pregnant.

'Neither have you, Gemma,' Jackie said, a smile lighting her dark face. 'And now that we know we're both god-awful liars, what are you doing here? And how long has it been? How's Rob?' Gemma's expression must have betrayed her, because Jackie said immediately, 'Oh, no, I've put my foot in it, haven't I?' She lifted Gemma's left hand and shook her head when she saw her bare finger. 'I'm so sorry, love. Whatever happened?'

'You couldn't have known,' Gemma reassured her. 'And it's been more than two years now.' Rob had found the demands of family life a bit more than he'd bargained for and hadn't proved much better as an absentee father. The child-support cheques, regular at first, became sporadic, then stopped altogether when Rob left his job and changed his address.

'Look,' said Jackie as the door swung open again and narrowly missed them, 'we can't stand about on the bleedin' steps all day. I'm just off duty, but I ran some paperwork over from Notting Hill as a favour to my sarge. Now I'm off home. Come with me and we'll have something to drink and a good old natter.'

Gemma had a moment's guilt, quickly buried as she told herself that she had, after all, followed Kincaid's instructions to the letter. And she could always quiz Jackie about Alastair Gilbert. Smiling, she said, 'That's the best offer I've had all day.'

Jackie still lived in the small block of flats Gemma remembered, near Notting Hill Police Station. It was a bit of an ugly duckling in an area of terraced Georgian houses, but Jackie's second-floor flat was pleasant enough. Wide windows opened on to a south-facing balcony, a profusion of green plants grew among the clutter of African prints, and bright-patterned rugs covered the casual furniture.

'Do you still share with Susan May?' Gemma called from the sitting room as Jackie disappeared into the bedroom, shedding her uniform sweater as she went.

'We rub along all right. She's had another promotion—fancies herself a bit these days,' Jackie said affectionately as she reappeared in jeans, pulling a sweatshirt over her tight curls. 'I'm starved,' she added, heading for the tiny galley kitchen. 'Hang on a bit and I'll put something together for us.'

When Jackie refused her offer of help, Gemma wandered out on the balcony, admiring the snapdragons and pansies that bloomed cheerfully in terracotta pots. She remembered that Susan, a willowy woman who worked as a production assistant for the BBC, was the one with the green fingers. When the three of them had gathered together for makeshift suppers in the flat, Susan had teased Jackie about her ability to kill anything by just looking at it.

This had been her patch, Gemma thought as she leaned over the railing and gazed out at the broad treelined streets—not all of it as elegant and pleasant as this, of course, but it had been a good place to start life as a copper, and she had grown fond of it. Once she'd walked a beat that stretched from the crayon-box of Elgin Crescent to the bustle of Kensington Park Road. It felt odd to be back, as if time had telescoped in on itself.

When she returned to the sitting room, Jackie had set out plates of sandwiches, fruit, and two bottles of beer. As they pulled their chairs nearer the window so they could sit in the last of the sun while they ate, Jackie echoed Gemma's thoughts. 'A bit like old times, isn't it? Now tell me about you,' she added, as she bit into an apple with a resounding crunch.

By the time Gemma had brought her up to date and Jackie had promised to visit Toby soon, they'd mopped up the crumbs. 'Jackie,' Gemma said tentatively, 'look, I'm sorry I didn't keep in touch. When I was pregnant with Toby it was all I could do to fall into bed at night, and afterwards...with Rob...I just didn't want to talk about it.'

'I understand,' Jackie's dark eyes were sympathetic. 'But I envy you your baby.'

'You?' It had never occurred to Gemma that her tough and self-sufficient friend might want a child.

Jackie laughed. 'What? You think I'm too crusty to want to change nappies? But there it is. And I'd never have thought you'd let a baby interfere with your career. Speaking of which,' she punched Gemma lightly on the arm, 'who would have thought you'd end up such a big shot, investigating a commander's murder. Tell me all about it.'

When Gemma had finished, Jackie sat quietly for a moment, swirling the dregs of her beer in its amber bottle. 'Lucky you,' she said at last. 'Your guv sounds like a good one.'

Gemma opened her mouth to protest, then closed it again. That was a can of worms she didn't dare open.

'I could tell you some stories about mine that would make your hair stand on end,' Jackie said, then added philosophically, 'Oh, well, I made my bed when I decided I wanted to stay on the street.' She finished her beer in one swallow and changed the subject abruptly. 'I saw Commander Gilbert at Notting Hill not too long ago—one day last week, I think it was. Can you believe he had a spot on his tie? Must have got caught in the crossfire of a canteen food fight, that's the only reasonable explanation.'

They both laughed, then, inspired by the mention of such juvenile behaviour, settled into a round of 'do you remember?'s that left them giggling and wiping their eyes. 'Can you believe how ignorant we were?' Jackie asked finally, blowing her nose on a tissue. 'Sometimes I think it's a wonder we survived.' She studied Gemma for a moment, then added more soberly, 'It's good to see you again, Gemma. You were an important part of my life, and I've missed you.'

Rob hadn't cared for any of Gemma's friends, especially those in the force, and after a bit she'd lost the energy to face the inevitable arguments that followed her contacts with them. Nor had he liked her to talk about her life before she met him, and gradually even her memories seemed to fade from disuse. 'I seem to have lost bits of my life in the last few years,' she said slowly. 'Maybe it's time I made an effort to find them again.'

'Come and have dinner with us sometime soon, then,' said Jackie. 'Susan would love to see you, too. We'll drink a bottle of wine to our misspent youth—and remember when all we could afford was the worst plonk imaginable.' She stood up and went to the window. 'How odd,' she said a little absently, 'I've just remembered that I thought I saw Commander Gilbert somewhere else recently. It must have been the wine that brought it to mind, because I'd just come out of the off-licence in the Portobello Road, and there was Gilbert talking to this West Indian bloke who's a known grass. At least I thought it was Gilbert, but a lorry came between us then and by the time the light changed, they'd both disappeared.'

'You didn't check it out?'

'You've been in CID too long, love.' said Jackie, clearly amused. 'Just who was I supposed to ask? Commander Gilbert himself? I know enough to keep my nose out of my elders' and betters' business, ta very much. Still,' she turned back

132

to Gemma and smiled, 'I suppose it wouldn't hurt to put in a word or two in certain quarters. I'll let you know if anything interesting turns up, shall I?'

Gemma hated the escalators at the Angel tube station. She was sure they must be the longest and steepest of any in London, and the prospect of facing that dizzying descent every day had almost deterred her from taking her flat. At least, she told herself as she hugged the rail, going up wasn't nearly as bad as going down—as long as you didn't look back.

A plastic bag wrapped itself around Gemma's legs as she emerged from the station. Disentangling herself, she saw rubbish blowing all along Islington High Street. A sheet of newspaper clung tenaciously to a nearby lamp-post, and a plastic bottle rattled discordantly along the pavement. The rubbish collection had failed again, Gemma thought, frowning in irritation, and she certainly didn't have time to complain to the council about it.

The sight of the black man sitting on the bench beside the flower stall snapped her out of her bad temper. Dwarfed by the towering glass office building behind him, he cradled a paper-wrapped whisky bottle against his thin chest and sang to himself as he smiled up at her. His ragged clothes looked as though they had once been of good quality, but they offered little protection from the wind that made his red-rimmed eyes water.

She stopped and bought a bunch of yellow carnations, then handed her change to the drunk before sprinting across the zebra crossing. Looking back, she had a glimpse of his head bobbing like a mechanical toy as he gabbled something incomprehensible after her. When she'd started in the force, a rookie constable, she'd almost unconsciously shared her parents' disdain for those who could 'better themselves if they made the effort', but experience had quickly taught her that the equation was almost never that simple. For some the most you could do was try to make their lives a little more comfortable, and if possible leave them a bit of dignity.

To her right as she entered the Liverpool Road lay the Chapel Market. It was closing time, and with an occasional cheerful curse the vendors were tearing down their stalls and packing up boxes. Too late to pick up anything there for supper, she'd have to stop in Cullen's or brave the crush in the enormous new Sainsbury's across the street.

One thing drew her to Sainsbury's, much as she disliked its sterile, gleaming interior.

The busker stood on his usual patch outside the doors, his dog watchful beside him. She always had a few coins for him, sometimes a pound if she could manage it, but this ritual was not motivated by pity. Tonight she stopped as she usually did and listened to the liquid notes spilling from his clarinet. She didn't recognize the piece, but it made her feel sweetly sad, leaving a gentle melancholy as the sound died away. The heavy coin clinked satisfyingly as she tossed it into the open case, but the young man merely nodded his thanks. He never smiled, and his eyes were as aloof as those of the mongrel lying quietly at his feet.

Laden carrier bags bumped her leg as she emerged from the supermarket and hurried up the Liverpool Road with her collar pinched together against the wind. Her anticipation built as she thought of catching Toby up in her arms, hearing him squeal with delight as she nuzzled his neck, breathing in the warm smell of his skin. Turning into Richmond Avenue, she passed the grammar school, gates shut against the darkening day, playground still except for the movement of an empty swing. Before she knew it Toby would be old enough to join the children there. Already his plump softness was melting away, little boy sturdiness emerging in its place, and Gemma felt a pang of loss for his babyhood. Thrusting back the guilt that always hovered near the surface of her mind, she assured herself that she did the best she could.

At least the move to the Islington flat had brought with it an unexpected benefit—her landlady, Hazel Cavendish, had offered to keep Toby while Gemma worked, and Gemma no longer had to depend on her mum or indifferent child-minders.

Thornhill Gardens came into view and Gemma slowed, catching her breath so as not to arrive on the doorstep panting. Almost home, and lights were coming on in the houses along the gardens now, offering a tantalizing vision of comfort and warmth behind closed doors. The Cavendishes' house backed up to the gardens, and Gemma's adjoining flat faced Albion Street, almost directly opposite the pub.

She let herself into the back garden by the gate at the side of the garage, not stopping to leave the groceries in the flat. She'd telephoned so that Hazel would be expecting her, and as she reached the back door she squinted at the small sticky note fluttering in the dimness. IN BATH, H., it read, and Gemma smiled as she looked at her watch. Hazel ran an orderly house, and by this time the children would have had their tea and been bustled upstairs to the bath.

A wave of warmth and spicy smells greeted her as she opened the door, a sure sign that Hazel was cooking one of her 'vegetable messes', as her husband affectionately called them. Hazel and Tim Cavendish were both psychologists, but Hazel had taken an indefinite leave from her lucrative practice to stay at home with their three-year-old daughter, Holly. They had absorbed Toby into their household effortlessly, and although Hazel accepted the going rate for child-minding, Gemma suspected it was more balm for her pride than a financial necessity for the Cavendishes. Following the distant sound of voices, she deposited her purchases on the kitchen table and dodged the toys littering the floor as she made her way upstairs.

She tapped on the bathroom door, and hearing Hazel's cheerful, 'Come on in,' she slipped inside. Hazel was kneeling by the old-fashioned claw-footed bath, the sleeves of her sweater pushed up over her elbows, her chin-length brown hair forming curly tendrils from the steam.

Both children were in the bath, and when Toby saw her he shrieked, 'Mummy!' and smacked his hands palm-down against the water.

Laughing, Hazel jumped back from the spray. 'I think you little munchkins are clean enough. Welcome home, Gemma,' she added, wiping the sudsy droplets from her cheek.

Gemma felt a sudden spasm of jealousy, but it faded as Hazel called out, 'How about giving a hand with the towels?' and she soon had her arms full of wet and giggling children.

When the children had been dried and dressed in their footed pyjamas, Hazel settled them with some toys on the kitchen rug and insisted on making Gemma some tea. 'You look knackered, to put it tactfully,' she said with a smile as she waved away Gemma's offer to help and busied herself with kettle and cups.

Gemma sank into a chair at the kitchen table and watched the children as they cranked toy cars up and down in the lift of a plastic garage with complete absorption. They played well together, she thought. Dark-haired Holly had inherited her mother's sweet disposition as well as her dimples. A few months older than Toby, she ruled him with a bossy kindness that he tolerated good-naturedly. Just now, though, with his still-damp hair sticking up in spikes, he looked a proper little imp.

'Stay to dinner,' said Hazel as she set a steaming mug before Gemma and slid into the chair opposite. 'Tim's got a therapy group tonight, so it will just be us and the kids. And as a further enticement, I'm making Moroccan vegetable stew with couscous. And besides,' she added with a pleading note, 'I have selfish reasons—I could use some adult conversation.'

'But I picked up some things at the supermarket...' Gemma made a half-hearted gesture in the direction of her carrier bags.

Wrinkling her snub nose, Hazel expressed her opinion of that. 'Macaroni cheese out of a box, I'll bet, or something equally ghastly. You need something that hasn't been thrown together at the last minute. Food is comfort for the soul as well as the body.' The last she intoned with great weight, then laughed. 'So says the philosopher of the kitchen.'

With a shamefaced smile, Gemma confessed, 'It was the first thing I saw on the shelf.' She stretched, relaxed now from the warmth of the room and the tea, and looked around the pleasant kitchen. The old glass-fronted cabinets had been rubbed with a soft green stain, the walls were covered with peach paper, and any spare spaces on counters and table held Hazel's baskets of jumbled knitting wool. Suddenly finding herself loath to leave, she said, 'It does sound lovely. Are you sure we wouldn't be imposing? I'm always afraid we'll wear out our welcome.' Seeing Hazel's emphatic reassurance, she added, 'And I'll admit it's been a hellish week.'

'Rough case?' Hazel asked sympathetically.

'You could say that.' Cradling the hot cup in her hands, Gemma told her about Alastair Gilbert.

When she'd finished, Hazel shuddered, concern evident in her expression. 'How awful. For them and for you. But there's more than that, isn't there, Gemma?' she asked, with the direct gaze that must have made her patients squirm. 'You disappear for days without notice, show up again, then leave Toby without a word of explanation—what's going on?'

Gemma shook her head. 'Nothing. It's nothing. I'll be all right.'

Shaking her head, Hazel leaned forward earnestly. 'Who are you trying to convince? You know it's not good to bottle things up. You don't have to be superwoman all the time. Let someone else share a little bit of the burden—'

'I don't need a therapist, Hazel,' Gemma interrupted, then instantly regretted it. 'I'm sorry, I don't know what's got into me lately. I've been sniping at everyone. You didn't deserve that.'

Sitting back with a sigh, Hazel said, 'I don't know—maybe I did. Old habits, you know. I'm sorry if I overstepped your boundaries, but I care about you, and I want to help if I can.'

The kindness in Hazel's voice brought an ache to Gemma's throat, and she felt a sudden longing to pour out her troubles and be comforted. Instead, she swallowed and asked tentatively, 'How could you bear it, Hazel? Giving up your job like that? Weren't you afraid of losing yourself?'

Hazel watched the children for a long moment before answering. 'It hasn't been easy, but I haven't regretted it, either. I've learned from experience that it's a great emotional risk to ground one's identity entircly in one's work. Life is entirely too tumultuous for that—you can lose a job or a career tomorrow, and then where are you? The same is true of marriage and motherhood. You have to rely on something deeper than that, something inviolate.' She looked up and met Gemma's eyes. 'Easier said than done, I know, and I'm not avoiding the personal question. I waited until fairly late to have a child, and as much as I enjoyed my work I decided that being with Holly the first few years of her life was an experience I wouldn't have a chance to repeat. I sometimes feel guilty about that, knowing so many women who don't have that option—like you.' Hazel's dimples appeared as she grinned

141

at Gemma. 'But then I'm not sure you'd take it if you could.'

Brow furrowed, Gemma studied her mug as if the contents held an answer. 'No way, I'd have said in the beginning. I saw being pregnant and having a baby as a bloody nuisance, to tell the truth—just another way I'd let Rob's carelessness spill over into my life. But now...'

Toby, perhaps sensing some current of unease in his mother's voice, stopped his play and came to stand beside her, butting his head against her arm.

Gemma cuddled him and tousled his hair. 'But now I don't know. There are days when I envy you.' She thought of Jackie Temple's unexpected revelation. Was anyone ever satisfied with her lot?

'And there are days when I think I'll go mad if I hear another toy advert,' countered Hazel, laughing. 'So I cook. That's my defence.' She stood up and carried their empty mugs to the sink. 'And I think it's time to switch from restoratives to sedatives.' She pulled a bottle of white wine from the refrigerator. 'This Gewürztraminer's lovely with the spices in North African food.' Retrieving a corkscrew from a drawer, she started to peel the foil cap off the bottle, then stopped and turned back to Gemma. 'Just one more thing. I won't push you, but I want you to know that I'm always here if you want to talk. And I'll not let the therapist get in the way of the friend.'

Gemma fell asleep that night in the curving leather chair in the flat, Toby sprawled across her lap, only to wake in the wee hours, chilled, numb from the weight of her son's relaxed body, with Claire Gilbert's face burned into her mind like the bright after-image of a flare.

Chapter Seven

The doorbell pealed as Kincaid and Nick Deveney waited on the steps of Dr Gabriella Wilson's creeper-covered cottage, a few doors up the lane from the Gilberts'.

Escaping gratefully after a morning of meetings at Guildford Police Station, they'd left Will Darling to collate the still-incoming reports. When Dr Wilson's name had appeared on the list of burglary victims gleaned from yesterday's house-to-house of the village, they'd made her their first priority.

As they drove into the village, Deveney had mumbled something around the cheese

143

roll he clutched in his right hand while changing gear with his left. Swallowing, he said more clearly, 'Kill two birds. And make Gemma happy, at any rate,' he'd added with a cryptic glance at Kincaid.

They'd begun to feel the cold by the time the door swung open. A small, competent-looking, middle-aged woman studied them. She seemed to have taken up where Kincaid and Deveney had left off, for she held half a sandwich in her left hand, a perfect half-moon-shaped bite missing from its edge. 'You'll be the police, I expect,' she said equably. 'I wondered when you'd get around to me again. Come in, but you'll have to be quick about it.' Turning, she led them down a passage towards the back of the house. 'I barely manage a bite as it is, between morning surgery and afternoon calls.'

Passing through a swinging door, they entered the kitchen and she gestured towards a table cluttered with papers and periodicals. Kincaid pulled out a chair, gingerly removing another stack of papers before he sat down. 'Dr Wilson, if you could—'

'I'm just Doc to everyone except the hospital administrators. They like to maintain a certain distance.' She chuckled as she sat down and picked up a cup of coffee that still had steam rising from the top. 'Ah, there's Paul now. My husband,' she added as a man came through the back door, wiping his hands on a towel.

'Hello.' He shook their hands as they introduced themselves. 'Sorry if I'm damp. I've had Bess out for her walk and it's a bit mucky. Had to hose her down just now in the garden.' Paul Wilson was dressed much like his wife, in serviceable trousers and pullover, but the resemblance went further than that. Short, stocky, and balding, he had about him the same friendly, no-nonsense air.

'Paul does mostly consulting now, so he's home quite a bit during the day,' volunteered Dr Wilson. 'Now, what can we do for you?'

'According to the statement you made, you were out on Wednesday night, Doctor,' said Kincaid, consulting his notes. 'You left the house about half-past six?'

'Patient went into labour. First baby, too, took most of the night.'

'And you didn't notice anything unusual at the Gilberts' as you were leaving?'

She swallowed the last bite of her sandwich and flicked a glance at the wall clock before answering. 'I also told your nice constable that I saw nothing out of the ordinary, but I suppose you have to be thorough. I have no idea if Alastair was at home then. It was fully dark, of course, and you can't see the Gilberts' garage from the lane in any case. What I do know,' she said before Kincaid could interrupt her, 'is that if I'd got home before all the commotion died down, I'd have insisted on seeing Claire Gilbert. It's unthinkable that she hadn't anyone with her.' She thumped her coffee cup on the table for emphasis.

'She's your patient, then?' asked Kincaid, jumping on the lead.

'They both were, but that's really not pertinent. I'd do the same for anybody.' She glanced at her husband and some of the starch seemed to go out of her. 'What a dreadful business,' she said on a sigh.

'And you, Mr Wilson?' asked Deveney. 'You were at home?'

'Until about half-past two in the morning, when my wife called me to pull her out of a ditch. It's not the first time,' he added affectionately. 'I've considered that a part of my job description for years, always keep a tow rope in the boot of the Volvo.'

'And you heard nothing unusual, either?' Deveney's voice held a touch of exasperation.

'No, I had the telly on in the back. It was only when I took Bess for her bedtime outing that I saw the lights flashing and went to investigate. I'm sorry.' He sounded genuinely apologetic.

Kincaid let the silence linger a moment, then said softly, 'I understand that you had a disagreement with Commander Gilbert recently, Dr Wilson.'

The doctor's coffee cup paused for an instant in its journey to her mouth, but she recovered quickly. 'Whatever gave you that idea?' She sounded amused, but she shifted slightly in her chair, turning her head so that her husband wasn't directly in her line of sight.

'Geoff Genovase told my sergeant that he overheard the tail-end of a quarrel between you.'

She relaxed a bit, sipping at the last of her coffee. 'Ah, that would have been the Saturday before last, when Geoff was here to mulch the beds. I wouldn't give too much credence to Geoff's account, Superintendent. The boy has a very active imagination—comes from playing too many of those silly computer games, if you ask me.'

'According to Sergeant James,' put in Deveney, 'Geoff had the very distinct impression that you'd had a row.'

Paul Wilson had been leaning against the counter with his arms folded, listening with an expression of friendly interest. Now he came to stand behind his wife, hands on the back of her chair. 'The commander's manner was often abrupt,' he said. 'Pookie's right, you know. I'm sure that Geoff misinterpreted something perfectly ordinary.'

'Excuse me?' said Kincaid, wondering if he'd missed something.

The doctor laughed. 'That's been my nickname since childhood, Superintendent. "Gabriella" was too big a mouthful for my brothers and sisters.'

The nickname suited her, he thought, without diminishing her dignity. She seemed a person to whom directness came naturally, and he wondered why she was evading the issue. 'Why did Commander Gilbert come to see you that day?' he asked.

'Superintendent, I'd be violating my patient's confidentiality if I told you that,' she said firmly, but she tilted her head back against her husband's hand as if drawing support from his touch. 'I can assure you it had nothing to do with his death.'

'Why don't you let me be the judge of that, Doctor? You have no way of knowing what may be important in a murder investigation. And besides,' he paused, looking at her until she dropped her gaze, 'you can't violate the confidentiality of a dead man.'

She shook her head. 'There's nothing to tell. There was no row.'

'You'll be late for your rounds if you don't get a move on, love,' her husband murmured, but Kincaid saw his fingers tighten on her shoulders.

Nodding, she stood up and helped him gather their dishes. 'Old Mrs Parkinson will be ringing any minute, wanting to know where I am,' she grumbled as she carried their plates to the sink.

'Just a moment, Doctor.' Kincaid still sat amongst the welter of paper, arms folded, even though Deveney had risen with the Wilsons. 'You reported a burglary several weeks ago. Can you tell me exactly what was taken?'

'Oh, that.' Dr Wilson dumped the plates in the sink and turned back to him. 'I wish now I hadn't bothered to phone it in. It's been more trouble than it's worth, what with the paperwork and everything, and we never had any hope of getting the things back. Well, you don't, do you?'

'It was only a few items of inexpensive jewellery and some keepsakes...mementoes, that sort of thing,' said Paul Wilson. 'I can't imagine why anyone would want them, and they left the TV and video. A very odd business altogether.'

'And you didn't see anyone or notice anything unusual about that time?'

'No suspicious men lurking about in the shrubbery, Superintendent,' said the doctor, shrugging into her coat. 'We certainly would have said if we had.'

'All right, Doctor, Mr Wilson, thank you.' Kincaid stood and joined Deveney at the door. 'We'll see ourselves out. But do please let us know if you remember anything.'

He and Deveney were only halfway down the front path when the doctor's car shot down the gravelled drive in reverse. She nodded to them as she went by, backed into the lane, and sped off towards the village.

'No wonder she ends up in the ditch,' Deveney said, chuckling.

Although the sun had come out while they were in the house, the garden still held a thin glaze of moisture. Heavy, bronze heads of hydrangeas hung over the path, leaving damp streaks on their trouser-legs.

'What do you suppose she's playing at?' Deveney continued after a moment. 'She knew Gilbert's death would release her from any obligation of confidentiality, especially about his medical condition.'

Kincaid pushed open the garden gate, then stopped and turned to Deveney as they reached the car. 'But Claire is still her patient, and I think it's *Claire*'s confidentiality she's protecting.'

'She could've just told us that he'd

come about his medical condition,' mused Deveney, 'and we would have gone merrily on our way.'

Kincaid opened the door and slid into the passenger seat, thinking about the slightly off-centre feel of the whole interview. 'I think the good doctor is entirely too honest for her own good, Nick,' he said as Deveney joined him. 'She couldn't bear to tell an outright lie.'

Next on their list of burglary victims was Madeleine Wade, owner of the village shop. They drove through the centre of the village and past the garage, and after a wrong turn or two found the shop, tucked away in a cul-de-sac halfway up the hill. Fruit and vegetables were displayed in boxes outside the door: lovely perfumed Spanish tangerines, cucumbers, leeks, apples, and the inevitable potatoes.

Nick Deveney picked a small, earthy pippin from the box of apples and brushed it against his sleeve. A bell tinkled as they entered the shop's postage-stamp interior, and the girl behind the counter looked up from her magazine. 'Can I help you?' she asked. Her soft voice held a trace of Scots. Straight fair hair framed a fragile-looking face, and she regarded them seriously, as if her question had been more than rote. Beneath the short sleeves of her knitted top her arms looked thin and unprotected. She seemed about the same age as Lucy Penmaric and made Kincaid think of his ex-wife.

The shop smelled faintly of coffee and chocolate. For its size it was very well stocked, even down to a small freezer case filled with good-quality frozen dinners. While Deveney handed his apple over for weighing and dug in his pocket for change, Kincaid flipped through his notebook, and when they'd completed their transaction, he took Deveney's place at the counter. 'We're looking for Madeleine Wade, the owner. Is she here?'

'Oh, aye,' said the girl, favouring them with a shy smile. 'Madeleine's upstairs in her studio, but I don't think she has a client just now.'

'Client?' repeated Kincaid, wondering bemusedly if the shopkeeper led a double life as the village prostitute. He'd known stranger combinations than that.

The girl tapped on a card Sellotaped to the counter top. REFLEXOLOGY, AROMATHERAPY AND MASSAGE, it read in neat calligraphy, and beneath that, BY APPOINTMENT ONLY, and a phone number.

Enlightened, Kincaid said, 'Oh, I see. She's quite the entrepreneur, isn't she?'

The girl looked at him blankly for

a moment, as if he'd exceeded her vocabulary, then directed, 'Just go round the side and ring the bell.'

Kincaid leaned a little more determinedly on the counter and ventured, 'You'd be about school-leaving age, I should think?'

She blushed to the roots of her fair hair and whispered, 'I did my GCSEs last year, sir.'

'Do you know Lucy Penmaric at all, then?'

Seeming to find this question less intimidating, she answered a bit louder. 'I know her to speak to, of course, but we don't hang about together, if that's what you mean. She's never had much to do with the village kids.'

'Stuck-up, is she?' Kincaid asked, inviting a confidence. Deveney, flipping idly through the postcards while munching his apple, gave every appearance of ignoring their conversation.

Frowning, the girl pushed her hair from her face. 'No, I wouldn't say that. Lucy's always nice enough, she just doesn't seem to mix with anyone.'

'That's too bad, considering what's happened,' said Kincaid. 'I imagine she could use a friend just now.'

'Oh, aye,' the girl said. With the first hint of curiosity she'd shown, she added, 'You'll be from the police, then?'

'That we are, love.' Deveney joined them, holding aloft his apple core. 'And you'll be doing us a great service if you'll toss this in the bin.' He winked at her, and she blushed again but took the apple core willingly enough.

Cocky bastard, thought Kincaid. He thanked the girl and she smiled at him gratefully. As he reached the door, he turned back to her. 'What's your name, by the way?'

She offered it to him on a whispered breath. 'Sarah.'

'That one's not likely to make a rocket scientist,' quipped Deveney as they left the shop.

'I'd say she's shy, not stupid.' Kincaid avoided a puddle as they rounded the corner of the shop. 'And I find it dangerous to underestimate people, though I dare say I've done it more than once.' He thought again of Vic, of the times she'd come home in a temper, threatening to darken her hair to brunette so that she wouldn't have to prove her intelligence to everyone she met. It occurred to him now that even though he'd sympathized with her, he'd been just as guilty as the clods he'd criticized—he hadn't taken her seriously until it had been much too late.

'*Touché.*' Deveney winced at the mild

154

reproof. 'I'll try to keep a more open mind.'

The side door proved to be at the top of an exterior staircase. It looked to Kincaid as though the stairs had been added fairly recently, perhaps in the process of converting the lower floor of the house into a shop. Both railing and door were painted a glossy white. As he pushed the bell, he murmured, 'She must be a good witch—she's got her colours right.'

The door opened as the last words left his lips. Looking at them enquiringly, Madeleine Wade said, 'Yes?' and Kincaid, tongue-tied, flushed as painfully as Sarah. While Deveney stumbled through the introductions, Kincaid examined the woman's clothes, a moss green and rose silk blouse with matching green silk trousers. Her hair was a stylish chin-length bob of a platinum shade he suspected owed more to art than nature. He looked everywhere except at her face until he had his own under control, for Madeleine Wade had an enormous hooked beak of a nose, resembling nothing so much as a caricature of a fairy-tale witch.

She smiled at them as if aware of their discomfort. 'Come in, please,' she said as she motioned them into the sitting room. Her voice was deep, almost masculine in timbre, but pleasant. 'Sit down and I'll fix you something to drink. I'm afraid I don't

155

use any caffeinated products, so you'll have to settle for herbal tea,' she continued as she moved to the small kitchen adjacent to the sitting room. Although he couldn't see her face, Kincaid fancied he heard a trace of amusement in her voice.

He and Deveney chorused, 'Fine,' then Deveney gave a quick grimace of disgust.

Under his breath, Kincaid said wickedly, 'Broaden your horizons, man. It'll do you good,' then looked around the room with interest. He became aware of music playing faintly but was unable to localize the source. At least he supposed you would call it music, for it consisted of tinkling sounds repeated in rhythmic patterns, like wind chimes moving to mathematical variations.

The flat had a comfortable and rather whimsical charm, with only the massage table on the far side of the sitting room indicating Madeleine Wade's use of the room for her business. A brightly patterned sheet draped the table, softening its clinical aspect, and the pine bureau on the far wall displayed a collection of plush animals as well as an assortment of oils, lotions and a pile of fluffy towels.

Kincaid moved to the end of the room, where two deep bay windows overlooked the shop front. He smiled as he looked at the curtains, made of the same fabric that covered the sofa and massage table. Primitively drawn farmyard animals cavorted across a cheerful white and red polka-dotted background, and he found the combination both odd and intriguing. A closer inspection revealed that the red dots were irregular in shape, as if they'd been finger-painted on, and the dogs and sheep in particular looked almost like the animals held seen in reproductions of cave paintings.

The left window sill held a multishaped and sized variety of corked glass bottles, filled with liquids in hues ranging from the palest green-gold to rich amber. Sprigs of herbs floated in some, and all sported rakish raffia ties.

The other sill held a red geranium in a terracotta pot and a marmalade cat curled on a cushion in the sun. When Kincaid gently rubbed a geranium leaf between his fingers, releasing the pungent, spicy scent, the cat stirred but didn't open its eyes. 'Is your cat always so oblivious?' Kincaid asked as a rattle of crockery told him that Madeleine Wade had returned.

'I don't think the apocalypse would faze Ginger, good-for-nothing beastie that he is. I keep him because the sight of him relaxes the clients.' Placing a tray bearing mugs and an earthenware pot on a low table before the sofa, she sat down and unhurriedly began to pour.

Kincaid watched from near the window as she concentrated on her task. All her movements were graceful and economic, and he found the contrast between her face and her self-assured poise oddly disconcerting. 'And the music?' he asked. 'Does that serve the same purpose?'

She sat back with her mug. 'Do you like it? It's structured to encourage the brain to emit alpha waves—at least that's the theory, but it's called angel music, and I think I prefer the more imaginative description.'

Having taken his seat in one of the simple farmhouse chairs beside the sofa, Deveney lifted his cup, sniffed, and sipped tentatively. 'What is this?' he asked, looking pleasantly surprised.

Madeleine Wade chuckled. 'Apple cinnamon. I find it a good choice for the uninitiated—familiar and non-threatening.' She turned to Kincaid, who had sat down opposite Deveney. 'And now what can I help you with, Superintendent? I'm assuming you're here about Alastair Gilbert's death?'

Kincaid took his mug from the tray and breathed the steam rising from its surface. 'We understand you reported a burglary some weeks ago, Miss Wade. Could you tell us about the circumstances?'

'Ah, the burglar-as-murderer theory is

it?' She smiled, showing teeth that were not well shaped but looked as though they had been cared for expensively. 'That's been the most popular hypothesis around the village—a vagrant, thinking the house empty, seizes the opportunity to pilfer it, then when caught red-handed by the commander, panics and kills him. That's all very convenient for everybody concerned, Superintendent, but I can see at least one logical flaw. My "burglary", if you want to call it that, for I never found any sign of a break-in, occurred almost three months ago. If any vagrant had been hanging about the village for that length of time, someone would have seen him.'

Although he privately agreed with her, Kincaid was beginning to form his own theory and merely countered with another question. 'If you hadn't a break-in, what alerted you to the fact that things were missing?'

The music had finished as they talked, and in the silence Kincaid heard the cat stir, then the sound of purring as it stretched and repositioned itself. It seemed to him that Madeleine imitated the cat, stretching out her long legs and crossing her ankles before she said, 'First it was an antique garnet ring, a gift from my mother on my twenty-first birthday. I thought I must

159

have misplaced it, that it would turn up, and didn't think too much about it. Then a few days later I discovered a brooch missing as well, and I began to worry a little and to look around. I discovered some small pieces of family silver missing, and a few other odd things—a ceramic egg coddler, for instance. Tell me why someone would steal a Royal Worcester egg coddler, Superintendent.'

'Have you any idea if all the things disappeared simultaneously?'

Madeleine considered his question for a moment before answering. 'No, I'm sorry, I'm afraid I can't be sure. I'd worn the ring more recently than I'd used the silver, but that's as far as I would be prepared to go.'

'And you noticed nothing out of order in the flat? No strangers about at that time?' Finding he didn't care for the strong cinnamon bite of the tea, Kincaid unobtrusively replaced his mug on the tray without taking his eyes from Madeleine.

She made a sweeping gesture with her hand, palm up. 'As you can see, my living quarters are quite small, just this room, the kitchen, and a bedroom. I chose to give up many of my possessions when I came here, and I'm naturally tidy, so it would be extremely difficult for someone to ransack my things without my knowledge. Yet I noticed nothing.' She gave a shrug almost Gallic in its eloquence. 'It reminds me of the brownie stories I heard as a child. They were benevolent elves, if I remember correctly, and I sensed no malice in this.'

Kincaid found her reference to her past and her last comment equally intriguing. While he was deciding which he wanted to pursue first, Deveney sat forward and said, 'But surely you have other people visiting your flat. Clients, friends—and what about Sarah, the girl who works downstairs? Could she have taken the things?'

'Never!' Madeleine stiffened, pulling her feet back from their relaxed position, and for the first time she looked awkward, as if she were too tall to sit comfortably on the sofa. Fiercely, she said, 'Sarah's helped me since she was fourteen. She's a good girl, and almost like my own child. Why would she suddenly take things from me?'

The reasons a seventeen-year-old girl might steal struck Kincaid as too myriad to list (the foremost being either drugs or a boyfriend using drugs), but he didn't wish to antagonize Madeleine further. And having met Sarah, he felt inclined to agree with Madeleine's assessment. For a moment he wished urgently for Gemma, who would have eased tactfully into such a suggestion, if she had made it at all.

'You can't be too cau—'

'I'm sure Miss Wade's right, Nick,' interrupted Kincaid, giving Deveney a sharp glance.

Deveney flushed and set his mug down with a noticeable thump.

'Tell me, Miss Wade,' said Kincaid, 'what exactly did you mean when you said you didn't sense any malice involved in the thefts?'

She looked at him for a moment, as if she were making a determination, then sighed and glanced away. Her flare of anger seemed to have burnt away the amusement he'd sensed in her manner, and now she spoke with quiet gravity. 'I was born with a gift, Superintendent. Not that it's so very unusual—I believe that many people have psychic talents, which they either use or suppress according to their degree of discomfort with the phenomenon. I also decided long ago that the vehicle used for expressing these talents is irrelevant. It doesn't matter whether one reads palms or predicts racing results, any more than it matters whether one writes a novel using a legal pad and pencil or the latest word-processing software. It comes from the same source.'

Although Kincaid had shown no sign of impatience, she glanced at him as if gauging his response and said, 'Bear with

162

me, please. You must understand that I am not condemning those who suppress their abilities.' Her eyes, green and direct, met his again. 'I was one of them. By the time I started school I'd learned that it wasn't acceptable to talk about what I could see and feel, at least not to adults. It didn't seem to bother other children, but if they should happen to mention it to their parents, I was no longer welcome. Children usually have a very well-developed sense of self-preservation, and I was no exception. I buried my difference as deeply as I could.'

Kincaid could all too easily imagine Madeleine as an awkward and remarkably plain child. Having no control over the features that would already have made her an easy target for ridicule, she would have controlled whatever else was within her power. And, he thought, no matter what the cost. 'You spoke in the past tense, Miss Wade. Are we to assume that things changed?'

'Things always change, Superintendent,' she said, and he heard the flicker of amusement return to her voice. 'But you're right, of course. I kept things buried for many years, toeing the more conservative end of the established line. I became an investment banker, if you can believe it.' Chuckling, she added, 'Sometimes it seems like a past life, and I'm not at all sure that I believe in reincarnation.' Then, growing serious once more, she said, 'But as the years went by I seemed to shrivel, wither away inside. Even though I often used my...talents...in my work, I refused to acknowledge what I was doing. Eventually I had a moment of epiphany, the cause of which need not concern you, and I packed it all in. Quit my job, gave up my flat on the river, donated my power suits to Oxfam, and came here.'

'Miss Wade,' Kincaid said carefully, 'you haven't told us exactly what these special abilities are. Can you see the past or the future? Do you know what happened to Alastair Gilbert?'

Shaking her head, she said fervently, 'I thank God every day that I don't have the power to see into the future. That would be an unbearable burden. Nor can I unravel the past. My small gift, Superintendent, is the ability to see emotions. I know instantly if someone is unhappy, hurt, afraid, joyous, contented. I've always disliked the term "aura". I suppose it does as well as any to describe what I see, but it's also a bit like describing colour to a blind man.'

Kincaid suddenly felt as vulnerable as if he'd been stripped of his clothes. Did she sense his hurt and anger, even his scepticism? He saw Deveney shift uncomfortably in his chair and knew he must be experiencing the same feelings. 'Miss Wade,' he said, attempting to focus his attention on something safer than himself, 'you didn't answer my question about Alastair Gilbert.'

'All I can tell you about Gilbert is that he was a very unhappy man. Anger seeped from him all the time, like water welling from an underground spring.' She folded her arms across her chest protectively. 'I find that sort of energy difficult to tolerate for any length of time.'

'Was he your client?'

She gave a peal of laughter. 'Oh, my, no. People like Alastair Gilbert don't come to the likes of me. Their anger won't let them reach out, search for help. They wear it like a shield.'

'And Claire Gilbert?'

'Yes, Claire is my client.' Madeleine leaned forward, arranging their mugs carefully in the centre of the tray, then looked up at Kincaid. 'I can see where you're going with this, Superintendent, and I'm afraid I can't co-operate. I don't know what my legal rights are—I've never been confronted with this situation before. But I do know that on moral grounds I must keep sacrosanct anything that my clients reveal during the course of

165

their treatment.' She gestured towards the massage table. 'Aromatherapy in particular is very powerful. It stimulates the brain and memory directly, bypassing the intellectual armour we build around our experiences. Often it enables clients to work out fears, past traumas, and it can be a very emotional catharsis. Any revelations made at these times could be misleading.'

'Are you telling us that Claire Gilbert made such revelations?' Deveney asked. It sounded to Kincaid as if he'd chosen aggression as the method of dealing with *his* discomfort.

'No, no, of course not. I'm merely illustrating why I find such self-imposed restrictions necessary when talking about *any* client—and Claire is no exception, despite the tragic circumstances.' She stood and lifted the loaded tray. 'I have a client due in just a few minutes, Superintendent. Finding policemen on the doorstep might be a bit off-putting.'

'Just one more thing, Miss Wade. How did Alastair Gilbert feel about his wife consulting you?'

For the first time, Kincaid sensed hesitation. Madeleine shifted her weight, balancing the tray on her right hip, then said slowly, 'I'm not sure that Claire discussed it with him. Many people prefer their visits to be entirely discreet, and I

166

honour that. Now if you don't mind...'

'Thank you for your time, Miss Wade,' Kincaid said as he rose and Deveney followed suit. She went ahead of them, depositing the tray in the kitchen, then came to see them out. Kincaid took the hand she offered. He found that women's handshakes often fell into two categories —either a limp, dead-fish touching of fingers or an overcompensating, knuckle-breaking grasp—but Madeleine Wade's strong, quick clasp was that of a woman comfortable with her place in the world.

He turned back to her as she opened the door. 'Did you ever think of going into police work?'

The curve of her lips as she smiled made her jutting nose seem more pronounced, and her husky voice held amusement once more. 'I did consider it, actually. The thought of having that secret edge was tempting, but I was afraid it would corrupt me in the end. I felt I could only find balance in offering healing and comfort to others, and I don't think that's in your job description, Superintendent.'

'Can you see guilt?'

She shook her head. 'I'm sorry. I can't help you. Guilt is a mixture of emotions—fear, anger, remorse, pity— much too complicated to separate into individual components. Nor would I implicate someone, even if I could. I don't want that power, that responsibility, on my hands.'

Deveney waited until they'd shut themselves in the privacy of his car before he exploded. 'She's just as batty as she looks,' he said vehemently, cranking the starter a bit too hard. '*Auras*, my grandmother's arse. What a load of bullshit.'

While Deveney groused, Kincaid thought about hunches. He suspected that all good coppers had them, even depended on them to some extent, but it was something no one discussed comfortably. They had all been on courses instructing them in the science of reading body language, but was that methodology just a means of fitting intuition into a more acceptable framework?

All in all, he thought it prudent to regard Madeleine Wade with an open mind.

The vicarage faced directly on to the village green, nestled between the pub and the little lane that led up to the church. Deveney, still muttering to himself, parked alongside the green. Kincaid stretched as he got out of the car, for the sun had warmed the afternoon air until it felt almost balmy for November. A light breeze had come up, and in it the green's emerald grass rippled in velvet waves.

Crossing the tarmac, they let themselves into the vicarage garden through the gate. The house drowsed in the high-hedged enclosure, its square and solid red-brick façade looking respectably suited to its role. The garden, on the other hand, flaunted itself, as if rebelling against such stuffiness. A riot of colour washed bravely against the subdued autumn background of hedge and trees. Everything that could still bloom did—impatiens, begonias, pansies, fuchsias, dahlias, primroses, verbenas, and the last of the roses, their heads full-blown on skeletal stems. Kincaid whistled in admiration. 'I'd say the vicar has a different gift.' Then, unable to resist the urge to tease Deveney just a bit, he added, 'I wonder how he gets on with Madeleine Wade.'

Deveney gave him an irritated look, and they waited in silence for a few moments in the porch. When it seemed certain that Deveney's assault on the bell was not going to produce a response, Kincaid turned away. 'Let's try the church.'

Letting Deveney precede him out through the gate, Kincaid gave the garden a last glance. The air shimmered slightly, as if it had been disturbed by their presence, then stilled. He shut the gate reluctantly and followed Deveney around the corner, then detoured a bit to read the noticeboard at the bottom of the lane. It proclaimed the activities of the Parish Church of St Mary and reminded Kincaid that the seasonal rhythms of his boyhood had been marked by the church calendar.

The churchyard lay on their left as they climbed, the muted grey headstones decorated with a confetti of fallen leaves. Beyond it, the church sat astride the hill at an angle that might almost have been construed as playful. Kincaid smiled—he had to credit the architect with good showmanship as well as a sense of humour, for the position commanded the best possible view of the village.

As they neared the church, Deveney pulled out his notebook and rifled through it.

'What's the vicar's name?' asked Kincaid.

'Fielding,' Deveney replied after flipping through another few pages. 'R. Fielding. Oh, hell.'

'R. Fielding O. Hell? Odd name for a vicar,' Kincaid said, grinning.

'Sorry, I've a stone in my shoe. I'll catch you up.' Deveney bent and began unlacing.

Kincaid found the porch door unlocked. Entering, he stopped for a moment and closed his eyes. Even blindfolded he would recognize that smell anywhere—damp and polish, overlain with a hint of flowers—ecclesiastical, institutional, and as comforting as childhood memories.

When he opened his eyes he found the usual stacks of leaflets in the narthex and a collection box. When a soft 'Hello, anybody about?' received no response, he wandered past the carved screens and into the dimness of the nave itself. Here the silence was almost palpable, and the only motion came from the dust motes stirring lazily in the rainbow-hued light that fell from the high windows.

The door creaked and Deveney's voice called, 'Any joy?'

Joining him a little regretfully, Kincaid said, 'No, but I don't think we've exhausted the possibilities.' He tried the door opposite the porch, and they entered a scuffed linoleum-floored hallway. To their left lay washrooms and a small kitchen, to the right a meeting room with stacks of plastic chairs. 'A new building,' Kincaid mused, 'but it's a clever extension—I didn't notice it from the outside. There's no one here, though. I suppose we'll have to try the good vicar again—'

The door to the ladies' toilet opened and a woman came out. Thirtyish, Kincaid guessed, with a friendly face and a mop of dark curls, she wore jeans and an old sweater, and in her rubber-glove-clad hands she held a utilitarian-looking brush and a jug of industrial-strength cleaner.

'Oh, hello,' she said cheerfully. 'Can I help you with something?'

'We were hoping to have a word with the vicar,' Kincaid ventured.

She looked rather helplessly at the objects in her arms. 'Just let me do something with this stuff, then. Won't be a tick.' Glancing up again, she must have seen their uncertainty, for she paused and smiled. 'I'm Rebecca Fielding, by the way.'

'Ah, yes,' Kincaid answered, returning the smile and wondering what other surprises the day might have in store. He supposed he shouldn't have been startled—ordained women were common enough in the Anglican Church these days, and in fact were rather tame news. He introduced himself and Deveney, and when Rebecca Fielding had disposed of her cleaning supplies in a small cupboard, they followed her into the meeting room.

An ancient-looking tea urn squatted malevolently on a trolley, taking pride of place over the scarred table and plastic chairs. 'A necessity of parish meetings, I'm afraid,' said Rebecca, eyeing it with distaste. 'I can't imagine why I went into this line of work—I never could stand the taste of stewed tea.' She separated two chairs for the men and one for herself, and when they were seated she became suddenly brisk. 'If this is about Alastair Gilbert, I'm afraid I can't help you. I can't imagine why anyone would do such a dreadful thing.'

'That's not exactly why we wanted to see you,' said Kincaid, liking the woman's easy, direct manner, 'although any light you could shed on the matter would be helpful. We'd like to ask you a few questions about the items you reported stolen.'

'That?' Her dark, straight brows rose in surprise. 'But that was ages ago! August, it must have been, and what on earth has it to do with anything?'

So the vicar had not been privy to the pub gossip, thought Kincaid, or else she was a very good dissembler. 'You know, I'm sure, that other people have reported items missing. There is some speculation that a vagrant was responsible for those thefts and that Commander Gilbert might have surprised him in the act.'

'But that's absurd, Superintendent. None of these incidents occurred at the same time, and besides, if there were anyone like that hanging about the village, I'd know it. The church porch is usually first choice of sleeping accommodations.' Smiling at them, she relaxed back into her chair and folded her arms loosely across her plum-coloured sweater. She had hooked her trainer-clad feet around the front legs of the chair, and her balanced posture made Kincaid think suddenly of a bareback rider he'd once seen in the circus.

'Did you ride as a child?' he asked. She had about her a certain scrubbed outdoorsiness, not exactly a toughness but rather an air of healthy competence. Her nails, he noticed, were short and a bit grimy.

'Well, yes, actually, I did.' She regarded Kincaid with a puzzled frown. 'My aunt owned a stable in Devon and I spent my summer hols there. How odd that you should ask. I've just this morning come back from her funeral. She died last week.'

'So you weren't here when Commander Gilbert died?'

'No, although the parish secretary called me yesterday with the news.' She shook her head. 'I couldn't quite believe it. I tried ringing Claire but only got the answerphone. Is she managing all right?'

'As well as can be expected, I'd say,' Kincaid answered vaguely, pursuing his own thought. 'Were the Gilberts regular members of your flock?'

Rebecca nodded. 'Alastair often read the lesson. He took the obligations attendant on his position in the village very seriously—' She broke off and rubbed her

174

face with her hands. 'Sorry, sorry,' she said through splayed fingers. 'That was very uncharitable of me. I'm sure he meant well.'

'You didn't like him,' Kincaid said gently.

She shook her head ruefully. 'No, I'm afraid I didn't. But I did try, honestly. Judging people hastily is one of my worst faults—'

'So when you dislike someone you go out of your way to make allowances for them?' Kincaid grinned at her in shared understanding.

'Exactly. And I'm afraid that Alastair was very good at taking advantage of me.'

'In what way?' Out of the corner of his eye, Kincaid saw Deveney shift impatiently in his chair, but he refused to be hurried.

'Oh, you know...the special service readings, opening the fête, that sort of thing—'

'Things that look important but don't require any real effort?' Kincaid asked wryly.

'Exactly. I could never imagine Alastair canvassing the village for a good cause or washing up teacups after a parish meeting. Woman's work. In fact—' Rebecca paused. A faint flush of colour crept into her cheeks and she stared steadily at her hands clasped on the table top. 'To tell you the truth, I don't think Alastair approved of me, though he never said it in so many words. I suppose that's one reason I went out of my way to be fair...proving to myself that I was above petty retaliation.'

'A forgivable vanity, surely,' said Kincaid.

She looked up and met his eyes. 'Perhaps. But it wasn't very tactful of me to speak about him so freely. This is a terrible thing to have happened, and I wouldn't want you to think I took it lightly.'

'Unfortunately, dying in a brutal manner does not automatically qualify one for sainthood, however much we might wish it,' Kincaid offered drily.

'Miss Fielding...uh, Vicar,' said Deveney, 'about the thefts. You reported no sign of a break-in. Could you tell us exactly what happened?'

Rebecca closed her eyes for a moment, as if summoning the details. 'It was a lovely warm evening and I'd been working in the front garden. When I came in I noticed that the back door was ajar, but I didn't think anything of it—I never lock up and that door has a rather stiff catch. It wasn't until later when I was dressing for dinner that I noticed my pearl earrings were missing.'

'And you were sure you hadn't misplaced them?' Kincaid asked.

'Definitely. I'm very much a creature of habit, Superintendent, and I always put them straight into the jewellery box when I take them off. And I'd worn them just two days before.'

'Was there anything else missing?' Deveney had his notebook out now, pen ready.

Frowning, Rebecca rubbed at the end of her nose. 'Just some childhood keepsakes. A silver charm bracelet, some school medals. It was quite odd, really.'

Kincaid leaned towards her. 'And you saw no one unusual about the place?'

'I saw no one at all, Superintendent, unusual or otherwise. I'm sorry, I'm afraid I've been a complete waste of time for you.' She looked genuinely distressed, and Kincaid hastened to reassure her as he rose.

'Not at all. And it gave me a chance to see the church. It's quite a gem, isn't it?'

'It was built by G.E. Street, the man who designed the London law courts,' Rebecca said as she led them into the corridor. 'It's a lovely example of Victorian church architecture but rather a sad story. It seems he meant it as a gift for his wife, but she died shortly after it was finished.' They had reached the porch, and as they stepped outside she stopped and looked up at the honey-coloured stone rising above them. Slowly, she said, 'I've felt very lucky to have come here, and I'd hate to see anything disrupt my village. One becomes proprietorial very quickly, I'm afraid,' she added with a smile.

Looking down the hill towards the vicarage, Kincaid said, 'You're the gardener, I take it?'

'Oh, yes.' Rebecca's smile was radiant. 'It's my temptation and my salvation, I'm afraid. The place was a wilderness when I came here two years ago, and I've spent every spare minute there since.'

'It shows.' Infected by her enthusiasm, Kincaid found he couldn't help grinning back.

'I can't take all the credit,' she hastened to reassure him. 'Geoff Genovase helps me at weekends. I'd never have managed the heavy work without him.'

Kincaid thanked her again and they turned away, but before they'd gone more than a few steps down the lane she called out to him. 'Mr Kincaid, the dynamics that make a village a functioning organism are really quite fragile. You will be careful, won't you?'

'That explains why she'd missed out on the gossip,' said Kincaid as they walked down the lane. While they'd been inside

178

the sun had dropped in its swift afternoon progress, the light had faded from gold to a soft grey-green, and the shadows stood long on the ground.

'What does?' Deveney looked up from the notebook page he'd been scanning as they walked.

'The aunt's funeral.' Kincaid put his hands in his pockets and kicked at a stone with his toe.

'What the hell difference does it make?' Deveney asked, sounding a bit frayed. 'Do you always go round the mulberry bush like that in interviews? Talk about circumlocution.'

'I don't know what difference it makes. Yet. And no, I don't always waffle on, but sometimes it's the only way I know to get under the skin of things.' He stopped as they reached the bottom of the lane and turned to Deveney. 'I don't think this is going to be a straightforward case, Nick, and I want to know what these people thought of Alastair Gilbert, how he fitted into the fabric of the community.'

'Well, we're certainly not making much progress on the vagrant theory,' Deveney said disgustedly. 'We've one name left, a Mr Percy Bainbridge, at Rose Cottage. It's just next to the pub, so we might as well leave the car.' As they crossed the road and walked along the edge of the green, he added, 'This is our most recent report, by the way, just last month.'

Rose Cottage might once have been as charming as its name implied, but the canes arching over the front door were bare and dry, and only few dying chrysanthemums graced the path. Deveney pushed the bell, and after a few moments the door swung open.

'Yes?' enquired Mr Percy Bainbridge, wrinkling his nose and pursing his thin lips as if he smelled something distasteful. As Deveney made introductions and explained their mission, the lips relaxed into a simper, and Bainbridge said with fruity affectation, 'Oh, do come in. I knew you'd be wanting a word with me.'

They followed him down a dark, narrow hallway into a sitting room that was over-warm and over-decorated—and smelled, Kincaid thought, faintly of illness.

Bainbridge was tall, thin and stooped, with a chest so concave it looked as though it might have been hollowed out with an ice-cream scoop. Skin yellow as parchment stretched over the bones of his face and his balding skull. A death's head with dandruff, thought Kincaid, for what was left of the man's hair had liberally sprinkled the shoulders of his rusty black coat.

'You'll have some sherry, won't you?'

said their host. 'I always do at this time of day. Keeps the evening at bay, don't you think?' He poured from a decanter as he spoke, filling three rather dusty cut-crystal glasses, so that they could hardly refuse the proffered drinks.

Kincaid thanked him and took a tentative sip, then breathed an inward sigh of relief as the fine amontillado rolled over his tongue. At least he'd be spared having to tip his glass into a convenient aspidistra. 'Mr Bainbridge, we'd like to ask you a few—'

'I must say you took your time. I told your constable yesterday to send someone in charge. But do sit down.' Bainbridge gestured towards an ancient brocaded sofa and took the armchair himself. 'I quite understand that you are at the mercy of the bureaucracy.'

At a loss, Kincaid glanced at Deveney, who merely gave him a blank look and a slight shake of the head. Kincaid sat down gingerly on the slippery fabric, taking time to adjust his trouser creases and find a spot on the cluttered side table for his sherry glass. 'Mr Bainbridge' he said carefully, 'why don't you begin by telling us exactly what you told the constable?'

Bainbridge sat back in his chair, his gratified smile pulling at his already too-tight skin until it looked as though it must melt, like wax under a flame. He sipped at his sherry, cleared his throat, then brushed at a speck on his sleeve. It was clear, thought Kincaid, that Percy Bainbridge intended making the most of his moment in the limelight. 'I'd had my tea and finished with the washing up,' he began rather anticlimactically. 'I was looking forward to settling in for the evening with my beloved Shelley—' pausing, he gave Kincaid a ghastly little wink '—that's the poet, you understand, Superintendent. I don't hold with the television, never have. I am a firm believer in improving the mind, and it is a proven fact that one's intellect declines in direct proportion to the number of hours spent in front of the little black box. But I digress.' He gave an airy wave of his fingers. 'It is my habit to take some air in the evening, and that night was no exception.'

Kincaid took advantage of the man's pause for breath. 'Excuse me, Mr Bainbridge, but are you referring to Wednesday, the evening of Commander Gilbert's death?'

'Well, of course I am, Superintendent,' Bainbridge answered, his good humour obviously ruffled. 'Whatever else would I be referring to?' He took a restorative sip of his sherry. 'Now, as I was telling you, although the night was quite foggy and close, I stepped outside as usual. I had gone as far as the pub when I saw a shadowy figure slipping up the lane.' His eyes darted from Kincaid to Deveney, anticipating their reaction.

'What sort of figure, Mr Bainbridge?' Kincaid asked matter-of-factly. 'Was it male or female?'

'I really am unable to say, Superintendent. All I can tell you is that it appeared to be moving furtively, slipping from one pool of shadow to the next, and I am unwilling to embellish my account for the sake of drama.'

Deveney sat forward, his notebook open. 'Size? Height?'

Bainbridge shook his head.

'What about hair and clothing, Mr Bainbridge?' tried Kincaid. 'You may have noticed more than you realize. Think back—did any part of the figure reflect light?'

Bainbridge thought for a moment, then said with less assurance than he had displayed so far, 'I thought I saw the pale blur of a face, but that's all. Everything else was dark.'

'And where exactly was the figure in the lane?'

'Just beyond the Gilberts' house, moving up the lane towards the Women's Institute,' answered Bainbridge with more confidence.

'What time was this?' Deveney asked.

'I'm afraid I can't tell you,' Bainbridge's thin lips made a regretful little *moue*.

'Can't?' Kincaid said on a note of disbelief.

'I retired my watch when they retired me, Superintendent.' He tittered. 'I lived my life a slave to the clock and the bell—I thought it time I had my freedom from such constraints. Oh, there is a clock in the kitchen, but unless I should have an appointment I don't pay it much attention.'

'Do you think you could make an estimate as to the time on Wednesday evening, Mr Bainbridge?' Kincaid asked with forced patience.

'I can tell you that it wasn't too long afterwards that the first of the panda cars arrived at the Gilberts'. Half an hour, perhaps.' Having placed the sherry decanter conveniently within arm's reach, Bainbridge wrapped his long fingers around its neck. 'Care for some more sherry, Superintendent? Chief Inspector? No? Well, you won't mind if I do?' He poured himself a generous measure and drank. 'I've become quite a connoisseur since my retirement, if I say so myself I've even put some bottle racks into the pantry—had young Geoffrey in to help me—as the cottage doesn't have a cellar, of course.'

Kincaid felt the prickle of sweat under his arms and between his shoulder-blades. The heat of the room had combined with the flush from the sherry to make him a bit queasy, and he felt an unexpected surge of claustrophobia. 'Mr Bainbridge,' he began, wanting to finish the interview as quickly as possible, 'we want to ask you a few questions about the thefts you reported in—'

'Don't tell me you've got on to this burglar business, as well? No, no, no, I tell you. It's absolute twaddle.' Pink splotches appeared on Percy Bainbridge's cheeks, and the knuckles wrapped around the stem of his sherry glass turned white. 'I heard them last night in the pub, the fools. You don't really think some stranger appeared in the village and just happened to bash the commander in the head, do you, Superintendent?'

'I'll agree it's not very likely, Mr Bainbridge, but we have to follow—'

'I'd look a bit closer to home if I were you. Oh, she's a cool one, is Claire Gilbert, I grant you that. Butter wouldn't melt in her mouth. But I can tell you,' he leaned towards them and put his finger beside his nose, 'that our Mrs Gilbert is no better than she should be. If I were you, I'd have a look at what she gets up to with that partner of hers, and I said as much to Commander Gilbert not too long ago.'

'Did you now?' said Kincaid, forgetting his discomfort. 'And how did the commander receive your advice?'

Bainbridge sat back a bit and smoothed the fringe of hair behind his ear. 'Oh, he was very appreciative, man to man, you know.'

Kincaid leaned forward and dropped his voice, as if inviting a confidence. 'I didn't realize you were on such friendly terms with Alastair Gilbert. Got on together well, did you?'

'Oh, yes,' said Bainbridge, beaming. 'I think the commander was much misunderstood by the hoi polloi of the village, Superintendent. He was a man of purpose, of direction, a man who counted in life. And I think he recognized a kindred soul when he met one.' One eyelid dropped in what might have been a wink, and Bainbridge finished off his sherry in one swallow.

'Did the commander ask you to substantiate your allegations about his wife?' Kincaid asked a bit more sharply.

'Oh, no, it wasn't like that at all.' Bainbridge shook his head in aggrieved agitation. 'I merely expressed my concern that his wife should be spending so much

186

time alone with a man like that. Well, I ask you, what can they be doing all day? It's not as if it were a real job, is it, Superintendent?' His enunciation became more absurdly precise as he compensated for the slurring effect of the sherry.

'And what did you do before you retired, Mr Bainbridge?' asked Kincaid. He tried to visualize the man as a navvy and failed miserably.

'I was a teacher, sir, a moulder of young minds and morals. At one of the best schools—you would recognize the name if I told you, but I don't like to make much of myself.' He simpered and smoothed the lank fringe of hair again.

Kincaid let a note of severity creep into his voice. 'Tell me, Mr Bainbridge, could the shadowy figure you saw have been Malcolm Reid, Claire Gilbert's partner? Think very carefully, now.'

The colour drained from Bainbridge's cheeks, leaving them more pinched than before. 'Well, I...that is...I never meant to imply... As I told you, Superintendent, the figure was very vague, very elusive, and I couldn't swear to anything at all.'

Exchanging glances with Deveney, Kincaid gave him a slight nod.

'Mr Bainbridge,' said Deveney, 'if you'll just answer a few more questions, we won't

187

take up any more of your time. What exactly went missing from your cottage last month?'

Bainbridge looked from one to the other as if to protest, then sighed. 'Well, if you must drag all that up again. Two silver picture frames with inscribed photos of some of my boys. A money clip. A gold pen.'

'Was there money in the clip?' asked Kincaid.

'That was the odd thing, Superintendent. He didn't take the money. I found the notes lying neatly folded, just where the clip had been.'

'Nothing more valuable than that?' said Deveney with obvious exasperation.

Affronted, Bainbridge puffed out his thin chest. 'They were valuable to me, Chief Inspector. Treasured keepsakes, mementoes of the years devoted to my charges...' Reaching for the decanter, he refilled his glass, this time not bothering to offer them any. Kincaid judged that Mr Percy Bainbridge had reached the maudlin stage and that no further useful information would be forthcoming.

'Thank you, Mr Bainbridge. You've been very helpful,' he said, and Deveney stood up so fast he bumped the coffee table with his knees.

They hastily said their goodbyes, and

when they reached the end of the cottage walk, Deveney wiped beads of perspiration from his brow. 'What a dreadful little man.'

'Undoubtedly,' answered Kincaid as they walked to the car. 'But how reliable a witness is he? Why didn't your constable report his "shadowy figure" story? And could there by anything to this business about Claire Gilbert and Malcolm Reid?'

'Proximity's made for stranger bedfellows, I dare say.'

'I suppose so,' said Kincaid, glad that the twilight hid the flush creeping up his neck.

They walked on to the car in silence, and when they'd shut themselves into the still-warm interior, Deveney stretched and said, 'What now, guv? I could use a real drink after that.'

For a moment Kincaid gazed into the deepening dusk, then said, 'I think you should give Madeleine Wade a call, ask her if Geoff Genovase has done any odd jobs for her. I'm beginning to get an idea about our village brownie.

'And sound out the village on the subject of Mr Percy Bainbridge—the pub ought to do nicely for that. I'd like to know if he has a reputation for moonshine and how chummy he really was with Alastair Gilbert. Somehow I can't quite picture that alliance. As for Malcolm Reid and his relationship with Claire Gilbert, we may have more success if we talk to him at the shop again tomorrow, rather than at home.'

'Right.' Deveney glanced at his watch. 'I should think the evening regulars would be drifting into the Moon about this time. Will you be coming along with me, then?'

'Me?' Kincaid answered absently. 'No, not tonight, Nick. I'm going to London.'

'All in order,' read the note the major had left on the kitchen table. 'Will maintain routine unless notified otherwise.' Kincaid smiled and picked up Sid, who was rubbing frenziedly about his ankles and purring at a volume that threatened to vibrate the pictures off the walls. 'You've been well looked after, I see,' he said, scratching the cat under his pointed black chin.

In the months since his friend Jasmine had died and he'd taken in her orphaned cat, he and his solitary neighbour, Major Keith, had formed an unlikely but useful partnership. Useful for Kincaid, as it allowed him to be away without worrying about Sid—useful for the major in that it gave him an excuse for contact with another human being that he would not otherwise have sought. Kincaid theorized that it also allowed Harley Keith to maintain a secret and unacknowledged relationship with the cat, a tangible evocation of Jasmine's memory.

Putting Sid down with a last pat, he turned out the lamp and went to stand on his balcony. In the dim light he could see the red leaves on the major's prunus tree hanging limp as banners on a still day, and pale splotches in the garden beds that would be the last of the yellow chrysanthemums. Suddenly he felt bereft, his grief as fresh and raw as it had been in the first weeks after Jasmine's death, but he knew it would pass. A new family occupied the flat below his now, with two small children who were only allowed to use the garden under the major's strictest supervision.

The cold crept into his bones as he stood a moment longer, irresolute. He had phoned Gemma from Guildford Station, then again from Waterloo, listening to the repeated rings until long after he'd given up hope of an answer. He hadn't admitted how much he'd hoped he might talk to her, perhaps even see her, hoped that in the course of going over the day's notes he might somehow begin to right whatever had gone wrong between them.

Chapter Eight

The burring sound came from a great distance, its insistent repetition dragging her up from the cottony depths of sleep. Her arm felt leaden, treacle-slow, as she freed it from the duvet and felt for the telephone. 'Hello,' she mumbled, then realized she had the handset the wrong way round.

Once she'd got it right side up, she heard Kincaid saying cheerfully, 'Gemma, I didn't wake you, did I? I tried to ring you last night, but you weren't in.'

Focusing on the clock, she groaned. She'd overslept by an hour and she had absolutely no memory of turning off the alarm. Fuzzily, she was trying to remember whether she had set it when she realized Kincaid was saying, '...meet me at Notting Hill.'

'Notting Hill? Whatever for?' She shook her head to clear it.

'I want to have a look at some records. How long?'

Making an effort to pull herself together, she said, 'An hour.' Quick mental arithmetic confirmed that she should be able to shower, leave Toby with Hazel and get the tube to Notting Hill. 'Give me an hour.'

'I'll meet you at the station, then. Cheerio.' The line clicked and went dead in her ear.

She hung up slowly, piecing together the wine drunk at Hazel's, the first part of the night spent sleeping in the chair, Toby in her lap. This was the first night she'd slept in her own bed for a week—no wonder she'd been so exhausted.

With that thought, memory returned to her sleep-fogged brain, and she realized that Duncan was no longer her comfortable, dependable friend and partner but an unknown territory to be navigated with the greatest care.

She might never have been away, thought Gemma as she walked into Notting Hill Police Station. The blue wire chairs in reception were the same, as was the black-and-white speckled lino on the floor. She had always loved this place, had forgiven it the awkward partitioning of its interior for the symmetrical grace of its exterior. As it was a listed building, no changes were allowed to the outside and very few to the inside, so the staff managed as best they could.

As she stood awaiting her turn at reception, she imagined the rhythms of the four

193

hundred officers moving through the four floors, the gossip, the boredom, the sudden spasms of frantic activity, and she felt a moment of acute longing for her old life. It had all seemed so much less complicated then.

'The Superintendent said to send you up to CID as soon as you came in,' said the friendly but unfamiliar girl behind the counter. 'He's in Interview Room B. First floor.' Gemma thanked her with tactful restraint, considering that she could have found CID drugged and blindfolded.

Kincaid looked up and smiled as she opened the door. 'I brought you some coffee. Sniffed out the good stuff, too, from the department secretary's office.' He gestured at a still-steaming mug standing on the table beside a stack of file folders. His chestnut hair, which always started out the day neatly brushed, fell over his forehead in a comma—due no doubt to the recent exercise of his habit of running his hand through it when he read or concentrated.

As she pulled out the chair opposite and sat down, he tapped at the open folder before him. 'It's all here.'

Gemma forced herself to concentrate. If he had intentionally set out to distract and disarm her he couldn't have succeeded better. His thoughtfulness in timing the coffee with her arrival, his attempts at cheerful normality, and worst of all, that damned wayward lock of hair. She clasped her hands tightly around the mug to keep from reaching out and brushing the hair back, then said, 'What's all there?'

'The death of Stephen Penmaric, twelve years ago this coming April.'

'Penmaric? But that's—'

'Lucy Penmaric's father. They lived here in Notting Hill, in Elgin Crescent. He was struck and killed crossing the Portobello Road, on his way to get some medicine for Lucy at an all-night chemist.'

'Oh, no...' Gemma breathed. Now she understood Claire Gilbert's oblique comment during their interview, and her heart ached for mother and daughter. 'That's too much for anyone to bear, surely. But what has it to do with this?'

'I don't know.' Kincaid sighed and pushed the hair back from his forehead. 'But Alastair Gilbert was Superintendent here then. A Sergeant David Ogilvie was the investigating officer.'

Gemma closed her mouth when she realized she was gaping, then said, 'I spoke to Ogilvie yesterday at divisional headquarters. He's a chief inspector now, and he was Gilbert's staff officer.' She recounted the interview, then her meeting with Jackie Temple.

'They go back a long way, then,' said Kincaid. 'And it most likely has nothing to do with anything...but I think we should have a talk with David Ogilvie about it.'

'What about Stephen Penmaric? Did they find out who ran him down?'

Kincaid shook his head. 'Hit and run. It was late at night, there were no witnesses. The copper on the beat saw tail-lights disappearing around the corner, but by the time he radioed for help the car had vanished.'

'How dreadful for Claire. And for Lucy.'

'He was a journalist, and from what Lucy told me I'd say that, unlike Alastair Gilbert, he was sorely missed.' Gathering up the loose papers, Kincaid closed the file and stacked it neatly with the others. 'Come on,' he said, standing up. 'Let's walk for a bit.'

It promised to be another clear day, and even in mid-November the trees arching over Ladbroke Grove made a lacy canopy of green. Gemma had followed Kincaid without question and now paced beside him, breathing the still air deeply but hugging her coat together against the cold.

He glanced at her as if gauging her mood, then said, 'I wanted to see it—the house in Elgin Crescent. For some reason I felt a need to meet the ghosts.'

'Only Stephen's dead,' Gemma said logically.

'You could argue that the Claire and Lucy of twelve years ago no longer exist either, if you wanted to get into the semantics of time.' He flashed her a grin, then sobered. 'But I don't want to argue with you at all, Gemma.' His steps slowed as he spoke. 'I admit I had a double motive—I wanted a chance to talk to you. Look... Gemma...if I've done something to offend you, it wasn't intentional. And if I've taken our partnership for granted in the past, I can only say I'm sorry, because the past few days have made me realize how much I depend on your support, on your interpretation of things, on your gut reaction to people. I need you on this case. We need to be communicating, not bumping around in the dark like blind fish in a barrel.' They reached an intersection and he stopped, turning to her. 'Can't we be a team again?'

Thoughts rattled around in Gemma's head, as disorganized as her emotions. How could she explain to him why she'd been so angry when she didn't know herself? She knew he was right—they were likely to make a real balls-up of the case if they kept on as they were—and she also knew neither of them could afford that. She, who prided herself on her professionalism above all else, had been behaving like an ass, but the words of an apology stuck in her throat and refused to budge.

Finally, she managed a strangled, 'Right, guv,' but she kept her eyes firmly on the pavement.

'Good,' he said. Then as the light changed and they stepped into the street, he added so softly that she wasn't sure she'd heard him correctly, 'That's a start.'

As they turned into Elgin Crescent a few minutes later, she searched for a safe subject. 'It's got more yuppified since I left.' Every house in the terrace boasted a different-hued stucco unified by gleaming white trim, and each sprouted its baby satellite dish and displayed a plaque announcing the possession of an alarm system.

Kincaid consulted a scrap of paper, and they soon found the house where the Penmarics had occupied the top-floor flat. 'And this is one of the victims,' Kincaid said as they surveyed the peach exterior and brilliant black front door. 'Lucy said it had a yellow door.' He sounded disappointed.

'I suppose it's a good thing'—with her toe Gemma poked at a bit of plasterboard that had strayed from the rubbish tip and the scaffolding in the garden next door—'this gentrification. Improves the neighbourhood and all that, but somehow I miss the character of the old one. It was comfortable and just a wee bit shabby, somewhere you could come home, take your shoes off and eat your chips right out of the paper.

'But this, now,' she gestured at the curve of the terrace, 'this is intimate dinner parties after work with wine and just the right gourmet goodies from Fortnum's. Not exactly conducive to ghosts.'

'No ghosts,' Kincaid agreed as they turned away and retraced their steps. 'We'll have to try further afield.'

Gemma hadn't expected to find herself in David Ogilvie's office again so soon, but this time she pulled out her notebook with a sense of relief and let Kincaid conduct the interview.

'Do you remember the Stephen Penmaric case?' Kincaid asked, when they had concluded the formalities.

Ogilvie drew his dark brows together in a puzzled frown. 'Claire Gilbert's first husband? Of course I do. Hadn't thought of it in years, though.' His smile seemed merely a baring of teeth. 'What are you on about? You think Claire had some old flame with a penchant for getting rid of husbands?'

Kincaid chuckled appreciatively. 'It's as good as anything we've come up with so far.' Shifting position slightly, he clasped his hands around his knee and regarded Ogilvie with what Gemma thought of as his getting-down-to-business expression. 'I've read the files, of course,' he said. 'Inconclusive as hell. You were the investigating officer, and you and I both know,' his smile suggested an understood camaraderie, 'that the officer in charge of a case can't put *impressions* in a report, but that's exactly what I want from you now. What *didn't* you say? What did you think of Claire? Was Stephen Penmaric murdered?'

David Ogilvie leaned back in his chair and steepled his fingers together before replying with deliberation. 'I think now exactly what I thought then. Stephen Penmaric's death was a tragic accident. There was nothing in the report because there was nothing to find. You know as well as I do,' he added with evident sarcasm, 'the odds for tracing an unwitnessed hit-and-run. And I don't see how any of this could possibly have any bearing on Alastair Gilbert's death.'

'Did Gilbert know Claire Penmaric before her husband's death?' countered Kincaid.

'You're not suggesting that Alastair had

200

anything to do with Penmaric's death?' Ogilvie's eyebrows rose in an expression of incredulous surprise. Tufts of hair on the inner edge of the brows grew straight up, giving them an odd, hooked aspect, making Gemma think absently of horns. 'Surely, Superintendent, you're not that desperate. I realize that you're under some pressure to solve this case, but no one who knew Alastair could possibly think him capable of bending the law to suit his own ends.'

'Chief Inspector, I'm at liberty to think whatever I like. And I have the advantage of not having known Commander Gilbert well, so that I'm not inclined to let personal opinions cloud my judgement.'

Gemma looked at Kincaid in surprise. It wasn't like him to pull rank, but Ogilvie had certainly deserved it.

Ogilvie's lips tightened, and although his olive colouring made it difficult to be sure, Gemma thought his cheeks darkened slightly with an angry flush. After a moment, however, he said civilly enough, 'You're quite right, Superintendent. I apologize. Perhaps one should stretch one's parameters.'

'I'm trying to form a clear picture of Alastair Gilbert, and I thought it might be helpful to learn a bit of his history. It seemed logical to suppose that he might have met Claire during the investigation of her husband's death.'

'Alastair did meet Claire during the course of the investigation,' Ogilvie conceded. 'Young, pretty and very much alone in the world—not many men would have resisted the temptation to offer her comfort and support.'

'Including Gilbert?'

Shrugging, Ogilvie answered, 'They became friends. More than that I can't tell you. I've never been in the habit of prying into the private lives of my superior officers—or anyone else's, for that matter. If you want the more intimate details, I'd suggest you ask Claire Gilbert.'

Gemma glanced at Kincaid, wondering how he would react to Ogilvie's thinly veiled disdain, but he merely smiled and thanked him.

They said good-bye, and as they left the building, Gemma said, 'I wonder why he dislikes us so much?'

'Are you feeling paranoid today?' Kincaid gave her a sideways grin as they walked down the steps. 'I suspect it's nothing personal—that David Ogilvie dislikes everyone equally. But why don't you stop by the station again? Have a word with your friend Jackie if you can track her down, see what she thinks about Chief Inspector Ogilvie.

'Then meet me at the Yard and we'll

take a car from the pool for the drive back to Surrey.' For a few minutes they walked in silence, then, as they reached the intersection where their ways parted, he mused aloud, 'I do wonder, though, if Ogilvie was entirely immune to Claire Penmaric's appeal.'

Jackie Temple eased a finger into the waistband of her uniform skirt and took a deep breath. She found it difficult to believe that anyone who walked as many miles a day as she did could possibly put on weight, but the physical evidence was undeniable. Time to get out the sewing box and hope that the seam held a generous amount of fabric, she thought with a sigh. She did so look forward to her elevenses, and she only had a few blocks to go before she reached the stall just off the Portobello Road where she usually stopped for her break. Ordering one sticky bun rather than two with her tea would make her feel as though she'd taken a stand against the creeping pounds, but she'd be ravenous by the time she finished her shift at three.

Slowing her pace, she scanned the knot of pedestrians blocking the pavement just ahead. It sorted itself out quickly enough—just a case of too many people going in opposite directions at the same time—and left her free to pursue her thoughts. In her years of walking the beat she'd developed a facility for dividing her mind. One half was ever-alert for anything out of the ordinary in her territory. It responded to greetings from familiar residents and shopkeepers, made routine checks, noticed those loitering a bit too conspicuously, and all the while the other part of her mind lived a life of its own, speculating and daydreaming.

She thought of her unexpected meeting with Gemma yesterday. Although she had to admit she envied her friend's status as a sergeant in the CID just a bit, she'd never really wanted to do anything more than walk a beat. She'd found her niche, and it suited her.

Not that she'd mind having Gemma's figure, she thought with a smile as she passed the homoeopathic chemist's and saluted Mr Dodd, the owner. In fact, she mused as she turned the corner and saw the stall's cheerful red awning ahead, it seemed to her that Gemma was thinner than she remembered and had a transparent quality, as if she were stretched beyond her resources. Jackie suspected that this was not entirely due to pressure of work, but she'd never been one to force confidences.

A few minutes later, holding her steaming tea in its polystyrene cup in one hand,

and her solitary and virtuous bun in the other, Jackie leaned her back against the stall's brick wall and surveyed the street. She blinked as she saw a flash of red hair, then a familiar face coming through the crowd towards her. It occurred to her that she should feel surprise, but instead she had an odd sense of inevitability. She waved, and a moment later Gemma reached her.

'I was just thinking about you,' said Jackie. 'Do you suppose I conjured you up, or is this one of those coincidences you read about in the tabloids?'

'I don't think I'd last long as a genie,' Gemma answered, laughing. Her cheeks were pink with the cold, and her copper hair had been teased from its plait by the wind. 'But maybe you should nominate your guv'nor. He has you timed down to the minute.' Eyeing Jackie's bun, she pinched a currant from it. 'That looks wonderful. I'm starved. One thing about CID—you learn never to pass up an opportunity for a meal.'

As she examined the stall's menu board, Jackie studied her. Gemma's loosely cut rust-coloured blazer and tan chinos looked casual yet smart, something that Jackie felt she never quite managed to achieve. 'Nice outfit,' she said, when Gemma had ordered tea and a croissant with ham and cheese. 'I guess I'm just fashion-impaired, which is probably one reason I stayed in uniform.' With a mouthful of bun, she added, 'You look much better today, by the way, roses back in your cheeks and all that. I'd just been thinking that you looked a bit done-up yesterday.'

'Put it down to a good night's sleep,' Gemma said easily, but she looked down, twisting the ring she wore on her right hand. Then she smiled brightly and changed the subject, and they nattered on about mutual friends until Gemma's sandwich was ready.

When Gemma had taken a couple of bites and washed them down with tea, she said, 'Jackie, what do you know about Gilbert and David Ogilvie?'

'Ogilvie?' Jackie thought for a moment. 'Weren't he and Gilbert partners? That was before our time, but it seems to me there was some rumour about bad blood between them. Why?'

Gemma told her what they had learned about Stephen Penmaric's death, then added, 'So it seems that both Gilbert and Ogilvie met Claire at the time of the investigation, then a couple of years later she married Gilbert.'

Jackie licked the last of the crumbs from her fingers. 'I know who might be able to help—you remember Sergeant Talley? He's been at Notting Hill for donkey's years and knows everything about everybody.'

'He told me where to find you.' Gemma looked down at the croissant in one hand and the tea in the other. 'Here.' She handed the croissant to Jackie and fished her notebook from her handbag. 'I'll stop back at the station and see if I can—'

'Wait, Gemma, let me do it,' Jackie said, the temptation of a second bun forgotten. 'You've got to understand about Talley. He may be the world's worst gossip, but he doesn't see himself that way. He'd never be willing to drag up any dirt on someone in our nick to an outsider—and you're an outsider now.'

'Ouch.' Gemma winced.

'Sorry,' Jackie said with a grin. 'But you know what I mean.' And it was true, she thought. She could see in Gemma now what hadn't been apparent yesterday—the focus, the drive that made her CID material. It was not so much that Gemma had changed, for those qualities had always been there, but rather that she'd found the job which utilized her talents, and in doing so had moved away from Jackie and the life they'd shared.

'You wouldn't mind talking to him about it?' Tucking her notebook under one arm, Gemma retrieved her croissant and nibbled at it again.

'I'll try to get him in the canteen for a cuppa when I get off shift, get him reminiscing. And I don't mind a bit,' Jackie added slowly. 'You've got my curiosity roused. I hope this detective stuff isn't catching.'

'He's got a record.' Nick Deveney looked up at Kincaid and Gemma as they entered the incident room at Guildford Police Station. He and Will Darling had been bent over a computer printout, and the quick smile he gave Gemma was his only greeting. 'I didn't manage to get in touch with your friend Madeleine Wade until this morning, and it turned out he worked for her, too. Did some heavy lifting in the shop and a bit of painting at the flat.'

Wondering at the barb implied by the emphasis on 'your friend', Gemma glanced at Kincaid, but he only looked amused. 'Who has a record?' she asked. 'What are you talking about?'

'Geoff Genovase,' said Will. 'Done for burglary five years ago. He was managing a hi-fi shop in Wimbledon, and it seems he and a mate from the shop decided to liberate some of the merchandise in the supplier's warehouse. Unfortunately they hadn't quite got the knack of disabling alarm systems, so Genovase did time in one of Her Majesty's best hotels.'

Gemma sat down in the nearest chair. 'I don't believe it.'

'He did some sort of odd job for everyone in the village who reported a theft,' said Deveney. 'Coincidences like that don't manufacture themselves. And if he did the others, why not the Gilberts', only this time something went wrong.'

She thought of the gentle young man who had fed her cheese and pickle so solicitously, whose face had lit with eagerness when she enquired about his computer game. 'Why didn't you tell me?' Her voice rose as she turned on Kincaid.

His face registered surprise as he looked up from the printout he'd taken from Deveney. 'It was just a hunch. I had no idea it would pan out.'

'I've applied for a warrant,' said Deveney. 'Hope we don't have to search the whole bloody pub.'

Kincaid returned the printout to Will, and stood staring into space, his eyes slightly unfocused. After a moment he straightened and said decisively, 'Listen, Nick, I'm not willing to drop everything else to run with this. I still think we should follow up on Reid and the London angle.' He turned to Gemma. 'Why don't you and Will go to Reid's shop in Shere and have a word with him while Nick and I handle the search?'

Her anger rose with frightening speed, closing her throat, making her heart pound, but she fought it back and managed to say evenly, 'Um, could I have a word, guv?' Kincaid raised an eyebrow but followed her into the empty corridor, and when the door clicked shut she said through clenched teeth, 'Shall I assume you have some reason for this?'

'What?' he said blankly.

'Sending me off on some fool's errand while you and Nick Deveney take the important job. Do you think I'm not capable of being objective. Is that it?'

'Christ, Gemma,' he said, backing up a step. 'I've tried to sort things out, but you're as prickly as a bloody hedgehog these days. What am I supposed to do with you? Ask your permission before I decide how to conduct an investigation?

'I have two reasons, in fact, if you want to know.' He ticked them off on his fingers. 'One, you haven't met Malcolm Reid and I wanted your reaction to him, wanted to know if you thought there was anything in Percy Bainbridge's allegations that Claire's having an affair with him. Two, you've established a positive contact with Geoff Genovase, and I'd like to keep it that way. You know as well as I do how useful that can be in an interrogation, and going in with a search warrant is certainly not going to reinforce his confidence in you.' He took a breath. 'Is that good enough for you, or do I need more?'

The anger drained away as quickly as it had come. She leaned against the cool wall and closed her eyes, feeling deflated and shaken.

An echo of his words took her back, and for a moment she was a child again, in her tiny bedroom above the bakery. She'd had one of her frequent and furious rows with her sister, and her mother had come in to her, sitting down on the bed where she lay with her hot, tear-streaked face buried in the pillow. 'What am I to do with you, Gemma?' her mum had said with weary exasperation, but the fingers stroking her hair had been gentle. 'If you can't learn to control that redheaded temper, love, you'd best learn to apologize gracefully. And if you have a particle of the sense God gave you, you'll do both.' It had been good advice—given from experience, Gemma had realized as she grew older—and she'd tried to take it to heart.

She opened her eyes as a breath of air touched her face. Kincaid had turned away, his hand on the doorknob, face set in a tight scowl. Gemma reached out and touched his arm, attempting a smile. 'You're right, of course. Guess I did overreact a bit. Look... I know I've been an awful bloody cow lately.' She glanced away, bit her lip. 'Duncan...I'm sorry.'

Tall and tanned, his close-cropped silver-blond hair moulded to his finely shaped head, Malcolm Reid was a sight to make any woman's heart flutter. He would make a perfect complement to Claire Gilbert's fair, delicate prettiness, and Gemma could easily imagine why tongues would wag.

He'd greeted them pleasantly, offering coffee from a sleek, German pot plugged into an outlet at the back of one of the display counter tops.

'I thought this was all just for show.' Gemma gestured at the kitchen area as she accepted a mug.

'Might as well make use of the facilities.' Reid grinned as he pulled up wrought-iron stools for Will and Gemma. 'Actually, this is very much a working kitchen. My wife uses it for demonstration cooking classes, but she has nothing on just now. "Healthy Cooking from the Mediterranean" finished last week, and "Italian Classics" starts this coming Tuesday.'

The names of the courses conjured up exotic ingredients, warm climates awash with garlic-laden smells, and Gemma felt a shiver of longing. Although her parents had turned out excellent baked goods, their business had left them little time or energy for anything but the most conventional of English cooking, and Gemma hadn't had much opportunity to venture further afield. 'Sounds lovely,' she said a bit wistfully.

'It is.' Malcolm Reid regarded her with interest. He'd propped himself against the counter top with an air of much practice, cradling his coffee in both hands. 'You should give it a try sometime. Now how can I help you?'

Will shifted position on a stool seat not made for thighs the size of hams. 'Mr Reid, can you tell us what you were doing on Wednesday evening?'

Reid's mug made an almost imperceptible pause in its journey to his mouth. He took a sip, then said, 'Wednesday evening? Are you asking me for an alibi? I know, I know,' he held up a hand before they could speak, 'I heard it from your...chief inspector, wasn't it? Routine enquiries, just like the telly, not to worry. I must say I don't find that reassurance very comforting, but I've no reason not to tell you. I'm afraid you may find it rather a disappointment, however.' He looked at Gemma, a gleam of humour in his eyes. 'I closed up the shop at half-past five and went straight home, where I spent the entire evening with my wife.'

Will nodded encouragingly. 'Your wife

will verify this, Mr Reid?'

'Of course she will. Why shouldn't she?'

'Mr Reid,' began Gemma, wondering how she might ease into this tactfully, 'does your wife get on well with Claire Gilbert?'

'Val?' Reid appeared genuinely puzzled. 'Val's known Claire longer than I have. That's how Claire came to me as a client—she'd taken one of Val's classes.'

'Were both your wife and Alastair Gilbert comfortable with your working relationship with Claire?'

For a moment Reid looked at her blankly, then his face hardened. 'Just what exactly are you getting at?'

Might as well be hung for a sheep as a lamb, thought Gemma, since her attempt at tact had not been a resounding success. 'Apparently, Mr Reid, there have been some rumours in the village that your relationship with Claire Gilbert was a little more personal in nature and that her husband was made aware of that.'

'Bloody hell,' exploded Reid, his knuckles white on the coffee mug. 'I hate bloody gossip. It's so insidious, and one's so bloody powerless against it. You're damned as a sneak if you say nothing, damned even more if you speak out or challenge the whisperers—"methinks he doth protest too much".

'It's all nonsense, and nonsense about

Alastair, too.' Suddenly he relaxed and sighed. 'Oh, it's not your fault, Sergeant. Sorry if I took it out on you. But tell me you don't have to thrust this on Claire, too. Surely she's had enough to deal with as it is.'

Painfully aware of its inadequacy, Gemma trotted out her stock answer. 'This is a murder investigation, Mr Reid, and the truth must take precedence. I dislike—'

She was spared finishing by the opening of the shop door, and she recognized Claire Gilbert's voice even as she turned.

'Malcolm, I—' Claire stopped in mid-stride as she took in Will and Gemma, but Gemma had the distinct impression that she had been about to rush straight into Malcolm Reid's arms.

'Claire, what are you doing here?' Reid crossed to her and took her hands, his face creased with concern. 'You've no business being out.'

Letting go of Reid's hands after a brief contact, Claire recovered enough poise to greet Will and Gemma with her usual graciousness. 'I'm so sorry, I hope I didn't seem rude.' She nodded at them, with a half-smile for Will. 'It's just that I couldn't bear it anymore. We've had the phone off the hook to stop it ringing, and the constable is still on the gate, but they're waiting out there in the lane, watching us.'

A shudder ran through her body and she clasped her hands together tightly.

'Here. Sit,' Reid instructed her as Will slid from his stool and positioned it for her. 'Who's watching you? What are you talking about?'

'Reporters.' Gemma made a face. 'Like bloody vultures. But it will pass, Mrs Gilbert, I promise you. They have relatively short attention spans—I'm surprised they've stuck it out this long, actually.'

'So how did you escape the siege?' asked Will.

The half-smile flashed again. 'I put my hair up under one of Alastair's caps to complete the disguise.' Claire gestured at her clothes, and only then did Gemma notice she'd exchanged her usual elegant attire for jeans and an old tweed jacket. 'Then I sneaked out the back and through Mrs Johnson's garden, slouched across to the pub, and borrowed Brian's car.' Her voice held a note of sheepish pride as she added, 'It felt quite unexpectedly liberating, to tell you the truth.'

The clothes made Claire look younger, bringing out what Gemma had begun to recognize as her toughness, as well as emphasizing her fragility. Would she continue to shed her respectable-suburban-housewife trappings like a snake sloughs an old skin?

'But why are *you* here?' She turned to Will and Gemma as if the thought had just occurred to her. 'I don't know why you'd need to talk to Malcolm.' She hugged herself as if cold, and a note of fear crept into her voice as she added, 'Has something happened? What's go—'

'Routine enquiries,' Reid said with a grin before Gemma could answer. 'Nothing to worry about. Right, Sergeant?'

'Mrs Gilbert,' said Gemma, 'could I have a word with you?'

Having suggested a walk, Gemma led the way across the bridge and took the path along the little Tillingbourne River. Birches grew right along the water's edge, and their bare silvery branches reached towards the sky as if seeking the last of the pale sun.

Gemma wondered how best to frame her questions. Claire seemed at ease, content to walk in silence. She smiled at Gemma, then stooped for a stone and stood weighing it in the palm of her hand. Shaking her head, she bent and looked for another one. The wind parted her hair as she knelt, revealing a flash of pale and slender neck. The sight made Gemma feel oddly and uncomfortably protective, and she looked away.

Claire found another stone, stood up and skipped it expertly across the water. When the last set of ripples had stilled, she said, 'I haven't done that in years—I'm surprised I remember how. Do you think it's like riding a bike?' Then, as if continuing a conversation, 'Thank God for Becca. I don't know what I'd do without her. She'll make all the arrangements for the funeral when...when they release Alastair's body.'

'Becca?'

'Our vicar, Rebecca Fielding.'

Gemma saw an opening. She was willing to abandon Malcolm Reid for the moment in order to delve into the past. 'I don't suppose experience makes these things any easier. I didn't know about your first husband when we talked the other day. I'm sorry.'

'There's no need for you to be—you couldn't have known. And Stephen was always a great one for getting on with things. I tried to remember that on those days it didn't seem worthwhile getting up.' Claire stopped and turned towards the river. Hands shoved in her trouser pockets, she stared into the water where it ran like molten pewter over the stones. 'But that all seems a very long time ago. I'm not even sure I know her any more, that distant Claire.'

'That was when you met Commander Gilbert, after Stephen died?'

Claire's smile held no mirth. 'Alastair thought I needed looking after.'

'And did you?'

'I thought I did,' answered Claire, walking again. 'Stephen and I married very young, just out of school. Childhood sweethearts. He was a journalist, you know, a brilliant one.' With a glance at Gemma she added fiercely, 'We had a *good* life. And after Lucy was born it was even better, but it wasn't what you'd call secure, living from assignment to assignment.

'So there I was, my husband dead, my parents dead, no job skills at all, and a five-year-old daughter to care for. Stephen had a bit of life insurance, not enough to last more than a year or two even if we pinched every penny.' The path had narrowed and now stopped abruptly against a stone wall. Claire turned and started back. 'Alastair seemed safe.'

Gemma followed her silently as they reached the road again and crossed over. They followed the lane leading to the church, skirting the tubs of bright flowers that half blocked the pavement.

What would she have done without her job and her parents' support when Rob left? Would she, like Claire, have chosen security had it been offered her? 'What about David Ogilvie?' she asked. 'Was he in love with you, too?'

'David?' Claire stopped with her hand on the church gate and gave her a startled glance.

'We had to interview him as your husband's staff officer. There was something in what he *didn't* say that made me wonder.'

'Oh, David...' Claire said with a sigh that echoed the creak of the gate. As they picked their way through the tall grass surrounding the gravestones, she plucked a blade and twisted it in her fingers. 'David was...difficult. At the time I convinced myself that I was just another of David's potential conquests, a notch on his belt. He was very much against my marrying Alastair, but that I put down to peacock rivalry. You know how men are when they feel their territory's threatened.' They had come to the river again, and stopping on the little wooden footbridge, Claire ran her fingers over the grass's feathery head, stripping it bare. She watched the seeds drift down towards the water. 'But looking back on it now I'm not sure that was true. I'm not sure of anything.'

'That must have caused friction between them, and yet they had to keep working together,' said Gemma, thinking of the bad blood Jackie had mentioned. 'Did the three of you remain friends?'

'David never spoke to me after Alastair

and I were married. I don't mean that quite literally—when we were thrown together in social situations he made civil responses—but he never spoke to me again as a friend.'

It still hurts after all these years, Gemma thought as she watched the tightening of Claire's lips and heard the careful control in her voice. Perhaps she should have asked a different question—was Claire in love with David Ogilvie when she married Alastair Gilbert?

Chapter Nine

'Got the list?' Kincaid asked as they pulled into the empty pub car park. Deveney had asked to drive the Rover from the Yard pool, finding it a damn sight better than his heaterless Vauxhall.

Deveney patted his pocket. 'Every last trinket. It does make an odd assortment when you put them all together.' He killed the engine and looked around as he unsnapped his seat-belt. 'The little van Brian uses for running about seems to be missing. Hope someone's here.'

As they left the car, he glanced through the window at the back of the pub, then said, 'We're in luck, at least as far as Brian's concerned.'

As they made their way single file along the path that ran from the car park around to the front door, he added, 'Okay if I handle him?'

'Be my guest,' said Kincaid.

The pub's door and windows were thrown open to the mid-afternoon air. They found Brian whistling as he wiped down the bar, preparing for the evening customers. The room smelled of lemon polish. 'You back for the night, Superintendent? And your sergeant, too?' He flipped his towel over his shoulder and began sliding clean glassware into the racks. 'My son will be pleased. She seems to have impressed him no end.'

'It's Geoff we want to talk to you about, Brian,' said Deveney. 'Why don't we have a seat?'

As gentle as Deveney's words had been, he might as well have punched Brian Genovase in the gut. The colour drained from his face, and he froze with one hand on the glass rack, his big body still with dread. 'What's happened? I just sent him over to the shop for some lemons—'

'Nothing's happened to him, Bri. Just come and sit down and let me explain.'

Brian followed him slowly to the nook beside the bar, the forgotten tea towel

222

hanging jauntily over his shoulder. When Kincaid had pulled up a stool and joined them, Deveney said, 'We have reason to believe Geoff may have had something to do with the string of thefts in the village. We need—'

'What do you bloody mean *you have reason to believe?* You've looked him up, found out about that shop business, and you're persecuting him. Well, it's not bloody fair and I bloody well won't have it.' Brian pushed against the table, trying to rise, but they had boxed him in.

'I'm afraid it's not that simple, Brian,' Deveney said. 'We'd never have run a check on him if we hadn't discovered that Geoff worked for everyone who reported things missing. He's the only common factor. We have to follow through, if only to clear him.'

It dawned slowly on Brian. His eyes widened with shock and his lips went bloodlessly white. 'You think Geoff murdered the bugger,' he said hoarsely.

'The sooner we get on with this, the better, Brian. We have a warrant, and we'll have to search his room. If it turns out to be a coincidence, we can cross him off and no one need be the wiser. If you'll just show us—'

'You don't understand. Geoff's had this problem since he was a kid. He takes things, but there's no meanness in it. He doesn't even do it for the money, he just keeps them.' Brian leaned towards them, entreating.

'What happened in Wimbledon, those two yobbos who worked as assistants in the shop blackmailed him into helping them. They'd seen him take a tape that belonged to the owner, said they'd report him if he didn't join in.'

'You're telling me that Geoff is a kleptomaniac?' Deveney sounded surprised, but Kincaid merely nodded as Brian confirmed his suspicion. He'd come across the magpielike pattern once when he'd worked in burglary—that time it had been an older woman in a posh neighbourhood, who visited her neighbours regularly for tea.

'He saw a doctor while he was serving his sentence, and he's seemed so much better since he came home.' Brian slumped in his seat as if all the fight had gone out of him.

'I'm sure they must have told you that the disorder is very difficult to treat,' Kincaid said. 'You must have wondered when things began to go missing.'

Brian didn't answer, and after a moment Deveney said softly to Kincaid, 'Let's get this over with. We'll find the room on our own.' They left Brian motionless at the table, his head sunk in his hands.

'Looks like he's been in the army,' said Deveney. 'Too neat.'

'Or prison.' Kincaid ran his hand over the smoothly tucked corner of the single bed. Fantasy posters covered the walls, but rather than being stuck up with the usual drawing-pins, they were framed in simple unvarnished wood. 'Do-it-yourself, I should think,' Kincaid said to himself.

'Hmmm?' Deveney looked up from the computer monitor. He'd been staring, mesmerized, at the everchanging mandala pattern of the screen saver. 'He mustn't have meant to be away long if he's left things running. We'd better dig in.'

'Right.' Kincaid sat down at the desk and opened the first drawer. He found snooping through the minutiae of people's lives both distasteful and weirdly fascinating, but the enjoyment always brought with it a slight stirring of guilt.

The top drawer held tidily organized desk paraphernalia, a few letters on flowery stationery, computer game manuals. In the bottom drawer he found a faded photograph of a young woman, dressed in the hip-hugging bell-bottoms of the late sixties. Bare midriff, long straight brown hair parted in the middle, huge bangle earrings, a serious and slightly bored expression. He wondered who she

225

was and why Geoff Genovase had kept the photo.

A bookcase by the window held mostly paperbacks—fantasy, sword and sorcery, a few historical novels. Kincaid thumbed through them, then stood at the window, gazing at the tiled roof of St Mary's rising disembodied over the vicarage hedges. He tried to analyse the difference between the order of this room and that of Alastair Gilbert's study. Gilbert's spoke of control exerted for its own sake, while this room evoked a carefully guarded and deliberate serenity, he decided after a moment.

'Pay dirt,' said Deveney, sounding less than jubilant. Kneeling on the carpet, he lifted a carved wooden box from the bottom drawer of a pine chest and brought it to the desk. He swore softly as he opened it. 'Bloody hell. Poor Bri.'

The bits of jewellery were neatly arranged on the velvet lining.

They found Madeleine Wade's silver and Percy Bainbridge's photos behind a shoebox on the shelf in the small wardrobe.

'He didn't make much effort to hide things,' Deveney said as he pulled the list from his pocket.

'I'm not sure hiding's the point of this.' Kincaid fingered an intricately carved antique brooch, then a pair of delicate pearl and gold filigree earrings. 'Do these pearl earrings match the vicar's description?'

Deveney ran down the list. 'Looks like it.'

'But there aren't any others. Unless we've missed them, Claire Gilbert's aren't here.'

'So maybe he threw them in a hedge somewhere, panicked after what he'd done,' said Deveney. Then he added, as they heard faint voices from downstairs, 'Sounds like the prodigal's returned. We'll radio the station for the lads to come and take this place apart board by board. It's time we had a word with wee Geoff.'

Brian Genovase held his son in a bear hug, and at first sight Kincaid thought he intended restraint. But as they came closer and Brian stepped away, Kincaid saw that the young man was trembling so violently he could barely stand unaided.

'Geoff.' Deveney's flat tone told all, and Geoff's knees buckled as Kincaid watched.

'Good God, man, he's going to pass out.' Kincaid leaped towards him, but Brian had already grasped his son around the waist and guided him to a bench.

'Head down, between your knees,' ordered Brian, and Geoff obeyed, his blond curls swinging near the floor. His breath whistled audibly.

Deveney slipped out of the door, and when he returned a few moments later, he said, 'I'm sorry, Bri. We'll have to take him along to headquarters. I've radioed for a squad car,' he added quietly to Kincaid.

Brian stood with his hand on Geoff's shoulder. 'You can't. You can't take him away from here. You don't understand.'

'We'll have to charge him, Brian,' Deveney said gently. 'But I promise you he'll come to no harm at the station.'

Geoff lifted his head and spoke for the first time, his teeth clenched to stop them chattering. 'It's all right, Dad.' He brushed his hair from his face and took a shuddering breath. 'I've got to tell the truth. There's nothing else for it.'

Brian Genovase insisted on accompanying his son to Guildford Police Station. By the time they climbed into the back of the panda and Deveney joined the driver in the front, a handful of neighbours had gathered and stood watching from a distance. Doc Wilson hurtled by the green in her little Mini, then braked hard as she peered at the police car.

Kincaid wished now that he hadn't sent Gemma to interview Malcolm Reid, but he'd had no way of anticipating Geoff's quaking terror. Glancing at his watch, he hoped she'd at least be back at the station by the time they were ready to begin the interview.

He retrieved the Rover and was reversing it from its space in the car park when he saw a blur of motion in his mirror and heard a thumping on the boot. A moment later Lucy Penmaric pounded on his window, shouting at him. When he'd killed the engine and rolled down the window, the words became comprehensible.

Between sobs she wailed, 'Why are they taking him? You mustn't let them—please don't let them take him away from here. He couldn't bear it.' As he slipped out of the car to stand beside her she clung to him, pulling at his sleeve with force enough to rip it.

'Lucy.' He clasped her hands in his, holding her clenched fists tightly. 'I can't help you if you don't calm down.' She gulped, nodding, and he felt her hands relax a bit. 'Now. Take it slowly. Tell me exactly what's wrong.'

Still hiccuping, she managed, 'Doc Wilson stopped at the house. She said they were taking Geoff away in a—' before her face contorted again.

Kincaid squeezed her hands. 'Hush now. You must help me sort this out.' She seemed a frightened child, far removed from the poised young woman he'd seen on the night of Alastair Gilbert's murder.

'We just need to ask him a few questions, that's all. There's nothing to—'

'Don't treat me like a baby. You think Geoff killed him! Alastair. You don't understand.' She wrenched her hands free and pressed her knuckles against her mouth, fighting for control.

'What don't I understand?'

'Geoff couldn't hurt anybody. He won't even kill spiders. He says they have as much right to exist as he does.' Her words poured over one another in her eagerness to explain. *"Might is not right."* He says that all the time—it's from his favourite book. And *"The end never justifies the means."* He says we can always find a peaceful solution.'

Kincaid sighed as he recognized the quotations. It had been one of his favourite books, too, and he wondered how much of the young King Arthur's vision he had managed to retain in the face of everyday policing.

'Maybe Geoff wouldn't hurt anybody,' he said, 'but would he take things that didn't belong to him?'

Lucy's eyes flitted away from his. 'That was a long time ago. And he didn't hate Alastair for what—'

'Hate Alastair for what, Lucy?'

'For being a cop,' she said, recovering quickly. She scrubbed at her face and sniffed. 'Though he probably should have, after the way they treated him.'

Kincaid regarded her quizzically for a moment, then decided to let that one pass for the time being. 'I'm not talking about what happened when Geoff was sent to prison, Lucy. I'm asking about here, now, taking things from the people he works for in the village.'

In a small, bewildered voice she said, 'Geoff?'

'Nothing terribly valuable, mostly keepsakes, really. Do you know that he may not be able to help himself?' He touched her cheek. Her eyes looked enormous and dark, even in the fading light, and the pupils were dilated with distress.

She shook her head. 'No. I don't believe it. It's just jumble sale stuff he collected for the game.'

'What game?' He could read her withdrawal in the half step she took away from him and the tight set of her mouth. 'Lucy, if you don't tell me, I can't help him. I have to know what this is all about.'

'It's just a computer game we were playing,' she said, shrugging. 'Roles, you know, and a quest. In the game you have to find certain objects, talismans, to help you along the way, and Geoff said that if we had *representations*, it would help us visualize better.'

'And these things that Geoff *collected* were the representations?' When Lucy nodded, he said, 'Would he have taken things from your house, too?'

'Never!' Her hair swung as she shook her head.

Such fierce loyalty was admirable, thought Kincaid, but he wondered if it was justified.

'It wouldn't have worked, you see,' she said earnestly, trying to convince him. 'It can't be your own things—that would negate any help they might provide in the quest.'

Deciding to accept Lucy's explanation of game logic for the moment, Kincaid went back to something that had been niggling at him. 'Lucy, what did you mean when you said Geoff couldn't bear to be taken from here?'

She hesitated for a moment, then said slowly, 'He's frightened. I don't know why. Brian says it has something to do with being in prison, but he never leaves the village if he can help it, and sometimes on bad days he doesn't leave the pub. And he doesn't like serving behind the bar—says the noise makes him feel funny—and that gets right up Brian's nose when he's short-handed,' she added with a ghost of a smile. 'I wish I could—'

A small white van turned into the car

park and jerked to a stop beside them. The windows were darkly tinted, so Kincaid didn't recognize Claire Gilbert until she jumped out and started round the van's bonnet towards them. In her casual clothes she looked almost as young as her daughter, but her expression was both frightened and furious.

'Lucy! What are you doing out? I've told you—'

'They've taken Geoff away. They think he's stolen things and that he killed Alastair.' She stepped forward until her nose nearly touched her mother's. 'And it's all your fault.'

Claire recoiled visibly, but when she spoke her voice remained level and controlled. 'Lucy, that's enough. You have no idea what you're talking about. I'm sorry about Geoff, and I'll do whatever I can to help him, but right now I want you to go home.'

For a moment mother and daughter stood face to face, the air between them vibrating with tension, then abruptly Lucy turned on her heel and walked away.

Claire watched until Lucy disappeared into the lane, then she sighed and rubbed at her face as if to ease strained muscles.

'What's all your fault?' asked Kincaid, before she could regain her equilibrium.

'I haven't the slightest idea.' She leaned

against the van and closed her eyes. 'Unless... Did she say you thought Geoff had stolen things?'

'We discovered that Geoff had worked for everyone in the village who reported jewellery and other small items missing over the last year.'

'Oh, dear.' Claire mulled this over for a moment. 'Then it may be that she's angry with me because I mentioned my missing jewellery. But it never occurred to me that Geoff might be responsible, and I still don't believe it. And I won't even consider the possibility that Geoff killed Alastair.'

'Have he and Lucy been friends long?'

Claire smiled. 'Lucy and Geoff formed an odd alliance from the time we came to the village. Lucy must have been eight or nine, and Geoff well into his teens, but there's always been something a bit childlike about him. Not childish,' she clarified, frowning, 'but he has a sort of innocence, if you know what I mean.

'He even looked after Lucy for me until she was old enough to stay alone in the house. Of course, when Geoff left school and took that job in Wimbledon they drifted apart a bit, but since he's come back they've seemed closer than ever.'

Kincaid wondered if they were sleeping together—Lucy was over the age of consent—but his instinct told him no. There had been something almost monastic in the atmosphere of Geoff's room. 'It must have been hard for Lucy when he went to prison.'

'They wrote to each other. It was a difficult time, but she never talked about it. Lucy's always been a bit of a loner. She gets along with kids at school and in the village well enough; she just never forms close attachments. Geoff seems to be her anchor.' She looked towards the pub. Dusk had crept up on them, and light shone visibly from the back window. 'Look, I must see if there is anything I can do for Brian. He'll be frantic with worry.' She stepped forward, but Kincaid touched her arm.

'There's nothing you can do here. Brian's gone to headquarters with Geoff. They'll make him cool his heels in reception, but he insisted on it.'

'He would.' In the light spilling from the pub, her shirt flared white between the lapels of her jacket. Kincaid saw it rise and fall as she sighed. 'And you're right, of course. I need to deal with my own child.'

Kincaid sat with his hand on the key for a moment, started the car, then turned the engine off and reached for his pocket phone instead. When he had Deveney on the line, he said, 'Don't start without me, Nick. I'll be along in a bit.'

The first customer's car pulled into the pub car park as he pulled out, but the houses clustered around the green looked dark and silent, as did the shop when he reached it. He could just make out the CLOSED sign, but yellow light filtered through the curtain chinks in the upstairs windows.

The stairs were inky, invisible but for the white rail under his hand, but he persevered to the top and knocked smartly on Madeleine Wade's door. 'You really should do something about a light,' he said when she answered.

'Sorry,' she said, frowning at the fixture. 'Must have just burned out.' She motioned him inside and shut the door. 'Should I assume this is a social call, Superintendent, since you are unaccompanied by minions?'

He gave a snort of laughter as he followed her into the kitchen. 'Minions?'

'Such a nice word, isn't it? I do like words with descriptive power.' As she spoke she rummaged in various cupboards. 'Most people's vocabularies are dismally bland, don't you think? Ah, success,' she added as she fished a corkscrew triumphantly from a drawer. 'Will you have some wine with me, Mr Kincaid? Sainsbury's is remarkably upmarket these days. You can actually get something quite decent.'

Madeleine filled two slender glasses with a pale gold chardonnay, then led the way back to the sitting room. Candles burned, adding their flickering light to that of two shaded table-lamps, and the music he'd admired before played softly in the background. 'Expecting a client, Miss Wade?' he asked as he accepted a glass and sat down.

'This is just for me, I'm afraid.' Slipping out of her shoes, she tucked her feet up on the settee, and the marmalade cat jumped up beside her. 'I try to practise what I preach,' she said with a chuckle as she rubbed the cat under its chin. 'Stress reduction.'

'I could do with a bit of that.' Kincaid sipped his wine, holding it for a moment in his mouth. The flavours exploded on his tongue—buttery rich, with a touch of the oak found in good whisky, and beneath that a hint of flowers. The sensation was so intense that he wondered if he were experiencing some sort of perceptual enhancement.

'Lovely, volatile molecules.' Madeleine closed her eyes as she sipped, then gazed at him directly. In the candlelight her eyes looked as green as river moss. 'How can I help you, Mr Kincaid?'

It occurred to him that in the few minutes he'd been in the flat, he had ceased to regard her as homely. It was not that her features had altered but rather that the normal parameters of judging physical beauty seemed to have become meaningless. He felt light-headed, although he'd barely touched his wine. 'Are you a witch, Miss Wade?' he asked, surprising himself, then he smiled, making a joke of it.

She returned the smile with her characteristic wry amusement. 'No, but I've considered it quite seriously. I know several, and I incorporate some aspects of their rituals into my practice.'

'Such as?'

'Blessings, protective spells, that sort of thing. All quite harmless, I assure you.'

'People keep assuring me of a lot of things, Miss Wade, and quite frankly, I'm getting a bit fed up.' He set his glass on the table and leaned forward. 'There's a conspiracy of silence in this village. A conspiracy of protection, even. You all must have known Geoff Genovase's history, must have considered the possibility that he might be responsible for your thefts. Yet no one said a word. In fact, you were reluctant to talk about the thefts at all. Were there others that went unreported, once the word got out?'

He sat back and retrieved his glass, then said more slowly, 'Someone murdered Alastair Gilbert. If the truth goes undiscovered, that knowledge will eat away at this village like a cancer. Each person will wonder if his friend or neighbour deserves his loyalty, then wonder if the friend or neighbour suspects him. The snake is in the garden, Miss Wade, and ignoring it won't make it go away. Help me.'

The music tinkled in the silence that followed his words. For the first time, Madeleine didn't meet his eyes but stared into her glass as she swirled the liquid slowly around. At last, she looked up and said, 'I suppose you're right. But none of us wanted the responsibility for harming an innocent.'

'Things are never quite that simple, and you are perceptive enough to be aware of that.'

She nodded slowly, acquiescing. 'I'm still not sure what you want me to do.'

'Tell me about Geoff Genovase. Claire Gilbert described him as *child-like*. Is he simple, a bit slow?'

'Just the opposite, I'd say. Highly intelligent, but there is something a bit child-like about him.'

'How so? Describe it for me.'

Madeleine sipped her wine and thought for a moment, then said, 'In the positive

239

sense I'd say that he has a very well-developed imagination and that he still has the capacity to enjoy the small things in life. On the negative side, I think that he may not always face things in an emotionally adult way...that he retreats to his fantasy life rather than face unpleasantness. But then most of us have been guilty of that at one time or another.'

Especially lately, thought Kincaid, then wondered if she could read his flicker of embarrassment. 'Madeleine,' he said, deliberately dropping the formality of 'Miss Wade', 'can you see the potential for violence?'

'I don't know. I've never been presented with a clear before and after example. I can sense chronic anger, as I told you yesterday, but I have no way of knowing when, or if, it will explode.'

He said casually, swirling his wine as Madeleine had done, watching its legs make ribbon patterns on the inside of the glass, 'And is Geoff angry?'

She shook her head. 'Geoff is *frightened,* always. Being here seems to ease him— sometimes he just comes and sits for an hour or so, not speaking.'

'But you don't know why?'

'No. Only that he's been that way as long as I've known him. They came to the village some years before I did. Brian

240

gave up a job as a commercial traveller and bought the Moon.' She shifted a little in her seat, and the cat stood up, giving her an affronted look before jumping to the floor. 'Look,' Madeleine said abruptly, 'if I don't tell you this, that nasty Percy Bainbridge probably will, and I'd rather you heard it from me.

'You might say that Geoff had good reason to hate Alastair Gilbert. When Geoff got into trouble, Brian begged Alastair to help him. He explained about the blackmail and Geoff's illness, explained that Geoff would never have participated voluntarily. Just a good word in the magistrate's ear might have lightened Geoff's sentence, perhaps even got him off on probation. But Alastair refused. He went on about the sanctity of the law, but we all knew that was just an excuse.' Her lips twisted in a grimace. 'Alastair Gilbert was a self-righteous prig who enjoyed playing God, and Geoff's trouble gave him an opportunity to exercise his power.'

They went into the interview room together, Kincaid and Gemma and Nick Deveney. Kincaid had asked Deveney to let Gemma conduct the interrogation and had briefed her on the results of their search. 'I'll be prepared to play bad cop if necessary,' he'd told her, 'but terrified

241

as he is already, I'm not sure that would be a very effective strategy.'

Geoff Genovase sat huddled on the hard wooden chair, looking defenceless and uncomfortable in faded jeans and a thin cotton T-shirt. The room's uncompromising light gave Kincaid his first opportunity to study him closely. High, flat cheekbones gave the young man's face a slightly Slavonic cast, and his eyes, though wary, were large, dark-lashed, and a true, clear grey. It was an honest, guileless visage, with no hint of meanness. Kincaid wondered, as he often did, at how easily one's perception of others was influenced by the simple combination of genes that made up a human face.

'Hello, Geoff.' Gemma sat directly opposite him, elbows on the table. 'I'm sorry about all this.'

He nodded and gave her a shaky smile.

'I'd like to get this business sorted as quickly as possible, so that you can go home.'

Kincaid and Deveney had flanked her but sat back a bit, allowing Geoff to focus on her.

'I'm sure this must be difficult for you,' Gemma continued, 'but I need you to tell me about the things we found in your room.'

'I never meant to—' Geoff cleared

242

his throat and started again. 'I never intended keeping them. It was just a game, something to—' He stopped, shaking his head. 'You won't understand.'

'A game you played with Lucy?'

This brought a nod. 'Yes, but how did you—' Beads of sweat broke out on his upper lip. 'Lucy didn't know,' he said, his voice rising. 'Honestly, I never told her the t-truth about where the talismans came from. Sh-she would have been really angry with me.'

'Lucy told us a little bit about the game. She also told us she thought you collected the things from jumble sales.' A hint of disapproval crept into Gemma's voice. 'She trusted you.'

'Lucy knows about...this?' Geoff whispered, ashen. When Gemma nodded confirmation, he closed his eyes for a moment, clenching his fists in a gesture of despair.

Gemma leaned even nearer, until her face was a mere foot from his. 'Listen, Geoff, I understand that you meant to help Lucy. But how could you play with things that were tainted by dishonesty—lying *and* stealing?'

A pulse ticked in the hollow of Geoff's throat, and the rise and fall of his collar-bone was sharply visible beneath the black-and-white dragon painted on his T-shirt.

Gemma, pale and tired but resolute, held his gaze transfixed.

She had a rare and instinctive talent for forming a connection and getting right to the emotional heart of things, and when Geoff's eyes filled with tears and he covered his face with his hands, Kincaid knew she had done it once again.

'You're right,' he said, voice muffled. 'I hated taking things from my friends, but I couldn't seem to help it. And the game wasn't working. I told myself I didn't know why, but I was too ashamed to admit it. I kept telling Lucy she wasn't trying hard enough.'

'Trying hard enough at what?'

Geoff lifted his head. 'Becoming the character. Transcending the game.'

'And what would happen then?' asked Gemma, sounding only reasonably curious.

Shrugging, he said, 'We'd live *this* life on a different level, be more engaged, more dedicated—I can't explain. But then that's only my idea, and it's probably total bullshit, anyway.' He sat back in his chair, looking tired and defeated.

'Maybe,' said Gemma softly, 'and maybe not.' She pushed a wisp of hair back into her plait and took a breath. 'Geoff, did you take anything for the game from Lucy's house?'

He shook his head. 'I don't go there

if I can help it. Alastair doesn't—didn't approve of me.'

Kincaid had no trouble imagining how Alastair Gilbert would have felt about Geoff or what he might have said.

'Maybe Wednesday night was an exception,' persisted Gemma. 'Maybe there was something you needed, and Lucy wasn't home. You've slipped in and out of other people's houses easily enough—we have the evidence of that—maybe you thought you'd just nip in for a minute and no one would be the wiser. Except Alastair came home unexpectedly and caught you. Did he threaten to send you to jail again?'

Geoff shook his head, more vehemently this time. 'No! I never went near there, I swear, Gemma. I didn't know anything had happened until Brian saw the police cars, and then I was frantic because I thought something must have happened to Lucy or Claire.'

'Why?' asked Gemma. 'Why not assume that the commander, a middle-aged man in a high-stress job, had dropped dead of a massive coronary?'

'I don't know.' Geoff wound a finger in his hair and tugged at it, a curiously feminine gesture. 'I just didn't think about him, I suppose because he's not often home that time of day.'

'Really?' Gemma sounded puzzled. 'It

245

was almost half-past seven when the nine-nine-nine call came through.'

'Was it?' Shifting in his chair, Geoff rubbed a thumb against his bare wrist. 'I didn't realize. I haven't worn a watch since I bid Her Majesty's hospitality farewell,' he said with an unexpected trace of humour.

'You know I have to ask you this.' Gemma gave him an answering smile. 'Where were you between six o'clock and half-past seven on that Wednesday evening?'

Geoff dropped his laced fingers into his lap. 'I'd finished in Becca's garden—about five, I'd say it was—then I came in and had a bath to get the muck off.'

He's on firm ground now, thought Kincaid, watching Geoff's relaxed posture.

'And after that?' asked Gemma, settling a bit more comfortably into her chair.

'I got on-line. I'd been looking for some communications software that might perform a little better than what I've been using. Brian stopped by for a word at one point, but I'm not sure when.'

Kincaid met Deveney's eyes. The on-line connection shouldn't be difficult to check, but how could they be sure Geoff hadn't left the computer downloading automatically while he ran across the road for long enough to kill the commander?

'I'd just finished when I heard the

sirens, then Brian came upstairs to tell me something had happened at the Gilberts.'

That struck Kincaid as a bit odd. With a bar full of able-bodied customers, why had Brian felt it necessary to inform his son before he charged across the road to investigate?

'Anyone else see you?' Gemma asked hopefully, but Geoff shook his head.

'Can I go home now?' he asked, but his tone held little optimism.

Gemma glanced at Kincaid, then studied Geoff for a moment before she said, 'I want to help you, Geoff, but I'm afraid we may need to keep you a bit longer. You understand, don't you, that if your neighbours identify the things we found, we'll have to charge you with burglary?'

Will Darling stood in the corridor outside the interview room, looking as relaxed as if he'd been napping on his feet. 'Brain Genovase asked for a word with you in private, sir,' he said as Kincaid came out and shut the door. 'I've put him in the canteen with a cuppa—thought it might be a bit more comfortable there.'

'Thanks, Will.' Kincaid had left Gemma and Deveney to take Geoff's statement, in hopes that he might catch up on his own paperwork, but he should have known it wasn't a likely prospect.

The smell of hot grease made his throat close convulsively. It also made him realize, with a stomach-turning queasiness, that he was ravenously hungry. Vaguely, he remembered lunch, and a look at his watch told him it was after eight o'clock.

The room was almost empty and he quickly spotted Brian, who sat staring fixedly into his cup. Kincaid got himself a cup of tea so dark it might have been coffee and joined Brian at the small orange-topped table. 'Disgusting colour, isn't it?' Kincaid asked, rapping the table with his knuckles as he sat down. 'Reminds me of baby food. Always wondered who's in charge of the decorating.'

Brian looked at him blankly, as if trying to decipher a foreign language, then said, 'Is he all right? I've called our solicitor, but he's not in.'

'Geoff is making a statement just now, and he seems to be coping reasonably—'

'No, no, you don't understand,' said Brian, pushing his cup out of the way. The spoon fell from the saucer with a clatter. 'I know you think I'm behaving like a broody old hen over a grown son, but you don't understand about Geoff.

'You see, his mum left us when Geoff was only six. The poor kid thought it was his fault, and he was terrified I'd leave him too. I had a good job then as a commercial traveller, and I could afford to pay someone to stay with him when I was away, but he'd panic every time. At first I thought he'd get over it, but instead he got worse. Finally I quit the job and invested my savings in the pub.'

'And did that help?' asked Kincaid, giving his muddy tea a desultory stir.

'After a bit,' said Brian, sitting back in his chair and regarding Kincaid levelly. 'But it was only then that I began to find out what she'd done to him. She told him it was his fault she was leaving, that he wasn't good enough, didn't "measure up". And before that, she did...' He shook his head, reminding Kincaid of a frustrated bull. 'She did vile things to a small boy. I'll tell you, Superintendent, if I ever find that bitch, I'll kill her, and then it'll be me you'll have warming your cell.' He stared aggressively at Kincaid, chin thrust forward, then when Kincaid didn't respond he relaxed and sighed. 'I felt responsible. Do you understand that? I should have seen what was going on, should have stopped her, but I was too caught up in my own misery.'

'You still feel responsible for him.' Kincaid made it a statement.

Brian nodded. 'He got better over the years. The nightmares stopped. He did well enough at school, even though he didn't make friends easily. Then when he went to prison it started all over again. "Separation anxiety," the prison doctor called it.

'Superintendent, if Geoff is sent to prison again, I don't think he will recover.'

A movement caught Kincaid's eye and he looked up. Will Darling threaded his way through the tables towards them like a barge easing its way down the Thames. 'Sir,' he said as he reached the table, 'there's a...um, delegation of sorts...to see you.'

They were crowded into the tiny reception area—Doc Wilson, Rebecca Fielding, and behind them, a head taller, Madeleine Wade. The doctor had evidently appointed herself spokesperson, for as soon as he came into the room, she marched up and buttonholed him. 'Superintendent, we want a word. It's about Geoff Genovase.'

'You couldn't have had better timing,' Kincaid said, smiling. 'You've saved us asking you to come in, as we need you to identify your things officially.' He looked over his shoulder. 'Will, is there somewhere more comfortable—'

'You don't understand, Mr Kincaid.' The doctor sounded exasperated, as if

250

he were a recalcitrant patient. The vicar looked worried, and Madeleine looked as though she was enjoying the whole thing but trying not to show it.

Stepping forward, Rebecca put a hand on the doctor's arm. 'Mr Kincaid, what we're trying to tell you is that we don't wish to press charges. We'll be glad to identify the things for you, but it won't make any difference.'

'What the—' He shook his head. 'I don't believe this. Madeleine?'

'I'm with them all the way. We'll say we lent him the things and just forgot, if necessary.' She gave him a conspiratorial grin.

'What about Percy Bainbridge?'

'Percy has a tendency to be a bit difficult, all right,' said the doctor, 'but Paul's having a word with him just now. I'm sure he'll manage to sort him out.'

'And if he doesn't?' Kincaid eyed them sceptically.

The doctor smiled, and he recognized the battle light in her eyes. 'We'll make his life hell.'

Kincaid rubbed the stubble on his chin between thumb and forefinger. 'What if you're wrong about Geoff? What if he went into the Gilberts' house that night and killed the commander?'

Madeleine stepped forward. 'We're not

wrong. I promise you, Geoff isn't capable of killing anyone.'

'You have no evidence,' added the doctor. 'And if you try to pin this on him, I guarantee you'll have half a dozen people suddenly remember they saw him doing something else.'

'This is all a bit feudal, don't you think?' When no one responded, Kincaid said on a surge of anger, 'You do realize what you're doing here? You're taking the law into your own hands, and you have neither the knowledge nor the impartiality to do so. This is what our justice system is designed to prevent—'

'We are not willing for Geoff Genovase to be sacrificed in order to test the fairness of the law, Superintendent.' The doctor's brows were set in a straight line, and the faces of the others were implacable.

Kincaid glared at them for a moment, then sighed. 'Will, take care of the formalities, would you? I'll just tell Brian he can take his son home.'

Kincaid scooted in beside Gemma on the bench before Deveney or Will could outmanoeuvre him, then smiled at the disappointment on Deveney's face. They had adjourned to a pub near the station, hoping to organize strategy as well as fill their stomachs.

'The chief constable's been on the blower,' Deveney said conversationally when they had ordered and were sipping appreciatively at their drinks.

No one looked thrilled at the prospect of hearing what that exalted figure had to say, but Kincaid set down his pint and took the plunge. 'All right, Nick, put us out of our misery quickly, then.'

'You'll never guess.' Deveney pulled down the knot on his tie and unbuttoned his collar. He's "very anxious for a resolution", and he would be "most pleased" if we were to find reason to charge Geoff Genovase with Gilbert's murder. Allay any suspicion on the part of the public that we're sitting around on our duffs, you know.'

Gemma spluttered into her drink. 'Is he daft? We don't have a shred of evidence. Turning the burglary file over to the CPS is embarrassing enough—trying to bring a murder charge against him at this point would make us laughing-stocks.'

'Not daft, politically minded,' snorted Deveney.

'Gemma's right, you know,' said Kincaid. 'It's all completely circumstantial, based on the assumption that Geoff *might* have taken Claire Gilbert's earrings, which we did *not* find in his possession. For all we know she lost them or accidentally knocked them down the bloody drain in the lav.

'We've checked his prints with the unknowns found in the Gilberts' kitchen, and there's not a smudge with a remote resemblance. Nor has forensics come up with any hair or fibres that might provide a link.'

Deveney grinned. 'So we assume that in the few minutes it took Geoff to download a file, he equipped himself with hat, gloves and protective clothing, nipped across the road and killed the commander, then disposed of Claire's earrings, the murder weapon, and the aforementioned protective clothing on his way back to the pub. Although, of course, we've searched every square inch in between and turned up sweet eff-all.' This brought a chorus of groans and much rolling of eyes. 'Is that all the appreciation I get for a feat of intellectual daring?' Deveney winked at Gemma, and Kincaid saw her look quickly away.

Before anyone could make a proper rejoinder, the barmaid brought their dinners. They tucked in like starving sailors, and for a while the clink of cutlery was the only sound at the table.

Kincaid watched as Gemma ate her chips and plaice with quiet concentration. He was comforted simply by her proximity. She didn't flinch if his knee occasionally brushed hers under the table, and he wondered if it heralded a thaw. Looking up at him, she gave him an unguarded smile, and he felt a wave of desire so strong it left him shaking.

'You know,' said Deveney, pushing his plate away, 'if that's the chief's line on this, maybe our village committee was right in refusing to throw Geoff to the wolves.'

'So now we're the wolves?' asked Kincaid a bit testily. 'Would we let someone we thought innocent serve as a scapegoat?'

'Of course not,' said Deveney, 'but these political agendas can very easily get out of hand. We've all seen it happen.' He looked questioningly around the table and they all nodded grudging confirmation.

Will wiped up the last bit of his shepherd's pie with his last chip, then pushed his plate away and regarded them gravely. 'It seems to me that we're all mincing around the real question like little ballerinas. And that is, regardless of the nature of the evidence, do we think Geoff did it?'

Watching his tablemates, Kincaid wondered fleetingly if the four of them were just as guilty of Star Chamber behaviour as the villagers. But they were all good, honest coppers, and none of them could do their jobs without exercising their judgement. Indecision would paralyse them. 'No,' he said, breaking the silence. 'I'd say it's highly unlikely, at the very least, and I'll not stand by and see him go down for a crime he didn't commit.' Beside him, he felt Gemma relax as she nodded agreement, and Deveney followed suit. 'Will?' Kincaid asked, unable to read the constable's expression.

'Oh, aye, I'd agree with you on that. It's too tailor-made by half. But I wonder if we won't wish we'd found such an easy solution by the time this is all over.' He drained his pint and added, 'And what about Percy Bainbridge's mysterious shadow?'

Kincaid shrugged. 'Could have been anybody.'

'More likely a product of Percy's imagination, dredged up purely for the drama,' said Deveney.

'You're not going to like this,' Gemma said slowly, 'and I don't like it either. But what if Gilbert went ferreting because he didn't like his stepdaughter having a...relationship with Geoff? And what if he found out that Geoff was responsible for the thefts? And then what if Gilbert told Brian that he intended to turn Geoff in? Brian had good reason to hate him already. What would he do in order to protect his son?'

'You're right,' Deveney said after a moment. 'I don't like it a bit. But it's the nearest thing to a motive we've come up with so far.'

Kincaid yawned. 'Then I suggest the first thing on our list tomorrow should be discovering if Brian can account for himself the whole of Wednesday evening. We'll keep picking at Malcolm Reid, too. There's something in that situation that bothers me. I just can't quite put my finger on it.'

'Let's call it a night, then,' said Deveney. 'I'm knackered. I've booked you a couple of rooms in the hotel on the High Street.' He put his hand over his heart and grinned at Gemma. 'And I'll sleep better knowing you're near at hand.'

The hotel turned out to be presentable, if a bit fusty. Having bid the lingering Nick Deveney a definite good night, Kincaid followed Gemma up the stairs at a respectable distance. Their rooms were opposite each other, and he waited in the corridor until she'd turned her key in the lock. 'Gemma—' he began, then floundered.

She gave him a bright, brittle smile. If she had allowed a chink to show in her defences at the pub, she'd pulled her armour firmly into place again. 'Night, guv. Sleep well.' Her door clicked firmly shut.

He undressed slowly, hanging up his shirt and laying his trousers across the room's single chair as if his salvation depended upon a perfect crease. The combination of alcohol and exhaustion had produced a numbing effect, and he felt as if he were watching his own actions from a distance, knowing them to be absurd. But still he kept on, order his only defence, and as he hung his overcoat on a peg in the wardrobe a crumpled paper poppy fell to the floor.

He'd worn it last Sunday, a week ago, when he'd walked up to St John's, Hampstead, to hear the major sing the Fauré Requiem in the Remembrance Day service. The soaring voices had lifted him, stilling all worries and desires for a brief time, and as he climbed into the narrow hotel bed he tried to hold the memory in his mind.

It came to him as he drifted in the formlessness just before sleep. He scrambled out of bed, upsetting the flimsy lamp on the nightstand in his haste. When he'd righted the lamp, he flicked it on and began digging through his wallet.

He found the card easily enough and sat squinting at it in the dim light that filtered through the pink, fringed lampshade. He hadn't been mistaken. The telephone number on the business card he'd picked up at Malcolm Reid's shop was the same as the one he remembered seeing pencilled in Alastair Gilbert's diary, next to the notation 6:00 on the evening before Gilbert died.

Chapter Ten

The press had decamped, the constable had been relieved of his post at the gate, and the lane seemed to dream peacefully undisturbed in the morning sun. As they let themselves through the Gilberts' gate, Kincaid muttered something that sounded to Gemma like '...this Eden...'

'What?' she said, turning back to him as he fiddled with the latch.

'Oh, nothing.' He caught her up and they walked abreast along the path. 'Just a half-remembered old quote.' As they rounded the corner, Lewis stood up in his run, but his deep intruder-alert bark changed to an excited yapping when Kincaid spoke to him.

'You've made a conquest,' Gemma said as he walked to the fence and scratched the dog's ears through the wiring.

He turned and met her eyes. 'One, at least.'

Gemma flushed and cursed herself for having put her foot in it once again. While she was still trying to think of a suitable reply, the kitchen door opened and Lucy called out to them. She came out on to the step, conspicuous in all the glory of her baggy red jersey, crumpled socks, and a tartan skirt barely long enough to earn its name.

'Claire's gone to see Gwen before church,' Lucy said as they reached her, and on closer inspection Gemma could see goose-pimples on the expanse of bare flesh between hem and sock.

'Gwen?' asked Kincaid.

'You know, Alastair's mum. Claire always goes on Sunday morning, and she thought it a good idea not to break the routine. Do you want to come in?' Lucy opened the door and made way for them.

Once in the kitchen, she sat down at the table by a half-empty bowl of cereal but made no move to resume eating. 'I'm glad you've come,' she said a bit awkwardly, clasping her hands in her lap. 'I wanted to thank you for what you did yesterday, letting Geoff go home and everything.'

'Geoff's friends were responsible for that. He seems to have quite a few.'

Kincaid pulled up a chair in the breakfast area, and Gemma did the same, but she still found it odd to be sitting so casually in this room.

'I don't think he realized until last night. He never thinks he deserves people caring about him.'

Watching the expression on the girl's heart-shaped face, Gemma wondered if Geoff felt he deserved Lucy's love—for she suddenly had no doubt that love him Lucy did and with all a seventeen-year-old's capacity for passion.

'Lucy,' said Kincaid, 'do you think you could help us out with something, since your mother's not here?'

'Sure.' She looked at him expectantly.

Gemma wondered how Kincaid meant to handle this. When they'd stopped in at the station, a quick check of Gilbert's impounded diary had confirmed Kincaid's memory. When he asked, with exaggerated patience, why he hadn't been informed of the connection, the constable in charge mumbled something about 'just assuming the commander had rung his wife'.

'First rule of a murder investigation, mate,' Kincaid had said, an inch from his face, 'which you should have learned at your guv'nor's knee. Never assume.'

Now he tackled the other, unspoken, assumption first. 'Is your mum in the

261

habit of working late, Lucy?'

She shook her head, her hair swinging with the movement. 'She likes to be here when I get home from school, and she never misses it by more than a few minutes.'

'What about the night before Alastair died? Was there anything unusual about that?'

'That would have been Tuesday.' Lucy thought a moment. 'We were both home by five or so, and then later Mum watched an old movie with me.' She shrugged. 'Nothing out of the ordinary.'

Kincaid straightened the table-mat, aligning it precisely with the edge of the table. 'Did Alastair ever ring your mum at the shop?'

'Alastair?' She looked baffled. 'I don't think so. Sometimes he'd have his secretary ring here and leave a message on the answerphone if he was going to be delayed. And sometimes he didn't let her know at all. Alastair wasn't one to put himself out for people,' she added. 'Even when Mummy broke her wrist last summer, he didn't leave work. Geoff went with me to pick her up from hospital. I only had my provisional licence then.'

'How did it happen?' asked Gemma.

'Driving along the road that runs through the Hurtwood. She said she hit a monster pothole, and the steering-wheel jerked so hard it snapped the bone in her wrist.'

'Ouch.' Gemma winced at the thought.

Grinning, Lucy added, 'It was her right hand, too. I had to do everything for her for weeks, and she didn't like it a bit. Poor Mum. Kept her from biting her nails, though.'

Kincaid glanced at his watch. 'I guess we'd better not wait for her any longer. Do you mind if I make a quick call from Alastair's study, Lucy?'

When he'd gone, Lucy smiled a bit shyly at Gemma. 'He's very nice, isn't he? You're lucky to get to work with him every day.'

Nonplussed, Gemma searched for a response. A week ago she would have agreed easily, perhaps even a touch smugly. She felt a pang of loss so sharp it took her breath away, but she managed a smile. 'Of course I am. You're quite right,' she said finally, trying for conviction, then did her best to ignore Lucy's puzzled expression.

'Well?' said Gemma when they reached the lane again. 'I think we can be fairly sure it was Malcolm Reid that Gilbert called.'

'I should've twigged sooner,' Kincaid said, his face set in an irritated frown.

Gemma shrugged. 'That's a bit pointless. Like saying you should remember what

263

you've forgotten. What's next?'

'I've got the Reids' home address, but first, let's give Brian a try.'

Leaving the car in the lane, they walked to the pub, but found it shut up tight. Kincaid's knock on the door brought no response. 'First thing Sunday morning's not the best time to beard a publican in his den, I suppose. I remember Brian saying he wasn't a morning person.' Turning away, he added, 'We'll have to come back, but just now let's pay a call on Malcolm and the missis.'

'I think that must have been it.' Gemma looked back at the gap in the hedge they'd just shot past. 'Hazel Patch Farm. I saw a little hand-lettered sign on the gatepost.'

'Bloody hell.' Kincaid swore under his breath. 'There's no place to reverse.' He shifted down another gear and crept around the hairpin bends, searching for an accessible drive or farm track. They were high in the tree-crowned hills between Holmbury and Shere, and Gemma supposed they'd done well to find the place at all with only the blithe directions of the Holmbury St Mary garage attendant to guide them.

A passing place presented itself, and with a little judicious manoeuvring, Kincaid managed to turn the car round. Soon they were nosing in through the farm gate, and he pulled the car up in a gravelled area just inside the hedge.

'Not exactly a working farm, I'd say,' he commented as they got out of the car and looked about. The house stood back beneath the trees, and what little remained visible beneath the cover of the creeping vines seemed unassuming enough.

Malcolm Reid came to the door in frayed jeans and an old sweater, looking considerably less like a *Country Living* fashion plate than he had in the shop, but perhaps, thought Gemma, even more handsome. If he was surprised to have his Sunday morning at home interrupted by uninvited coppers, he managed to conceal it, and the two sleek springer spaniels at his heels sniffed at them with equal politeness. 'Come through to the back,' he said pleasantly and led them down a dim passageway.

Entering before them, he said, 'Val, it's Superintendent Kincaid and Sergeant James.'

Anything else he might have attributed to them, Gemma lost, as she was too busy gaping with delight to take in the conversation. They stood in a terracotta tiled kitchen, and it was much less intimidating than she would have imagined from the high-tech displays in the shop.

Dusty-blue cabinets, a sunflower-yellow Aga as well as a gas hob, copper pans hanging from a rack in the ceiling, and all open to a solarium whose windows looked down the steep hillside to the Downs rolling away in the distance.

Kincaid gave Gemma a gentle nudge and she focused on the woman rising from amidst the pile of newspapers that covered most of a comfortable-looking settee. 'You've caught us at our Sunday morning vice,' she said, laughing as she came towards them with her hand outstretched. 'We read them all—the high, the low, the insufferably middlebrow. I'm Valerie Reid.'

Even barefoot, dressed in leggings and what looked to be one of her husband's cast-off rugby shirts, the woman radiated sex appeal. Dark hair, dark eyes, olive skin, and a flash of brilliant white smile made her seem as Mediterranean as her kitchen, but her accent held an incongruous trace of Scots burr. 'Do you like it?' she said to Gemma, gesturing at the kitchen. She hadn't missed Gemma's rapt stare. 'Do you cook—?'

'Darling,' said her husband, 'they are not here to talk about cooking, difficult as that may be for you to imagine.' He gave her shoulder an affectionate squeeze.

'Nevertheless, they cannot talk without

266

something to eat and drink. There are wholemeal scones still warm in the oven, and I will make some *latte.*'

Kincaid opened his mouth to protest. 'No, really, that's quite—'

'Sit,' ordered Valerie, and Kincaid obediently sat in a clear spot on the settee. Gemma lingered in the kitchen, sniffing as Valerie opened the Aga's warming oven.

'You're wondering how I manage not to waddle,' said Malcolm as he joined Kincaid. He pointed at the dogs, who had stretched out on the tiled floor in a patch of sunlight. 'If it weren't for running those two up and down the bloody hills twice a day, I probably wouldn't be able to get through the door, much less into my clothes. Val's cooking is quite irresistible.'

The hiss of the espresso machine filled the room, and when Valerie had filled cups Gemma helped her carry coffee and scones into the solarium. Once settled in a comfortable slip-covered chair, Gemma tasted her scone as Valerie watched expectantly.

'Wonderful,' said Gemma sincerely. 'Better than anything from a bakery.'

'It takes ten minutes to mix these from scratch, yet people buy *mixes* from the supermarket.' Wrinkling her nose disdainfully, Valerie sounded as if she were talking about black-market racketeering. 'Sometimes I think the English are hopeless.'

'But you're English, aren't you, Mrs Reid?' asked Gemma through a mouthful of crumbs.

'Valerie, please,' she said, helping herself to a scone. 'My parents are Anglicized Italians. They settled in Scotland and opened the most British of cafés, on the anything-you-can-do-we-can-do-better principle. This they even extended to the naming of their children.' She tapped her chest. 'You'd think Valerie was bad enough, but they called my brother *Ian*. Can you imagine anything less Italian than Ian? And they learned to fry everything in rancid grease, in the best British fashion. But I forgave them, because every summer they sent me to Italy to stay with my grandmama, and so I learned to cook.'

'Val.' Malcolm's voice held amusement. 'Give the superintendent a chance, would you?'

'I'm so sorry,' said Valerie, sounding not the least bit abashed. 'Do get on with whatever it is you need to get on with.' She settled back into her nest of papers, cup of *latte* in one hand, scone plate balanced on her knee.

Kincaid smiled and sipped his coffee before replying. 'Mr Reid, I believe you told us that you'd had no contact with Alastair Gilbert before his death?' Before Reid could affirm or deny this rather open-ended question, Kincaid continued, 'But I think that in fact you misled us. You had an appointment with Gilbert at six o'clock the evening before he died, which he confirmed by telephone. Just what was Gilbert's urgent business with you, Mr Reid?'

A smooth bluff, thought Gemma, but would it work?

Malcolm Reid glanced openly at his wife, then rubbed his palms against the knees of his jeans. 'Val said at the time that it wasn't a good idea, but I simply didn't want to complicate things any more than necessary for Claire. She's had a difficult enough time as it is.'

When Reid didn't continue, Kincaid said, 'You have to let us do the interpreting. We'll make every effort to cause Claire as little distress as possible, but the only way she can get on with her life is to have this business resolved. Surely you can see that?'

Reid nodded, glanced at his wife again, started to speak, stopped, then finally said, 'I find this all very awkward and embarrassing.'

'What my husband is trying to tell you,' said Valerie, matter-of-factly, 'is that

Alastair had developed some wild idea that Malcolm was having a passionate liaison with his wife.'

Reid gave her a grateful look as he nodded in agreement. 'That's right. I don't know what put it into his head, but he was behaving quite oddly. I had no idea how to deal with him.'

'Oddly in what way?' asked Gemma, having finished her scone and rescued her notebook from the depths of her bag. 'Was he violent?'

'No...not physically, at least. But he didn't seem quite rational. One minute he'd be demanding proof and threatening me, then the next he'd be smiling and jocular, and sort of...ingratiating.' Reid gave a slight shudder. 'I can't tell you how creepy it was. He kept talking about his *sources.*'

'Did he mention anything, or anyone, in particular?' Kincaid sat forward intently.

Shaking his head, Reid said, 'No, but he was almost...gloating. As if he were enjoying his secrets. And he kept saying that if I'd just tell him the truth, he wouldn't take any action against me.'

Kincaid raised an eyebrow at that. 'Very magnanimous of him. What did you do?'

'Told him there was nothing to tell and that he could bloody well bugger off. He shook his head, as if he were disappointed in me. Can you imagine that?' Reid's voice rose incredulously.

'And that's how he left you?'

'No.' Reid rubbed his hands against his jeans again and smiled a bit crookedly. 'It's too melodramatic—I feel an ass just repeating it. "Malcolm, my boy, I promise you'll regret this," he said as he reached the door. Just like some character in a bad film.' One of the spaniels raised its head at the change in Malcolm's voice and gave him a sleepy, puzzled look. Reassured, it flopped down again with a gusty sigh.

'What did you do then?' asked Gemma. 'That must have made you feel a bit odd.'

'Laughed it off, at first. But the more I thought about it, the more uncomfortable I felt. I tried to ring Claire, but no one answered, and once Alastair had had time to get home, I was afraid that my ringing up would only aggravate him further.'

'But you discussed it with her the next day.' Kincaid made it a statement rather than a question.

'I never had the chance. She was out on a consulting job in the morning, and we only met briefly in the shop at lunchtime, when there were customers waiting. When I returned from my afternoon appointment, Claire had left for the day.'

'And since then?'

Reid shrugged. 'It seemed pointless to worry her with it. How could it possibly matter now?'

The look Kincaid cast at Gemma conveyed his scepticism, but he merely said, 'And on Wednesday evening, Mr Reid, you said your wife had a cooking class, I believe?'

Valerie responded before Reid could get a word in. 'No, no, Superintendent. The classes are all finished until next week. On Wednesday night Malcolm was at home with me. We had vermicelli abruzzesi and a salad.'

'Do you always remember what you had for dinner on a particular night, Mrs Reid?' asked Kincaid.

'Of course,' she said, rewarding him with a brilliant smile. 'And that was a new recipe I'd been wanting to try, but I'd had a bit of trouble getting the courgette flowers.'

'Flow—?' Kincaid shook his head. 'Never mind. Is there anyone who can corroborate this?'

'Not unless you count the dogs,' said Malcolm, with a weak attempt at humour.

'Well, I appreciate your frankness.' Kincaid set down his empty cup and rose, nodding at them both. 'And your hospitality. We'll let you know if we have further questions.'

Valerie Reid stood up quickly. 'If you must go so soon, I'll see you out. No, darling,' she added as Malcolm started to get up, 'I can manage perfectly well.'

When they reached the front door, she came out with them, pulled the door to, and stopped, hand on the knob. 'Superintendent,' she said quietly, 'Malcolm...my husband sometimes has a tendency to behave nobly. I admire this in him, but I am not willing to see him sacrifice himself to a code of honour.' She bit her lip. 'What I'm trying to say is that if you're interested in Claire Gilbert's lover, you'd do better to look a bit closer to home.'

With that she slipped back inside and shut the door firmly, leaving them standing in the dim and dappled shade.

'And what do you make of that?' Kincaid said when they'd buckled into their seats and eased out into the road again. 'A well-coordinated cover-up, wife supporting husband despite his erring ways?'

Slowly, Gemma shook her head. 'I don't think so. Maybe I'm naïve as a just-hatched chick, but I can't see Malcolm Reid as a straying husband. They have a good life, and the affection between them seems genuine.'

'He was embarrassed by Gilbert's accusations, but he wasn't a bit nervous. Did you notice?'

'What about the lover Valerie mentioned?' asked Gemma. 'Do you suppose she just made it up to stop us harassing Malcolm? Who could it be?'

'Percy Bainbridge?' suggested Kincaid. 'Though I'm inclined to think he prefers schoolboys.'

Gemma took it up. 'The vicar?'

'Now, there's a thought. She is rather lovely.' He gave her a swift sideways glance, accompanied by a raised eyebrow.

Wondering what the vicar looked like, Gemma felt a twinge of jealousy. 'What about Geoff?' she countered. 'Maybe she's cradle-snatching? Or maybe it's—'

'Brian?' They said it in unison on a rising note of incredulity. Kincaid looked at her and they both grinned.

'Great minds,' he said as he changed down into another gear.

'But I'd never have thought it. Brian doesn't seem Claire's type at all, while Malcolm seemed tailormade for her.'

'One should never fail to take proximity into account,' Kincaid said levelly, his eyes on the road. 'Or the unpredictable nature of the human heart. What—' His phone trilled, and he paused while he slipped it out of his pocket, flipping it open with a deft one-handed manoeuvre. 'Kincaid.'

After listening for a moment, he said, 'Right. Right. I'll pass it along,' then disconnected.

He gave Gemma a regretful glance. 'It looks like I'll have to manage Brian Genovase without you. Jackie Temple's been trying to reach you—says she needs to see you urgently.'

Gemma watched Will's big, square hands lying easily on the steering wheel and wondered if others found him as restful as she did. A call to Guildford Police Station from the mobile phone had brought him to the village, ready to run her into Dorking for the quickest train to London. He'd made no attempt to disturb her preoccupied reflection, yet his silence held no hint of injured feelings.

She looked out of the window again as the car swooped round a curve. Tall, silver-trunked trees closed in on either side of the road, and the falling leaves flickered and swirled through the air like swarms of golden bees. The beauty of it pierced Gemma unexpectedly—sharply, sweetly—and for a moment she felt as exposed and transparent as a jellyfish.

She must have made some involuntary sound, because Will glanced at her and said, 'You all right, Gemma?'

'Yes. No. I don't know.' She took a breath, then said the first thing that came into her head. 'Will—do you think we ever *really* know anyone? Or are we so blinded by our own perceptions that we can't see past them? I've been imagining Brian as a loving father who might do anything to protect his son. But that was only one dimension, and it kept me from seeing the possibility that he might be Claire's lover, a man who could have killed Alastair Gilbert for reasons that had nothing to do with his son. And I didn't see Claire as—oh, never mind.'

Will chuckled. 'You didn't see Claire as flesh and blood, as a woman with needs so strong she'd be willing to court social condemnation, at the very least, to satisfy them.'

'You never seem surprised,' said Gemma.

'No, I suppose I'm not, but I'm no cynic, either. This job teaches us not to have faith in people. But in the end, what else is there? I'm still willing to give the benefit of the doubt.'

'That's a fine balance,' Gemma said slowly. But was she capable of achieving it? She studied Will covertly through her lashes, wondering if she'd been deceived by her perceptions once again

276

and his placid exterior concealed something entirely different.

His quick glance caught her off guard and she felt herself colouring. 'This isn't really about Brian, is it, Gemma?' he asked. Before she could protest, he added, 'You don't have to tell me. But remember, if you ever need someone to talk to, I'm available.'

By half-past one, Gemma was ascending the steps at the Holland Park tube station, fortified by a cheese and tomato roll bought from the buffet trolley on the train. A brisk walk brought her to Jackie's flat and she stood on the pavement for a moment, catching her breath and admiring the way the tendrils of creeper flamed orange against the brown brick.

Jackie answered the bell with a smile of pleasure. 'Gemma! When I couldn't get you at home I tried the Yard, but I wasn't really expecting you to turn up on the doorstep like a lost pilgrim. Come in.' She wore a brightly coloured dressing-gown and her tight curls looked damp from the bath.

'They said it was urgent,' Gemma explained as she followed Jackie up to the first floor.

'Well, I expect I did lay it on a bit.' Jackie looked sheepish. 'But I thought they wouldn't take me seriously, otherwise. Have a seat and I'll get you something to drink.'

When Jackie returned from the kitchen with two glasses of fizzy lemonade, cold from the refrigerator, Gemma said, 'What's it all about, Jackie? And why aren't you at work?'

Jackie curled up on the settee, her dressing-gown spreading around her like the robes of an exotic princess. 'I go on at three. They've changed my shift. I'll have to get dressed and be off in a few minutes. They said you weren't in London—I haven't brought you all the way from Surrey, have I?'

Gemma gave her friend a quizzical look. 'Jackie, if I didn't know better, I'd think you were stalling. And, yes, I did come up from Surrey. Now spill it.'

Jackie sipped at her drink, wrinkling her nose as the bubbles got up it. 'I feel a bit of a silly cow, to tell the truth. I'm probably making a mountain out of a molehill. You know I said I'd have a word with Sergeant Talley?'

Gemma nodded encouragement.

'Well, he got quite shirty with me. Told me to mind my own business if I knew what was good for me. I hadn't expected that, and it got my back up a bit. There are a couple of blokes on the beat that have been at Notting Hill as long as Talley, so this morning I ambushed one of them when he came off duty. Bought him breakfast in the café next to the station.' Jackie paused and drained half her drink.

'And?' Gemma prompted, her curiosity thoroughly aroused.

'He said that the way he heard it, the bad blood between Gilbert and Ogilvie had nothing to do with a woman. Rumour had it that Gilbert blocked Ogilvie's promotion, told the review board that he thought Ogilvie was too much of a maverick to make a good senior officer. They'd been partners, and it was common knowledge among the lads that Gilbert was incompetent and Ogilvie had covered his ass more than once.' Jackie shook her head in disgust. 'Can you imagine? Ogilvie did get promoted eventually, when Gilbert was no longer his senior officer, but I doubt he ever forgave Gilbert.'

'Do you suppose Ogilvie hated him enough to murder him, after all these years?' Gemma thought for a moment, frowning. 'From what I've learned about Alastair Gilbert, I wouldn't be surprised if he blocked Ogilvie's promotion out of spite, because he was jealous of him. This all happened about the time they both met Claire, didn't it?'

'I think so, but I'm not sure. You'd have

to check the records. Gemma—'

'I know. If I don't let you get ready, you'll be late.' Gemma picked up her empty glass, intending to take it to the kitchen.

'That's not it.' Jackie glanced at the clock on a side table. 'Well, only partly, anyway.' She stopped, smoothing the folds of her dressing-gown with her fingers, then said hesitantly, 'I have some connections on the street, some sources. You know, you work a beat long enough—you accumulate them. When I got curious about this business I started asking some questions, putting out some feelers.'

When Jackie paused again, her eyes on the fabric beneath her fingers, Gemma felt a prick of apprehension. 'What is it, Jackie?'

'You'll have to decide what to do with this, whether to turn it over to Complaints and Discipline.' She waited until Gemma nodded assent before continuing. 'Remember I said I thought I'd seen Gilbert talking to a snitch? Well, Gilbert was much too far up the ladder to be running informers, so I asked my bloke if he'd heard Gilbert's name in connection with anything dirty.'

'And?' Gemma prompted.

'Drugs, he said. He'd heard hints of some high-up bloke running protection for the dealers.'

'Gilbert?' Gemma's voice rose in an incredulous squeak.

Jackie shook her head. 'David Ogilvie.'

Going back to the Yard had been a mistake, thought Gemma as she walked slowly up Richmond Avenue in the dark. She'd been inundated by piles of paper, and by the time she'd accomplished her own task of looking through every record pertaining to Gilbert and Ogilvie, her eyes burned and her back ached with fatigue. She'd missed Toby's tea, and now, too tired to shop on the way home, she'd have to settle for whatever she could find in her meagre store cupboard.

Thornhill Gardens came into view, an even darker void against the black bulk of the surrounding houses. She picked her way along the pavement until she reached the Cavendishes' pathway, then stopped. The sitting-room blind hadn't been pulled quite to the sill, and through the uncovered space she could see the blue flickering light of the telly. But there was an added glow, yellow-warm and wavering. Candles. For a moment she fancied she heard laughter, soft and intimate. Gemma shook herself and marched up the path, but her knock was tentative.

'Gemma, love!' said Hazel when she opened the door. 'We weren't expecting you tonight.' She looked rumpled, relaxed, and slightly flushed. 'Come in,' she said, shooing Gemma into the hall. 'The children were knackered, poor dears—I took them to the Serpentine today and wore them out—so we got them down early. Tim and I were just watching a video.'

'I meant to phone,' said Gemma, then as Hazel started towards the stairs, 'Wait, Hazel. I'll just nip up and get Toby. You go back to your video.'

Hazel turned. 'You're sure?'

'Positive.'

'All right then, love.' Padding back in her stockinged feet, Hazel squeezed Gemma's shoulder and gave her a quick peck on the cheek. 'I'll see you in the morning.'

Toby lay sprawled on his back, arms flung up in the air as if he'd been doing star jumps in his sleep. He'd kicked his covers off as usual, which made it easier for Gemma to slip her arms under him, one hand cradling the back of his head. When she lifted him he barely stirred, and his head flopped against her shoulder as she positioned him in her arms.

She'd turn in early, too, she thought as she carried Toby across the garden, balancing his inert weight against her hip as she let herself into the flat. Then she could get up and enjoy spending some time with him in the morning before she had to leave for Holmbury St Mary again.

But after she had tucked Toby into his own small cot, she went round the flat tidying, unable to settle to anything. Finally, when she had exhausted her repertoire of chores, she searched the fridge until she found a piece of cheddar that hadn't been attacked by mould, then unearthed a few stale biscuits in the cupboard.

She ate standing at the sink, looking out into the darkened garden, and when she'd finished she poured a glass of wine and eased into the leather chair. *Old maid habits*, she thought with a wry grimace. Soon she'd be wearing cardies and flannel pants, and then what would become of her?

Jackie usually saved the area near the top of the Portobello Road for the end of her shift. It had been a long time since she'd worked evenings, though, and she wasn't used to the eerie emptiness of the culs-de-sac at this time of night. The little antique shops that bustled with customers during business hours were dark and barred, and bits of rubbish rattled along the gutters.

As she turned left into the last street,

the streetlamp at its end flared and died. 'Shit,' said Jackie under her breath, but she always finished her rounds, and she wasn't about to let a case of the rookie spooks stop her doing it tonight. She imagined herself telling her guv'nor that she'd done a bunk because the street was dark and empty, then giggled to herself at the thought of his response.

She'd be home soon enough. Susan, who had to rise with the birds to get to her job at the BBC, would be fast asleep but would have left out a snack and a nightcap for her. Jackie smiled at the prospect. A hot bath, a warm drink, and then she'd curl up with the Mary Wesley novel she'd been saving. There was something rather liberating about being awake in the small hours while the rest of the world slept.

She stopped, head cocked, listening. The hair on the back of her neck rose in an atavistic response. That soft shuffle behind her—could it have been a footstep?

Now she heard nothing but the slight sigh of the wind between the buildings. 'Silly cow,' she said aloud, chasing the shadows. She walked on. A few more steps and she'd reach the bottom of the cul-de-sac, then she'd start the last leg back to the station.

This time the footfall was unmistakable, as was the raw and primitive terror that left her knees like jelly. Jackie spun round, heart pounding. Nothing.

She unclipped her radio and thumbed the mike. Too late. She smelled him first, a rancid sweetness. Then the metal burned cold against the base of her skull.

Chapter Eleven

Kincaid had seen Gemma into the car with Will Darling, then watched as they sped away round the green. She looked back once, but by the time he'd lifted his hand to wave to her, she had turned away. A moment later the car disappeared from sight.

He crossed the road and stood for a moment at the end of the path leading to the pub, collecting himself for the task ahead. Deveney had been called out to a shop burglary in Guildford, which left Kincaid on his own to question Brian Genovase. But perhaps he could turn that to his advantage by making the interview as informal as possible.

The wind had risen from the west, shivering the leaves of the old oak, and the pub sign creaked on its hinges as it swung. Looking up at the lovers silhouetted against the moon, Kincaid thought that the image was perhaps more apt than they'd realized.

He found Brian alone, preparing for Sunday lunch. 'Roast beef and Yorkshire pud,' said Brian by way of greeting. He finished lettering the blackboard with a flourish. 'We always do Sundays properly. You'll do well to get a table early.' His words were friendly enough, but as he spoke he gave Kincaid a wary glance.

'I'll keep that in mind, but first I'd like a word with you before you get too busy.' Kincaid slid on to a bar stool.

Brian stopped in the midst of setting up a rack of clean glassware. 'Look, Mr Kincaid, I appreciate what you did for my lad last night. You were decent to him, which can't be said of the last lot. But I don't know what else I can tell you. Geoff's been round to the folk in the village already this morning, told them he'd work free in order to make some reparation for what he did. And first thing tomorrow we'll get him started again in counselling. It seems this is going to be a long process. I should have—'

'Brian.' Kincaid cut him off. 'This isn't about Geoff.'

Brian stared at him blankly. 'Not about—'

'I'm afraid we never quite finished our

official inquiries. Can you tell me what you were doing on Wednesday evening, between about six o'clock and half-past seven?'

'Me?' Brian's mouth dropped in astonishment. 'But...I suppose you have to ask everyone?'

'You'd just got lucky up to now,' Kincaid said with a smile. 'Were you here?'

''Course I was bloody here. Where else would I be?'

'By yourself?'

Shaking his head, Brian said, 'John was on the bar, and Megan was here, the girl that helps out in the kitchen. It was a busy night for middle of the week.'

'Did you leave at any time, even for a few minutes?' asked Kincaid. 'Think carefully now. It's important to be accurate with these things.'

Brian frowned and rubbed his chin. 'There's only one thing I remember,' he said after a moment. 'Somewhere between about half-six and seven I went to the store-room and broke out a new case of lemonade. I can't have been away from the bar much more than five minutes.'

'Can you reach the store-room from inside the pub?'

'No. You have to go the long way round, through the car park.' Then Brian added, with the air of sharing a confidence,

'Bloody miserable when it's raining, I can tell you.'

'Did you see or hear anything unusual, however small?'

'Only the mice. We lost our mouser a few months back. It's time we found a new puss. Usually they come to us, but not one's turned up so far. Maybe the word hasn't gone round that the position's vacant.' Brian grinned, obviously regaining his equilibrium.

Good, thought Kincaid. Now that he'd got him relaxed and a bit pleased with himself, it was time to hit below the belt. 'Brian, I've gathered the impression that you and Claire Gilbert are quite good friends.'

Brian took a glass from a tray and slotted it into the rack, almost concealing his momentary hesitation. 'No more than most neighbours. We help each other out when needed.' He kept his eyes on his task as he spoke.

'How did her husband feel about that?'

'I don't know why he should have been bothered one way or the other.' Irritation edged Brian's voice, but he still hadn't met Kincaid's eyes. 'Now, if you don't mind—'

'I think he might have been quite bothered, actually,' Kincaid interrupted. 'It seems that Alastair Gilbert was irrationally jealous of his wife. He might have misinterpreted the most innocent of gestures.'

'I hardly knew the man.' Brian's brows were drawn together in a scowl, and the glasses clinked dangerously as he slid them into position. 'He didn't frequent the pub, and he certainly didn't consider me his social or professional equal. He called me a bloody shopkeeper once, and him a farmer's son from Dorking.'

Resting his elbows on the bar, Kincaid leaned close to Brian and said, 'You knew him well enough to ask him for help when Geoff got into trouble, and he turned you down flat. You hated him, didn't you, Brian? No one could say you didn't have good cause.'

The wineglass in Brian's hand cracked, the head separating from its stem and falling unscathed to the bar. Blood welled from his thumb and he held it to his mouth for a moment, glaring at Kincaid. 'All right, I hated him. What do you want me to say? He was a bastard who didn't deserve to breathe the same air as Claire and Lucy. But I didn't kill him, if that's what you're getting at. He laughed at me when I asked him to help Geoff—treated me like I was some kind of scum. I might have been tempted then, but I didn't touch him, so why should I have done it now?'

'I'll give you two good reasons,' Kincaid said. 'He found out what Geoff was up to and told you he intended to take action. I think he would have wanted to gloat over it a bit first, would have enjoyed making you squirm. Gilbert liked playing the petty tyrant, didn't he, Brian? And you could have shut him up once and for all.'

'But I didn't—'

'And what if he suspected you were dallying with his wife? Gilbert was not the sort of man to step nobly aside, was he? I think he'd have been determined to make your life as miserable as possible, no matter the cost.'

'But he didn't—'

The kitchen door swung open. Through it came a thin girl enveloped in a white chef's apron several sizes too large for her. 'Could you give me a hand with the veg, Bri?' she asked, then, as she took in Kincaid and the tense atmosphere, 'Oh, sorry.' The smell of roasting beef reached Kincaid's nose, and he swallowed involuntarily.

'I'll be right there, Megan.' Brian gave her a quick smile and turned back to Kincaid as she disappeared into the kitchen. 'Look, Superintendent, this is all nonsense. You can't seriously—'

The front door opened and a group dressed in Sunday best came in, laughing

290

and calling greetings to Brian. Kincaid met Brian's eyes and smiled. 'I'd better get that table, hadn't I?' He knew when to beat a graceful retreat.

Kincaid found himself outside the Moon once again, but this time he was stuffed to popping point with roast beef and Yorkshire pudding. Although the state of his stomach made him long for nothing more taxing than a nap, he felt restless and unsettled as he contemplated the afternoon stretching before him.

He'd reached the point in this case where he hadn't an idea what to do next, but he knew that his mounting frustration was counterproductive.

What he needed was a walk. It would help clear his mind as well as lessen the impact of his Sunday lunch. Having been informed of several promising routes by some of the regulars in the bar, he changed into the trainers and lightweight anorak he kept in his overnight bag.

The westerly wind had brought clouds with it, but Kincaid judged the weather not seriously threatening. He chose the way that led through the village and up the hill, past Madeleine Wade's closed shop. Soon the track left the paved road and he climbed steeply, past the silent cricket pitch, following the signposts designating the Greensand Way, as he'd been instructed. Winded, he reached a large level clearing, the junction of many paths running through the Hurtwood. A good metaphor, he thought, for the many avenues this case seemed to be taking, but he'd be damned if he could see how they all came together.

He took the Greensand Way, walking easily at first on the sandy path, studying his surroundings. An evocative name, Hurtwood, bringing to mind images of injured trees, but one of his garrulous lunchtime friends had informed him that the name came from the old word for bilberries. He wondered if the thickets of brambly plants he saw were indeed *hurtberries*.

One usually thought of autumn as crisp, but this wood was a soft symphony in greens and browns. The heather lining the path had dried to a crumbly brown, yellow and brown leaves carpeted the path under his feet, and the bracken had dried to the colour of new pennies. He shied away from the comparison with Gemma's hair that came to mind and picked up his pace a bit.

Soon the path narrowed, and the ground dropped away on his left; through the gaps in the trees he could see all the way across the Surrey Weald to the South Downs. He made a deliberate effort to stop his mind circling, and for the next half-hour he just walked, climbing more and more often as the path became steeper.

Rounding the bend, he came to a halt, balancing on his toes from the abrupt change in momentum. A giant splay of tree roots grew out of the hillside, blocking the path. Surely this was not still the Greensand Way? He must have missed a signpost somewhere. Suddenly aware that he had neither map nor compass, he decided that retracing his steps would be the wisest course, but first he picked a dry spot on one of the roots and sat down for a moment's breather.

As his breathing slowed, the quiet closed in, broken only by birdsong and the occasional rumble of a jet taking off from Gatwick. No sound reached the forest floor from the gently swaying treetops, but when a leaf drifted down from a branch above his head, he could have sworn he heard it rustle as it touched the ground.

Kincaid ran his fingers over the lichens on a gnarled stick, wondering if Alastair Gilbert had ever taken time to feel the texture of bark or listen to the leaves fall. Strict agendas for professional and social success usually didn't leave much room for contemplation.

He'd tried hard not to let his personal feelings about the man cloud his view of the case, but perhaps he'd have been better off starting with his own judgement. That was the key, after all—what kind of man Gilbert had been and what consequences had unfolded from his actions. For Kincaid had no doubt that Gilbert's murder had been committed by someone who knew him, had in fact never given the intruder theory more than a cursory consideration.

What had Brian Genovase been about to say when Megan opened the door? Had Gilbert not suspected Brian of having an affair with his wife? Thinking about it, Kincaid felt fairly certain that Valerie Reid had steered them in the right direction, whatever her motives. Brian had never asked him the obvious question of an innocent man wronged by gossip—*Who the hell told you that?*

But if Brian and Claire were lovers, and Brian had killed Gilbert in a confrontation, why had he been so worried about Lucy and Claire? Shaking his head, Kincaid crumbled bits of bark off the stick with his fingers. Could Brian have murdered Gilbert in the few minutes he'd been away from the bar and disposed of the murder weapon? The lads had searched the premises thoroughly, looking for Claire Gilbert's missing earrings, and hadn't turned up anything that fitted Kate Ling's description of the instrument.

It seemed to Kincaid that this was exactly the scenario they'd constructed for Geoff. Only if the crime had been premeditated and carefully planned could either Geoff or Brian have pulled it off, and he felt sure that Gilbert's murder had been committed in a moment of rage. It had been a passionate crime. *A crime of passion,* in fact.

That left Malcolm Reid. If one assumed that Valerie was covering up for him, then Reid would have had the time to commit the murder and the leisure to dispose of the weapon and anything else incriminating. But since Reid seemed to have been open with his wife about Gilbert's accusations, what had he to gain by killing him? And besides, Kincaid, like Gemma, had difficulty seeing either of the Reids as consummate liars.

He'd stripped his little stick down to the bare, smooth wood, but he felt no nearer to uncovering the truth. Tucking the stick in the pocket of his anorak, he stood up and brushed off the seat of his trousers as he started back down the path. The only thing for it was to intensify the search of the paper trail, go back over every bit of information once again.

It was only then, having explored all the

apparent options, that the thought came to him. And as little as he liked it, he knew he'd have to follow it through.

When he came again to the junction of paths in the clearing, he chose the right fork, hoping it would bring him down at the other side of the village. A few minutes' walk proved him right, as the gentle descent brought him out into the clearing at the top of the Gilberts' lane. Before him lay the village hall, still ornamented with the coloured lights left over from Guy Fawkes night. The announcer's wooden platform remained in place as well, but the bonfire's ashes were long cold. The wind brought the dank scent to him, and he gave the scorched grass a wide skirting.

Resignedly, he returned to the pub kitchen and questioned John and Megan about Brian's movements on Wednesday evening. He didn't expect them to contradict Brian's story, but procedure must be observed.

Megan, wiping her sweaty face with the tail of her apron, declared that Brian couldn't have been away from the bar for more than three or four minutes, and had come back, whistling, with a case of lemonade. John said that, frankly, it had been a bugger of a night, and he hadn't noticed Brian's absence at all.

Kincaid thanked them and, as the sun had by that time definitely disappeared over the yardarm, wandered into the bar and ordered a pint of Flowers bitter. He carried his drink to the nook by the fire and sat quietly, watching the evening customers trickle in. Brian ignored him quite successfully, while John, a rangy, greying man who wore waistcoats with his jeans and boots, gave him an occasional, curious glance.

The warmth from the fire's embers felt good, and Kincaid stretched his legs out beneath the table, enjoying the pleasant tiredness that results from physical exercise. Looking about him, he wished suddenly that he were here on holiday, that he could enjoy this village and its inhabitants without ulterior motive, and that he might be accepted simply as himself.

Smiling at the futility of his desire, he thought he might just as well wish for a case in which the victim had been a saint and he disliked all the suspects equally. Things would be so much simpler, but in his experience, saints seldom got themselves murdered.

Through the bodies clustered at the bar, he caught an unexpected glimpse of Lucy. She must have come in the back way or from upstairs, as he couldn't have missed her if she'd come in the front door. She was speaking to someone, and as the crowd shifted he saw that it was Geoff.

In jeans and a flannel shirt several sizes too large, she looked innocently child-like, but as Kincaid watched she moved a step closer to Geoff, putting her hand on his waist in a gesture both provocative and possessive. Geoff smiled down at her, but did not return the touch, then at a summons from Brian they both disappeared into the kitchen.

Kincaid finished his drink in undisturbed solitude and slipped out through the door, his departure apparently unremarked. He left his car parked by the green and walked through the dark village, retracing the beginning of his afternoon walk.

Madeleine Wade's stairs were still unlit, but this time he climbed with some familiarity. When she opened the door to his knock, he smiled and said, 'You can compare me to a bad penny if you like.'

'I'd already opened the wine and set a place for you.' She stepped aside to allow him in, and he saw that she had opened up the small gateleg table that stood next to the settee and pulled up the two rush-seated chairs. The table was indeed set with plates, cutlery, and wineglasses for two.

He took a slow step forward, aware of the hair prickling at the back of his neck. 'Sometimes you quite frighten me, Madeleine. Are you dabbling now in foretelling the future?'

She shrugged. 'Not really. I just had an odd feeling tonight and decided to risk making a fool of myself. After all, if I were wrong, no one would ever know but me, and you have to admit it's a rather effective parlour trick.' In a voice rich with amusement, she added, 'I could say the same of you, you know.'

'I frighten you?' he asked, surprised.

'Sometimes I feel a bit like a mouse fascinated by a snake—it's such fun, but I never know when you're going to pounce. Come sit down and I'll pour the wine. It's had long enough to breathe.'

'I promise I didn't come with pouncing in mind,' he said as he took the place she indicated at the table. 'And as long as we're being so honest, I must say that I haven't quite got used to the feeling of being an open book, and I'm not at all sure that I like it.' This time the music playing in the background was classical—Mozart, he thought, a violin concerto—and the candles burned on windowsill and table.

'You're coping admirably,' she said as she carried in a tray from the kitchen. She set a platter on the table, then filled his wineglass before seating herself.

Kincaid whistled as he read the bottle's

label. 'You didn't find this at Sainsbury's.' The platter looked an equal treat—cheeses, smoked salmon, fresh fruit and biscuits. 'You'll spoil me,' he said, sniffing the wine before taking his first sip.

'Oh, I don't think there's much chance of that.' Madeleine watched the deep purple-red stream of wine as she filled her glass. 'You won't be around long enough to spoil. You'll bring this case to a conclusion—I have no doubt.' She met his eyes. 'Then you'll go back to whatever life you lead when you're not working, and you'll forget all about Holmbury St Mary.'

For a moment Kincaid fancied he heard a trace of regret beneath the amusement in her voice. 'I'm not sure I have a life when I'm not working,' he said as he positioned a slice of salmon on a biscuit. 'That's the problem.'

'But that's your choice, surely?'

Kincaid shrugged. 'So I thought. It seemed enough for a long time. In fact, after my wife and I split up, anything seemed preferable to going through that sort of emotional turmoil again.'

'So what happened to change things?' Madeleine asked as she spread a crumbly white cheese on a biscuit. 'You should try this one. It's white Stilton with ginger.'

'I don't know.' Kincaid polished off his salmon while he considered her question.

300

'Last spring I lost a friend and neighbour. I suppose it was only when I couldn't seem to fill the hole she left that I realized I was lonely.' He felt astonished even as he spoke. These were things he hadn't really articulated to himself, much less shared with anyone else.

'Sometimes grief takes us by surprise.' Madeleine lifted her glass and held it in both hands, tilting it gently. Tonight she wore tunic and trousers in olive-green silk, and the wine looked blood dark against the earthy green. Kincaid heard the experience in her voice, but he didn't ask what loss she'd suffered.

When he'd sampled the Stilton, he said, 'Do you suppose Claire Gilbert will grieve for her husband?'

Madeleine thought for a moment. 'I think that Claire did her grieving for Alastair Gilbert a long time ago, when she discovered that he was not what she'd thought.' Behind her, the farmyard animals seemed to cavort across the curtains in the flickering light. 'And I don't think she ever stopped grieving for Stephen. She hadn't time to do it properly when she married Alastair, but we often make choices out of necessity that we later regret.'

'And have you?'

'More times than I can count.' Madeleine smiled. 'But never because the wolf was at my door, like Claire. I've been financially fortunate. My family was comfortably off, then I went straight from college into a well-paid job.' With a delicate twist of the stem, she picked a grape from its cluster. 'What about you, Mr Kincaid? Have you made decisions you've regretted?'

'Out of the necessity of the moment,' he said softly, echoing her earlier words. Had she sensed what was on his mind and led him to this, all unsuspecting? 'I'd say this was odd, except I'm beginning to think that nothing concerning you is quite...ordinary. Yes, I made that sort of decision once, and it concerned Alastair Gilbert.'

'Gilbert?' Madeleine spluttered, choking on her wine.

'It was years ago—probably quite near the time that Gilbert met Claire. I was on a development course, just after I'd been promoted to inspector, and he was the instructor.' Kincaid stopped and drank some wine, wondering why he had got himself into this tale and why he felt compelled to continue. 'We had the weekend at home in the middle of a two-week course. That Sunday evening, just as I was about to leave for Hampshire again, my wife told me that she desperately needed to talk.' Pausing, he rubbed his cheek. 'You have to understand that this was very out of the ordinary for Vic—she wasn't a "tempest-in-the-teapot" type at all. I rang Gilbert, told him I had a family emergency, asked for a little leeway in returning. He told me he'd see me thrown out of the course.' He drank again, swallowing the bitterness that rose in his throat.

'I think he'd already taken a dislike to me because I hadn't sucked up to him, and I wasn't experienced enough then to know that the threat was mostly hot air.'

'So you went?' Madeleine prompted when he paused again.

Kincaid nodded. 'And when I came home she was gone. Of course, I've enough perspective now to realize that it wouldn't have made any difference in the long term. She wanted me to choose her over the job, and if I'd stayed with her on that Sunday, she'd have picked another occasion for the same test—when I had an important case, perhaps.

'But for a long time I needed someone to blame, and Alastair Gilbert provided a very convenient scapegoat.' He smiled crookedly and began spreading cheese on a biscuit.

Madeleine refilled his glass. 'It doesn't take Sherlock Holmes to deduce that others besides you and the Genovases will have had scores to settle with Gilbert. How do you know where to start?'

'We don't. The man was like a bloody virus—he infected everything he touched. How could we possibly trace every contact he ever made?'

'I can sense your frustration rising,' Madeleine said, smiling. 'And that wasn't my intent.'

'Sorry.' Studying her as she concentrated on arranging slivers of salmon on a biscuit, he found himself intensely curious about this woman, but he hesitated to test her boundaries. After a moment, he said carefully, 'Madeleine, are you ever really comfortable with anyone?'

'There have been a very few exceptions.' She sighed. 'The needy are the worst, I think, those that cry out constantly for attention, for affirmation of their right to exist. They are even more disturbing than the angry.'

'Is that what Geoff is like?'

Shaking her head, she said, 'No. Geoff isn't a *sucker*—that's how I think of them—or if he is, he only takes his security from a select few. His father, and perhaps Lucy.'

Kincaid thought of the scene he'd witnessed in the bar. 'Madeleine, how do you think early emotional, and probably sexual, abuse would affect a young man's responses to sex?'

'I'm no psychologist.' She bit into a slice of green apple.

'But you're probably more perceptive than most.' He gave her an encouraging smile.

'If you're talking about Geoff, and considering his history I assume you are, I'd say there are two likely avenues. He might become an abuser himself. Or...' She gazed into space, frowning, as she thought. 'He might associate sex with failure and abandonment.'

'So that he'd never take that risk with someone he cared about?'

'I wouldn't take my word for it. That's pure amateur speculation.' Pushing her plate away, she sat back and cradled her wineglass.

'Tell me more about what you do in your professional capacity, then,' Kincaid said, still nibbling. 'Do you treat injuries with massage therapy?'

'Sometimes. It's not just a relaxation technique—it stimulates the body's lymphatic system to function more efficiently, and that speeds up toxin disposal and healing.' Madeleine spoke directly, almost earnestly, and without what he was beginning to recognize as her self-protective veneer of amusement.

'I'll take your word for it. I hope you'll be around if I should ever need your ministrations. You must have been a godsend to Claire when she had that bad break.' He tossed it in casually, hoping Madeleine wouldn't read the stab of guilt he felt at this betrayal of their mutual trust.

'The collar-bone gave her hell. It's surprising how much trouble a silly thing like a clavicle can be.' She smiled easily at him.

Much as it went against his inclination, he let it slide. There were other sources of information, and pursuing it now wasn't worth the loss of Madeleine's confidence. 'I broke mine when I was a kid. Fell off a chair, of all things, but I don't remember it. My mum says I was a right little pain in the bum about it—wouldn't keep my sling on.'

They talked on, refilling their glasses as Madeleine opened a second bottle of wine, and he told her things about his childhood in Cheshire that he hadn't remembered in years. 'I was lucky,' he said at last. 'I had loving parents, a safe and stable environment filled with the love of learning for its own sake. I see so much—so many kids never have a chance. And I don't know if I could give a child what my parents gave me. This job's not conducive to family life...ask my ex-wife.' He tried on a grin and glanced at his watch. 'Bloody hell. Where did the time go?'

'Would you make the same choice again, between a relationship and your job?'

Pausing with his glass halfway to his mouth, he stared at her.

'There is someone, isn't there?' Madeleine asked, and her green eyes held him like a vice.

He put his glass down, the wine untasted. 'Was. I thought there was. But she changed her mind.'

'How do you feel about that?'

'You know,' he said with certainty.

'Say it anyway.'

He looked away. 'Pissed as hell. Betrayed.' His mouth had gone dry from the wine, and he rubbed a hand across it. 'It was so good—we were so good together. How could she slam the door in my face?' He shook his head and stood a bit unsteadily. 'I think I'd better go before I get maudlin on you. And I think I'm well over the limit. It's not gone closing time quite yet—hopefully Brian will take pity and put a poor copper up for the night.'

He raised the dregs of wine in his glass to her. 'You are a witch, Madeleine. You've bewitched me into crying on your shoulder, and I can't remember when I've inflicted that on anyone—and you're still as enigmatic as the bloody Cheshire Cat.'

Madeleine saw him to the door, and

just before closing it she reached up and touched his cheek. Using his name for the first time, she said, 'Duncan. Everything will sort itself out. Be patient.'

The light narrowed to a slit, disappearing with a click as the door shut, and Kincaid found himself alone in the dark.

Brian gave him a bed with good grace, and as Kincaid carried his bag up and undressed it came to him that he hadn't answered Madeleine's question. What if Gemma were to change her mind—would he make the same choice he'd made with Vic? Was he capable of putting anything before his job? Would he be willing to risk hurting her, and himself?

He fell quickly into the heavy but unrestful sleep brought about by the consumption of too much alcohol. His dreams were strange and disjointed, and when his pager started its strident beeping in the small hours of the morning, he woke with pounding heart and a mouth like sandpaper.

He fumbled for the pager's off switch, then squinted blearily at the LED readout. Swearing under his breath, he sat up and turned on the light. What on earth could Scotland Yard want with him at this time of the night? Any call concerning a breakthrough on the Gilbert case would have come from Guildford. And what had prompted him to drink so much? He was not ordinarily given to such excess. Madeleine, he thought with a wan smile, must have a wooden leg. He retrieved his jacket from the chair back and patted the pockets for his phone, then realized he must have left it in the car. *Bloody hell.*

In dressing-gown and slippers he made his way down the stairs to the phone in the alcove next to the bar. When the switchboard put him through to the duty sergeant at the Yard, he listened in growing dismay. When the sergeant had finished, Kincaid said, 'No, don't. I'll take care of it myself. Right.'

Hanging up, he stood for a moment numb with shock, then made an effort to pull himself together. He looked at his watch. If he drove like all hell was after him, he could make it to London by daylight.

Chapter Twelve

Kincaid pulled up in front of Gemma's garage flat at exactly seven o'clock. Red-eyed and stubble-chinned, he climbed stiffly out of the car, dreading what he had to do.

His light tapping brought Gemma to the door, blinking at him in sleepy confusion. 'What are you doing here? I thought you were in Surrey.' Peering at him a bit more closely, she added, 'You look absolutely dreadful, guv. No offence.' Yawning, she stood aside to let him in. She wore a tatty, candlewick dressing-gown in an unflattering maroon which made her tousled copper hair look orange by contrast.

'Toby's still asleep,' she said softly, with a glance in the direction of his room. 'I'll make us coffee, then you can tell me about it.'

'Gemma.' Kincaid reached out and held her shoulders as she started to turn away. 'I've got some very bad news. Jackie Temple's dead.'

He'd never thought to see that blank, stunned look on Gemma's face, as if she'd just been slapped with an open palm.

'What? Jackie can't be dead. I just saw her yes—'

'It must have happened just as she finished her beat last night. She'd checked in by radio about a quarter past ten. When she didn't log in after her shift and they couldn't raise her by radio, they sent a patrol out to look for her.'

'What...?' Her pupils had dilated until her eyes looked like black holes against the chalk of her skin. Through the thick, nubby fabric of the dressing-gown he felt her begin to tremble.

'She was shot. In the back of the head. I doubt she knew anything at all.'

'Oh, no.' At that Gemma's face crumpled and she covered it with her hands.

Kincaid drew her to him and held her, stroking her hair and murmuring endearments. She smelled faintly of sleep and talcum powder. 'Gemma, I'm so sorry.'

'But why?' she wailed into his shoulder. 'Why would anybody want to hurt Jackie?'

'I don't know, love. Susan May, her flatmate, asked that you be notified, but when the call came through to the Yard, old George happened to be on the desk and he rang me instead.'

'Susan?' Gemma pulled away from him and stepped back. 'You don't think... Surely it was just some yobbos doing a burglary... Oh, my God...' She fumbled behind her for a chair and sat down hard. 'It wasn't, was it? You don't think it had anything to do with—'

Toby padded out of his room, looking like a chubby yellow bunny in his pyjamas. 'Mummy, what's the matter?' he said sleepily, butting up against her.

Gemma gathered him into her lap and rubbed her face against his hair. 'Nothing,

311

sweetheart. Mummy just has to go to work early, after all.' She looked up at Kincaid. 'You will go with me to see Susan, won't you?'

'Of course.'

She nodded, then said, 'I'll tell you about...yesterday on the way.' Studying him for a moment, she added, 'They rang you in Surrey? This morning?'

'About half-past four.'

'Who's Susan, Mummy?' asked Toby. He squirmed around until he could straddle her knees, then made swooping motions with his arms. 'Look, Duncan, I'm an aeroplane.'

'A friend of a friend, lovey. Nobody you know.' Gemma's eyes filled with tears and she scrubbed at them, sniffing.

'I'll wait outside until you're ready,' said Kincaid, suddenly feeling that he had intruded long enough.

'No.' Gemma set Toby down and patted his bottom. 'I'll change in Toby's room. You can play aeroplane with him in the meantime. Then I'm going to get you both some breakfast.' With a critical glance at him and an attempted smile, she added, 'You look like you're running on fumes.'

A half-hour later, Gemma had showered and dressed, then lent Kincaid the use of her tiny bathroom to shave and put on a clean shirt. As he sat at the half-moon table finishing off buttered toast and hot coffee, he felt considerably more human. With Toby, dressed now in corduroy overalls and little trainers, playing happily at his feet, Kincaid wished that he might be there under different circumstances.

He accompanied Gemma across the garden and was briefly introduced to Hazel, then Gemma kissed Toby good-bye and they were on their way to Notting Hill.

As they crept through the rush-hour traffic, Gemma told him haltingly about Jackie's revelations of the previous day.

Kincaid whistled when she'd finished. Ogilvie bent? You think Gilbert found out somehow and Ogilvie decided to shut him up?'

'And Jackie.' Gemma's mouth was set in a straight, uncompromising line.

'Gemma, Jackie's death probably had nothing to do with this at all. These things happen, and they are usually utterly senseless. We both know that.'

'I don't like coincidences, and this is too much of a coincidence. We both know that, too.'

'I don't know anything more than I've told you. Don't you think we should stop in at Notting Hill and get the details before we talk to Susan May?'

Gemma didn't answer for a moment,

then she said, 'No. I'd like to see Susan first. That's the least I owe her.'

Glancing at her profile as he idled at traffic lights, he wished he could offer her some comfort. But despite his reassuring words, he didn't like this coincidence either.

He found a kerbside parking spot near the flat, and as they walked up to the door he saw Gemma pause and take a breath before ringing the bell. The door swung open so quickly that Kincaid thought the woman who answered must have been standing just inside it. 'Can I help you?' she said brusquely.

'I'm a friend of Jackie's, Gemma James. Susan asked to see me.' Gemma held out her hand and the woman took it, her face breaking into a smile.

'Of course. I'm Cecily Johnson, Susan's sister. I was just on my way out to the shops for her. Let me tell her you're here.'

The word that came to Kincaid's mind as they followed Cecily Johnson up the stairs was *handsome*. She was a tall woman, large-boned, with café-au-lait skin, fine dark eyes, and a wide smile. They waited on the landing for a moment while Cecily went in. Returning to them, she said, 'Go right in. I'll leave you to it.'

Susan May stood with her back to them,

314

staring out of the sitting-room window at the small balcony with its bright pots of pansies and geraniums. In silhouette, she looked a more slender, willowy version of her sister, and when she turned Kincaid saw that she had the same creamy skin and dark eyes, but she didn't quite manage a smile.

'Gemma, thanks for coming so quickly.'

Gemma took her outstretched hands and squeezed them. 'Susan, I'm so—'

'I know. Please don't say it. I haven't quite reached the point where I can deal with condolences yet. Sit down and let me get you some coffee.' As Gemma started to protest, she added, 'It helps if I have something to do with my hands.'

After Gemma introduced Kincaid, Susan went into the kitchen and returned a moment later with a tray. She made inconsequential small talk while she poured, then sat gazing into her cup.

'I still can't believe it,' she said. 'I keep expecting her to walk in the door and say something silly, like "It was all a big joke, Suz, ha-ha." She liked practical jokes.' Putting down her cup, Susan stood up and began pacing, twisting her hands together. 'She left her dressing-gown on the floor by her bed again. I was always fussing at her to pick things up, and now it doesn't matter. Why did I ever think it did? Can you tell me that?' She stopped as they had first seen her, her back to them, facing the terrace. 'They've given me indefinite "compassionate" leave from work. To do what? Coming home to this empty flat in the evenings will be bad enough; the thought of spending days here alone is unbearable.'

'What about your sister?' asked Gemma. 'Can she stay with you for a bit?'

Susan nodded. 'She's packed her kids off to Grandma for a few days. She'll help me go through...Jackie's things. She... Jackie, I mean...hadn't any family, so there's no one else to see to things...' Susan stopped, and for a moment Kincaid thought she would lose control, but she managed to go on. 'She didn't want to be cremated. She actually worried about it, and I used to laugh at her. Do you suppose she knew... I'll have to try to find a cemetery that will take her. Then I'm going back to work—I don't care how callous anyone thinks me.'

She turned around and faced them. 'Jackie talked about you a good bit in the last few days, Gemma. It meant a lot to her to see you again. I know there was something she was anxious to talk to you about, but I don't know what it was—only that I heard her mumble something about "bad apple where you'd least expect it"'

'I saw her yesterday. Before her shift. She told me—'

'You saw her? How did she—what did she—' Susan swallowed and tried again. 'She didn't happen to say anything about me, did she?'

Kincaid saw Gemma hesitate, then quickly collect herself. 'She talked about your promotion. She was really proud of you.'

The front door opened and Cecily came in with a shopping bag full of purchases. Twisting her hands together again, Susan smiled at her sister, then said to Gemma, 'You will let me know, won't you, if you find out...anything?'

'We'll be in touch.' Gemma stood up and gave her a quick hug. Cecily let them out and they descended the stairs in silence.

By the time they reached the street, tears were streaming down Gemma's face. 'It's not bloody fair,' she said furiously as she got into the car. 'Susan should have seen her last, not me.' She slammed the door so hard the car shook. 'It's not bloody fair. Jackie shouldn't be dead—and if it's because of me, I'll never forgive myself.'

'We're treading on very delicate ground here,' Kincaid said as he pulled into the Notting Hill Police Station car park. 'We have absolutely no grounds for pursuing inquiries concerning the involvement of a senior Met officer, other than an unsubstantiated rumour. I'd suggest that we begin with discretion.' He pulled the car into an empty space, then thought for a moment, drumming his fingers on the steering wheel. 'I think we'll have to disclose Jackie's interest in the Gilbert case in order to justify our poking our noses into her murder, but I don't know that we need go any further at this point.'

Gemma nodded, then fished a tissue from her bag and blew her nose.

'We could just say that Jackie told you she'd heard something dodgy about Gilbert, but that you don't know what it was. Then in the meantime, let's see if we can trace Ogilvie's movements last night and the night of Gilbert's murder, but in a roundabout way. That'll be enough to get the wind up him, if he's dirty.'

'Chat up his secretary, why don't you?' Gemma suggested. 'She has an eye for a pretty face.'

Kincaid glanced at her, wondering if the comment was a dig or an attempt at banter, but she was examining her fingernails with great concentration. 'Who was the sergeant that Jackie said stonewalled her?' he asked.

'Talley. I remember him from my days here.'

'I think we might want to have a word with him, too.' Watching her, Kincaid wished again he could find something to say, some comfort he might offer without sounding condescending, but no words seemed adequate. He resisted the urge to touch her shoulder, her cheek. 'Are you ready?'

She nodded. 'As I'll ever be.'

'This is a stroke of luck,' Kincaid murmured to Gemma as they were shown into Superintendent Mark Lamb's office. He and Lamb had met on their first development course, but it had been several years since they had bumped into each other.

'Duncan, old chap.' Lamb came around his desk, beaming, and pumped Kincaid's hand. 'The Yard's wonder boy in the flesh. Do have a seat.'

Kincaid introduced Gemma with a small, unworthy spark of satisfaction, for although he and Lamb were the same age, Lamb was decidedly losing his hair and gaining a paunch.

When they had spent a few minutes chatting about mutual acquaintances, Kincaid explained their interest in Jackie Temple.

Lamb sobered immediately. 'You never think something like that will happen at your station. Brixton, maybe, but not here. Jackie Temple was one of my best officers—level-headed and well liked by the public as well as her fellow officers. You know how it is—sometimes coppers starting out have a lorry load of good intentions and not a particle of common sense, but Jackie had both from the very beginning.'

Now Kincaid noticed the hollows under his old friend's eyes, and the slept-in state of his jacket. He had probably been up all night. 'Was there any indication of a burglary in progress?'

Lamb shook his head. 'Sweet eff-all. Nor has forensics turned up anything useful so far.' Glancing at his watch, he added, 'We should be getting the autopsy report any time now, but I'll guarantee you right now that from the powder burns on the scalp and the size of the entrance wound, she was shot at point-blank range. She never had a chance.'

Kincaid saw Gemma's fists clench convulsively in her lap. 'So what do you make of it, Mark?' he asked.

Lamb straightened a picture frame on his cluttered desk-top. Wife and kids, thought Kincaid, but he could only see the back of the frame. 'This is a tough patch,'

320

Lamb said slowly, 'with its gentrified neighbourhoods and its ethnic population, but we try to keep it clean.' He looked up and met Kincaid's eyes. 'Much as I hate to admit it about my own territory, this reeks of a gangstyle execution.'

With Lamb's permission, they found Sergeant Randall Talley having a tea break in the canteen. 'That's him,' said Gemma, nodding in the direction of a small, grizzled man in his fifties sitting alone at a table.

When they reached him, Gemma held out her hand and introduced herself, adding, 'Do you remember me, Sergeant Talley?'

Studiously avoiding her hand, Talley glanced at her, then looked away. His eyes were a light, faded blue. 'Oh, aye. And what if I do?'

Seeing Gemma's surprise and confusion, Kincaid pulled out a chair for her and one for himself. Talley was obviously not the sort of man who would allow himself to be questioned by a former subordinate, but perhaps rank would induce a bit more co-operation. 'Mind if we sit down, Sergeant?'

'You can do as you like.' He finished his tea in a deliberately long swallow and pushed his chair back from the table.

'Break's over for me.'

'We'd like to ask you a few questions, Sergeant. We've cleared it with your guv'nor. You were one of the last people to talk with Jackie Temple, and we thought she might have said something that would give us a lead to her murder.'

'She was shot down in the street by a bunch of effing thugs! How the hell should I know anything about that?' He glared at them with bulldog aggressiveness, but there were tears in his eyes. 'And you have no bloody jurisdiction over Jackie Temple's murder.'

'But we do have jurisdiction over Alastair Gilbert's,' Kincaid said. 'And Jackie had been asking questions about Alastair Gilbert. She told the sergeant here, in fact, that you very nearly boxed her ears for it.'

'Why shouldn't I? She had no business digging for dirt on a senior officer, dishonouring his memory. Gilbert was a good man.'

Kincaid raised an eyebrow. 'Ah, a supporter in a legion of detractors. That's a nice surprise. And what do you think about Detective Chief Inspector David Ogilvie, Sergeant?'

The whites of Talley's eyes showed. 'I've never heard a word said against DCI Ogilvie, not that I'd repeat it if I had.' He pushed his chair back and stood up. 'Now, I have better things to do with my time than spread scurrilous gossip, even if you do not. Good day to you.' He turned smartly and left them, threading his way through the scattered tables until he reached the door. Watching his rolling gait from behind, Kincaid wondered if Talley had spent his formative years in a less landlocked locale.

'Well, well,' Kincaid said to Gemma as they looked at each other wide-eyed. 'If you ask me, I'd say the man's bloody terrified.'

'You don't suppose...' Gemma said slowly. 'The bad apple Jackie mentioned... you don't suppose it could have been Sergeant Talley?'

The placard on Ogilvie's secretary's desk read HELENE VANDEMEER. Gemma had got it right, for a smile like a beacon lit up Mrs Vandemeer's middle-aged and unassuming face when Kincaid introduced himself.

Sounding genuinely regretful, she said, 'Oh, I'm so sorry, the chief inspector's away just now,' when Kincaid asked to see Ogilvie. 'He left on Friday to teach a training seminar in the Midlands, and he won't be back until...' she flipped a page, and then another, on her calendar

'...Wednesday. He'll be so sorry to have missed you.'

Absolutely heartbroken, thought Kincaid as he smiled back at her. As Gemma took the small cubicle's only chair, he propped one hip on the corner of Mrs Vandemeer's pristine desk. She would have been Gilbert's secretary as well, he remembered, wondering if she had been hired for her habits, or if she had acquired them through association. 'Do you have the number where he might be reached?' he asked. Then he added confidentially, 'It's about Commander Gilbert. You see, we hadn't really checked on what the commander might have done between the time he left the office that day and the time he arrived home. We thought DCI Ogilvie might be able to throw some light on the matter.'

'Oh, dear. I'm afraid he won't be much help to you, then. He had a meeting with a local citizens' group after lunch that day, and it must have dragged on a bit, because he never made it back to his office. And the commander...' Helene Vandemeer took off her glasses and pinched the bridge of her nose, as if it suddenly hurt. 'The commander left here on the dot of five, just like always. He put his head round my door and said, "Cheerio, Helene. See you tomorrow."' She looked up at Kincaid, and he saw that her unmasked eyes were a startling, true violet. 'Do you think I might have been the last person to speak to him?'

'That's difficult to say,' Kincaid temporized. 'You're sure the commander didn't say anything about what he meant to do that afternoon or anything else unusual?'

Looking as if she could hardly bear to disappoint him, Helene shook her head. 'I wish I could help you, but I can't think of a thing.'

'You've been terrific,' he said warmly, avoiding Gemma's derisive glance. 'If you could just give us that phone number...' As she wrote, he added nonchalantly, 'That citizens' meeting DCI Ogilvie had that afternoon, you don't happen to remember what the group was called?'

'Let me think.' Glasses firmly in place again, Helene frowned, then gave him a brilliant smile. 'I've got it. The Notting Hill Association for Noise Reduction. NHANR. They're petitioning for traffic reduction on certain streets.'

Taking the phone number she'd jotted down for him, he said, 'Thanks, love,' and left the room on Gemma's heels.

When they were barely out of the door, Gemma whispered, 'You might as well hand out doggie treats while you're at it.'

The suspicion of a dimple intimated that

she was taking the mickey, so he answered in mock defence. 'Hey, it was your idea. And it got results, didn't it?'

He pulled out his cell phone as he left the building and began to dial, and only when he reached the pavement did he realize that Gemma was no longer by his side. Looking back, he saw her standing just at the top of the steps, looking stricken. 'Gemma,' he began, but just then the Yard answered, and by the time he'd finished his call, she had caught him up.

'What's next, guv?' she asked, determinedly businesslike.

After a moment's hesitation, he said, 'Let's get a bite of lunch. Then I'd like to take a look at something, just to satisfy my curiosity.'

They stood at the top of a tiny, cobbled mews, not far from Notting Hill Police Station. Kincaid had finagled David Ogilvie's address from a mate at the Yard. On either side the houses stretched away like chocolate-box confections—peach and yellow, terracotta and pale sherbet green. Some had shiny black wrought-iron railings, others windowboxes overflowing with bright flowers, and like Elgin Crescent, every house sported a burglar alarm and a baby satellite dish.

Kincaid whistled softly. 'You can almost smell the money. Which one is Number Ten?'

Walking on a bit, Gemma said, 'Here.' It was a deeper shade of yellow, with glossy black trim.

Peering through a gap in the ground-floor curtains, Kincaid caught a glimpse of a sleek contemporary sitting room, and beyond it a garden. He stood back and let Gemma have a look. 'I certainly couldn't have managed this on a chief inspector's pay. Somehow I doubt if our friend David invites the lads over for a beer after work—what do you think?'

Gemma looked up at him. 'I'd say it's time we called in C&D.'

'My sentiments exactly.'

Once back at the Yard, they settled into Kincaid's office for an afternoon of tedious telephoning. First Kincaid checked in with Guildford CID, and finding Deveney still out on the burglary case, spoke to Will Darling. 'Go back over everything with a fine-tooth comb, Will. We're missing something—I can feel it—and it's probably as obvious as the nose on your face. The lad in charge of effects made a sloppy call on the commander's diary—let's make sure that was the only instance.'

A call to the chairman of the NHANR—

'We call it *Nanner*' the man had cheerfully informed him—confirmed that David Ogilvie had indeed had an appointment with their group after lunch on the day of the commander's death but revealed that Ogilvie had only stayed half an hour.

Kincaid raised an eyebrow as he hung up the phone. 'So what did he do for the rest of the afternoon? Tell me that,' he demanded as much to himself as to Gemma.

Next, Gemma rang the Midlands training centre and managed to elicit the fact that Ogilvie had not finished his lecture until almost a quarter to ten the previous night. She shook her head as she hung up and relayed the information to Kincaid.

'He'd have had to fly to make it back to London in time to shoot Jackie,' said Kincaid, 'and while he may live above his means, I haven't seen any evidence of superhuman powers.' He sighed. 'Still, that doesn't rule out the possibility that he might have hired someone to do it. If he's bent, he'll have the connections.' He looked at Gemma sitting the other side of the desk, her face lit by the watery, late-afternoon sunlight slanting through the blinds. 'Are we chasing our tails, Gemma? If Gilbert found Ogilvie out and threatened to expose him, why the hell would Ogilvie bash his head in in his own kitchen, rather than arranging something much less risky?'

'Should we be back in Surrey grilling Brian Genovase like the Spanish Inquisition? But we've no hard evidence, and I still just can't quite see Brian for it.'

'There's Jackie,' she said flatly.

He rubbed his fingers over his cheekbones, stretching the tired muscles around his eyes. 'I haven't forgotten Jackie, love. Let's take this whole Ogilvie mess to the chief and let him contact Complaints and Discipline. And I don't think we'd be amiss in mentioning Sergeant Talley, while we're at it.'

Chief Superintendent Denis Childs having agreed that the Ogilvie matter was best turned over to C&D, Kincaid followed Gemma back to his office with a feeling of relief. 'Let them put the squeeze on Ogilvie, up the pressure a bit. Then we'll ask him where he was the afternoon Gilbert died.' He unfastened his collar button. 'But for now let's call it a day.'

Gemma had hung her bag on the coat stand, and it seemed to him that she stood now a little aimlessly, as if she didn't quite want to go. 'We could go down the pub for a drink, if you like,' he said, trying to banish entreaty from his voice.

She hesitated and his hopes rose, but

after a moment she said, 'I suppose I'd better not. I've spent little enough time with Toby lately as it is. It's just that I'm not sure I want to be—'

The phone rang, startling them both. Kincaid jerked the handset out of the cradle, held it to his ear. 'Kincaid.'

Will Darling's voice came over the line. 'You were right, guv, but I don't know what it means. There was a number pencilled on the back of a dry-cleaning ticket crumpled up in Gilbert's pocket. I kept looking at it, thinking the sequence was wrong for a phone number. Then, bingo, the old light-bulb went on, and I thought, *It's a bloody bank account.* I checked it against the Gilberts' joint account at Lloyds—no match. Took me all afternoon, but I found the branch that uses that number sequence in Dorking, and I ran a bit of a bluff. Told them I was Darling's Jewellery in Guildford, and I had a cheque in my hand for the sum of a thousand pounds and wanted to verify sufficient funds in the account to cover it. Name of Gilbert, account number so-and-so—'

'And?' Kincaid hurried him.

'They said no problem—*Mrs* Gilbert's account contained sufficient funds to cover the cheque.'

330

Chapter Thirteen

When Gemma slipped quietly into Kincaid's office the following morning, he was sitting exactly as she'd left him the night before—one elbow on the desk and his fingers thrust through his hair, staring down at a pile of reports. With his tie loosened and his shirt suspiciously rumpled, he looked even more exhausted than he had yesterday.

'You did go home, didn't you?' As she hung her coat on the stand, Gemma felt a stab of guilt thinking of the few hours she'd managed away from the Yard. But even though she'd got back to her flat, she'd tossed and turned, her sleep interrupted by dreams of Jackie holding a fair-haired child. Finally she had risen and knelt beside Toby's cot, resting her palm on the flat of his back so that she could feel the gentle rise and fall of his breathing. By the time the oblong of the garden window began to pale, her legs had long gone numb.

Kincaid looked up and smiled. 'Scout's honour. Couldn't seem to sleep, though, so I came back in the small hours.'

He stretched, cracking his knuckles, and pushed the papers away. 'I'm beginning to feel like a bloody ping-pong ball with this case. London-Surrey, Surrey-London.' He swivelled his head back and forth as he spoke. 'We find out yesterday that there's some funny business going on with the Gilberts, then first thing this morning a bloke from C&D calls, says when they tried to contact David Ogilvie this morning, they discovered he's disappeared from his training course. Seems he was supposed to teach a final workshop today and he just didn't show up. His hotel room's been cleaned out, too.'

Gemma sank into a chair and whistled softly. 'Maybe he left a message and it got lost somehow. You know, family emergency or something.'

'Playing the devil's advocate?' Kincaid sat up a bit straighter.

'It is possible,' Gemma countered.

'But highly unlikely.'

Conceding, Gemma nodded. 'So where is he, and what are C&D doing about it?'

'Tracing primary contacts, making the most obvious enquiries. They don't feel they have enough on him to pull out all the stops yet. What I'd like to know is what precipitated such a flight. If he arranged Jackie's death, why wait almost two days before panicking?'

'Why panic at all?' Gemma traced a circle in the dust on Kincaid's desk, then drew another. 'Unless we stirred the mud more than we intended yesterday. But in that case, who tipped him off?' She connected the circles with a wavy line, then wiped the smudge from her fingertip.

'Could be as simple as his secretary, nice Mrs What's-her-name, telling him we were enquiring about his movements on the night Gilbert died, but I'd have expected a cooler response from an experienced copper like Ogilvie—a good bluff at the very least.'

Gemma nodded. 'Cool personified, is Ogilvie. But what about—'

'Talley? The converse, I should think. C&D will begin on him today, and their wheels grind very fine indeed. But in the meantime, there's not much we can do that end.' Kincaid yawned.

'What's next then, guv?' asked Gemma.

'You can make us some coffee, there's a good girl,' Kincaid said, grinning at her.

It was an old running gag between them, and this morning Gemma didn't feel inclined to disappoint him. 'You can make your own bloody coffee, sir,' she answered, not quite managing a scowl. 'I'll make some for myself, though, and if you're very nice to me I might just

333

spare you a cup.' Rising from the chair, she added, 'But seriously—'

'Back to Surrey, I think. Do you want to go with Will to interview the bank manager in Dorking?'

He phrased it as a request, rather than an order, and the gesture touched her more than she expected. 'Okay.' She perched on the arm of her chair. 'You don't want to ask Claire about it first? Could be there's a perfectly simple explanation.'

Kincaid shook his head as he rubbed at the tension lines between his eyes. 'No.' He dropped his hand, looking up at Gemma with no trace of the mischief he'd displayed a moment earlier. 'Claire's not telling us the whole story, Gemma. I'm sure of it, and I don't like it one bit. I think it's time I had another little talk with Dr Gabriella Wilson.'

After a good look at her boss in the light of the Yard car park, Gemma insisted on driving the Rover they'd requisitioned from the pool. Kincaid was asleep before they'd crossed Westminster Bridge, and nothing disturbed him as they inched their way south through the clamour of London traffic. Glancing at him as she waited at another interminable traffic light, Gemma thought of the last time she'd watched him sleep, defenceless as a child, and for the first time doubt assailed her. Should she have listened, at least, to what he had to say?

Kincaid stirred and opened his eyes for a moment, as if an awareness of her regard had reached him when the sound of honking horns and squealing brakes could not.

Gemma gripped the wheel and concentrated on her driving.

'Fancy a bite of lunch first?' asked Will Darling as he whipped the car into a space in the Dorking car park, beating another eager motorist to it.

Gemma and Kincaid had swapped cars as soon as they arrived at Guildford Police Station, Gemma going with Will and Nick Deveney with Kincaid in the pool Rover.

'It's not gone twelve yet.' Gemma gave the frustrated driver an apologetic smile as she got out and joined Will on the pavement.

'Tell that to my stomach.' Will took her elbow, steering her towards the High Street. 'I know a good pub.'

'Somehow that doesn't surprise me. But no fish and chips,' Gemma admonished, remembering the last lunch they'd shared. As they walked along the busy street, bumping shoulders with the crush of lunchtime shoppers, she realized she was hungry. She couldn't remember what she'd eaten since hearing the news about Jackie yesterday morning, but she supposed she must have gone through the motions.

It was indeed a nice pub, and a favourite with the locals, as the early crowd demonstrated. When they'd placed their meal orders at the bar and settled into a corner table with their drinks, Will said, 'You know the first rule of good policing: *Eat first.* You never know when you might have another chance.'

'You've certainly taken it to heart.'

'Could be the army had something to do with that.' Will stared out of the window as he sipped the foam from his pint. 'Living on the edge tends to make priorities easier to recognize.'

'On the edge?' Gemma repeated, puzzled.

'I served in Northern Ireland for two years.'

The barmaid brought their food—jacket potatoes with prawn mayonnaise for Gemma, chicken basket for Will. As Gemma mixed the topping into her potato, she glanced up at Will through the rising steam. She imagined him in fatigues and boots, still looking like a red-cheeked Surrey farm boy.

'When I went over I was just as ambitious as you,' continued Will when he'd swallowed a mouthful of chicken.

'Don't bother arguing,' he added with a grin. 'Women don't reach your rank in the Met otherwise. You want to make DCI, don't you, or even superintendent?' He waved a chip at her for emphasis. 'So did I, only I had my sights set on a county force, preferably this one.'

Gemma paused with her fork half-way to her mouth. 'I don't understand, Will. Surely it's not too late. You're only...what?' Remembering what he'd said about his birthday, she did the maths in her head. 'Thirty-four? And you're a good cop—I don't have to tell you that.'

'Thanks all the same.' Wiping his fingers with his napkin, Will smiled at her. 'And I imagine I'll eventually rise up a rank or two by the sheer force of attrition above me. The thing is, it doesn't really matter to me any more. Two of my best mates were working routine border checks one night.' He put his hand on his pint but didn't lift it. 'Unfortunately, the last lorry they stopped happened to be carrying a bomb.' His voice level, only the stillness of his hand on the glass betrayed him.

'Oh no,' Gemma breathed.

Will shrugged. 'We'd all been grousing about our posting. The usual complaints— boredom, lousy food, shortage of girls.' A hint of a dimple appeared in his cheek. 'We were going to have such great adventures when we got out. My mum used to tell me that it was the journey that counted, not arriving at the station. It's a well-worn platitude, I know, but that day I saw the truth of it.'

Gemma put her fork down beside her half-eaten potato. 'They told you about Jackie, didn't they?'

'Yeah.' Will reached across the table and touched her hand. 'I'm sorry, Gemma.'

Finding she couldn't meet the frank sympathy in his eyes, she picked up her fork again and pushed at her food. She thought of Jackie's stubborn refusal to leave her beat, because she had loved what she called 'everyday policing', the regular contact with the people for whom she was responsible. 'Jackie would have liked you, Will,' Gemma said. Watching him as he returned his attention to his lunch, she wondered if he, too, had felt somehow responsible for his friends' deaths.

The nameplate on the bank manager's desk read AUGUSTUS COKES, and he so befitted the image it conjured up that Gemma wondered if names left an inescapable imprint, like an extra chromosome. A small man with a round, bespectacled face and thinning hair, he rose to greet them with an expression of puzzled concern.

338

'This is most unusual,' he said, when they had introduced themselves. 'I don't know how I can help you, but fire away.'

Gemma settled herself a bit more comfortably in the hard chair and brushed at the lapel of her jacket. Taking her cue from Will's slight nod, she began, 'I'm afraid it's a bit delicate, Mr Cokes. You see, it concerns a murder investigation. You will have read about the death of commander Alastair Gilbert in the papers, I'm sure.' Watching Cokes's full, pink lips assume a fishlike gape, Gemma pressed on. 'It's come to our attention that the commander's wife, Claire Gilbert, kept an account here, and we believe there may be some...irregularities. We'd like to—'

'Well, I never. A commander's wife—a common criminal. Who'd have thought it?' Cokes shook his head with relish, lips pursed now in a tut-tut pout. 'And such a well-bred woman, too.'

Will answered Gemma's querying glance with a look of surprised incomprehension.

'Whatever are you talking about, Mr Cokes?' asked Gemma. 'We haven't suggested that Mrs Gilbert has done anything criminal. We'd just like to clear up some questions about Gilbert himself.'

'But the other policeman—' Cokes looked from Gemma to Will. 'The one who came in last week.'

'What other policeman?' Will asked patiently.

'You people really should learn to co-ordinate your efforts a bit better,' Cokes said a little smugly, as if he were beginning to enjoy their discomfort. 'No wonder they have all those exposés on the telly.'

'I think we should start from the beginning, Mr Cokes.' Will pulled out his wallet and extracted the photo he and Gemma had shown around with so little success at the Friary. 'I take it that you met Mrs Gilbert personally?'

'When she opened her account. I often handle new accounts—it keeps my hand in, and I like to know a bit about the customers.' Cokes took the photo from Will and examined it for a moment before handing it back. 'Oh, yes, that's Mrs Gilbert, all right. She's quite unmistakable. Of course, I did wonder when she asked that her statements be sent to her at work.'

'At work?' repeated Gemma. 'Did she say why?'

'I'd never have asked—we respect our clients' privacy—but she told me quite confidentially that she meant to save up enough money to surprise her husband with a holiday.' The echo of Claire Gilbert's charm still resonated in the man's voice and faintly wistful expression. 'You can imagine how surprised I was when the first policeman came inquiring about her. And even then I'd no idea her husband was a policeman.'

Will sat forward, and the standard-issue visitor's chair creaked dangerously. 'Tell us about this other policeman, Mr Cokes. When did he come to see you, and what did he want with Claire Gilbert?'

Cokes made a little humming noise as he squinted at his desk calendar. 'We'd had our regional branch meeting on the Tuesday last week, and I think it was the day after. Wednesday, it would have been, just before closing. He requested a personal interview with me, but once we were alone in my office he showed me his ID and said he was investigating something very hush-hush.' Leaning forward, Cokes lowered his voice. 'A cheque fraud ring. He said they hadn't any hard evidence to connect our customer, but a quick look at her file would probably clear the matter up. Of course, I told him that much as I wished to assist the police in any way, I was also under an obligation not to divulge details of a customer's account.' Cokes gave a sniff of disapproval.

'So you're telling us that this policeman did *not* see Claire Gilbert's file?' Will asked.

Cokes cleared his throat and slid the

paperweight on his desk over a fraction of an inch. 'Well, I can't be absolutely certain...' he said, refusing to meet their eyes. 'I was called out of my office for a few moments, a little problem that needed my immediate attention...'

'Don't tell me,' said Gemma. 'You just happened to leave Claire Gilbert's file on your desk. How tactful of you.'

'Well, I...' Cokes's upper lip glistened with perspiration. 'It seemed the best solution at the time.'

'I'm sure.' Gemma smiled at Cokes, thinking that she doubted Claire Gilbert would have seen his solution in quite the same light. 'This policeman, Mr Cokes. What was his name?'

Cokes cleared his throat again. 'I don't remember. I only saw the ID for a moment, and I was so startled that it quite flew out of my head.'

'What Force did he say he was with?'

Cokes shook his head. 'I couldn't say. I'm sorry.'

Persisting, Gemma said, 'Then tell us what he looked like, Mr Cokes. Surely you can remember that?'

'Thin and dark.' Moistening his pink lips, Cokes added, 'There was something a bit predatory about him.'

Kincaid filled Deveney in as they drove

towards Holmbury St Mary. The morning overcast had lifted to a high haze that muted the landscape and burned his tired eyes as he squinted at the road. 'Claire Gilbert's had two broken bones in the last year or so, and perhaps other injuries as well. The wrist and the collarbone just happen to be the ones I heard about in casual conversation. It's enough to raise the possibility of spousal abuse.'

'Are you telling me that you think Commander Gilbert *beat* his wife?'

Kincaid glanced at Deveney. 'Don't look so shocked, Nick. It happens all the time.'

Deveney shook his head. 'I know. But I wouldn't have thought—'

'You think Gilbert's uniform and position gave him some sort of automatic immunity?'

'I think if you mean to get anything out of Doc Wilson, you'll get short shrift,' Deveney countered. 'But if you're right, it gives Brian Genovase a damned good reason to want to bash Gilbert's head in. Unfortunately, we still haven't found a shred of physical evidence to connect him to the scene.

'The records of the on-line service confirm what Geoff told us, by the way, and our interviews with the other customers in the pub that night confirm Brian's account of his movements. So that leaves us with a less-than-ten-minute window when either Brian or Geoff could have popped across the lane and done the dirty.'

Kincaid changed down as they entered the village. 'That leaves the Ogilvie end. I'll be damned if I know how he fits into it, but I'm sure he does.' He grinned at Deveney. 'Maybe I should take lessons from Madeleine Wade.'

'You seem destined to catch me in the middle of my lunch,' Doc Wilson said when she opened the door. 'Oh well, can't be helped, I suppose,' she added resignedly as she stepped back and Kincaid and Deveney crowded into the hall with its welter of gum boots, dog leads, and walking sticks.

On reaching the kitchen Kincaid and Deveney once again went through the ritual of clearing a place to sit while the doctor wasted no time getting back to her lunch.

'Leftover beef from Sunday's joint,' she waved her fork at her plate when they were settled opposite her, 'with horse-radish. Clears the sinuses. Paul's gone to London for the day, by the way, if it was him you were wanting. Took Bess with him for the run.'

Kincaid wasn't fooled by her inconsequential chatter—the glance she'd given

344

him had been sharp as a needle. 'No, it was you we wanted a word with, Doctor. It's about Claire Gilbert. I understand that she's had several broken bones recently. Weren't you concerned about this sudden tendency towards accidents?'

The doctor very deliberately finished her roast beef and pushed her plate aside before answering. 'Really, Superintendent, you'll have to ask Claire about her medical history, not me.'

'We could get a warrant,' Kincaid said, 'and force disclosure, but I'd hate to have to resort to that. Very unpleasant for everyone concerned.'

'I don't like being bullied, Mr Kincaid, no matter how charmingly it's couched. You must do whatever you think necessary, but I'll not willingly divulge anything confidential about my patient.' The doctor folded her arms across her nondescript jumper, her mouth clamped in a stubborn line.

Kincaid met her look. 'Look, Doctor, let's not beat about the bush. We have very good reason to think that Claire Gilbert was being beaten by her husband, and I believe that you came to the same conclusion. That day Geoff overheard you quarrelling with Gilbert—it was about Claire, wasn't it? Did you confront him with your suspicions? He'd not have taken kindly to your interfering in his business.'

'I'll give you that Alastair Gilbert could be difficult,' she said, her mouth still set. 'But I'll not discuss Claire with you.'

'Alastair Gilbert was more than difficult the last few weeks of his life. He'd started to behave in uncharacteristic ways, and I think he had become so consumed by jealousy that he was no longer rational. Gilbert used his control, his appearance of remaining above emotion, as a method of dominance. The fact that he allowed himself to be drawn into an out-and-out row with you is an indication of how far he'd slipped. Surely you must realize that it's vital we know the truth about what happened that day.'

'So that you can put pressure on Claire?'

'We are talking about a murder, Doctor, and I have a duty to make whatever enquiries I think can help bring the matter to a conclusion. I'll have to question Claire in any case, and I'd prefer to do it with the benefit of your advice. I'm sure I need not remind you that you have an obligation of care as well as one of confidentiality.'

The doctor met his eyes for a long moment, then her mouth relaxed and her shoulders slumped a bit. 'Claire is very vulnerable right now, Mr Kincaid. If you go stomping about making damaging allegations about her husband it could cause her serious harm.'

'Then help me out. Deny that you believe Claire Gilbert was physically injured at any time by her husband, and I'll leave it alone.'

The silence stretched until Kincaid could hear his own breathing and the rasp of tweed against tweed as Deveney shifted in the chair beside him. He waited, thinking of the time he'd stared down a bulldog as a child, until the doctor looked away. Still she didn't speak.

Kincaid stood up. 'Thank you, Doctor. You've been most helpful. We'll see ourselves out.'

'I have to hand it to you,' Deveney said when they reached the car, 'that was rather cleverly done.'

Grimacing, Kincaid said, 'Doesn't make me feel any better about it. But the good doctor is as perceptive as she is honest, and if she was worried enough about Claire to confront Gilbert directly, you can be sure she had good cause.'

'So you got the confirmation you wanted.' Deveney settled into the passenger seat.

'Confirmation of a suspicion only, not proof.'

'Still,' Deveney said as Kincaid turned the key in the Rover's ignition, 'the suspicion's enough to put Claire Gilbert squarely in the frame.'

Chapter Fourteen

Gemma asked Will to drop her off in Holmbury St Mary on his way back to the station, as Kincaid had told her he'd meet her in the village. It was almost two o'clock, and the sun had seared through the morning's haze. She stood on the edge of the green for a moment after Will drove away, turning her face to the light until stars blossomed behind her closed eyelids. Mid-November was seldom so generous, and one couldn't expect it to last. This was a day for sailing model boats on the Serpentine, a day for storing memories of warmth to last through the long winter days ahead.

She heard the whir of wheels on pavement, and, opening her eyes, she found that a jaunty little red Vauxhall had pulled up beside her. The woman driving rolled down her window and leaned out. 'You looked a bit lost. Can I help you?' She had a slightly husky, melodious voice, a bob of platinum hair, and the largest beak of a nose Gemma had ever seen.

Embarrassed at being caught standing about daydreaming like an idiot, Gemma stammered, 'I'm not—I mean, I'm quite all right, thank you. Just waiting for someone.'

The woman studied her until Gemma looked away from her penetrating gaze. 'You must be the elusive Sergeant James. I've heard about you from Geoff, among others. I'm Madeleine Wade.' She put her hand out of the window and Gemma grasped fingers as strong as her own. 'If you're looking for your superintendent, I haven't seen him lately. Cheerio.' With a wave Madeleine put the car into gear and pulled away, leaving Gemma gaping after her.

She closed her mouth with a snap, wondering why she felt as if she'd just been unzipped and put back together again. And had she heard an emphasis on the *your* before *superintendent,* or was she imagining things? With a shrug she crossed the road and went round to the pub car park, but there was no sign of the Rover.

Slowly, she walked into the lane and stared at the Gilberts' house. Would she be stealing a march on Kincaid if she took the opportunity to have a word with Claire Gilbert? She felt she and Claire had established a rapport of sorts and that perhaps she had a better chance of winning Claire's confidence alone.

Letting herself in through the gate, she bypassed the dark, austere front door that seemed to her to symbolize Alastair Gilbert's presence in the house, and took the path to the back garden.

The sight that greeted her might have graced a painter's canvas. A white wrought-iron chair had been pulled out into a sunny patch on the green square of lawn. In it sat Claire, wearing a high-necked Victorian blouse and skirt like a drift of wild flowers. Lucy sat on the ground beside her, head against her mother's knee. Lewis gambolled about with a tennis ball in his mouth, which he promptly dropped in his eagerness to greet Gemma.

'Sergeant,' said Claire as Gemma crossed the lawn, 'get another chair and join us. It's positively indecent, isn't it, for November?' She turned a palm up to the flawless azure sky. 'Have some lemonade. It's the real thing, not the fizzy stuff from a bottle. Lucy made it herself.'

'I'll just get you a glass,' said Lucy with a smile, and pushed herself up with graceful ease. 'No, Lewis,' she scolded as she pulled over a chair for Gemma. 'She doesn't want to play with you just now, silly beast.' The dog cocked his head and panted, the pink of his lolling tongue bright against his dark muzzle.

'I feel an absolute layabout,' said Gemma, but she sank into the chair gratefully.

Claire closed her eyes. 'Sometimes it's the best option, and we don't take it often enough.'

'Everyone seems to be telling me that today. Is there a conspiracy?'

Claire laughed. 'Did you grow up having "the devil finds work for idle hands" drummed into you, too? Funny how hard it is to shake those things off.'

Lucy returned with a glass of lemonade for Gemma and resumed her place beside her mother's chair. 'Shake what things off?' she asked, looking up at them.

'Things we learned at our mothers' knees,' Claire answered lightly, running a hand through her daughter's hair. 'How to listen, how to please, how to do what's expected of us. Isn't that right, Sergeant?' She gave Gemma a quizzical glance. 'I can't keep calling you "Sergeant"—it's Gemma, isn't it?'

Gemma nodded, thinking of her mother's outspoken independence (bloody-mindedness, her dad had been known to call it). Yet even with that influence, Gemma had tiptoed around Rob's every whim as if he were royalty. The memory made her wince.

351

Where did such behaviour come from, and how did one guard against it?

'I'd better get ready,' said Lucy, breaking into Gemma's reverie. 'Dog drool doesn't exactly suit the occasion.' She stood up and brushed at her skirt.

'Occasion?' asked Gemma.

'We're taking Gwen out for tea and Mum says I have to wear something "appropriate". Don't you hate that word?'

'It's dreadful,' Gemma agreed with a smile. 'How's his mother coping, by the way?'

'I'll be along in a minute, love,' Claire said to Lucy, then turned back to Gemma. 'As well as can be expected. The shock seems to have made her a bit fuzzy. Sometimes she seems to forget what's happened, but when she remembers she's worrying herself over the funeral.' Claire gazed at the trees that climbed the slope behind the garden. When the kitchen door had banged behind her daughter, she said, 'Since we have no idea when the coroner will release the body, Becca thinks we might hold a small memorial service without making a feast for the press.' With a hint of a smile, she added, 'I think Alastair would have felt quite let down, actually, not to be shown proper respect. Black armbands and pallbearers, and all the gallant officers in uniform.'

Claire finished the last of her lemonade and glanced at her watch. 'I suppose I'd better get into something more suitable myself before I drive to Dorking to pick up Gwen.'

'I did just want a word,' said Gemma, 'if you could stay a bit longer.'

Claire sank back into her chair and looked at Gemma attentively.

'It's about your bank account, Mrs Gilbert. The one you opened in Dorking. Why did you have all the correspondence sent to you at work?'

'Bank account?' said Claire blankly, staring at Gemma. 'But how—' She blinked and looked away, and after a moment smoothed down the fabric of her skirt where she'd bunched it with her fist. 'I was a very well-supervised only child, and I married Stephen at nineteen, straight from my parents' arms to his. Except for that short period of time after Stephen died, I have never lived alone.' She met Gemma's gaze again, her eyes fierce. 'Do you understand what it's like to want something just for yourself? Have you ever felt that? That's all I wanted, something no one else could touch. I didn't have to ask permission to spend it, didn't have to justify myself. It was glorious, and it was my secret.' Glancing down at the hands she'd clenched into tight fists again, she took a breath. 'How did you find out about it? Malcolm wouldn't have told you.'

'No,' Gemma said softly, 'he didn't. We found the account number in your husband's pocket.'

Gemma sat at the picnic table in the front garden of the pub, watching the life of the village revolve around her. Brian went by in the small white van; Claire and Lucy left in their Volvo; Geoff stopped and spoke to her as he went to help the vicar in her garden.

After a bit she closed her eyes, willing herself not to think—not about Jackie, not about Alastair Gilbert, not about... anything. The sun felt hot on her skin, and it was only the coolness of the shadow falling across her face that made her open her eyes with a start.

'Care to tell me about it?' asked Kincaid.

'Where did you—I didn't see you drive past.'

'Obviously.' He raised an eyebrow as he slid on to the bench opposite her.

Nettled by his teasing, Gemma launched into an account of her trip to Dorking with will, then, a bit more hesitantly, her call on Claire.

Kincaid's only comment was the raising of his eyebrow a fraction of an inch higher. In an expressionless voice he told her about his interview with the doctor.

When he'd finished she stared at him for a moment, then said flatly, 'You're not serious.'

'I wish I weren't.'

'But how could he possibly hurt her? She seems so...fragile.' In her mind Gemma heard the sound of bone snapping, and she saw again Claire's neck beneath her parted hair, delicate as the stem of a lily.

Kincaid looked down at his hands, fingers splayed on the rough wood of the table. 'I can't be sure, but I have a feeling that Claire's illusion of fragility made her all the more appealing as a victim.'

The thought made Gemma feel ill, and she crossed her arms protectively over her stomach. 'You have no proof.'

'That's what Nick said.' He shrugged. 'I've been wrong before. But I'll have to confront her with it. I don't think she's told you the whole truth about the bank account, either. You think it was Ogilvie the manager met?'

It was Gemma's turn to shrug. 'Who else could it have been? No one would ever describe Gilbert as predatory. Maybe we've been wrong about Brian and Claire. She and David Ogilvie go way back; maybe they took up where they left off years ago.'

'But if Ogilvie were Claire's lover, why

would he be snooping into her bank account—'

'In either case, how did Gilbert come by the account number? Unless the two things aren't connected at all, and Claire was simply careless. Maybe she left her chequebook in her handbag—people get careless when they've grown accustomed to a deception—and Gilbert found it.'

'Or maybe Claire and Ogilvie planned to get rid of Gilbert, and Ogilvie thought she might be double-crossing him, so he checked up on her.' Kincaid looked quite pleased with himself at this last flight of fancy.

'I don't believe that Claire Gilbert deliberately planned to kill her husband, no matter what he did,' Gemma said, feeling unreasonably irritated with him.

Kincaid sighed. 'I don't want to believe it either, but we have to consider all the options. If she did kill him, I don't believe she could have done it alone. That's what made us rule her out in the beginning. Whatever else you might say about Gilbert, he was no softie, and I don't think she could have sneaked up and hit him on the back of the head without his reacting in time to save himself.'

Glancing at his watch, he said, 'Look, Gemma, I have an idea. We can't talk to Claire until she comes back from Dorking.

I checked in with the Yard just now when I ran Nick back to Guildford, and there's no word on Ogilvie's whereabouts, so we've reached a standstill on both fronts for the moment.' He squinted up at the sun. 'Come for a walk with me.'

'Walk?'

'You know,' he mimed walking with his fingers on the tabletop, 'locomotion with two legs. I think we have time before the light goes. We could climb Leith Hill. It's the highest point in southern England.'

'I don't have any boots,' she protested. 'And I'm not dressed for—'

'Live dangerously. I'll bet you've got trainers in your overnight bag in the boot, and I'll lend you my anorak. It's warm enough, I don't need it. What have you got to lose?'

And so Gemma found herself striding along the road beside Kincaid, the nylon of his anorak swishing as she swung her arms. They left the road just past a tidy place called Bulmer Farm, and shortly they were climbing on the signposted path. At first, the land fell away on their right, the slope carpeted with russet leaves and punctuated by the skeletal trunks of pale-barked trees. Soon, however, the banks began to rise steeply on either side, and the path became a muddy rut.

Gemma hopped from dry spot to dry spot, rabbit-like, grabbing vegetation to steady herself and cursing Kincaid for his longer legs. 'This is your idea of fun?' she panted, but before he could answer they heard a humming noise behind them. It was a mountain biker, kitted out in helmet and goggles, barrelling full tilt along the path towards them. Gemma sprang to one side and scrambled up the bank, clutching a tree root as the biker whizzed by, splattering them with mud.

'Bloody bastard,' she seethed. 'We ought to report him.'

'To whom?' asked Kincaid, eyeing the mud on his trousers. 'The traffic police?'

'He'd no right—' Gemma said as she let go of the tree root and began to descend gingerly towards level ground. Then her feet shot out from under her. She twisted violently in mid-air and landed hard on one hip and one palm. Her hand stung like fire, and she snatched it up, swearing viciously.

Kincaid came and knelt beside her. 'Are you all right?' The expression on his face told her he was biting back laughter, and that made her more furious.

'Don't you know better than to touch a nettle?' he asked, taking her hand and examining her palm. He rubbed a smear of mud from her finger with his thumb, and his touch made her skin burn almost as fiercely as the nettle.

She withdrew her hand and pulled herself up, balancing carefully, then stepped for the next spot of dry ground.

'Look for a dock leaf,' Kincaid said from behind her, amusement still colouring his voice.

'Whatever for?' Gemma asked crossly.

'To stop the stinging, of course. Didn't you ever have holidays in the country as a child?'

'My mum and dad worked seven-day weeks,' she said, standing on her injured dignity. Then after a moment she relented. 'Sometimes we went to the seaside.'

It came back to her with the smell of salt air and candy-floss—the bite of the water, always too cold for anyone sensible to bathe in, the feel of wet bathing dress and sand against her skin, the squabbling with her sister on the train home. But afterwards had come hot baths and soup and drowsing before the fire, and for a moment she felt a stab of longing for the unquestioned simplicity of it all.

When they reached the summit a half-hour later, she sat down gratefully on a bench at the base of the brick observation tower and let Kincaid fetch tea from the refreshment kiosk. Her thighs ached from the climb and her hip from her fall, but as she looked out across the hills she felt exhilarated, as if she'd reached the top of the world. By the time he returned with steaming polystyrene cups, she'd caught her breath and she looked up at him and smiled. 'I'm glad I came now. Thanks.'

He sat on the bench beside her and handed her a cup. 'They say that on a clear day you can see Holland from the top of the tower. Are you game?'

She shook her head. 'I'm not very good with heights. This will do well enough.'

They sat for a while in silence, sipping the steaming tea and looking at the hazy smudge of London sprawling across the plain to the north. Then Gemma brought her knees up and swivelled around on the bench, tilting her face up to the sun.

Kincaid followed suit, then shaded his eyes with his hand. 'Do you suppose that's the Channel, just on the horizon?' he asked.

Gemma felt the tears smart behind her lids and leak from the corners of her eyes. She found she couldn't speak.

Looking at her, Kincaid said anxiously, 'Gemma, what is it? I didn't mean—'

'Jackie...' she managed, then gulped and tried again. 'I've just remembered. Jackie told me she meant to go there for her next holiday. She'd always wanted to see Paris. She and Susan were going on to take the Chunnel train across to France. If I hadn't—'

Kincaid took the cup from her shaking hands and set it on the bench. He put the flat of his hand against her back and began to rub in slow circles. 'Gemma, it's right to grieve, but you can't go on blaming yourself for Jackie's death. In the first place, we're still not positive there's a connection. And even if there is, Jackie was an adult and responsible for her own decisions. She helped you because she wanted to, not because you made her, and she went further than you'd asked because *she* was curious. Don't you see?'

She shook her head mutely, her eyes squeezed tightly shut, but after a few minutes she relaxed against his hand and the tightness in her chest began to subside. Opening her eyes, she glanced at his face. His concern for her was evident in the crease between his brows, and it seemed to her that he'd acquired new lines around his eyes. She thought of him driving up from Surrey so that she wouldn't receive the news about Jackie's death from an impersonal phone call. Such consideration deserved better treatment than she'd given him lately.

'The sun's starting to sink,' he said. 'Dusk will come on fast. We'd better start down while we can see where we're going.'

They managed the last few hundred yards of the trail in gathering gloom, and by the time they reached the village, lights had begun to glow in a few of the houses.

Kincaid looked at Gemma hugging his anorak tighter around her as they faced into the wind. She hadn't spoken on the way back from the tower, but he sensed no hostility towards him in her silence, only a withdrawing into herself. She had smiled at him and taken his hand willingly in the rough spots.

'Claire should be well back by now,' he said. 'Let's try the house first.'

'Like this?' Gemma gestured at her mud-spattered trousers and shoes.

'Why not? It will give us an air of country authenticity.'

The gate creaked as they let themselves into the Gilberts' garden, and the shrubbery assumed shapes of unexpected menace in the dim light. Kincaid stopped when they rounded the corner into the back garden, not sure at first what felt odd. He held up a hand to halt Gemma and peered towards the dog's run. Was that a shadow or a still, dark shape?

'Lewis?' he said softly, but the shape didn't stir. Kincaid's heart lurched in his chest. 'Stay here,' he hissed at Gemma, but he felt her at his heels as he sprinted across towards the enclosure.

The dark shadow coalesced as he drew closer, became a sleek, black dog splayed on its side. Kneeling, Kincaid thrust a hand through the octagonal space in the wire, scraping the skin from his knuckles. His straining fingers touched the dog. The coat felt warm, and under his hand the flank rose gently.

'Is he...' Gemma didn't finish her sentence.

'He's breathing.' Kincaid saw a smudge on the concrete near the dog's head. He looked up at the dark windows of the house. 'Something's wrong, Gemma. You stay—'

'I'm bloody not letting you go in on your own,' she whispered. 'So don't even think about it.'

They crossed the lawn together. When they reached the kitchen door, Kincaid eased it open and they moved through the cloakroom as silently as wraiths. In the kitchen they stood in the dark, just touching. Kincaid turned fall circle, willing his eyes to adjust, willing his ears to pick up a sound over the thumping of his heart.

After a long moment his pulse began to slow, and beside him he felt some of the tension drain from Gemma's body. The noise came just as she drew breath to speak. His arm shot around her and he clamped his hand over her mouth, feeling the bite of her teeth against his palm as she gasped in surprise.

He heard it again, the faintest suggestion of a creak. The hair on the back of his neck rose. 'The mobile phone,' he breathed at Gemma. 'In my jacket, in the car. Go—'

The voice came from the darker oblong of the doorway into the hall. 'I wouldn't do that, if I were you.'

Chapter Fifteen

'DCI Ogilvie, I presume?' Kincaid's voice sounded easily conversational, but Gemma could feel the tension in the hand across her mouth. She reached up carefully and tapped his hand, letting him know she understood, and it dropped away. He took a small step away from her and continued, 'You've saved us a lot of trouble looking for you.'

'Don't move,' the man said sharply. A click, and the light came on in the hall behind him, silhouetting his body but leaving his face in shadow. The light sparked from an object in his hand—flat and compact, it looked like a toy. A gun.

Gemma thought desperately of the firearms chapter in her criminal investigation text, trying to place the gun—semi-automatic, a Walther, maybe—while at the same time a small, detached part of her mind wondered what difference it made. She couldn't judge the calibre. From where she stood the opening at the end of the barrel looked big enough to swallow her.

He moved another step into the room, throwing the gun into darkness again, but Gemma kept her eyes fixed on the spot where she knew it must be. 'The pair of you are too clever by half,' he said, mocking them. 'Now, the question is, what do I do with you?'

'Why not slip out the front as we came in the back?' asked Kincaid. He might have been enquiring about tomorrow's weather.

'I tried.' There was a trace of humour in Ogilvie's voice, for Gemma had no doubt now that it was him. 'Damn Alastair and his paranoia. The front door has to be opened with a key, and I don't happen to have it. And the windows seem to be stuck shut. So you can see my predicament. You two are all that stand between me and a tidy exit.'

Gemma's tongue felt as if it had been glued to the roof of her mouth, but she tried to match Kincaid's matter-of-fact tone. 'There's no point in killing us, you know. We've turned everything we know over to C&D.'

'Oh, but there is, Sergeant. I'd intended to brazen it out, come up with some plausible excuse for my sudden absence. They'll not find anything concrete on me. But now that you've seen me here—'

'Why are you here?' asked Kincaid. 'Satisfy my curiosity.'

Ogilvie gave an audible sigh. 'Bloody Alastair managed to acquire some rather damaging evidence of my activities. I thought it prudent to get it back, but unfortunately he seems to have been more devious than I gave him credit for, and I've run out of time.'

Gemma's eyes had adjusted to the dim light well enough to see the planes of Ogilvie's face and the glint of teeth as he spoke. He'd traded his usual Bond Street attire for nondescript jeans and anorak, and he looked even more dangerous without the civilized veneer. The gun made a small arcing movement as he shifted his aim from her to Kincaid and back again.

Kincaid moved a step nearer and put his arm around her, his fingers resting lightly on her shoulder. He meant more than comfort, she was sure, but what did he want her to do? All the *should* haves ran through her mind. They should have called for back-up when they found the dog. She should have stayed outside, but would she have known Kincaid was in trouble before it was too late?

She felt Kincaid's hand tense, then freeze as Ogilvie drawled, 'However, I've had a good run, and I have a considerable bit of money tucked away on the Continent. I think I might prefer to retire DCI Ogilvie and start afresh, rather than pop holes in you two. It makes such an unpleasant mess, and while I may have walked the other side of the line a few times, I haven't resorted to murder. But I can't have you raising the alarm too soon, can I? Sergeant—'

'What about Jackie?' Gemma burst out. 'Doesn't having her gunned down in the street count? Or was that all right because you didn't get your hands dirty?'

'I had nothing to do with that,' said Ogilvie, sounding irritated for the first time.

'And Gilbert?' asked Kincaid. 'Did you come here looking for the evidence before, and he surprised—'

There came the unmistakable sound of car tyres on gravel, then the slamming of a door. Ogilvie swore, then laughed softly. 'Well, I suppose we might as well turn on the lights and have a party. The more the merrier.' Stepping forward, he flipped the light switch, and Gemma blinked as Claire's copper-shaded lamps came on.

'Move!' he barked at them, motioning towards the far side of the kitchen with the gun. 'Away from the door.' He smiled then, and Gemma shivered, for the light in his eyes reminded her of drawings she'd seen of Celtic warriors going into battle. David Ogilvie was enjoying himself.

Voices, then footsteps. The cloakroom door opened. Claire Gilbert came through into the kitchen, saying, 'What's going—?' She stopped as she took in the tableau before her. 'David?' Her voice rose into a squeak of surprise.

'Hello, Claire.'

'But what... I don't understand.' Claire looked from Ogilvie to Gemma and Kincaid, her face slack with incomprehension.

'I'd say "long time no see", but it's not exactly true on my part.' Ogilvie shook his head regretfully. 'You know you made the wrong decision all those years ago, don't you, love? It would have cost me my promotion either way—Alastair was vindictive as well as jealous—but at least I might have had you to console—'

'Mummy!' Lucy burst into the room with a wail of distress. 'Something's wrong with Lewis. I can't wake—' She skidded to a stop beside her mother. 'What—'

'He's only drugged,' said Ogilvie. 'You really should teach him not to accept steak

368

from strangers. He should come round in a bit.' He turned his attention back to Claire. 'But you were *afraid* of me. Do you remember telling me that, when you broke the news you were going to marry Alastair? You said I had a wild streak, and you had to consider Lucy's need for a stable home.' He gave a snort of derision.

Claire drew Lucy close. 'I only did what—'

'He blackmailed me into following you. His suspicion consumed him like a disease—he was riddled with it. For months I spent my off-duty hours watching your every move. You really lead a rather dull life, my love, with the occasional exception.' Ogilvie smiled at Claire. 'You'd better be glad I didn't tell him everything I discovered.'

His sharp black eyes came back to Gemma and Kincaid. 'Now, this has been quite pleasant, but I think we've chatted long enough. There's an upstairs bedroom with a locking door, I believe?'

Claire nodded confirmation.

'All together now, like good girls and boys.' Ogilvie motioned towards the hallway with the gun.

The cloakroom door banged again. They all turned like marionettes, waiting.

'Mrs Gilbert, the door was standing open, and you've left your—' Will Darling came to a halt just inside the kitchen. 'What the hell...' In a fraction of a second he took in the scene, then he spun around and dived for the door.

The gun cracked, and Will went down with a shout of pain. Rolling, he clutched at his thigh, and Gemma saw the bright stain blossom and spread on the light fabric of his trousers. Her ears ached from the sound, and she swallowed against the acrid smell of gunpowder.

Too much blood, she thought wildly. *Oh, please God, don't let it be the femoral artery. He'll bleed to death.* She tried to remember her first-aid training. *Pressure. Apply pressure directly to the wound.* Ignoring Ogilvie, she grabbed a tea towel from the cooker and ran to crouch beside Will. Folding the cloth into a thick pad, she pressed it against his leg with all her weight. Will tried to push himself up, then fell back with a grunt of pain. He grabbed Gemma's arm, pulling at her sleeve. 'Gemma, help me. I've got to call for back-up. What hap—'

'Shhh. You'll be all right, Will. Lie still.' She glanced at Ogilvie then. His lips were clamped in a thin white line, his arm rigid. It could go either way, she thought. He'd broken the barrier that separated most people from the possibility of violence; now anything might happen.

'Listen, mate.' Kincaid took a slow step towards Ogilvie, then another. 'You can see there's no point going on with this. What are you going to do—gun us all down? You're not going to hurt Lucy or Claire, so give it up.'

'Back off,' Ogilvie turned the gun on Kincaid, raised it level with his heart.

Kincaid stopped, hands up, palms out. 'Okay. You could lock us up, but you can't leave the constable here without medical help. He was doing his job—you want that on your conscience?' He took another step towards Ogilvie, palms still out. 'Give me the gun.'

'I'm telling you—' Ogilvie raised his left arm to support his right.

Firing stance, thought Gemma, watching in helpless, furious dismay. *No.*

'The car lights,' said Will. The tug at her sleeve was weaker. 'She'd left the car lights on.' His face was white now, covered with sweat, and the towel under Gemma's hands felt warm and wet.

'Somebody help him,' Gemma said, clenching her teeth to stop them chattering.

Claire thrust Lucy behind her and stepped forward. 'David, listen to me. You can't do this. I know you. I may have been wrong about Alastair, but I'm not wrong about you. If you shoot him you'll have to take me next. Give it up.'

Gemma heard Lucy whimper, but she couldn't look away from the frozen triad of Kincaid, Claire and Ogilvie.

For a moment she thought she saw a tremor run down Ogilvie's arm and his finger tighten on the trigger, then he smiled. 'There is something to be said for a graceful defeat. And I suppose that one body on your kitchen floor was more than enough for you to have to deal with, my dear.' He transferred the gun to his left hand and handed it butt first to Kincaid, but he kept his eyes on Claire. He added softly, a little regretfully, 'I could never refuse you anything.'

Claire stepped up to him and laid the back of her hand against his cheek. 'David.'

Gun still raised, Kincaid backed across the kitchen, scrambled for the phone on the breakfast table, and punched 999.

Kincaid stood alone in the Gilberts' kitchen. Gemma had gone with Will in the ambulance, and a squad car had picked up the unresisting David Ogilvie. Alerted by the lights and sirens, Brian had come across the road and shepherded a shaken Claire into the conservatory with a stiff drink.

The adrenalin rush had taken its toll on Kincaid as well. He raised a hand, wondering if the tremble he felt were visible. It would be, he thought, by the time he reached the station and began interviewing David Ogilvie. Later he would think about the possible consequences of what had happened.

He heard the cloakroom door creak and a soft step, then Lucy entered the kitchen. She still wore her afternoon outfit, a high-waisted, calf-length dress in dark green. It made her look innocently old-fashioned and far removed from the currents of violence that had flowed through this house. He smiled at her.

'Mr Kincaid?' She came to him and touched him lightly on the arm. On closer inspection he could see the tear streaks on her cheeks and a slight swelling of her eyelids. 'It's Lewis. I still can't wake him and I don't know what to do. Do you think you could have a look at him?'

'Let's see what we can do.' He followed the bright path of her torch across the garden and knelt beside the dog.

Crouching next to him, Lucy said, 'I've called the vet and left word with his answering service, but they said he may not be back for hours yet.'

Kincaid felt the dog's respirations again, then pulled back an unresponsive lid and examined the eye with the aid of the torch. 'It's too bloody dark out here. Even with the torch I can't make anything out. Shall we get him inside?'

'Oh, please,' said Lucy. 'I tried to lift him, but he's a bit much for me to manage on my own.'

Kincaid slid his arms under Lewis and heaved himself up. 'There, just steady him.' The dog's body felt reassuringly warm. Together he and Lucy crossed the garden and manoeuvred through the doors, then Kincaid carefully eased the dog on to the kitchen floor, half in Lucy's lap.

He pulled back the dog's lip and examined the gum. 'See, there? His gums are pink and healthy looking. That means he's got good circulation. And his breathing's regular,' he added, watching the steady rise and fall of Lewis's chest. 'I don't know what else we can do until the vet comes, except maybe keep him warm. Have you a blanket?'

Lucy looked up from stroking the dog's ears. 'There's a quilt on the foot of my bed. Would you—'

'I'll be right back.'

Finding Lucy's room easily enough, he stood in the doorway for a moment as he surveyed it in surprise. Except for a motley collection of stuffed animals on the bed, there was none of the clutter he associated with teenagers' rooms—no posters of rock bands or fashion models, no piles of clothes making an obstacle course of the floor. It had, in fact, the same air of simplicity as Geoff's room at the pub, and Kincaid wondered if Lucy had been influenced by him or if it were a natural expression of her own personality.

The furniture looked old but well loved, and an Irish wool blanket in lovely shades of lilac and green covered the single bed. He picked up the faded and tattered quilt that lay neatly folded on the bed's foot, yet still he lingered.

Framed newspaper and magazine clippings covered the wall above the small desk—the simple wooden frames more of Geoff's handiwork, thought Kincaid. Moving to examine them more closely, he saw that all the articles bore the byline of Lucy's father, Stephen Penmaric.

Hanging shelves either side of the window held books, and most prominently displayed was a set of C.S. Lewis's *Narnia* books, complete with dustjackets. Pulling one from the shelf, he checked the copyright and whistled. They were first editions, and in flawless condition. His mother would likely give her first-born grandchild for these.

Beside the books rested a small cage filled with cedar shavings and a wire wheel. He tapped on it and was rewarded by a scuffling sound and the emergence of a tiny white mouse. It blinked its ruby eyes at him and scurried back under cover.

Kincaid switched off the light and carried the quilt downstairs.

Lucy looked at him expectantly as he entered the kitchen. 'Did you meet Celeste? I forgot to tell you about her. I hope you're not afraid of mice.'

'Not at all. I kept them myself, until they had an unfortunate encounter with the family cat.' He knelt and tucked the quilt around Lucy as well as Lewis, for it felt chilly near the tile floor. 'You don't look very comfortable there. Will you be all right?'

'I couldn't bear to leave Lewis.' She glanced at Kincaid from under her lashes, then said hesitantly, 'Mr Kincaid, who was that man? He seemed so familiar, but I couldn't quite place him.'

'He worked with your stepfather and was a friend of your mother's after your dad died.' He'd leave it to Claire to explain the intricacies of that relationship, if she wished.

'I couldn't help but notice your C.S. Lewis books. Did you know they're quite valuable?'

'They were my dad's. He named me after Lucy in the stories.' She gazed past Kincaid, and the hand stroking the dog's head went still. 'I always wanted to be like her. Brave, courageous, cheerful. The other children were tempted, but never Lucy. She was good, really good, all the way through. But I'm not.' She turned to Kincaid, and it seemed to him that her eyes held a sadness beyond her years.

'Maybe,' he said slowly, 'that was an unreasonable expectation.'

'Looks like we've got this one nailed,' said Nick Deveney to Kincaid. They sat in the Guildford Police Station canteen, having a quick sandwich and coffee while David Ogilvie waited in Interview Room A.

'He hasn't admitted to anything,' Kincaid answered through a squishy bite of cheese and tomato. 'And I don't think we're going to rattle him by making him wait. He's been on the other side of the table too often.'

'No way he can wiggle out of Gilbert, after what he's done. Jackie Temple may be a bit more difficult, if he can prove he was lecturing that evening.' Deveney grimaced. 'God, I hate to see a copper go bad. And shooting another officer—' Finding no words to express his disgust, he shook his head.

'He wouldn't have known Will was a cop,' Kincaid said reasonably, then wondered why he was defending Ogilvie, and why Ogilvie's ignorance should make what he'd done any less reprehensible. 'Any news of Will?'

'He's in surgery. Fractured femur, they think, and ruptured femoral vein.'

Finishing his sandwich, Kincaid rolled the clingfilm into a tiny ball. 'He was fast. Faster than I was. If I'd got out and called for back-up, none of it might have happened.'

Deveney nodded, not bothering to excuse him. 'You get slow in CID. You lose your edge. You spend too much time writing bloody reports, sitting on your backside at a desk.'

'I don't think you'll find that David Ogilvie's gone soft at all,' said Kincaid.

Ogilvie looked none the worse for wear. He'd hung his anorak neatly over the back of his chair, and his white cotton shirt looked as crisp as if it had just come from the laundry. He smiled at Kincaid and Deveney as they came in and sat opposite him. 'This should be an interesting experience,' he said as Deveney turned on the tape recorder.

'I should think you're about to have quite a few new experiences,' said Kincaid, 'including a very long stay in one of Her Majesty's finer accommodations.'

'I've been intending to catch up on my reading,' countered Ogilvie. 'And I have

378

an exceptionally good solicitor, who is on his way here, by the way. I could refuse to say anything until he arrives.'

And why doesn't he? Kincaid wondered as he tried to read the expression in Ogilvie's dark eyes. David Ogilvie was highly intelligent as well as experienced in the rules of interviews. Did he want to talk, perhaps even need to talk?

Kincaid cast a warning glance at Nick Deveney—this was definitely an occasion when aggression wouldn't get them anywhere. 'Tell us about Claire,' he said to Ogilvie, leaning back in his chair and folding his arms.

'Have you any idea how lovely she was ten years ago? I could never fathom what she saw in him.' Ogilvie sounded incredulous, as if the years had not dimmed his amazement. 'It can't have been sex—she always came to me starved, and I think she must have kept up her ice-queen façade until after they were married. Maybe she sensed that was what he wanted...I don't know.'

So that had been the way of it, thought Kincaid. 'I take it he didn't know she was sleeping with you?'

Ogilvie shook his head. 'I certainly didn't tell him.'

'Not even after she told you she meant to marry him?'

'Don't insult me, Superintendent. I wouldn't stoop to that.'

'Even though it might have botched things for Gilbert?'

'To what end? Claire would have despised me for betraying her. And I think by that time he was so determined to have her that it wouldn't have stopped him. She was his porcelain prize, to be shown off as his latest accomplishment. The phrase "trophy wife" might have been invented for Gilbert and Claire, but he underestimated her. I've often wondered how long it took for him to realize he'd got a real person.' Ogilvie's face had relaxed as he talked about Claire, and for the first time Kincaid could imagine what she might have seen in *him*.

'You had no contact with her?'

'Not until tonight.' Ogilvie sipped from the cup of water on the table.

Kincaid sat forward, hands on the table. 'What evidence did Gilbert have against you?'

'Trying to take me by surprise, Superintendent?' The mocking wariness returned to Ogilvie's mouth. 'I think that's something I'd prefer to discuss with my solicitor.'

'And the nature of the activities in which you were involved?'

'That as well.'

'Jackie Temple believed you were taking protection money from the big-time drug dealers. Is that why you had her killed?'

'I told you before. I had nothing to do with PC Temple's death, and that's all I intend to say on the matter.' Ogilvie's mouth was set in a stubborn line.

Deveney moved restively in his chair. 'Tell us about the day Commander Gilbert died,' he said. 'What happened after you went to the bank?'

'The bank?' Ogilvie repeated, sounding unsure of himself for the first time.

Sweat, goddammit, thought Kincaid, and smiled at him. 'The bank. The bank where you conned the manager into letting you see Claire's file.'

'How in bloody hell...' Ogilvie shrugged. 'It doesn't matter, I suppose.' He sipped at his water again and seemed to collect himself before continuing. 'The problem with following Claire was that I couldn't take a chance on her recognizing me, so I could never get too close. I'd seen her make stops at that bank several times, and I knew they did their personal banking at the Midland in Guildford. For all I knew she was simply running errands for Gilbert's mother, but I noticed that she always came from work and returned there, and that made me wonder. By that time the game had grown a bit stale, and I was intrigued.

'Oh, it was a game at first, I admit, a chance to use old skills, feel the edge of things again. And it was a challenge—give Alastair enough to keep him off my back, yet not enough to compromise Claire too badly. He should have blackmailed a less biased snoop.'

Deveney rubbed one thumb with the other. 'I should think you'd have relished the opportunity to get even with her, after she threw you over for him.'

'And satisfy bloody Alastair Gilbert in the process? He *wanted* me to tell him his wife was cheating on him. He seemed to get some sort of perverse satisfaction out of it.'

Kincaid leaned forward. 'Was she?'

'I don't intend to tell you that, either. What Claire did was her business.'

'But you told Gilbert about the bank account.'

'It seemed harmless enough. I telephoned him that afternoon, told him I wanted to talk to him and that I'd meet his train in Dorking. I gave him the information and told him I was finished. In months of watching Claire, that was the only thing I'd come up with, and for all I knew she was saving up to buy him a bloody birthday present. I'd had enough.'

'And that was that?' Kincaid raised a sceptical eyebrow.

'He agreed,' said Ogilvie, his eyes shuttered.

Kincaid leaned forward and thumped his fist on the table. 'Bollocks! Gilbert would never have agreed. I know that for a fact, and I didn't know him half as well as you. I think he laughed at you, told you he'd never let you off. And you believed him, didn't you?' Kincaid sat back again and stared at Ogilvie, playing out the scenario in his head. 'I think you followed him home from Dorking that evening, hoping for an opportunity. You left your car in the pub car park, where it would be unremarkable, or up at the end of the lane. You rang the doorbell and made an excuse, told him there was something you'd forgotten to mention, while you saw that no one else was home.

'And I think it was *you* Gilbert underestimated. He turned his back on you, and that was the end of it.'

The silence in the room grew thick. Kincaid imagined he heard their hearts beating in opposition and the sound of the blood pumping through their veins. Sweat stood out now on Ogilvie's brow, glistening like oil.

Ogilvie moved, wiping his hand across his face impatiently. 'No. I did not kill

383

Alastair Gilbert. And I can prove it. I drove straight back to London, as I had an evening appointment with a painter to discuss the decorating of my flat.' He smiled. 'An alibi from an unbiased witness, Superintendent. You'll find it stands up.'

'We'll see about that,' said Deveney. 'Anyone is susceptible to a payoff. As you should know.'

'A dirty blow,' said Ogilvie. *Touché,* Chief Inspector. But if we're trading points here, I must say that in my old nick we at least gave the accused a cup of coffee. Do you think you could manage that?'

Deveney glanced at Kincaid, grimaced. 'I suppose so.' He spoke into the tape recorder, giving the time and noting that they would take a brief recess, then switched it off.

When the door had closed behind him, Ogilvie gave Kincaid a considering look. 'Off the record, Superintendent?'

'I can't promise that.'

Ogilvie shrugged. 'I'm not about to make a grand confession. I have nothing to confess, except that I'm tired. You seem like a sensible man. Let me give you a bit of advice, Duncan. It's Duncan, isn't it?' When Kincaid nodded, he went on. 'Don't let bitterness damage your judgement. I should have had Gilbert's job. I was the better qualified, but he was better at sucking up to the powers that be, and he sabotaged me.

'After that I started to feel I deserved more, that the system owed it to me, and that was how I excused the little infractions. Then you begin to justify it in other ways—the stuff goes on no matter what we do, you say, so why not benefit from it?' Ogilvie paused and drained his water cup, then wiped his mouth. 'After a while it wears on you, though, like a sickness. I knew I needed to get out, but I kept putting it off. I never meant for anyone to get hurt. That constable—how is he?'

'They say he's in surgery, but it sounds as though he'll be all right.' How easy it was to fall from grace by increments. Kincaid looked at Ogilvie, wished he'd met him a dozen years ago, untarnished. 'But that doesn't excuse what you did. And Jackie Temple—you may not have ordered her death, but she was killed because she asked questions about you. In my book that makes you guilty as hell.'

Ogilvie met his eyes. 'I'll have to live with that, won't I?'

No matter how hard they tried to make the waiting room look comfortable and homelike, they couldn't disguise a hospital. The smell crept under the doors and through the ventilation system, as pervasive as smoke. Gemma sat alone in the corner of the sofa, waiting. She felt very odd. Time seemed fluid, erratically arbitrary. Her eyes trained on the pattern in the wallpaper, she heard the gunshot and saw Will fall, again and again, as if a film were looping inside her head.

She remembered a kind-faced sister ordering her down to the cafeteria for a supper she hadn't been able to eat, but she had no idea how long ago that had been. Surely Will must be out of the theatre soon, and someone would come.

Her trousers were splattered with mud and streaked with blood across the knees and thighs. Still huddled in Kincaid's anorak, she was grateful for its warmth, but she kept fingering the stiff, stained cuffs, a voice in her head repeating *Will's blood, Will's blood,* like an incantation.

Her head jerked up. Had she been asleep? The voices and footsteps were real; she hadn't been dreaming. She stood up, her heart racing, as Kincaid and Nick Deveney came through the door.

'Gemma, are you all right?' Kincaid asked. 'It's not bad news about Will, is it?'

Weak-kneed, she sat again, and Kincaid took the chair beside her. She shook her head. 'No. It's just... I thought it must be the doctor... Sorry. You didn't see anyone as you came in?'

'No, love.' Kincaid glanced around the empty room. 'Doesn't Will have family?'

'He told me his parents died,' said Gemma.

Deveney made a face. 'He won't have told you how.' When Gemma and Kincaid looked at him expectantly, he sighed and examined his fingernails. 'They were devoted to each other, his parents. And to Will. They took it hard when he was posted to Ulster. Just after Will came home his mum was diagnosed with Alzheimer's, and a few months later, his dad with terminal cancer.

'His dad shot his mother, then himself. Will found them, curled up on the bed like lovers.' Deveney cleared his throat and looked away.

Kincaid said, 'Oh, Christ,' but Gemma found herself unable to speak at all. Poor Will. And now this. It wasn't fair. The door opened and her heart jerked again. This time she couldn't stand.

The doctor still wore his pale green overalls, and he'd pulled his mask down below his chin like a bib. Tubby and balding, with spectacles that glinted in the light, he smiled at them. 'It was quite a job patching your boy up. He lost a lot of blood, but I think we've got him stabilized.

I'm afraid it will be tomorrow before you can see him.'

The wave of weakness that washed through her made Gemma feel faint. She let Kincaid and Deveney thank the doctor and guide her, unresisting, towards the hall.

'Ogilvie's solicitor showed up,' Deveney said to Gemma as they walked. 'Slick as an American politician, and probably as rich. He shut Ogilvie up in a hurry, but we'll get him for this. And for Gilbert, no matter what he says about an alibi.'

'I wouldn't be so sure,' Kincaid said slowly, and they stopped, looking at him. 'You remember, Nick, Ogilvie saying that Gilbert underestimated Claire? I think perhaps we have, too.'

Chapter Sixteen

Gemma woke before daybreak. For a moment she felt disoriented, and then the patch of light beside the strange bed solidified into a net-curtained window, lit by a street-lamp. The hotel in the High Street in Guildford, of course. The events of the previous day began to click into place. Will, lying in hospital. David Ogilvie had shot him.

She lay in bed, watching the window pale to pearl-grey. Getting up, she washed, then dressed in the change of clothes she carried in her bag. Slipping a note under Kincaid's door, she left the hotel and started walking down the High Street towards the bus station. No cars passed, no pedestrians peered into the windows of the shut-up shops, and Gemma felt eerily alone, as though she were the last person in the world.

Then she passed a greengrocer's van unloading, and the driver called out a cheerful greeting. Turning into Friary Street, she looked up and saw a brilliant rose stain spreading across the sky from the east. Her spirits lifted, her step quickened, and soon she reached the station and found a taxi to take her across the mist-shrouded river and up the hill to the hospital.

'You're too early, love,' the sister said kindly. 'We haven't finished our morning routine yet. Just have a seat and I'll fetch you when you can see him. Or better still, go downstairs and get yourself some breakfast.'

Gemma hadn't realized until the sister spoke that she was starving. She took the advice, eating bacon and eggs and fried bread without a twinge of guilt, and when she went back upstairs the sister took her into the ward. 'Not too long, now,' the sister cautioned. 'He's lost quite a bit of blood, and he'll tire easily.'

Will's bed stood at the end of the ward, the curtains half drawn. He appeared to be asleep, pale and vulnerable beneath the white sheet. Slipping quietly into the chair beside the bed, Gemma found herself feeling unexpectedly awkward.

He opened his eyes and smiled at her. 'Gemma.'

'How are you feeling, Will?'

'I'll not be able to get through airport security without a medical card—they put a pin in my leg.' The smile widened almost to a grin, then he sobered. 'They haven't let anyone tell me anything. That was Ogilvie, wasn't it, Gemma? Will they get him for Gilbert and your friend, too?'

'I don't know. They're checking his statement now.'

'Is Claire all right?' He shook his head in admiration. 'Wasn't she a cracker, the way she stood up to him?'

'You were the brave one, Will. I'm glad you're all right. I should have—'

'Gemma.' He raised his hand from the sheet to halt her. 'Bits of last night are fuzzy, but I remember what you did. The doctor said you saved my life.'

'Will, I only—'

'Don't argue. I owe you, and I won't forget it. Now, tell me everything from the beginning, blow by blow.'

She hadn't reached his own part in the drama when his eyelids drooped, fluttered, drooped again. Leaning over, she kissed him lightly on the cheek. 'I'll be back, Will.'

'How is he?' Kincaid asked as they left Guildford Police Station. Gemma had met him there after her visit to hospital, looking considerably brighter than the evening before. For a moment he felt jealous of her concern for Will, then he chided himself for such small-mindedness, wondering if he were not compensating for his own sense of failure.

'Game enough, even if a bit thin around the edges,' answered Gemma, smiling. 'But the sister told me afterwards it'll be a slow job, mending that leg.'

'You mean to visit him,' Kincaid said as he opened the Rover's door, making every effort to sound casually unconcerned.

'As often as I can,'—she glanced at him as she buckled herself into the passenger seat—'once this case is finished.'

Ogilvie's painter had been found and interviewed first thing that morning, and he had, indeed, confirmed Ogilvie's alibi. Deveney was now digging with bulldog determination, trying to find a hole in the man's story or a connection between the two men. A second futile search of Gilbert's study had been made after Ogilvie had been taken into custody and they could only hope that C&D would have better luck turning up Gilbert's evidence of Ogilvie's corruption.

As if aware of his thoughts, Gemma said, 'You believe Ogilvie, don't you, guv?' as they swung around the roundabout and headed towards Holmbury St Mary. 'Why?'

Shrugging, Kincaid said, 'I'm not sure I know.' Then he grinned at her. 'The infamous gut feeling. Seriously...he lied about some things, and I could tell. Gilbert's response when he told him he'd not do his dirty work any more, for instance. But I don't think he's lying about Gilbert or Jackie.'

'Even if you're right about that, and I don't grant it to you, why Claire?'

He thought he heard a trace of resentment in her voice. Sighing, he thought he couldn't blame her. He liked Claire Gilbert, too—admired her, even. And maybe, just maybe, he was wrong. 'In the first place, there's no physical evidence to place him there—not a hair or a fibre in that kitchen.

'Then think about everything we've

learned about Alastair Gilbert. He was a jealous and vindictive man with a megalomaniac's thirst for power. He enjoyed inflicting pain on others, whether physical or emotional. Who would have borne the brunt of it?' He glanced at Gemma's profile, then said emphatically, 'His wife. I've always said this murder was committed in rage, and I think Claire Gilbert hated her husband.'

'*If* you're right,' said Gemma, 'how are you going to prove it?'

Claire met them at the back door with an anxious expression. 'I've called the hospital and they're being very tight-lipped about Constable Darling. Have you heard anything?'

'Better than that,' Gemma reassured her. 'I've seen him, first thing this morning, and he's doing fine.'

Kincaid paused in the cloakroom, running his eye along the mackintoshes hanging on a row of hooks. When he saw what he was searching for he didn't know whether he felt jubilant or sorry.

'And... David?' Claire asked as they entered the kitchen. She looked at Kincaid.

'He's still helping us with our inquiries.'

Lewis was lying on Lucy's quilt, but this morning he lifted his head and thumped his tail. Kincaid knelt and scratched his ears. 'I see this patient is improving, too, though he's not entirely back to his rambunctious self.'

'Lucy insisted on staying up with him all night. It was only after the vet came an hour ago that I was able to convince her to curl up on the sofa in the conservatory.' Claire hesitated, fingering the silk scarf bunched in the neck of the crisply tailored white shirt she wore. 'About David...he was a good man, once. Whatever has happened to him in the last few years, I still can't imagine him capable of...killing anyone.'

'I'm inclined to agree with you,' Kincaid said, feeling Gemma's sharp glance.

Claire gave him a relieved smile. 'Thank you for coming to set my mind at rest. Can I get you a coffee or some tea?'

Kincaid took a breath. 'Actually, we'd like a word with you. Somewhere a bit more private, if you wouldn't mind.'

Her smile faltered, but she agreed readily enough. 'We can use the sitting room. I'd rather not disturb Lucy just now.'

They followed her into the room that had seemed so welcoming the night Alastair Gilbert died, leaving the door just slightly ajar. The fire was cold in the hearth, and the red walls seemed tawdry in the thin daylight streaking through the shutters.

Kincaid sat stiffly on the armchair's

chintz seat. He had rehearsed angle after angle, how he might surprise her, trick her, but in the end he began simply.

'Mrs Gilbert, I've learned several things this last week that have led me to believe your husband physically abused you. Perhaps this happened only on one or two occasions, perhaps it had been going on from the very beginning of your marriage. I don't know.

'I do know, however, from sources other than David Ogilvie, that your husband suspected you of having an affair. He went so far as to accuse Malcolm Reid, and he threatened him.'

Claire put a hand to her mouth, pressing hard on her lips with her fingers. Reid hadn't told her, thought Kincaid. What else had Claire Gilbert's friends kept from her in their desire to protect her? And what had she kept from them?

'But Reid was guilty of no more than helping you hide financial assets, and he told Gilbert where to get off. How close did your husband get to the truth, Claire? Did he threaten Brian, too?'

The silence stretched as Claire twisted her hands together in her lap. This was the watershed, Kincaid knew, and he had to remind himself to breathe. If she denied her relationship with Brian, he had no other lever to use and no evidence against her but his own wild suppositions. Her face seemed shuttered and remote, as if none of this quite touched her, then she took a little breath and said, 'David knew, didn't he?'

Kincaid nodded and made an effort to keep the relief from his voice. 'I think so, but he didn't tell us.'

'It was no great middle-aged passion, you know, Brian and me,' she said with a trace of a smile. 'We were lonely, both of us, and needy. He's been a good friend.

'And Malcolm. I never told Malcolm the whole truth about Alastair, only as much as I could bear. I said I was tired of being condescended to, of being treated like a chattel, and Malcolm helped me any way he could. I was so careful not to take that chequebook home. I even hid it away in a secret place in the shop, in case Alastair managed somehow to search my desk. He was very plausible when he wished it, you know. I imagined that he might come in when he knew I would be out on a consultation, and tell Malcolm I'd rung and asked him to pick something up. What could Malcolm do?

'And then, of course, I wondered if my paranoia had reached epic proportions, if I was becoming mentally ill.' She shook her head and gave a strangled laugh. 'But I know now that not even my paranoia did

396

justice to Alastair.'

Her words poured out in a torrent of release, and it seemed to Kincaid that the façade Claire Gilbert had built around herself was cracking before his eyes. Emerging from the splintered shell was the real Claire—frightened, angry, bitter, and no longer the least bit remote.

'It didn't occur to him to wonder why I brought home so little money, because he didn't think my work worth anything. That, of course, was the only reason he tolerated my working at all, and I'm not sure that would have lasted much longer. 'I have an old schoolfriend in the States, in North Carolina. I thought that when Lucy finished school I'd have enough money put by, and we would just...disappear.'

'What about Brian?' asked Gemma, sounding as though she'd decided he needed a partisan voice.

Slowly, Claire said, 'Brian would have understood. Things with Alastair had... escalated...in the last year. I was afraid.'

Gemma leaned forward, her cheeks pink with indignation. 'Why didn't you just leave him? Tell him you wanted a bloody divorce and be done with it?'

'You still don't understand, do you? *"It sounds so easy,"* you're thinking. *"No one with half a backbone would put up with that sort of treatment.*" But things never start out that way. It's a gradual process, like learning a foreign language. One day you wake up and find you're thinking in Greek, and you hadn't even realized it. You've bought his terms.

'I believed it when he told me I couldn't manage on my own. It was only when I started working with Malcolm that I began to see it might not be true.' Claire stopped, her face intent, her eyes focused on something they couldn't see. 'It was the beginning of a sort of resurrection, a rebirth of the person I'd had the potential to become before I married Alastair.' She sighed and looked at them again. 'But I'd learned enough over the years to try to keep those changes to myself.'

Softly, Kincaid said, 'It didn't work, did it? You've had two broken bones in a little over a year.'

Claire cradled her right wrist in her left hand, an instinctive, protective gesture. 'I suppose he could sense that my centre of attention had shifted. I'd ignore the subtle signals that were usually all he needed to manipulate me, until finally he would explode.'

'Was that the beginning of the violence?'

She shook her head, and when she spoke her voice was barely audible. 'No. That started almost at the beginning, but

398

little things, things he could laugh off. Pinching...shaking. You see, I discovered as soon as we were married—' Claire stopped and rubbed a hand across her mouth. 'I don't know a delicate way to say this. Sexually, he wanted...he only wanted me to be compliant. If I expressed any desires or needs of my own, or even enjoyment, it made him furious—he wouldn't come near me. So when I began to find him...distasteful, I would pretend to be eager, and he would leave me alone.

'Do you see? It was a very complicated game, and finally I grew tired of playing. I rejected him outright, and that's when he began accusing me of having a lover.'

'Did you?' asked Kincaid.

'No, not then. But it made the possibility real for me. If I had sinned in fiction, why not in fact?' She smiled, mocking herself. 'Somehow it made it easier to justify.'

Starved, thought Kincaid, remembering the word David Ogilvie had used. Starved for tenderness, starved for affection, in Brian she had found both. But did she count it worth the cost?

'Claire.' He waited until he had her full attention. 'Tell me what happened the night Alastair died.'

She didn't answer, didn't raise her eyes from her clasped hands.

'Shall I tell you what I think?' Kincaid

399

asked. 'Lucy went to the shops in Guildford alone that afternoon. We had a positive identification of her, but no one remembered seeing you. Your husband had told you he had a meeting that evening, but much to your surprise, he walked in only a few minutes past his usual time. He had just met Ogilvie at Dorking railway station, and Ogilvie had told him about your secret bank account.

'Gilbert was livid, beyond anything you'd seen before. How dare you go behind his back, make a fool of him?' Kincaid paused. He had seen the quickly aborted gesture, the nervous raising of her hand towards her throat. 'Untie your scarf, please, Claire.'

'Wh-what?' She cleared her throat.

'Untie your scarf. You were hoarse that night—I remember feeling surprised at the huskiness of your voice. This morning I realized you've kept your throat covered all this last week with scarves and turtleneck jumpers. Let me see it now.'

He thought she might refuse, but after a moment she reached slowly up and untied the tag ends of the scarf She unwound the two loops around her throat, then pulled, and the silk cascaded to her lap.

The thumbprints were clear, either side of her windpipe, the purple fading into an unlovely shade of yellow.

Kincaid heard Gemma's intake of breath.

Slowly, deliberately, he said, 'Alastair came home and put his hands around your throat, squeezing until things began to go dark. Then something distracted him for a moment, and he turned away from you. He wasn't afraid of you, after all. But you knew this time he had lost all reason, and you were afraid for your life. You picked up the closest thing to hand and hit him. There was another hammer, wasn't there, Claire, lying handy in the kitchen?

'And when you realized what you'd done, you put on that old black mac hanging in the cloakroom and carried the hammer up the lane. Percy Bainbridge saw you, a dark shadow slipping by. Where did you put the hammer, Claire? In the ashes of the bonfire?'

Still she didn't speak, didn't look up from her hands. Kincaid went on, gently. 'I don't believe you'll let anyone else take the blame for this—not Geoff, not Brian, not David Ogilvie. What I don't understand is why you didn't claim self-defence in the first place.' He gestured at her throat. 'You had irrefutable evidence.'

'I didn't think anyone would believe me.' Claire's words came so softly she might have been speaking to herself. 'He was a policeman, after all. It didn't occur to me that I had proof.' She raised her head and smiled at them. 'I suppose I wasn't thinking very clearly. It happened just as you said, only I didn't mean to kill him. I only wanted to stop him hurting me.'

She sat up on the edge of the sofa and her voice grew louder, as if practice made it easier to say the words. 'But yes, I did kill him. I killed Alastair.'

She's too calm, thought Kincaid, then he saw that her hands were still clenched in her lap. Her knuckles were white from the pressure, as were her short-bitten nails. An odd habit for such a well-groomed woman, he thought, and then it came to him with sickening clarity.

The pathologist, Kate Ling, describing the tiny rips in the shoulders of Gilbert's shirt. Rips Claire couldn't have made. And Claire hadn't been protecting herself at all with her manufactured story of missing jewellery and open doors.

He swallowed against the sudden lurch of nausea, then looked at Gemma. Did she see the truth? If only he knew, should he, could he, let Claire get away with her deception?

The door opened and Lucy came in, shutting it carefully behind her. In her green dress, with her dark-honey hair sleep-tangled and her feet bare, she looked like a wood nymph.

'I've been listening,' she said as she came to stand beside Kincaid, facing her mother. 'And it's not true. Mummy didn't kill Alastair. I did.'

'Lucy, no!' Claire started to rise. 'Stop it this minute. Go to your room.'

Gemma put out a restraining hand, and Claire sank back to the edge of the sofa, looking up at her daughter. When Lucy stood implacable beside Kincaid, Claire turned to him, hands outstretched in entreaty. 'Don't pay any attention to her. She's upset, distraught. She's just trying to protect me.'

'It happened just the way she said,' Lucy continued. 'Except that I came home from Guildford. I wondered why Alastair's car was in the garage when Mummy had said he'd be late and why the cloakroom door wasn't quite shut.

'They didn't hear me come in. He had his hands around her neck and he was shouting at her in a sort of hoarse whisper. His face was red and the veins on his neck were standing out. I thought she was dead, at first. She looked limp, and her face had gone a funny colour. I screamed at him and grabbed him by the shoulders, trying to pull him away.' Lucy stopped and swallowed, as though her mouth were dry, but she didn't take her eyes from her mother's face. 'He swatted me off as though I was a fly and went straight back to choking her.

'I'd left the hammer out on the work top. I'd been hanging a new piece Geoff had framed for me. I picked it up and hit him—Alastair, I mean. After the second or third time he fell.'

Lucy swayed slightly. She reached out and rested light fingers on Kincaid's shoulder, as if the mere human contact was enough to keep her steady. Her mother watched her, transfixed, powerless to stop her now.

'I don't remember much after that. When Mummy could breathe again, she made me strip off my clothes and my trainers. We put them in the washer with some other dirty things and some enzyme liquid—you know, the sort of stuff that takes the bloodstains out. She told me to dip my hands in it, too, before I went upstairs for clean clothes.

'When I came down again, the hammer was gone. She told me we'd say we'd found the door open, and some of her jewellery missing. When the washer finished its cycle we put the clothes in the dryer, then she called the police.'

'She's a child,' Claire said, looking at Gemma, then Kincaid. 'She can't be held responsible for this.'

Lucy's fingers tightened on Kincaid's

shoulder. 'I'm seventeen, Mum. I'm legally an adult. I don't think I *meant* to kill Alastair. But the fact is that I did.'

Lucy went to her mother and put her arms around her, but she looked at Kincaid as she spoke. 'I tried not to think about it, to pretend it hadn't happened. But that's what I'd done for years. I knew about Alastair, and Mummy knew I knew, but we didn't talk about it. Maybe none of this would have happened if we had.'

'Sir.' Gemma's whisper was urgently formal. 'I'd like a word with you.' She nodded towards the door, and they left mother and daughter together as they rose and went into the hall.

'How can we let her do this?' she hissed at him when they'd closed the sitting-room door behind them. 'Gilbert was a beast. She only did what anyone might have done in the circumstances, but this will ruin her life. She's paying for Claire's mistakes.'

Kincaid took her by the shoulders. He loved her then, for her prickly defence of the underdog, for her generous spirit, for her readiness to question the status quo, but he couldn't tell her.

Instead, he said, 'I thought the same thing, when I realized what had happened. But Lucy's right, and she's taken it out of our hands. We have to let her make her reparation. It's the only way she'll be able to live with herself.'

He let her go and leaned against the wall, tiredly. 'And we can't compromise ourselves, not even for Lucy. We swore to uphold the law, not to pass sentence, and we dare not cross that line, no matter how good our intentions. I don't want Lucy to suffer any more than you do, but we have no choice. We must charge her.'

Chapter Seventeen

Leaving Gemma with Claire, Kincaid had taken Lucy into the station himself. Having changed into jeans and sweater and said a brief good-bye to Lewis, she sat quietly resolute beside him.

'I've been thinking,' she said as they came into the outskirts of Guildford, 'that maybe now I can finish the game.' She'd looked at him and seemed to hesitate. 'You know,' she said slowly, 'if you'd been more like *him*, it would have been much easier to go on pretending, not facing up to things. But you remind me a bit of my dad.' And having given him the highest compliment in her vocabulary, she administered the *coup de grâce*. 'Will you come and visit me, wherever I am?'

Now, having taken on, not unwillingly, an obligation of honour to Lucy, he had given her into the capable hands of Nick Deveney and her family solicitor. He doubted a jury would do more than slap her wrist—abused women had been known to get probation for shooting their sleeping husbands—or the Crown Prosecution Service might throw it out altogether. Her toughest battle would be with herself, but she would have the support of those who cared for her, he felt sure.

As he drove back along the winding road to Holmbury St Mary to pick up Gemma, he couldn't shake the aching, persistent sadness lodged under his breastbone. It was all mixed up together—his regret for Lucy, for Claire, even for David Ogilvie.

And Gemma. The thought of working with her every day, of being so close and yet not close enough, was like rubbing salt in a wound. But the alternative, not seeing her at all... He thought of David Ogilvie's admonition against bitterness, and knew that was a path he would not allow himself to follow.

A recklessness possessed him as he thought of the way he'd lived for so long, isolated behind walls of his own making. He wouldn't give up on Gemma, nor would he go back to what he had been before he took her into his bed.

As he reached the green, he had a sudden desire to see Madeleine Wade one last time. He passed the Gilberts' lane and drove through the village, turning into the street that led up the hill to Madeleine's shop, and past that, the Hurtwood.

He saw from the window that Madeleine was presiding over the shop counter herself, and he felt a pang of disappointment that he would not see her flat again. She looked up as the bell jangled and said, 'I'm so sorry.'

'The news has travelled already, I take it?'

'Like the proverbial wildfire.'

'I came to say goodbye.'

She came around the counter and held out her hand to him. 'I wouldn't worry too much about Lucy. She's strong, and she'll manage to be what she wants to be.'

'I know.' Her fingers felt warm in his grasp. 'You could give her a lesson or two.'

Madeleine smiled. 'I might just do that.'

He drove with such precision, thought Gemma, watching his absorbed face in the flickering light of the street-lamps. It seemed to her that they were always coming and going together in cars, while their lives remained stuck in a sort of limbo between journeys.

She'd spent the quiet hours of the afternoon with Claire, sitting at the kitchen table drinking endless cups of weak tea, talking mostly of inconsequential things. Once, though, Claire had looked up from the dregs in her cup and said, 'I'll be charged, too, won't I, as an accessory after the fact?'

Gemma nodded. 'I'm afraid so. They'll be sending someone for you from Guildford Police Station.'

'I'm glad, really,' Claire had said. 'It's a relief to have it over. Now the truth is out, we can get on with learning to be ourselves.'

Gemma thought of Will, to whom the truth seemed to come so easily, and of the chaste goodbye she'd bid the disappointed Nick Deveney. She looked at Kincaid again and wondered if she had the courage to face her own truth.

'Come in for a bit,' she said when he had pulled the car up in front of the flat and killed the engine. Through the screen of leaves in the dark garden she could see a light shining in the nursery window of the big house. Toby was still awake, then, but she was content to postpone seeing him.

'It's been a rough day, Gemma, and I know you're tired,' Kincaid answered, sounding exhausted himself. 'Some other—'

'Please. I'd like you to.' She rummaged in her handbag for the heavy key, and when she got out of the car he followed her obediently.

Once inside, she dumped her bag and coat on the chest by the door and bustled around the flat, closing blinds and lighting lamps. 'There, that's better,' she said as she glanced around with satisfaction. Hazel must have been in the flat, for it looked swept and tidy, and a vase of deep yellow roses stood on the low table. Hadn't she read somewhere that yellow was the colour of mourning?

'I'll get us some wine.' She uncorked a nice bottle of Burgundy she'd been saving, then stood on tiptoe as she retrieved her best glasses from the kitchen cupboard's top shelf.

Kincaid, having positioned himself against the long window counter, safely avoiding her whirlwind of activity, watched without saying a word. Accepting his glass, he said, 'Gemma—'

'I wanted to talk to you.' Her words came out in a rush. 'But I don't know how to begin. What's happened the last few days...has made me think about a lot of things.' Unable to meet his level gaze, she turned away, reached out, and touched the yellow petal of an opening rosebud. 'I want you to understand that my job is very important to me and that I have other obligations, commitments. There's Toby, and I've promised to see Will whenever I can—'

'Gemma, stop it. You don't have to apologize to me or make excuses for what you feel or don't feel. You have every—'

'No. Let me finish.' She turned back to him, brushing the hair off her face impatiently. 'You don't understand what I'm trying to tell you. I saw everything as black or white. You or the job. I was afraid that I would let what I felt for you consume me. I was afraid of losing myself, losing everything I've worked to become.

'Except...' She paused, staring at her dark and wavering reflection in the smooth surface of her wine. 'I saw Claire Gilbert find her strength, begin taking back her life, even after all she's been through. I realized that we always have a choice, and that *I* can choose not to let go what I've made of myself.'

Gemma looked up at him, swallowed, took a breath. She could hear the pulse in her ears. 'I'm not doing this very well. What I'm trying to say is that I think I have to take that risk. I don't want to spend the rest of my life looking in other people's windows, wondering what it would be like to be loved.

'What happened to Will...and Jackie...it

411

could have been you. The chance we have is so fragile...I don't want to pass it up.'

She had run out of words and could only wait now for his answer. Seconds passed as he looked at her without speaking, his face expressionless. Panic made her blood run cold. Had she left it too late?

Then he smiled, the familiar mischievous grin, and lifted a questioning eyebrow. 'Nothing ventured, nothing gained?'

Gemma nodded, unable to speak.

Raising his glass to her, he said softly, 'Cheers, my love.' He drank, then set his wine carefully on the half-moon table. 'How long before we have to collect Toby?'

The publishers hope that this book has given you enjoyable reading. Large Print Books are especially designed to be as easy to see and hold as possible. If you wish a complete list of our books, please ask at your local library or write directly to: Magna Large Print Books, Long Preston, North Yorkshire, BD23 4ND, England.

This Large Print Book for the Partially sighted, who cannot read normal print, is published under the auspices of

THE ULVERSCROFT FOUNDATION

THE ULVERSCROFT FOUNDATION

. . . we hope that you have enjoyed this Large Print Book. Please think for a moment about those people who have worse eyesight problems than you . . . and are unable to even read or enjoy Large Print, without great difficulty.

You can help them by sending a donation, large or small to:

The Ulverscroft Foundation, 1, The Green, Bradgate Road, Anstey, Leicestershire, LE7 7FU, England.
or request a copy of our brochure for more details.

The Foundation will use all your help to assist those people who are handicapped by various sight problems and need special attention.

Thank you very much for your help.